"This is painful and powerful reading; both the pain and the power grapple without respite for the reader's heart and soul. Both win."

– The Whig-Standard, Kingston

"Richards has the ability to make us see and smell New Brunswick. Further, he makes us feel the pain in the lives of his characters and in a community where everything is 'sad and wrong' . . . Richards shows a kind of compassion in compulsive violence, and a kind of beauty in ruin. Here is a major voice in the land."

– Ottawa Citizen

". . . he is a major writer, a voice to be reckoned with."

– The Globe and Mail

"Magnificent . . ."

– The Edmonton Journal

David Adams Richards was born in Newcastle, New Brunswick, in 1950. He attended St. Thomas University in Fredericton, and in 1973 was awarded the Norma Epstein prize for the first five chapters of *The Coming of Winter* – a novel that was subsequently published (1974) and later translated into Russian (1979). Much praised by critics, Richards has sometimes been called the most under-rated of Canadian writers. He has published a collection of short stories, *Dancers at Night* (1978) and three other novels, *The Coming of Winter* (1974), *Blood Ties* (1976), and *Road to the Stilt House* (1985).

David Adams Richards

Lives of Short Duration

New Canadian Library No. 187

McClelland and Stewart

ISBN: 0-7710-9336-5

McClelland and Stewart Limited
The Canadian Publishers
25 Hollinger Road
Toronto, Ontario
M4B 3G2

Book design by Michael Macklem

*For Richard Parks, Paul Richards and to
the memory of Gary Barnaby (1958-80)*

Printed and bound in Canada

Graduation

Child of mine
child of mine

came the song.

Georgie's girl was pregnant. She was going to pack her suitcase and leave forever, money or no money. But Georgie kept shouting: "We got her all—eh there Lois?"

The girl cursed. She kept looking at her feet. There were bugs about her.

Lois said: "Georgie, you just shut yer goddamnable mouth, we're having a party."

"Money or no money," the girl managed to say.

Lois looked at the girl, her undernourished body. She was three months pregnant, her thin arched back hooked so that the spine showed. It was late. Under the floodlight they'd set up the flies were buzzing. The men George had invited to the party had taken sides in the argument, a few for George and a few for the girl—actually a few more for George because it was his party. It was his house also, now. The roasting pit still crackled with flame.

One of the men said: "Georgie can burn the bridge if he wants—its not up to her. Well, let me ask a civil question, is it up to her or is it up to George. I say it's up to Georgie—eh Georgie?"

Lois watched.

"No arguments," she shouted. "We're having a goddamn party."

Her blouse was opened. You could see the rose tattoo above her left breast and her hair was up in twenty curlers. From her tight shorts. But George wasn't going to argue. With a swing at his girlfriend, just to show who was boss, he walked onto the span that crossed the river carrying a canister of gasoline and a pig's head impaled on a stick. Everyone was yelling. The pig's head, with its relaxed grin impaled upon a spruce stake that Georgie had cut, had grinning eyes (as if it too was happy to have itself cooked and eaten—you might so think anyway). And then George with his medallion jiggling, singing:

Pearl Pearl Pearl—oh don't you marry Earl,
He will lay you on your back and he will twiddle with your ——
Oh Pearl you are a —— girl.

5

On into the night.

"George, you jeeser, we're tryin to have a good time," Lois yelled.

The long span shuddered when Georgie walked on it, and underneath the river silent, still swelled with rain water. The body of the girl shivering.

"Money or no money George," she said. "You act crazy—I'm leavin."

George waved his fist at her and poured gasoline over the span.

"Get back here George—or ya'll get no more wine from me, boys oh boy," Lois said.

"Yes—come on back here Georgie," one of the men said.

Donnie was running along the opposite shoreline. He was yelling: "Oh —Lester isn't home he isn't, Lester isn't." His voice, his arms waving. "Lester isn't home—"

The men all looked confused now. George himself looked confused. But he tried to light a match. The span swayed—you could hear the ropes. Leona, the youngest of Lois' three children, ate a piece of pork, with her pretty party dress on, her hair in bows. Across the river, along the hollow, the American camps. The Americans had come up from the pools for the evening, one, a professor of theology from Maryland, having taken a four-pound grilse from Simon's pool in the dying moments of the evening. You might think. It was dark. The rain that had sent them into the house had stopped, yet water still lay along the summer hedges, the smell of lilac.

"Get me some toilet-paper," George said, as if he were angry.

"I have no paper to get ya," Lois yelled. "And none of you jeesers make a move for paper," she yelled to the men. Some were wanting to go for toilet-paper and others weren't. George was at the centre of the span, the pig's head tilted. Under the bridge the pleasant moving shadows of water.

"Some just like to take charge," George yelled. "But I'm going to burn down this span if it takes till doomsday—doomsday, you hear me— doomsday." And then the song, "Oh Pearl Pearl Pearl," coming and going with the rhythm of the pig's swaying head.

"Goddamn George, you ruin everything," Lois shouted. "But ya aren't ruinin my fun, you hear that—you aren't ruinin my fun."

Slowly with a furl and then a bright purple rush along the walkway the gasoline caught, and Georgie laughed: "Got it done—got the job done boys."

Lois herself gave a yell, lifted her left leg and kicked at the air. Georgie's girl was crying. The fire brightened her hair, shone against her. George ran as the span caught, veering this way and that, his own shirt-sleeve on

6

fire—him laughing, the pig's grinning head swollen.

George stood with his mouth opened slightly. The spruce splay the pig's head rolled on, careened in the centre of the span. All Lester Murphy's buildings, his gazebo behind the brick wall with pagoda lights, took on in the flaring withering flame a dormant oppressive shape, and then eerily was blackened out as the fire grew. Little by little you could see the span swaying, fire creating wind, then sinking. Donnie waved.

George took his wine, picking it up out of the dirt behind the roast pit, and walked over to the porch. He giggled slightly, then became quiet. Donnie walked back and forth on the other side of the river.

"Fuckin retard," George said when he noticed him. Then he loked at his grand-daughter, still sitting with a piece of charred pork in her hand, chewing unconsciously.

Georgie's girl—a girl he'd managed to bring home when he came back from some city or other last summer—a girl who'd grown up in town 30 miles below here and whose own parents had kicked her out until Lois had won the $50,000 on Atlantic loto and she'd invited them here for a champagne breakfast, stayed near the riverbed, her arms wrapped about her stomach, the faded beach-robe like the thousands of garments somehow boughten to be needless. At intervals, and quite suddenly, she'd look up at the fire, her face betraying a childish enthusiasm.

"And you went to technical school—and what in God's name did you do in technical school except smoke dope?" George said under his breath, watching that roast pit that still somehow had the flavour of lukewarm blood. Lois stood, her hands on her thighs, her shoulders tilted backward, watching the fire and shaking her head. Four men stood at various distances from each other, but all somehow in close proximity to Lois.

"Bradley," Lois yelled. "Bradley—you little jeeser, where are you?"

"I'm not doin nothin," Bradley said.

"Ya—well get the hell away from those marshmallows—we aren't going to have any marshmallows tonight."

"Why not?"

"Because we aren't—because we aren't."

She shook her head.

"Some span, eh boys," George said watching it. He grunted, was quiet. There was a smell of grease; some plywood boards floated along the water like vessels in distress crying from bow and stern.

"Didn't I say I was gonna burn that—didn't I say when I moved inta this place I was gonna burn that?" George turned about, moving slightly on his hips. He kept mashing his hands together—looking at them they

7

seemed like strange powerful things. He shrugged, picked up a strand of grass, blew on it, made a sound and turned to Leona, who was staring up at him. "That's what ya do when ya fart eh," he said. The little girl in her happy party dress, with the very words *happy party dress* written upon it, that Lois had picked up for her, chewed quietly and looked across the river.

"We got a fuckin arsonist across that river," George said.

"You know what my teacher says, Uncle Georgie?" she said.

"No—what does yer teacher say?" George said, still looking at his hands, smelling them. He seemed confused and touching his leg quickly he took his hand away and looked at it.

"My teacher says—she says I'm the most wonderful little creature, I'm the most *splendid* little creature, and I got four stars."

"Me hands Jesus near burnt," George said suddenly. He grunted, shook his head.

The men stood like Toms in heat all at a distance from each other, staring at Lois, whose breasts were visible in the flashes of light, who still kept her hands on her thighs, one heel arched.

"Yes me hands burnt, dear," he said to Leona. "And where's that Packet," he said suddenly, in fury. "Eh, where is your uncle Packet—ya know where he is eh, oh oh oh, I could tell ya where he is, off with the squaw Emma Jane Ward, who should be strangled she's such a knowitall, strangled up, thumb prints on her, leave her on the road, what I say— and who did Little Simon get all mixed up with, follow around like a sick dog before he died—eh, boat-people girl, that's right—boat-people girl—oh, thought she was too good for him, much too good—for my son —yellow cocksucker, ya see her all yellow, stinkin yellow—yellow bum on her, dear—yellow everything—and that jeesless Packet wouldn't come ta no party—too good ta come ta any parties, even though his own flesh and blood goes around throwin parties, just like when I was in Toronto and he passed right through there—oh for Jesus sure, and now who've we got? Ya see Little Simon that day after he went and bought the one a present and she laughed right in his face, right up his gob and then went to work at McDonald's, which is good enough for the bastard, but I know —can't help but know, ya know what ya know—how in cocksucker can we get jobs in this country if they're lettin those no-nourished Pakistanis and Cambodian Jiggiboos in—I met a woman in TO—oh the very best of a place that cocksucker—makes disposable diapers, says they're all up there now makin disposable diapers, every one of them and she got so screwed up listenin to them talk that she missed the handle on the press and cut about nine fingers off, and Packet—burnt my hand dear, smell it," he said, holding his hand to her face.

The child looked up at him, almost a quarter-pound of pork on her plate, tilted, the mosquitos lighting in her hair with those pretty bows that Lois had put in when she'd washed her face with a face-cloth, saying: "Now someday dear you'll be far prettier than your mother."

The men talked silently now. Donnie from across the river was puffing on his pipe dramatically. He stared at the span, part of the structure sunken but remaining firmly clasped like the extended arms of two drowning lovers. And from the furls of escaping fire and ash the pig's head bobbed once, twice mischievously. The men standing there spoke quietly like thin-shouldered aunts visiting a household to cause intrigue. Since George had sold the three acres to the New York firm that owned the mines, and since Lois had won the $50,000 on Atlantic Loto, they'd been here most days and nights. And Lois stood, in her tight terrycloth shorts, without panties. One man chewed at his lip and pretended to be staring at the ground while looking at her. Behind them in the pit, half the pig loin in blackened tin foil.

Lois watched Donnie pacing back and forth, his hands behind his back. And she thought of the time Russell Peterson had taken his boots and shoes off in the winter, and had thrown them to the top of Alewood's store. Strange and ludicrous were his fattened and swollen feet and the dark pipe that ran up the side of Alewood's ruined building, which he'd tried to climb, the steps worn and decomposed with the imprint of a dead generation and the ghostly filament against the cracking windows at twilight, the smell of charred cardboard, and Donnie laughing because everyone else was, his fattened and swollen feet somehow catching the reddish flush and hue of the worn brick. And when he fell back into the snow Packet took him home.

One of the men went down to the water where Georgie's girl sat. He put his arms around her. Georgie had his head down, almost between his legs. When he'd look up he'd see the span and become startled and frightened and angry. The picnic table with pieces of meat and half-finished jugs of wine; and the two cars, one up on blocks sitting in the dooryard. And far away there were sirens.

"It weren't us," the man said to the girl. "I mean, you know yerself Georgie's on the wine—can't do anything with him when he's on the wine—it was him, not us." He put his arms around her and his thin leg touched her thin thigh and he could feel her shaking. She looked at him, nodding neither one way or the other.

9

He smiled slightly.

The man smiled, touched the sleeve of her beach-robe, almost playfully his fingers touched her arm.

Child of mine
child of mine—

came Anne Murray's advertisement from somewhere inside the house. "No—you and I had nothin, nothin in the world to do with the likes of this," he said.

"I don't care," she said, waving her hand. He stared at the flowered bikini bottoms she wore, the elastic pinching her thin hips and sharpened, jutting hip-bones, and smiled nervously. A tear of grease had spotted her belly just above the bikini bottoms.

"How's yer mother?" he asked. "By God, she's one lovely woman—you know that?"

Georgie's head was sunken between his legs and he could smell the sweat from his body mingling with the wet dark earth, where he saw a firefly flitting suddenly and made a grab for it.

"It went out on me," he mumbled. "Ya know Leona, it went out on me —oh there it is." He sat up too quickly and fell backward onto the porch. Lying there a second he smelled a cool breeze.

Night. Would he run again tonight, and hide searching for cover? Now that he'd this much wine he wouldn't—but tomorrow, or especially the day after—then he would, run searching for cover. And the nineteen-year-old German boy saying: "Kanada—ferry bad—Kanada" and Lester Murphy and him lying in a ditch in Holland. Suddenly there was a great energy in him and he sat up laughing and took a drink of wine. It settled in his guts, filling him.

"Boys, I think this is my night to howl, Leona—what dya say?" He grabbed his granddaugter around the waist and swung her a bit.

"And that span for all the rain was a pretty sickly easy fucker ta burn," he said. Here George was thinking. He tried to think. What was it? Yesterday, too hungover to vomit, or chance a vomit, he saw animals with bloody teeth crawling out of the socks he'd started to put on. Vermin limping on strange wings seemed to crawl toward him, but after a few dark ferreted things swam before his eyes they went away, and he didn't think for a time of anybody clawing at his back when he sat at the picnic table and tried to read Louis L'Amour.

"Anyway Leona dear—Donnie over there is a mental midget—been a retard all his life—oh I could tell ya so much about Donnie, and about the likes of Lester Murphy, who's all corrupt anyways and is caught at arsonin his own tavern just cause Ceril Brown had enough foresight to set up the disco—but when Donnie asked you ta go into the woods with him ta see those robin's eggs, I knew what he was up to—I knew—ya know what ya know."

She looked up at her grandfather in perplexity and then smoothed her dress.

"He gave them to me for *show and tell*," Leona said. "And my teacher—"

"Oh I know what he wanted to show and tell," George said. "Fuckin retard." He took another drink, looked in the opposite direction and then looked back at her.

"See, they're all lawyers and everything, eh—the Bryans, who own that big cottage I took ya to—"

"What cottage?"

"Well if I didn't take ya to it I was going to—it's easy enough to see that they wouldn't let you in anyway. Too good. But Murphy got them all started—Bryan who went to Ottawa—the whole works—and Lester thinks he's some damn good, not a bit shy of his house is he—how did Lester get his money, stole it—stole it." He was saying the words slowly, his broad shoulders seemed to slither away from him, his flabby chest with grey hair, and the chain of the gold medallion.

"Lois?"

"What?"

"Gimme the keys ta my car."

"Yer not gettin inside that car—not tonight, not gettin a sniff of that car."

"Gimme the keys to my jeesless car—I'm taking Leona for a ride."

"Over my dead body—over my dead body you're gettin her in that car."

"I'm takin her down to Bryan's—she wants to see Bryan's cottage, with the swimming-pools and the swimming-pools and everything—okay Lois?"

"No."

"Good enough then—I'll drink here all night long—"

"I don't care what you do," Lois said. "But yer not getting in that car—"

He rolled off the porch and into the dirt, face down. His burnt hand twitched. "Hey," he called to his girl, "hey there." "Help me up," he continued. "Someone help me up—or I'll—"

Bradley, Lois' second boy, came through the screen door. He had a bandage wrapped about his head and looked, with his delicate white face, like a young soldier about some bivouac during some useless retreat. He'd taken five stitches in the head after falling out of a canoe and hitting Kapochus rock. And he seemed to be quite proud of his bandaged head. His eyes were large and strangely illuminated. The night turning cool, and still damp, the dying smoke crept about him. He shivered.

"You want up," he said.

"You leave him be," Lois said. "Let him sleep." She was sitting now, with her feet spread on the picnic table drinking a beer. The fire flickered in her eyes.

"I'm gonna get him up if he wants up," Bradley said.

"You leave him be," Lois said. Her hair was dry now so her curlers were loose, and curls of hair came down against her cheeks.

"I'll lift him," Bradley said. George lay with his eyes open. He kept his eyes open when Bradley spoke, and blinked each time he heard Lois. "I'll lift him," Bradley said, sucking his teeth.

"You're into those damn marshmallows—I can tell—you're chewing those marshmallows, aren't ya?"

"No siree," Bradley said, chewing.

"Ya damn well are."

"No siree," Bradley said.

"I want a marshmallow," Leona said.

"No."

"Well, if he had a marshmallow I want one too—I want one too."

"Listen to your mother—eh Lois," one of the men said, who was helping himself to more wine.

"Ya can't have a marshmallow cause they're all gone anyways," Bradley said.

"Gone—what dya mean gone?"

"Oh for Christ's sake Lois, leave the little bugger alone—now he's helped us all night," George was saying.

"You roundheaded little jeeser—there must of been two pounds of marshmallows on the kitchen table," Lois yelled. "Do you want a good cuff across the head," she said looking at him and then at the bandage. She gritted her teeth, flared a match with her thumb and lit a cigarette. When she did her left breast was visible. The man with the wine and pork chops coughed and came to sit down beside her.

The girl (Georgie's girl) was drunk. She'd been drunk yesterday, and again this afternoon, when Lois brought the pig and they'd started drinking Alpine beer—and they had with them a good deal of hash-oil. Her feet touched the chilly water. There was a great deal of commotion on the roadway across the river. Sirens sounded. It was graduation night and so a hundred youngsters would be out in cars racing along the roadway, and at the Real Thing Disco they were having a wet-T-shirt contest, that the men had tried to talk Lois into entering because first prize was $200. But Lois had balked at the suggestion finally, earlier in the evening—though she herself admitted there was nothing wrong with this, she just couldn't see herself being wetted down by a youngster.

George had planned this party for a week. And he'd sent out invitations, to Ceril Brown—his old friends from the fifties (and any friends of Ceril Brown who'd want to come, George said). But as the day wore on it became evident that not even Ceril Brown, who happened to own the Real Thing Disco, and who perhaps had more money than anyone on the roadway, even Lester Murphy, would show up. George had watched the lane for three hours, and they didn't put the pig on till late, because George was sure everyone would be coming. And then he'd become angry, kept making threatening comments about Lester Murphy's span and, determined to show he didn't care, laughed loudly at his own jokes, made fun of his girlfriend and hit the wine early.

"Jesus Christ, we're havin a good time tonight, eh Lois?" he kept saying. He never mentioned Ceril Brown all evening but he'd asked Brown yesterday if he'd received an invitation.

"Certainly," Brown said. And Brown had looked at the man with him, the young Malcolm Bryan, and they'd smiled. George had a claw in his back ever since.

"I can earn a hundred bucks a day, no problem," he remembered saying later to Malcolm, who looked embarrassed to be talking about how much money a man earned. And yet George had thought for some reason that this was what Ceril Brown and Malcolm Bryan always talked about. And then when he fell asleep in the car, with his mouth open, Ceril Brown had to drive him home, with his shoes untied and his Louis L'Amour book in his back pocket. They helped him into the house, and he fell asleep on the couch—and when he woke up on the couch later he remembered Ceril and Malcolm laughing at him while he sang:

Pearl Pearl Pearl oh don't you marry Earl,
He will lay you on your back and he will twiddle with your ——
Oh Pearl you are a —— girl.

(Ha ha, what ha—was the expression he always finished that song with.)

Ceril Brown now wore Adidas and a jogging-suit. Every morning he ran two miles—he and his young girlfriend played tennis in the court Lester Murphy had donated to the village, and last winter both wore full-length fur coats. (Ceril Brown had divorced his wife—and she'd gone for a facelift in upper New York State.) Ceril Brown had his hair in a new way, a sort-of afro style. His hands were plump and white. So he'd come a long way from the days when he and Georgie had brought in pinball machines called Acapulco and Jamaica, and had sold Canadian rye whisky to young men with fiercely sad happy faces in the shed behind Loel and Mina Brown's.

"You know my Lois eh," he asked Malcolm.

"Of course—"

"I bet you do—know her well." (Ha ha, what ha)—and he'd slapped Malcolm's thigh so hard the young man winced. George had shook his head and he began to talk about Lois being *some kind of* —— and thought they'd all laugh at this. But they didn't. So George had laughed again, and then had told them there wasn't a man on the river he couldn't drink under the table, and then he'd fallen asleep, with the Louis L'Amour book sticking out of his back pocket.

Malcolm Bryan had grown up here in the summers, at the old Bryan homestead. George remembered his marks were always high eighties—his clothes were always high eighties also, George thought, even the gym clothes he wore now were high eighties—and when he graduated and went to university he went on a scholarship, though a small one, and now he was a member of the bar—had his own $75,000 home and was a member of the Liberal Party. And so he knew men much older than he, and more influential, and even Lester Murphy was his client, because of arson. Malcolm was known to be damn good at what he did. And George thought he too would be able to talk to them, have a drink with them, that they'd pat him on the shoulders—and of course the war. George wanted to talk about the war—about D-Day and crossing the road to the village, and meeting up, against fierce resistance, with A Company.

The two of them had wanted to play tennis, and George said he would go with them, play tennis also—but as he watched the ball being thwacked from one side of the net to the other—with Ceril shouting 30–love, he became agitated.

"Look Malc—I've got a party tomorrow night—we're going to have a fuck of a good time, why don't you pick up some little lady—"

"30–love," Ceril shouted.

"And come along with Ceril—Ceril never misses one of my parties—

never do ya Ceril?"

"What's that now?"

"I just tellin the young lawyer lad here—you never miss one of my parties—"

Malcolm's face was intense and competitive. His lips were thin, and he wore a protective medical strap around his right wrist. His legs were stocky, well formed, and the upper part of his body showed muscular training. He was already tanned, and perspiration wetted those few strands of hair that fell against his broad forehead. Now and then he'd squeeze the top of his nose with the thumb and forefinger of his left hand and press away a bit of mucus. George watched them, leaning against the mesh fence, or stared at his dusty untied shoes, the grass mounds, the medallion that dangled on his chest, his open shirt tucked loosely into his suit-pants so the shirt ballooned out at the back.

"Hey have you ever read *Torso*, Malcolm?"

"What's that?"

"A book about a woman being all chopped to pieces in Hamilton—I just thought you being a lawyer—ya might have read it."

"No—I haven't Georgie."

"No—well it's a pretty good book—tells everything about the murder —I loan it to young Dale Masey—he's readin it now—he's a pretty smart boy, he gets his money." He looked about. There was a cement truck winding its way slowly toward Cortes Road, there was the sound now and then of those spray planes taking off from the airstrip, that nubbed and whined in his ears like mosquitos, there were plates of grey clouds scudding over them, blocking the sun now and then. The Spalding tennis ball rolled over the net and bounced against the mesh next to him. He stumbled after it as it rolled past him along the upper grade of the court and then ran down toward centre court again. Malcolm reached it before he did. He looked at the fellow, smiled, and Malcolm smiled at him saying, "Excuse me Georgie." He shook his head as Malcolm served, seeing the intense muscles at the back of his legs, his blue Adidas shorts. The ball, returned hard by Ceril, whizzed past him before he had a chance to retreat into his corner, and Malcolm, backing up too, collided with him. George (the racket having hit him on his bald head) fell onto the warm asphalt.

"God—sorry—you hurt?" Malcolm said. There was a warm trickle of perspiration that rolled over his close-cropped sideburns. He tried to help him up. George smiled, his mouth hung open, and he laughed with his tongue out. There was a drop of blood. "I was never much good at this tennis thing," he said. "Don't worry though, I ain't hurt—take more than a fall down to hurt me," he said. "Eh Ceril—eh?" Malcolm's lips tightened, turning white and sad. He waited for George to leave.

And George returned to his corner again where one of his shoes rested against a mound of dirt and the other on soft blue gravel. And he stared at the mound of dirt and looked at the strands of grass and padded weeds growing beyond the mesh fence. And when the clouds blocked the sun, how cold, how sad and far away they seemed. And too he was hungry—

But how dangerous it was to be there, especially as both of them, he thought, were watching him—especially since Malcolm, and he just realized this, had made that kind effort to help him to his feet. He felt that he must say something nice. Something with humour in it that would make them laugh—and then they'd stop the tennis and go back to the car and have a drink of wine. How cold it looked when the wind blew against the weeds that grew up through the mesh fence, already slightly rusted. He looked at Ceril Brown's body, plump and sweating—he made much more frantic movements with his upper body than he did with his legs, and yes, he was growing a small goatee. When the ball hit the fence Ceril Brown slapped it down quickly with his racquet, caught it with his left hand and slammed it over the net again.

"Jeesus—I wish I could do that," George said. "I'll have to get in shape like you Ceril—do a bit of running—hey Malcolm, can you imagine me running?" Then he said: "I couldn't run nowhere, eh?"

"Well you should start Georgie," Malcolm said, without turning around. Again there were the blue sneakers, the blue shorts, the white socks, the muscular, well-trained, browned body. George nodded, at nothing. He put his fingers through the wire mesh and breathing deeply, gauging the distance beyond the wire fence (when he would have to let go of it) to the car, he began moving along the incline, now and then tramping on the laces of his right shoe. But when had this tennis started, he wondered? And yes, hadn't he seen the Vietnamese boat-people playing tennis—last week, weren't the young brother and sister here tossing the ball back and forth themselves? On the bench near the opened gate, that he'd have to slip through, lay Ceril's orange towel and Malcolm's green one. He'd forgotten about the two towels that they'd taken from the back seats with their racquets. They'd closed the door on him also—thinking he'd stay in the car—and they were already opening the presses of their racquets when he managed to get out of the car and stumbled with a warm beer in his hand toward them, waving. What was it? What would he do with a new child? Well? A certain depression filled him. He tramped into the soft parking-lot dust one step, two, let go of the outside

16

of the mesh fence. He'd have to cross the small dirt path to the new Eldorado, which sat twenty yards away, near the first of the power-lines. He could hear the power-lines humming, tick tick tick like so many grasshoppers. Well, what of it? He took a deep breath and lurched forward with his arms out, he could see the Eldorado moving up and down as he approached it. It was now summer again—so he'd been home a year, he thought. Near the power-lines the sharp yellow grasses looked like thin metal spears—and there was a stink in his mouth like excrement and piss. Of course they'd seen him walking, so instead of attempting to hide how he was stumbling he turned around at the last moment, gave a wave of his hand and fell against the car door.

"Made her, boys," he shouted. "Hey Malcolm—I made it—eh?" He laughed, shook his head; his mouth opened and he felt his tongue hanging out.

But neither Malcolm nor Ceril had watched him at all. Malcolm looked about. And then he hit the ball again, the Spalding ball.

"Who's winning?" George managed. "Who—who is winning?" he said.

The power-lines rose straight in the air, like so many crosses all the way to town—or at least all the way to Calvin Simms' Irving garage. The sun came out again, came softly through the trees, the light on their branches, and in the distance the McGraw hayfields; and they'd have a terrible time collecting hay this year because of the wet weather. In the other direction was the village—the newly built (and as yet not completely finished) Glad Tidings Tabernacle, where two ministers preached, and brought in guest speakers, ex-convicts and addicts who'd turned to God—and beyond that Bobby Simms' newly erected McDonald's, with over 30 billion sold.

Ho-ho. It was obvious now he'd done nothing with the money he'd received—and so what was all this damn talk for over twenty years about a restaurant of his own?

He scratched his nose and looked at the light blue car—and thinking suddenly that he was in the best place possible, and that he was travelling about today with Ceril Brown and Malcolm Bryan—whose father was an MP and who some day himself would be an MP and that he himself had a great number of parties, and people were always asking him for $10 or $20 to tide them over—he shouted, opened the car door, opened another pint of beer and took a large mouthful.

"Hey Malcolm," he said. They were drying themselves with the towels now, Malcolm patting his chest and belly and under his armpits. Georgie watched them.

"What's that George?" Malcolm said smiling. (You see he said "What's that George?" and smiled—he even waved his green towel, and probably—) George laughed, waved the warm beer. "When can I get down to your swimming-pool at the cottage and have a swim?" he said.

"Any time at all George," Malcolm said. "Come anytime."

"Very best," George said. "You got a woman yet?" he said.

"Oh yes," Malcolm said.

"Well, I was thinking you should come over and meet my daughter Lois—come on over."

"Oh I know Lois," Malcolm said.

George shook his head, coughed. The beer was very warm.

Malcolm sat on the bench facing Ceril. Ceril had his sweat-shirt off wringing it out, and Malcolm was looking up at him speaking. Then Malcolm, taking off his sneakers, dried his legs and laughed at something. George looked at his beer, studied it. Along the ground a little way off there was a small bird that'd been electrocuted on the power-line. It lay with its wings stiffened, and tiny flies crawled in its grey disordered feathers, and then the wind came again and smelled of something sweet and heavy. And oh there was that cement truck churning along toward town. Of course it wasn't impossible for him to get a restaurant—he could possibly swing a restaurant; but what right had McDonald's to come here just when he was ready to swing a restaurant?

Damn it all.

Summer again. No, you couldn't do that much in the summer. Not to worry about anything, have some parties. Behind the cluster of maple saplings rose the power-lines out of shale rock-beds, humming like so many grasshoppers, tick tick in the heat. A rusted barrel had been thrown oddly into those saplings, leaned against them, its rusted bottom smelling like burnt paper. Georgie's mouth was flat. He sipped on his warm beer. He thought of something; thought that actually at this spot—or just a little farther up, near the property once owned by Hitchman Alewood himself, the village benefactor, he had had his Hamburger Palace in the nineteen-fifties: when he and Ceril Brown had some parties together?

He was sitting in the car, smelling the seat-covers, the Louis L'Amour book sticking out of his back trouser pocket—the suit pants held up by a belt with a cowboy buckle. There were great patches of greyish sweat on on his shirt now. He breathed. The door was open and his feet rested on the ground. Ceril and Malcolm were still on the bench; Ceril was smoking a cigarette now, George could taste salt as he sipped on the beer, as he watched them. The Vietnamese boy, still wearing the black cotton pants of his homeland, was riding up the road on his second-hand bicycle; *and one day he'd seen the whole family, the mother with grey hair, riding second-hand bicycles.*

Ceril pinched the cigarette between his plump fingers. He pointed toward the Vietnamese boy, smiled and said something, bending his head slightly. Malcolm stood, with his sneakers in one hand, the tennis racquet in the other, flexed slightly, preening. He smiled, a smile which suggested to George that more things were possible for him than for anyone else— and they were too. Certainly he would be in Ottawa some day there could be no doubt of that—Ottawa (the boys in Ottawa). But George thought about this and the clouds blocked the sun suddenly. The feathers of the electrocuted bird fluttered, stiffened. Means, that George himself had taken an active role in politics in the nineteen-fifties, had worn buttons and had run for treasurer of the local Conservative Party—had lost and had taken a good deal of pleasure in the fact that he had lost. But, of course too, those were the days when he'd no clear idea of what he wanted to do with his life. He was still a young man then, home from the war. He knew also that being a member of the Conservative Party in this part of the province was synonymous with being second—and then to lose when running for treasurer, well that meant third at least, or just no-account. (But still it was keeping out of the clutches of Lester Murphy or the French.) And still there was, back then, a handful of men who said of him that he was the best man for the job. The loud talk, the phrases, the campaigning for the Conservatives, all came down to off-colour jokes told at the small party headquarters when he'd sat at the head table, and a group of men sat around on wooden chairs that squeaked.

He still held the pint of warm beer in his hand. Ceril Brown had put on a fresh T-shirt, with the letters UCLA on the front, and the number 36 on the back. It was a T-shirt that glittered, the letters UCLA glittered.

Not all the French were Liberal though—no, in Gloucester and other counties, in certain rural hideaways in little red and pink houses one or two pockets of French Conservatives sat at meetings themselves. Why George was angry when he thought of this he didn't know—yes he did. He did know? It'd be so much simpler if all the French were Liberal and all the English were Conservative, then people would know where they stood. Wouldn't they? But once—when he was in the northern part of the province on a deal (George went away three or four times a year on deals) he'd laughed about Trudeau not being able to handle his wife, let alone the country, and suddenly two Frenchmen that he'd hoped to get in a fight with, laughed, patted him on the left knee and agreed with everything he'd said—saying: the feeble talk of politics swims in the loins, the necessary talk of the partisan mob is interlaced with smugness and smut.

But what was wrong with Mr. Clark, clapping his hands to fiddle music at a rally, shown tasting French cuisine—why did George feel embarrassed when he saw the short-lived Prime Minister clapping his hands, one clap two, chuckling—they showed his feet tapping—one foot tapping; and tasting French cuisine? Why did that depress him? Perhaps it was the smile—oh, well—not everyone could smile as well as Mr. Trudeau, but was it the smile of a person who'd much rather, and instead of tasting French mocha balls and clapping his hands, be looking through the contents of a briefcase containing financial reports and information on how many cubic feet of gas they might successfully ship to the United States of America—but weren't they all like that, certainly Trudeau—and how ridiculous it was anyway to have to prove you were having a good time in front of a CBC cameraman who was thinking more about—

George was staring at the beer, piss-warm, the vexing colour of urine. His entire body twitched suddenly. The car smelled of suntan oil and it lubricated his nostrils. Ceril Brown's paunch shook slightly. George dropped his head; the electrocuted bird that had fallen from the stinging wire now lay near a small dusk-brown rock. George had forgotten about it, and now saw it again with its feathers twisted, a white piece of cartilage or bone.

He remembered his wife, Elizabeth Ripley Terri, wearing silver fingernail polish the last time he'd seen her—which was at Little Simon's funeral, Little Simon sunken into the cushions, the waxy colour not hiding the morbid greenness of the skin, the hands folded as if they'd nothing else to do but fold those wax fingers with bitten nails; Elizabeth Ripley Terri having the tenacity to bring with her, from Charlottetown, the little miniature poodle she called Mincy that peed over the new couch Lois had bought:

"Never mind that, Mummy—just never mind," Lois said. "Jeffrey, you get a wet cloth and clean that up."

"I'm not cleanin that up," Jeffrey saying.

"Clean it up."

"No way in the world."

"Listen you little redhaired jeeser, I'm tellin ya—it's me yer talkin to, boys oh boys."

"No way in the world—but I'll take the dog out and drown it for ya anytime—maybe tonight."

"My dear you just don't understand," Elizabeth Ripley Terri said as she looked over at George and George's girl who were sitting on the other side of the room. "This is a very expensive dog—and a very *important* present—extremely important—" she smiled.

"I'd say—oh it'd take about fifteen seconds ta drown her," Jeffrey said.

"You get a cloth an clean it up or you'll be the one drowned in fifteen seconds—I'm not having this place smell of piss at Little Simon's funeral —you hear me," Lois saying.

The dog yapped at everyone coming in or out of the house.

"George—my soul how are you doing?" Elizabeth asked. George sat in his black turtleneck with the medallion around his throat.

"You know me there—Ripley," he said, calling her by her maiden name, instinctively. He laughed loudly and shaking his head he grabbed his girlfriend around her waist. But somehow (he thought he'd have a great time showing off his girl in front of Elizabeth) he was embarrased by her. Her panty-hose were wrinkled, the new blue skirt she wore hung over her thin hips and she stared at Elizabeth with a moody frightened expression on her face. Elizabeth took out her cosmetic case, and staring in the mirror said, "Yes."

"Well I mean I don't change from day to day," George said. He had half a glass of rum in his hand and he clinked the ice in the glass. The little dog, with manicured furballs, gurred at him.

"Mincy," Elizabeth said, scratching the dog's ears with her silver-coloured fingernails and taking out a cigarette-case to light a cigarette.

"No—I don't change from day to day," George said. He smiled at his girl.

"Well some do and some don't." Elizabeth winked at Georgie's girl. The girl suddenly smiled. George stared at his drink. Now Elizabeth and the girl began talking.

"Well George—introduce us for heavens sakes," Elizabeth said.

"Beth," George mumbled.

"Pardon?"

"Her name—is Beth."

"Hello Beth," Elizabeth said, and then recognizing the name, she began at the dog's ears again. The thing hopped on her lap. She smiled, puffed her lips and kissed the dog and blew in its ear. When she did the dog yapped. She smiled and did it again. The dog yapped again.

"Play little boys—play little boys," Elizabeth said to the dog. "Come on, play little boys," she said. The little poodle began to whine frantically, hopping on and off her lap.

"Come on, Mincy dear—play little boys, come on—" Lois looked at it

21

—and Packet, wouldn't he have to fly back for this, was he now at 38,000 feet?—please Packet you must come back, ran through Lois' mind at that instant. She turned. The little female poodle had one leg lifted, like a male about to urinate against a fire-hydrant. "Play little boys—play little boys," Elizabeth said. "You see, you see," she said. Everyone laughed. Lois, her nose raw from crying, smiled.

"You see—you see," Elizabeth said. She clicked open the lighter with the letter E on it and lit her cigarette: "Of course at the first sight of blood she'll be locked in a room—I don't want a thousand males at my Mincy." She smiled, the cigarette quivered slightly. "Not at my Mincy."

She looked at the girl (George's girl) and the smoke drifted from her slightly parted mouth.

"And how's Lester Murphy?" she said suddenly, "*Is he still the old Lester I knew?*"

George wanted to get out of the Eldorado and go sauntering up to Malcolm and Ceril once more but his legs seemed to be quite weak. Now a patch of white gravel looking like a heap of salt came into focus, through the yellowed blood of his dirty sclera—along and away there were sounds of Indian children playing skip-a-rope; and he thought, and said: "Georgie—yer the only man I know ta take the bull by the fucking horns, eh boy." He shook his head and yelled: "Hey Malcolm—who takes the bull by the horns more'n me eh?"

Again and again—why was it so awful that no-one was listening to him? Elizabeth had worn a gold chain around her left ankle—a very thick ankle now, with two blue veins, and for some reason she signed the guest book at her own son's funeral right beneath Lester Murphy's name —scrawled out in her childish handwriting, which of course was more legible than Georgie's handwriting (so that when they'd been together he'd gotten her to do all the writing) was the name Ms. Elizabeth Ripley (Terri). George too was going to see the authorities about Little Simon's death, but he never did. But that day with her poodle playing tricks for the crowd, Georgie said to his girl, "Hand me the goddamn telephone, I gotta make a phone call—I wanta get to the bottom of this—"

"What?" his girl said.

"I just told you—as I told Lois last night, I want to get to the bottom of this—autopsy—that's all."

I'm drunk, he thought sitting, or rather lying, in the Eldorado, staring at the ceiling where two flies fornicated merrily, I'm drunk. He shook his head, drowsily, the wind over the stiffened feathers, the dead twigs of grass.

Death came from massive loss of blood and shock, *almost* instantaneously. The bullet cutting (scalding) through the aorta. Packet with his new-found Indian woman, Emma Jane Ward, flying home—over the 5000 miles, where in a bar in Victoria he'd watched the twenty-year-old boy with the tight impatient slacks of a bullfighter doing pirouettes for his lover, and then a few afternoons later that same boy with the silk blouse of a woman slicing his wrists while sitting on the flush in the men's washroom. Packet now no longer drank, what was wrong with Packet that he no longer drank? A few parties—what in God's name was wrong with a few parties?

Georgie's mouth hung open. He rubbed it, remembered the beer between his legs and drank from it, hoping that it would render him instantaneously sober. He could smell the stench of so many powdered bodies in the car, stale perfume from Ceril Brown's young girlfriend—pink tissues in a pick-one box on the dash, of old perfume from immaculately performed toilettes. The wire lines ran over the cut, those now-bleached stems and adolescent blueberry crops. White dirt mounds the colour of ash.

(George remembered: he was sitting in the Eldorado, and Ceril Brown yelled to him, asking him if he wouldn't mind bringing his deodorant over? No, certainly—deodorant? It was in the glove compartment. Suddenly George found himself looking for this deodorant, as if it were the most important task in the world. With the Louis L'Amour book still sticking up in his back pocket and the deodorant in his right hand—Irish Spring—he began crossing the lot again.

"Lies you mean," Ceril saying.

"No—not at all—but—*specific* generalities."

"Lies," Ceril said humorously.

George with his right hand outstretched holding the stick deodorant, tried to manœuvre his way by clutching onto the mesh fence once more; heard: "lies—" He moved toward them sweat rolling along his naked temples, his face appeared orange. Malcolm arched his back to the shoulder blades moved toward one another and you could see small golden-coloured hair just above his shorts.

"No mind of their own," Ceril saying.

Malcolm rubbed his shoulders and coughed slightly.

"Fuck, I can't stand a person without a mind of their own," George said. "Take Packet now—my son there—no mind of his own."

He handed the deodorant over, shook his head, spit a deal of spittle that stuck to his chin and hung there. He wiped it away watching Ceril lift his

23

UCLA T-shirt to rub the deodorant under his arms; there was a squelching and squeaking sound. But what struck him was the black, still sweaty cluster of hair near Ceril Brown's navel, and just as he was looking at this Brown rubbed the deodorant against those hairs—a yellow gauze came over them and twisted them, in one direction or another.

Lies, George heard. And suddenly (without wanting to) he asked, angrily, tapping Bryan on the shoulder:

"Are you fucking coming to my party tomorrow night or not—there, eh?"

"I think we'll make it," Malcolm said, staring at him a second (Malcolm's head jerked just slightly) and then he looked at the Pinto pulling in behind the Eldorado.

"Well—I mean I was just wondering," George laughed, his mouth hung open. He wanted to rub Malcolm Bryan's head, but something prevented him.

George remembered. That this ran through his mind, and he wanted them all to be happy and have a drink with him.

"And I had a son, shot himself—the authorities blocked it all the way —the investigation, and if it wasn't for me—"

Both of them stared at him. He didn't understand something, there was a scalding smell of asphalt. Two small tears came to the corners of his eyes.

"I still cry when I think of it," he said. "*Anyways*," he said (he paused and swallowed), "Anyways—you'll get to Ottawa Malcolm, any day now." He shook his head. No-one seemed to look at him and he wanted to tell them about the Vietnamese girl; how Little Simon bought her a present—and that he'd gone the next evening to the tavern—with Rance, and then he'd shot himself and anyone could understand why. Couldn't they understand why? He was talking again. He was blaming the Vietnamese girl. The authorities didn't take that into consideration.

"All cowards—they didn't haul her up in front of no judge, did they —no siree they didn't—I seen her old man, I phoned him—" he said. "Me—I phoned him—*ho ho through*, no authorities in that there were there." He shook his head. Malcolm could not seem to help, was staring away without a trace of passion on his face twisting his mouth. Ceril mumbled something. George laughed suddenly, fell back and gave a whoop.

"Anyways boys—we gonna have a drink or what," he said. He fell with a slight clatter against the mesh fence. "Packet now—can't have a drink with him, couldn't drink with him couldja—big feeling'd son of a

24

bitch don't drink no more—eh?" His head fell forward.

Malcolm smiled, nodded at Ceril. The asphalt blue and lonely and far away.

There was no denying it. He wanted to go back to the Eldorado and fall into the back seat. And wasn't this always the way with him—that now he really did want to go home, he had no way home, because now Ceril and Malcolm were talking to Ceril's ex-wife who'd just driven up in the Pinto.

Her hair was dyed light brown. Ceril was growing a goatee and he kept smoothing it with the fingers of his right hand. He looked at his ex-wife with malevolent eyes—clear black eyes. She patted Ceril on the stomach quickly—she too seemed to look at him with that bright malevolence as she patted him.

"Malcolm, what is he eating?" she said.

"God only knows, Karen," Malcolm said. Ceril chuckled. George kept lifting his head to watch them; he too let out a big breath and chuckled.

(George remembered: how positively some people lived—look you could see Karen adjusting the perfect strap on her halter top; and there was a good scent of suntan lotion from her also; as she patted her ex-husband's stomach she was telling Malcolm that Rosemary Alewood had invited her to spend a fortnight in Bar Harbour; and she actually used the word fortnight. Ceril smiled when she patted him, and Georgie's face stung suddenly—various pin-pricks, for there was that—

"And how's Rhonda, Ceril?" she said suddenly. It was playful, the voice was playful. George laughed and shook his head. Karen looked at him for a second and he saw his own reflection in her eyes, the skin even after the facelift with one or two crinkles. How sad it was that a few tiny drab strands of her hair wisped in the breeze. Ceril cleared his throat: "Rhonda's fine—very well, she's visiting her parents this afternoon—so you're away then," he smiled. "When we were together I could never get her out of the house—now she's a gallivanter—"

"A gallivanter," she said. "Anyway Ceril I was—about the?"

"Of course," Ceril said. "Oliver will open the safe for you—okay?"

"He's not there."

"Well he damn well should be."

"Yes my son and his father," she said. Everyone laughed. And Georgie laughed louder than everyone.

Her toes shone with clear toe-polish. George was drunk, he was so drunk—would he remember then, at three in the morning, when he woke on the couch too weak to vomit or chance a vomit, would he then remem-

25

ber running behind an alleyway that smelled of cooked stones when Kenneth Ward, and the Ginnish man, the one with the tattoo "Born to lose" on his left wrist, were after him, and backed into that alleyway that smelled of cooked stones and cardboard covering the windows he'd beaten them both; in those days when he and Elizabeth Ripley Terri were still together and he and Ceril Brown brought in pinball machines named Acapulco and Jamaica, with pictures of men playing roulette against a backdrop of sinister characters, palm trees and summer water?

"Priceless," Karen said. "You know me—I've never been upstaged."

George looked at her. Ceril was smiling slightly, his capped teeth seemed to be clenched together—she was talking about the trip to Bar Harbour, the trip with Rosemary Alewood, which would be Randolf Alewood's only child, George thought, and Ceril had teased her about the American men. So she'd just said that she'd never be upstaged. Her toes shone with clear toe-polish, though too there was the scent of Cutex.

"Oh play the field," George said. "Play the field—I've been wantin to put me arms around you for years," he said. She was holding prescription sunglasses in her right hand—where you could see the thumb tendon. She put the sunglasses on now and looked quizzically about, as if she'd forgotten something. The last time she and her husband had been together was at their son's wedding to Sandra Simms—a huge snowball of a wedding with 500 guests, and the lead singers from the choir in town and a great reception after, with a telegram from the premier—which was read twice. There was a vicious scar across her left wrist that had healed, blue-grey skin had grown across the wrist itself. No-one noticed it. She smiled.

"Well George—my goodness I didn't even notice you—when did you come home?"

"Oh I been home off an on for a year," George said. "I left out west there—they hired a couple of men to take over my job and I came home."

She smiled again, vaguely.

"Malc, tell your mum tomorrow night lobsters for sure—positive."

Georgie's eyes lost focus again. He'd been about to tell her what he did out west, how much he'd earned out there—which he'd not decided upon at the moment, but now she turned completely from him and was talking about lobsters to Malcolm.

"Lobsters," George muttered. "I can get you all the lobsters you need, tons of them—"

"Is your dad still in Ottawa?" Karen said. Just below Malcolm's blond stomach hair the now-flattened ruby appendix scar was visible.

"Oh yes," Malcolm said.

"I mean you can all come over tomorrow night ta my place for lobsters —you remember Lois there Karen—Lois my daughter there?"

"I should have *known* he'd still be there," she said. She clicked her teeth again slightly. It seemed as if both Malcolm and Ceril understood what she was saying about the business in Ottawa and the men in Ottawa. The bird had fallen, perhaps yesterday or the day before—the wires tick tick tick, you would think anyway, and then the smell of Cutex, coming to him now. You could see the line of her underwear below her white shorts, the dark flowers on her panties. He noticed it, somehow the cruelty of it. Amazing how they'd all grown older; how she wore those white shorts that hugged her buttocks and showed the painful traces of flowers —perhaps unaware that the sunlight abused her, that the traces of little roses were visible. His eyes were closed again, one damnable eye kept bothering him. The fingers of his right hand were intertwined through the mesh fence.

(They were all standing around the Eldorado, except he was sitting inside, on the passenger side with the door open, and when Ceril handed him the deodorant to put into the glove compartment he rubbed some across his chest between the chain of his medallion.) They were talking about something he didn't understand—though he'd have liked to have understood it, for it sounded quite important. Malcolm was telling them something, about who? Lester Murphy. But he'd missed it. In the reflection of her glasses he could see his own cowboy buckle. He wanted to sing: "Oh Pearl Pearl Pearl you are a ——— girl, don't you marry Earl, he will lay you on your back, and he will ———." Then everything was quiet, like the presbytery in London England he'd visited by mistake the day he'd bummed a half pack of cigarettes from an American soldier: "Kanada—ferry bad, Kanada" that German boy with the translucent ears like a comical satyr's, until he started running and then George (and what else could he do?) shot him through the pelvic girdle. The German prisoners cursing him, the Maritimers yelling—

He could hear the chain clinking against the dull teeth and the pedal scraping the chainguard. The Vietnamese boy, with his younger sister on the crossbar, had ridden up, with their tennis racquets—the girl held both tennis racquets, and the boy had laid his bike against the fence and had chained it to the mesh. George was fascinated by this. The girl was not more than five feet tall, and if he was not mistaken, which he wasn't, it was not tennis racquets they carried but badminton racquets. The girl was not more than five feet tall—and the boy, a good five six would scare him, George thought. The boy's hair fell across his eyes and he tossed his

27

head quickly. George met his eyes for an instant. He looked away. Little swirls of white dust blew along the ground. He stared at it, his eyes flitting. The girl held the gate open for the boy, and touched his arm as he slipped through it laughing. Georgie's eyes flitted, he said something undecipherable to himself that sounded like *a bunch of creeps.* No-one heard it. They were still discussing Lester Murphy, and Ceril Brown came up with the estimation that Murphy was worth in the vicinity of—

"I can earn a hundred bucks a day, no problem Malc," George said suddenly. He smiled, shook his head playfully. "Buy a coat from one man sell it to another, a suit from one lad see, and sell it to another—the profit's there—once I bought a leather coat from one lad at the tavern and sold it to another for $25 profit eh—and the stupid fuckers were sitting right beside each other—hello for free enterprise—*Karen me darlin that halter top is some sexy on you.*" He tapped his feet on the ground, snapped up a quart of wine from beneath the seat and hit the bottom of the bottle twice with the palm of his hand. Then unscrewing the top with a flick and feeling happy and sober he drained a quarter of it away immediately. Karen cleared her throat, the healed slash mark on her wrist, the dead skin glinted in his eyes. He remembered falling forward and seeing the finishing screws of the rocker panel. The wine seeped between his pantlegs and dissolved in a sweet circle in the dirt. Lester Murphy's faded sign just above the hollow read: "Atlantic Salmon Centre of the World."

The road signs told of bends and curves and deer crossings. He stared up at Karen's legs, the rough skin about her knees, the power-lines like a crucifixion all the way to Calvin Simms' garage.

"Poor Rhonda—I hear she had it rough," he heard Karen saying as Malcolm put on a fresh T-shirt. Ceril had left them for a moment and Malcolm, when his head popped out of his T-shirt, nodded. Georgie blinked. Karen sighed.

"Abortion is always rough," she whispered. She stroked Malcolm's brown arm. He nodded, his cheeks flattened. "But Ceril and I—well there's nothing but the *utmost* concern for one another." The voices were far away and whispering—painfully they whispered. George lay on his side sleeping—voice through the dead wine bottle over the stinking grasses in the heat, tick tick. Voice said, how properly open some people are—how amazing their lives, how all the essential steps are taken, they who have their own maids to take the children for walks. Voice said the badminton bird fluttered, the bushes smelled of the faeces of lost cats.

Voice said—

28

He heard Malcolm laughing.

"C'mon—I've heard your mother talking," the voice said.

Malcolm's slight laughter.

The voice said: utmost concern for one another. Another voice: granted you can't live for 25 years with a person—. Voice said: in Bar Harbour while Rosemary and I—

The light hair, those transparent grey hairs lost in the sweet breeze. She smiled, and her mouth trembled slightly. Voice said: certainly and Rhonda and I would have nothing but good things to say about one another—can you understand Malcolm? Of course. Voice saying: poor Rhonda. Yes, voice saying: I just wonder about her maturity, nineteen years of age. I understand: Malc by the way, Malc your mum took me through your new house.

Really.

Yes yes, how lovely—you've come a long way young man.

Slight laughter.

Voice saying: the litter of lost things in the damp undergrowth, the discarded materials of a generation stunk in his mouth. The Vietnamese girl laughed childlike. The badminton bird fluttered, the second-hand bicycle manacled to the fence. The mounds of shale that Ceril Brown walked over, on his way back from urinating in the bushes, crunched.

(God, Lois said, God—good God?

Father Barry stood behind the pit they'd dug out to roast the pig. When the fat dripped from the centre loin onto the coals there was a burst of flame and a smell of sweetened meat. By this time Jeffery, Lois' firstborn who'd come back on his minibike, and Bradley, with his bandaged head, looking like a lost soldier during some useless campaign or other, had managed to drag their grandfather a ways and set him on the porch. So Georgie was sitting quite steadily on the porch now beside his grand-daughter. His mind reeled with certain thoughts—the way Karen had walked to her car, those clogs sounding and the Vietnamese children talking in their strange, somehow frightful language. The smell of Cutex, like the smell of Kleenex dipped into Cutex put into plastic bags and breathed to get high. He himself had done that more than one time in the camps—the men in the camps, the girls wearing their leather boots and tight Levis in bars during frigid winters—yes it was then he'd taken the Cutex and breathed it. Now he remembered why the Cutex seemed so familiar and important, and strangely so violent—because wasn't it that way in Northern Manitoba when the two squaws were naked on the bed, one crying about her husband until the other one broke her teeth, and bleeding from the mouth everyone had sexual intercourse with her anyway? (In a way, to Georgie, that wasn't as bothersome as Karen seeming to want to enjoy herself last year with the man Robert who'd the *HMS Bonaventure* tattoo on his arm—that day coming from detox he'd seen them in the downtown office, Robert holding her purse and helping her on with her coat—was it before then or after, that she'd cut herself—and why did Robert have to hold her purse—why did that seem so unjust? A circus whirled in his brain, one that showed a trained monkey smoking a cigarette and bears that lay on the ground in their own heavy mess, eyes groggy with sorrow and discomfort—*member* that Georgie, *member*— perhaps it was only that he was coming from detox and everything was discomforting: "Now you'll have a bit of discomfort"—and that he'd wanted to go into that office and grab that purse away from the man with his *HMS* tattoo, the red insinuating purse—God, to think Karen might even buy that man a present—"Now you'll have a bit of discomfort"— and then the man came out of the office and holding Karen about the waist, his pantlegs billowing in the wind, said: "Oh my soul swearing— a girl like you" and there was laughter—why was it so terrible that neither of them noticed him as they hurried away?)

The memories of certain things.

Leona in her pretty party dress was telling Bradley what her teacher had said:

"G Hovus ya big baby suck up to the teacher," Bradley said.

George breathing deeply set his feet as far apart as he could. The span had collapsed. It no longer burned. Georgie's mouth hung open. So they'd put him in the car, in the Eldorado, and he sang. When he fell asleep certain of their phrases came to him—and he heard Malcolm saying something (it sounded like—Lois 'cunt, but would Malcolm say that —and Ceril snickering). When they'd helped him into the house he'd wanted them to stay; "have a good time." But they left him. Their bodies, like objects from a strange world, all moved away.

"Come back tomorrow night—come early, about six—come," he'd said. "You will won't you—you will won't you, Ceril—Ceril?"

It mightn't have been honest but Jeffery, Lois' firstborn, had seen a ten-dollar bill of Georgie's lying on the ground when they lifted him. Georgie was tapping his feet, calling them all miserable cocksuckers, the ten-dollar bill just beneath those feet.

Lois and Father Barry were talking and the men had gathered around her, shaking their heads.

"George," Lois yelled.

George lifted his head.

"Hey," Lois yelled. "They found Papa's body today—this afternoon at cold stream, you hear me George come here—they found Papa—and Lester Murphy was run down, you hear that you hear—George they found Papa."

George lifted his hand, waved and shrugged. The hand moved. There was the smell of pig.

"They found Papa," Lois screamed. "And Lester—was run over, he was run over George, phone Packet, for God's sake phone Packet will you."

Lois was crying. George lifted his hand as if to inspect it, and yawned. The little girl jumped off the porch and ran to her mother. He didn't know —he didn't remember anything immediately about the span. Lois was crying and shaking her head; she cried and began banging her head on the girl's (Georgie's girl's) shoulder, and the girl cradled her. Father Barry had his hand on Lois' shoulder and there was a smell of gas. Georgie rubbed his burnt hand across his bald head.

The men backed into the shadows.

Ursa Major in the sky was threatening. Father Barry was asking about the span.

"I didn't do nothin," one man said. "It weren't me, Father—oh Father it weren't—I didn't do nothin Father."

Lois cried. She kept trying to bang her head. From her twenty curlers the smell of hair rinse.

George kept rubbing his head. Perhaps he too would cry, at any moment. As a matter of fact he could feel his throat start to swell. "You get, you get out of my yard; I'll put ya out of me yard," George managed, to no-one in particular.

He managed a threatening gesture with his arms. Father Barry stared at him. George said:

"We were just havin a party—we were havin a party till you come here —ruinin everythin."

"George—" Georgie's girl said. Father Barry looked at the girl, smiled slightly.

And again there were sirens—all along the road. And at the Real Thing Disco owned and operated by Ceril Brown they were having a wet T-shirt contest, where the boys and girls would go—and where Georgie himself had gone to watch the wetting down of youngsters on that makeshift platform with the used crepe adorning the back wall and the girls' slackened wet breasts gone sexless—the outside afternoon winter light resolute

31

and determined, the flashes of sunlight when they went outside at twilight, and then darkness.

George was trying to think. Things whirled about him—there was another silence, to a drunkard the whirr of an untaped cassette. A grasshopper hung from a viny leaf and then made a slight slapping sound when it jumped.

(No, Karen walked on her clogs, she walked away. The grasshopper jumped, settled and moved its body slightly. Then he remembered pubic lice with their transparent claws moving on his flesh that morning in Toronto with the yellow light through the bathroom window, and the woman who worked making disposable diapers coughed and lit a cigarette. And that afternoon he'd waited for Packet to come by. The woman's face showing, who knows, some Spanish blood, earrings stretching her earlobes. He went into the drugstore and asked for blue ointment and a pretty teenager handed it to him. Perhaps she didn't hand the ointment to him; maybe she put it on the counter and slid it across to him. The smiling little animals looked up at him from his testicles, their claws moving like beasts in a horror show. The woman said:

"The yellow infected slant eyes are comin from all over Cambodia." And as he poured the homemade beer into her glass and prepared to watch the hockey game on her small black-and-white there were sirens in the streets. So then tonight he would connect all the millions of sirens together. He would connect them always.

"The yellow infected slant-eyes are put in goddamn $20,000 houses all over this jeezly country," the woman who made disposable diapers told him. There was a great yeast taste from the homemade beer and he'd swilled eleven pints of it before the hockey game came on. He'd wanted to tell the woman that the greatest hockey in the world was played in Montreal but the woman coughed and spat into a Kleenex. Later that night he watched an old war movie—the Americans moving through Europe. The American infantry moved through Europe and he drank homemade beer and left the porch light on for Packet.

Lois was banging her head quite a bit; at first on the girl's shoulder, and then on the picnic table—then she was backing up from everyone, clutching her stomach. The girl tried to hold her.

There was still a drowsy bit of smoke. The men huddled together in the shadows. Father Barry smoothed his receding hair. And Lois was trying to find something on which to bang her head. At the Murphy house Donnie was sitting on the porch. You could tell Donnie because he towered over everyone—there were four or five people sitting with him now. There was something acutely idiotic about his gestures. He sat on his porch steps and stared across at George, and George stared back at him.

"Don't try ta stare me down—ya'll never be able to—never," George muttered. Barry looked at him and then spoke to Lois. What was it? Oh yes, one of his friends had just said: "Oh Father it weren't us, Father—it weren't me." Georgie spat. Hadn't Georgie heard about Father Barry playing soccer in steel-toed boots against cub scouts in sneakers and shorts —or what had he heard, if it wasn't that Little Simon himself had been a cub scout the first year Father Barry started them—and hadn't he played soccer in his steel-toed boots—hadn't George heard that Little Simon wouldn't get out of Barry's way but kept blocking shots, until his ankles and shins were blue? Hadn't this happened—when Little Simon was what, seven or eight, Father Barry—Georgie imagined it somehow. Somehow there were only the two of them in the centre of the field, the short muscular priest and the child—and the child moving with those jerking unco-ordinated movements, his brown skinny legs—the cords at the back of his knees like some kind of chicken bones, in those dull shorts. Falling down and wincing and then shaking the hair out of his eyes, running at the priest again who rolled the black-and-white soccer ball, the Spalding soccer ball, over the dirt; pushing the child down.

"Oh Father—it weren't us, Father," the men said.

What was it?

He would get the keys to the car and go over to the Bryan's cottage and have a swim in the swimming-pool. They all knew him. And he could damn well cope with his father's body being found. So there was no use in Father Barry coming here and trying to blame him. The old lad was always as odd as a duck. If he was 82 years old and walked into the woods and didn't come out—well Georgie could have told them that he'd do that. Could have told them. Did tell them. More than once.

"I told ya," he shouted. "Didn't I tell ya about it—and everything about it Lois—oh make the big show, go round bangin yer head—make the big show—and you Father Barry—I go ta church too—oh ya—I go ta church," he said. "Didn't I tell you about everything—more than once?"

He held up his hand and nodded his head, which was still almost touching his chest. Donnie was still staring at him. But then Donnie stood and walked across his lawn so he was hidden by the brick wall. Half the span blocked the river and the water had risen above the front of the lawn, and was still rising. No-one noticed it. There was water near the old shed, supported by pit-props, the tattered shingles and the scent of dried manure. He closed his eyes and great red spots swam before him and then one red spot, and that red spot was on the chest of Lester Murphy, and Murphy was hauling George into a ditch in Holland and taking a bullet in the thigh for it. He shook his head quickly—his eyes fluttered. Lester Murphy always needed a cane after that—and yet?

There were people running about the yard now, and across at Murphy's there was an ambulance and an RCMP squad car.

There was a terrible thing happening. Everyone was saying that they needed Packet there. Someone had to go out and try to identify the body. Father Barry had come over to drive into town with someone.

George stood up. "I'll go," and tapped his chest. "I'll go," he said quite calmly as he started to walk toward Father Barry and Lois, who was still crying and shaking. He was quite steady on his feet, the wine bottle swaying limply in his hand. He was quite happy. Old Murphy was run down, he remembered someone saying. Lots of goings-on this evening.

"Is Murphy dead too?" he said.

"Yes," Georgie's girl whispered. "Yes."

"My God," he said. He felt that he too could cry. Might cry at any moment. Give him one more second. Terrible little feelings crowded him —the worst of them satisfaction. Both Brad and Jeffery had jumped into the dirt near the porch and were tussling with each other.

"I saw it first," Bradley was shouting.

"I did—you liar—liar."

"Don't hurt his goldarn head Jeffery—don't you touch his head—what are you fighting over—all of you get into the house—go to bed, now— go to bed." Then she managed to wink at Father Barry. "Rascals," she smiled.

"Now I have to get ready and go way down and identify a goldarn body or two," George said, looking at everyone. His mouth hung open and he shook his head.

"I'll beat you," Jeffery shouted.

"C'mon then, c'mon—yer rippin it—yer rippin it."

"It's me that'll have ta identify a goldarn body," George said.

"You get in the house—get in the house right now—what are you fightin over—look both of you all over dirt—"

"Listen to yer mother, eh Lois," one of the men managed from the shadows.

Father Barry seemed to be staring now in acute frustration at all of them. George looked at him, looked toward the lane when Nobel Simms drove in.

"C'mon now," Barry said. "Party's over—c'mon now."

Georgie looked about him. Lois had already gone over to Nobel Simms and was banging her head against him as he tried to catch her head between his hands. Nobel looked distractedly about, and then looked sadly away from her.

George looked about him. He suddenly felt that everything was sad, and wrong—things were not in their proper place at all. No-one stood where they were supposed to be standing. The floodlight the pieces of half-cooked pork lying dormant. Father Barry himself—a man who was energetic enough to set up a boy-scout camp—how bad that was. There was something terrible in all those men who set up boy-scout camps and taught children; 30 years of sweat and energy—that all seemed so nasty (still in Georgie's mind there was Little Simon blocking the soccer ball, the Spalding ball). Nastiness? Of course. It was as nasty and as improper as the whole evening itself. George felt he might like to hit something to try and make it proper—say, hit something and then Nobel would stop backing away from Lois who was now saying, "You understand Nobel—Nobel and I've been through the mill together—haven't we Nobel, been through the mill—Nobel."

Perhaps George wanted to hit Father Barry. Would that make the evening better?

"Tents," he mumbled. "Boy scouts," he muttered. "Hike—go for a hike—go for a hike."

The smell of wine and the whole night crowded him. "Mill," he heard. "The goldarn mill me and Nobel's been through."

He saw Jeffery and Bradley tearing at a $10 bill, both of them face down in the dirt. Leona with her pretty party dress hanging on to her mother.

"I can't take you to town in that condition," Barry said. He stared at George as if he were quite ashamed of him. Yet who was the worse, Georgie thought—or would think, that perhaps a man with receding hair who had the bad taste to take care of himself and to go on hikes with children he could push and order about—even bully—George did not think this; he felt something—only felt something—Little Simon pretending he was having a grand time at cub camp. He stared at Father Barry's shoes. Father Murtree had, for example, far nicer shoes.

"Oh," George managed. "It's not my fault—Lois tell him to take me to town—so I can identify my father—I only had one father ya know; it isn't as if a man was born with a chunk of fathers."

"You can't identify him," Barry said. "It's just articles—you must remember the man's been in the woods all year."

"Articles," George said brightening up. "I know his articles—I do hey Lois, tell him about how much I know his articles."

"George get into bed," Lois said.

"No."

"George get yer arse inta bed—now," Lois said, and then she said: "Sorry for swearin Father—I should shake my head for swearin."

"Oh," Georgie said. "Oh!"

Father Barry smiled. He was looking about him, smiling—and then he shrugged with his palms toward the sky—he was standing there with his shoulders hunched into a shrug of some kind, and he was smiling.

"Is this any way," George said, "fer a priest to go around actin?" There was something very bewildering—

"George," Georgie's girl said. "Please George."

"Go," George was yelling. "Go tie a slip-knot—go on, tie the old slip-knot—sheep shank—I remember—tie one—a big one—sheep shank—"

"Please George."

"Please George."

Lois in her tight terry-cloth shorts, without panties, was now bent over trying to make herself sick.

"Oh Papa," she groaned.

"There's nothing I can do about it Lois—nothing tonight," George heard himself sighing. He tipped the wine bottle and sighed again. Father Barry had gone.

"Who's with me?" George yelled, waving the wine. "I didn't do nothin—who's with me?"

He gave a whoop and giggled.

"We are George—we are boy," two of the men said from the shadows.

The noises grew. At first he didn't bother with them—they were like wind, like the whirring of an untaped cassette—but then; a slight noise and he would remember the gold ankle bracelet on Elizabeth Ripley Terri's ankle; his shoulders shivered—a frugal bit of pubic hair that strayed from Karen's shorts, with the flowered underwear, as she'd tried to tell them a story—of how she identified with comedies where women were always bright and happy, when the rocks smelled of ash and the refuse of a generation wallowed in the grasses near the mesh fence and his wine made a goblet in the dirt. Her clogs also, the morbidity of too much valium, the cramped skin behind her ear to show where the facelift ended (as if that in itself would improve the lot of a woman so conscious of nothing she'd already slashed her wrists—Robert saying: "Swearing these times a girl like you") and the tick tick of the power-lines heading all the way to town, or at least to Calvin Simms' Irving Garage.

Hadn't they all double-dated? Hadn't he tried to put his arm around Karen yesterday—"Karen me darlin that halter top is some sexy on you." She had taken his arm away as if he were nothing more than a slight child. He could do nothing more than smile, how his mouth hung open too much.

"Oh Georgie," she'd said. "I fly solo—you must know by now—"

Malcolm had smiled with her. George had said: "That's all right—eh Malc, did you know I was Ceril's best man, I wouldn't think of Karen as anything but my sister—my sister, we're just sisters—I mean—"

Yes—he'd been on the same Louis L'Amour book for ten days because of the noise, the dark ferreted noises all the time—noise jumping from the page at certain words, like *lonely gunslinger*. The words *lonely gunslinger* had made a terrifying noise in his skull. There was a bump on his head, and his hand was burnt. At this moment he'd no idea how either had happened. Midgets wrestled under the floodlight, and the floodlight shone whitely over the ground where Jeffery and Bradley were Scotch-taping the $10 bill together. Jeffery with his tongue sticking out of his mouth as he put the last piece of Scotch tape on.

"Poor Papa," Lois was saying now. Leona was sitting on her knee. Lois had her legs parted and was wiggling them. Georgie's girl was hunched over. She hadn't managed to remain standing when her uncle, Father Barry, was here, and she'd fallen down in front of him, though she'd managed to say, "Lois you tripped me." Father Barry had looked at her and yet her eyes at that instant flashed away noncommittally.

By now hash oil was being passed about again. The girl could no longer speak. The man who'd walked to the shore and had sat with her earlier was now rubbing her thin shoulder-blade just above her breast. The girl moved away from him. "Go on—go on," she managed.

Lois shook her head, her eyes flaring—cold and immediate. "C'mon now Lois—jus havin a party, jus bein friendly," the man said. There was a thin white stink from him, like the stink of a late winter twilight.

"Leave her the fuck alone," Lois said.

Leona looked up at her mother.

"Hey Georgie, the women are gettin upset—eh Georgie?" the man said. He laughed and moved away.

By now Bradley and Jeffery had the $10 bill well taped and Jeffery had put it into his back pocket. Bradley kept following him in and out of the house as they obeyed the men's orders to bring beer from the cooler.

37

"Poor Papa," Lois said, quite calm now. She flared another match and lit a cigarette, and inhaling quickly she said:

"You know, there was nothing but his *skeleton* left—a skeleton, Leona."

"What?" Leona said.

"Well, there's nothin but his skeleton left—his eyes and everything are gone," Lois said, thinking it over. "It makes you wonder, doesn't it—I mean about it?" She held the cigarette in her hand. Where had that Nobel Simms gone—why had she the feeling that everyone was leaving her as well, and why was this feeling so damning—and Packet, where was Packet? Nobel had stared at her as she'd banged her head against his warm chest—and had felt the vibrations of his heart, and she saw the clear intelligence in his face (which was different from so many—so many of the men and women with their haughty or vicious eyes mistaken for intelligence) and she knew she must do something to make him stay with her—just for one night. She began talking of how they'd been through the mill together; and she kept pressing her warm legs anointed with smoke and river against him—where had that Nobel Simms gone?

She spat, cursed almost playfully, smoothed her daughter's party dress and felt the child's slight kneecap with her fingers; she wiped her eyes quickly, took a sip of beer. Leona slouched between her legs.

"Just a skeleton and a skull," she said. "Of course Beth," she said to Georgie's girl, "he was nothing more than skin and bones the night he ran away was he—all sunken in, remember?"

The girl nodded. Lois inhaled some hash-oil, passed it back over her shoulder to George: "Listen darlin, don't get stung by a bee and have a miscarriage—okay," she said. She caressed the girl's head softly. There was moist warmth from under her armpits and down the small of her back. She wiped her eyes again, blowing her nose hoarsely. "God—I wonder what it's like to sit there and know you're going to die—I mean really die, like he did," she said. "That's something we should all think of —especially at times like this."

Lester Murphy had the biscuit too she thought. When she leaned her head back you saw the developing double chin she patted with her hand; her legs twitched slightly, lovingly to the music inside the house. Did Lester Murphy burn down his tavern because he'd nothing left and needed insurance money to put in some fund for his son? She didn't even know she'd asked this question out loud, and was surprised when she heard the nattering little men crowding about her.

"Fuck off," she said. "I know he wouldn't do that—he'd too much

38

money in the first place."

"Sure he did," one of the men said. "Ask Georgie about it—he'd know about it—Georgie—did Lester have any money or didn't he?"

"Not in my books he had any money—oh some a long time ago—"

"Who da fuck was Donnie's mother George, tell everyone that one—"

"He never married her—" George said. "And she was no relation to Ramsey Taylor neither—as everyone wanted to assume she was—"

"Tell us that one George."

"Not tonight boys—"

"C'mon George."

"Not tonight boys," George said. "Lester might have had money— could have, maybe he did—a long time ago—no more though—tavern was nothin—who went there—apartments—those were jokes—after the disco started he'd nothin—talked big—some like to talk big—donated things, anyone can donate things—but it was Ceril Brown who put him out of business— at one time that tavern needed five waiters—" George said.

The men nodded, looked at each other. But George knew it was a half-truth. "Lies," Georgie heard, and something stung him, came into his brain. The thousand times they'd sat about Ceril Brown's junkyard came to him with those antiquated useless commodities, the Indians coming back and forth with their catches of salmon and their jacked meat; and Ceril Brown's black eyes—ah yes even the poor Irish girl that had borne Donnie, a million Irish skulls in her brain, Dublin and Belfast shrieking out, and Lester putting her in a tub and bathing her fevered body in ice during her pregnancy as she gummed about the British—

Half-truths stung Georgie's brain and a certain rage took hold; the men seemed to close about him.

"Beautiful people—beautiful people Donnie eh," Lester would say.

"Oh oh oh, beautiful," Donnie would say. "Seems some are awful dirty when they're drinkin though—seems it is, seems Russell Peterson is awful dirty when he's drinkin—seems he sat his mother-in-law on his knee when he was drinking—and started singing dirty songs, and they called for that minister—from the Glad Tidings, and that fat minister— Lester you know that fat minister from the Glad Tidings came and Russell sat the minister on his other knee—his mother-in-law on one knee and the fat minister from the Glad Tidings on the other, singing dirty songs."

"Good," Lester would say. And looking out the window he'd see the youngsters that had come up from the junkyard to throw rocks and eggs at his house.

39

"We'll get Lester sooner or later—that bum boy for the Liberal party," Ceril saying, giving the group of half-breeds and youngsters who worked for him a sugary smile. "Some day we Conservatives will do things right."

"Lies," Georgie heard.

And the youngsters, who in those days worked for 30 or 40 cents an hour piling beer cases into tractor-trailers for Ceril Brown, would toss the rocks against the cold verandah of Murphy's house, until Murphy came out at them with his birch cane—

Georgie shivered violently. The men seemed to be crowding about him.

"We'll get him sooner or later—that bum boy for the Libral party," Ceril saying. (Ohh—George was thinking of that birch cane, also his wife Elizabeth, they seemed to fuse together.)

"That bum boy for the Liberal party—how do you think he came by his tavern—or the land for the cocksuckin fishing camps—" Ceril saying. "And Georgie here—Georgie saves his life in the war, why in fuck didja bother saving his life in the war—we should fire-bomb him Georgie—"

The half-breeds and youngsters nodding with peculiar interest.

"Lies," Georgie heard. Or what did he hear, if it was not the Irish woman screaming:

"Trees—trees trees trees trees trees trees—" and laughing.

"Trees trees trees," and Lester trying to carry her back into the house, she breaking away from him, her body in the transparent nightgown. "Trees trees trees," she laughing. "Kanada—ferry bad," that German boy saying.

Georgie's mind stung.

"And where there's not trees there's snow—isn't there—snow snow snow snow," she laughed and bit her finger until the blood came.

Oh oh oh, Georgie is thinking, why were the men crowding him, and who were the men talking about—"now you might feel some discomfort." One of the men was saying he could understand why Little Simon wanted to try playing Russian roulette, and that some day he might try it too, and not only might he try it but almost certainly he would try it, and if Little Simon was with Rance and Dale in the van that evening why were Rance and Dale too gutless to try it.

"You wouldn't try it."

"Certainly—give me the gun."

"Go way."

"Give me the gun."

"Go way."

George shivered. For an instant he couldn't see. There was a whir

40

somewhere a long way off, and somewhere the cement plant rose up corpulent and dirty, with one light in the back window. Why was there the smell of cement in the air?

"He's blocking me now," Ceril was saying, his smile sugary, "but my turn is coming—*our* turn is coming George." And Ceril's face went painfully away, and he saw Ceril Brown's hand patting him on the back when George admitted he'd saved Lester Murphy's life, and then blushed and couldn't look at anyone; and the youngsters nodded.

"A good Conservative like you," Ceril was saying. "Someday we'll be in office—someday it'll be our turn to do things right—"

Ooh, George was thinking. And one of the men was telling a funny story of what Little Simon did last year; and all the men were laughing about how Little Simon could play tricks on people and someone called him a genius for doing that sort of thing.

The men nodded, looked at each other.

"Tell us about Donnie's mother Georgie—tell us that one."

"Not tonight."

"Where is she—Campbellton or some place—in a nut-house or some-place—tell us that one."

"Not tonight boys," George said.

"How low can you go—burning down your own building for insurance —eh George?"

"The bastard just got what he deserved after what he done to me and Clarence Simms," George said suddenly.

"I thought he just did it ta Clarence Simms," Larry said. "Last time you told it, it was just Clarence Simms—"

"Well it was Clarence Simms," George said angrily. "But it wasn't only Clarence Simms you dumb prick, it was the whole jeesless works of us that had any common sense after the war—he did it more or less to the whole Conservative Party—when I ran for treasurer—remember Larry?"

"I remember."

"Goddamn right you remember—remember or get outta my goddamn yard—sayin I'm a liar."

"I said nothin," Larry said.

George pointed a finger at him. The men all looked at Larry.

"I said nothin," Larry said.

The men looked angrily at him—as if they were fed up with Larry.

"I'm just agreeing with ya," Larry said. He looked about. George looked at him and glowered. Larry smiled.

"Hey Georgie,' he said. Larry said, "Hey Georgie," and smiled. He

41

certainly didn't want to get out of the yard, but everyone seemed to be just a bit fed up with Larry—who they all called marble head. And Butch, the man who'd gone down to the water to sit with Beth, now looked disgusted. He took a drink of beer and then let it be known that he was going to walk off into the darkness by making certain preparations —tucking in his shirt was one of them, breaking wind was another.

Yawning. "Hey," George said to Butch. "Don't you go—don't *you* go."

"Oh," Butch said. "I'm just tired George—think I'll head it home."

"No," George said. "This is my yard here—and you can stay in my yard —and in my house for as long as you want."

The man flicked his hand. Larry looked at him. George looked at both of them—his flesh trembled with the sensation that the only way to make things proper was to swing out, hit something—then this night would be better.

"Hey," he said to Butch, "is Larry botherin you—you say somethin ta him Larry?"

"Like I was sayin," Larry said, "I'm jus standin here havin a good time —minding my own business, the subject of Lester Murphy was brought up and I was just listening, same as I always do."

"Same as you always do," Butch said, under his breath.

"Get the fuck outta my yard," George said. "Outta my yard Larry—"

"Why?" Larry said. (The whole thing was made more ludicrous because all this time Larry, who didn't have any teeth, was trying to suck down a pork chop.)

"Because no-one can trust ya—and I'm not havin a man in my yard I can't trust—next thing ya know you'll be after my money."

"No I won't Georgie, you know."

"I don't know," George said.

"Ya been hangin around too goddamn long," Butch said.

"What have you got to say about it?" Larry said.

"I'll say what I want to say about it—you comin in here and leeching off a man like George Terri—who was good enough ta let ya in here— and George just lost his goddamn father—you *understand*." Here Butch was crying and he started to swing at Larry. And just when Larry started to defend himself—started to throw Butch down, Georgie stepped in with boots and fists. Larry was hit hard.

"C'mon," Butch was saying. "C'mon—I ain't scared a you—c'mon." And George kept hitting Larry.

"Georgie," Lois yelled. "Georgie."

"I just lost my goddamn father—I just lost my goddamn father,"

George said.

"Ya lost yer goddamn mind," Georgie's girl said, "if ya ask me—but who asks me?"

"Now that Larry's out of the yard," Butch said, "George'll tell ya how Lester had a kid—go on, tell us George."

Larry stood just outside the last pine marker shouting insults at them. For a time. And then fed up with this he left. But something happened— the men weren't as happy after Larry left—things weren't as exciting.

"No way in the world am I tellin that story tonight," George said. He tried to think—

"Ha, ha," Butch said. "Tell about the time ya got—you and Ceril Brown got Donnie Murphy to eat his own shit—tell us about that one George."

"Stop talking about poor Lester Murphy," Lois said.

"Yes, just all shut up," Beth said.

"Poor Lester Murphy."

"Yes poor Lester Murphy."

"Huh," Butch said. "Tell them about it George—tell them where Murphy is, heaven or hell—dead or not dead—tell them."

George said nothing now. For some reason he was still wondering why he'd hit Larry and why he'd kicked him out of the yard. The thing was, Larry came early to help him set things up—and Larry suggested the floodlights because Bryans and Browns always had floodlights about their patios.

"Innocent are guilty," Butch said. "The way he treated Clarence Simms —innocent or guilty—eh boy?"

There was silence. "Whose wife did he fuck, eh George?" Butch said. "Whose wife—tell them—George."

There was silence. Butch put his hand to his mouth, then hauled at a tooth.

"I got a loose tooth here George," he said. George was looking away.

Look, they were saying to him, we all have to work. Old Simon worked every day of his life, and when he couldn't work any longer he went into the woods and died. I know how you feel but we were born to croak and that's what all of us should keep in mind.

So the conversation, disjointed, flaring now and subsiding, then seemed to rage about him.

"There's no man I respected more," George heard himself saying. He was busily searching for something in his pockets, only half realizing it.

Louis L'Amour. The top came off an Alpine beer—the beer cap flew up and the foam gushed and subsided. Suddenly the remaining half of the span was burning again. It was much brighter than the first fire. It lit up the entire house and its shadows danced on the house, on the small garden Lois had planted. There was a wicked heat on his back and he could see his shadow elongated—almost gargantuan it stood amongst the shadows of the flames, and to his right and left smaller shadows of the men, their mouths and hands moving cowardly. Someone was complimenting him on the blood on his pants—which must have been Larry's blood.

Bradley was handing him an Alpine beer. So that was the pop he'd heard. He tried to gesture, to say: "No—I don't want the beer—I have wine here," but he took the beer and held it. He nodded to one of the men about the blood and then to another—hoping this was what they'd expected.

Someone laughed. Bradley was standing very still beside him, the white bandage covered with bits of soot. What was he standing there for, looking up at his grandfather who seemed to be staring at the flood of insects beneath the light. God, you could smell pig's blood, half-cooked flesh—or rather flesh that was charred, with blood oozing through it. The men were content to eat the pork this way, and drunk enough to enjoy it.

"Did Larry start crying?" George asked, suddenly remembering something, how Larry covered his head and went "Oh oh" like that: "Oh oh."

Someone laughed. And George through half-closed eyes could see blood and burnt rind on Butch's tongue as he moved it over his lips. Butch was remembering something funny, which mightn't have been funny at all. The scene involved Clarence Simms watching his brother Bobby getting his hair styled at Great Expectations Hair Salon—and looking through the window at this, muttering:

"He's gone on over to the opposition—to my competition." A look of horror on his face, the apoletic look, and then turning away from it crushed, his dry lips trembling.

"I cut hair."

The man laughed, and he tried to mimic Clarence Simms' dry lips— "I cut hair."

George felt he must walk away, leave, but as he started to move the man grabbed at him. "George," he said, holding onto his shirt. "You know how I felt about Simon?"

George didn't look at the man. A great numbness closed in upon him. "Now you'll have a bit of discomfort." The man kept speaking. He saw the man's mouth open and close in various attitudes, all terrible—his shirt

44

with the cowboy laces. His small hands were pawing at Georgie's body.

"No no," George managed. "Okay then." Someone laughed. Why was that cutting-hair business so bad—or was it just whose hair was being cut —Bobby Simms. He remembered Bobby carrying an oven pan, with an apron on, his shirt-sleeves showing through the pants that hugged his paunch—the oven mitts? Bobby had just had his hair styled, and was asking George if there was any reason why he avoided the Knights of Columbus.

Georgie's suit-pants dragged over his shoes, the bottoms of these pants covered with mud. There was a streak of mud on his pants from his knee-cap to his ankle, and a rip as if someone had gouged it.

Bullet pierced the aorta—death was almost instantaneous. Oh yes, the flattened ruby appendix scar just above Malcolm's shorts when he stretched.

The man was holding onto him. He was saying, "I think the old bugger would have wanted you to have a party in his honour—that's what we're doin Georgie, we're all celebrating on account of Old Simon." He laughed in George's face and George could smell foul lukewarm breath. He pushed away, held the picnic table for a second. The man slapped him on the shoulder. "No—okay." Lonely Gunslinger.

"Hey George, how about my quarter for the beer—I didn't get a quarter yet—Uncle George?" Bradley was saying. He had his hand out. George fell, missing the edge of the picnic table by half an inch, and began to vomit almost immediately.

"I'm gonna ask him if he can change a $10 bill—that's what I'm gonna ask him," Bradley said after a moment.

"Oh no," Jeffery said. "Just leave him be."

"Well, I ain't followin you around all goddamn night."

"Don't then."

"Try me an see."

"Don't then."

"Try me and see," Bradley said. "Ya got a million places ta hide that knowin you—"

Lois said: "Poor Old Simon, he loved this house. Beth, I wonder how Packet's gonna recognize him—I don't want to start to cry again but he was always kind to me, Beth—hey did you hear somethin about Packet and Emma Jane gonna be married—I wonder—"

(They had left. They were all going into town. Lois promised the children ice cream and they too were gone. They'd all piled into one car. He was alone on the ground. They had rolled him over on his right side. There

45

had been a great deal of urgency and hurrying about him. The men all talking at once—arguing and laughing like corruptible thin-shouldered things. And then Lois was crying again. The whole troupe of them were gone into town to view the remains. Lois was crying and someone had handed her a pink Kleenex, and then Beth started crying.

My God your mother's a lovely woman. And before they'd left two of the men got out of the car and ran toward him. Oh, he thought, they're coming back to help me—Lois and Beth sent them. But the men were no more than fleeting shadows as they grappled the jug of wine left on the table and took it with them. And then everything was black. They had switched off the floodlight and he was alone.

Far away there was the laughter of children who'd graduated. Now and then a dog barked and another answered. A cricket twitched sleepily, and he could hear and smell coals falling and drying into ashes.

Oh, the fires in the winter. How lovely they were. And his father could walk in a straight line—straight through the worst cedar swamp, by taking readings from tree to tree.

"Don't be frightened George," he used to say. His father smelled of balsam. Ah, the fires in the winter, beyond the lake—cold cold fires beyond the lake, the clear ice when the snow blew across it, the blue ice with rounded air-bubbles—the fires, cold and far away beyond the lake where they went to fish through the ice.

"Are we lost Papa—are we?"

"Don't be frightened Georgie—no, we can never get lost."

"I can't do it Papa."

"What do you mean, you can't do it—can't do it—I did it when I was your age—Merlin did it when he was twelve years old."

Cold fires, the petrified smell of balsam. Ah his eyes—Old Simon's eyes—far far away.

"Check out, check out, check out the difference at Sobey's," came a commercial from somewhere inside the house. "Oh just you check out, check out, check out the difference at Sobey's." And then the first of the song again: "Oh where will you do your shopping today—what will you get and what will you pay?"

It made George think of sweet potatoes with rindy rust-coloured skins and just the suggestion of drying blood along the meat counter, the rows of chicken with purple bones at eleven in the morning and an old woman carrying a string shopping-bag counting her money before the livers of young cows. That too was as far removed from him now as the minister and his wife and daughter who went along the roadway to stop at no

46

given point to preach. The minister's wife had cake and Kool-Aid for people who would listen to her husband. The cakes had pink icing. After the preacher spoke he'd signal his wife to cut small slivers of the cake— signal her to hand one sliver to each of those who'd listened to him, and a glass of Kool-Aid. Until men came out of the woods one evening and stole his cake—the whole cake, and upset the jar of Kool-Aid. Near the grounds of the circus, on August nights, the preacher and his family could be seen amid the festive and the drunken, the cake with its pink icing and the jug of Kool-Aid resting on the table. Then later when another minister joined him and they were working for donations for their Glad Tidings Tabernacle they sold pamphlets they'd written, comparing circuses and movies with Sodom, and today with the Apocalypse—their cake with pink icing slowly became less and less a factor, until finally they had a microphone and amplifier—and shortly after that a tent. And now, finally, the Glad Tidings Tabernacle.

Freddie Silver and the whole crusade team were up tonight from somewhere in West Virginia. But if they could let him know one thing—could tell him one thing. Would he then go to their godawful meeting, smelling the privacy of other human bodies dressed for the occasion. (Ha ha what ha.) Georgie got a good kick out of the fact that not too far from the Glad Tidings Tabernacle—not very far at all away from it, not very far away from the Glad Tidings Tabernacle, you could witness the stony windows of a small bookstore, the wet clitoris of healthy women under plastic wrapping, touching penis of man or dog, a thousand faces of the occult leering in cauldrons of hair and blood. And biographies on Hollywood movie stars and drunken US senators turned Christian. Of weather almanacs and tips on yoga and meditations and the preparing of vegetarian diets. And questionnaires on sexual fulfillment, the same questionnaire for a proposed 4,000,000-copy sale, with top score *excellent*, as the young girls with trimmed pubic hair smiled almost joyous. To witness in the back room of that store, snug with wall-to-wall carpeting and a fish-tank with guppies, some with pretty green gills, the store owned by Ceril Brown, who sometimes held meetings there; the stag movies that Denby Ripley had rented out when he was younger, with titles like *The Lizard Queen*. There the guppies swam in a tank that was perpetually filtered. The faces of the occult with their eyes like rubies, and pictures of women gutted in blood smiling at the knife.

"Abortion is always rough," Karen said. Oh well, he certainly didn't mind if women went about having abortions. But what was it about Karen saying that? Could she ever really like Rhonda, and just go about saying,

47

"Abortion is always rough"? And Rhonda, what did he remember about Rhonda—not that he'd heard that she went away, and was whisked to some place in Quebec, to some room somewhere—he remembered her working in that store. She wore pigtails, and he remembered her relaxed stance, and she wore brown sexless $60 Wallabies. And he could not help staring at her—you know, and thinking that there was still the faint scent of knifed babies. It was absurd to think that. That she still carried the faint stench of knifed babies.

"Kanada werry bad," the German prisoner said. "Kanada—" And yet she was nervously ringing in the cash register, and he laid the book down for her to ring in: *Torso*.

"Volare Volare—woa woa woa woa," came the commercial from somewhere.

George was in the house. He didn't know why he was in the bathroom. It was raining again, and it was easy to sleep when it rained against the roofing, as the rain flowed along the gutters and the soil and vegetation was saturated. He was staring into the flush, yet now and again his eyes darted toward the mirror. He'd see himself. His tongue would somehow dart here and there, his eyes look away. There was clothing hanging on the small rack near the tub and a pair of Jeffrey's socks dripped a bit of dye. The green dye ran like two tear drops down the enamel. He felt himself belching again as he rested his hand against the wall and stared into the bowl where specks floated up milkily from the funnel. When he lifted his head the odour of bodies, of milky specks floating, and the sight of his burnt hand made him gag and then begin to vomit. On a small shelf above the flush was a rectangular box of prophylactics and a hairbrush with a clot of hair. Louis L'Amour. He had the bathroom light on. The rest of the house was dark and silent.

He was lying on the floor weakly. His gut churned and the place stank of wine—corrupted, and a pair of Lois' panties lay rumpled beneath the small rack. When he sat up he looked about for toilet-paper to wipe his mouth. There wasn't any. The light was so yellow. He was trying to re-member something. The bathtub faucet leaked, had worn the enamel brown and water sucked in the drain, and a long time ago Elizabeth Ripley Terri sprinkled clothes with water and ironed them and it sanctified the smell of things, made the long winter nights, before they had a tele-vision, calm, the sound of the heated iron and the smell of freshly ironed linen. But the day after Little Simon's funeral when Lois took her mother into town to buy her a present—he and Beth had to take care of the children. He watched them walk toward the car and then he wanted

48

pancakes for breakfast.

Beth said: "I don't have no pancakes to give ya—"

"I want pancakes," he shouted. "Jesus Christ."

"Don't shout at me if ya got a big hangover," Beth said.

And Elizabeth Ripley Terri was getting into the car. She must have heard him shouting. She opened her cosmetic case and smoothed her lipstick, her lips curled.

"I'll shout at anybody I fucking well want to shout at," George yelled, hoping the whole world heard him. Then he turned about and kicked the bucket of fat they kept in the corner. The dog Mincey, with the manicured furballs, gurred at him.

He snatched up Lois' panties and wiped his mouth. The material draped over his hand. The word *Love* was written on the crotch, in black, with the O widened. He wiped his mouth again, coughed and threw them toward the door. Standing, he flushed the toilet. Oh yes, Little Simon. He was quite calm now, staring vaguely into the toilet-bowl. He heard a sound—as if there were something down the hall. His limbs twitched but he was tired now. He wouldn't drink again tonight. (Ha ha what—ha.)

He'd put Little Simon's and Packet's head into the toilet-bowl, one at a time, and flushed the toilet, when they were youngsters. Ceril Brown and he were trying to telephone someone and Packet and Little Simon were playing, rolling about the floor. He'd dropped the telephone—and had dragged each of them to the toilet, Little Simon saying: "Ya ain't puttin my head in there—I ain't gonna put me head in—no *sir*—no sirree." George saying, "That'll teach ya some respect when Ceril and I are on the telephone talking business—eh Ceril, that'll teach them some respect." Packet said nothing. He stared at his father—looking at him so Georgie ducked his head good. Put it down and flushed it. He could see Packet's hair swirling in the whirlpool.

Then he went for Little Simon. Little Simon clung to the kitchen table, so it was dragged across the floor. He slapped Little Simon's hands. Then Packet came at him his head soaking and tried to stop him. George threw Packet down. Packet came at him again. Again George threw him. Ceril Brown kept looking at the phone-book, chewing expansively on a toothpick. Then he yawned. And Little Simon. The godawful screams.

"He's screamin Ceril just tryin ta be the big show," Georgie said. Ceril stared at the phone-book. Little Simon screamed. He snatched at everything—first the table then the doorknob on the closet door. His feet were kicking. One of his shoes came off and a picture of Roy Rogers fell out of his pocket. He clutched the banister knob and George had to thwack him

49

good.

Packet, up from the floor again, ran after them. George slapped his mouth. Little Simon held onto each rail of the banister.

"I ain't goin—I ain't goin," he screamed. Georgie was sweating and he smelled his young son's flesh. A picture of Roy Rogers' horse Trigger fell out of Little Simon's pocket.

"I ain't goin—I ain't—I'll be *good* I'll be *good* then—*okay*—I will— okay—Packet you tell him—*okay?*" he screamed. He clutched at the bathroom door-handle, a screw fell and it came off, and George staggered backwards, slapping the boy hard on the mouth; Little Simon held the doorknob—stared at it, and a gurgling came from his throat. Ceril Brown saying from the bottom of the stairs, "George I'll be off now for supper." There was a pause; "I'll be off now for supper," Ceril saying.

He turned off the light-switch and halfway along the upstairs hall he felt something on his right shoe. He bent over and picked up a piece of cloth, switched on the hallway light:

"Pope John Paul made an unplanned visit earlier this afternoon—" came the voice from somewhere. The voice sounded very pleased that John Paul had made this unplanned visit.

George was staring at Lois' panties, frilled with red lace. *Love* was written on the crotch in black, the O being widened, and there was a heady smell of perfume. Mingling with something soured. With what? His vomit. He shoved the panties into his pocket—tucked them away.

He woke sitting up in the chair. On the television a young woman was advertising tampons, saying that her life was different from her mother's. He watched her smile. The smile was faint, drifted away from her private real-estate office, and then they were back to the Pope. The Pope brushed his eyes, his lips trembled. The Pontiff's lips were trembling and a crowd of lepers, who stood frightened—one without a nose, one without a finger to his name—watched him. The Pontiff's lips trembled, and his ruddy pale cheeks curved. All along a muddy walkway the Pontiff moved, surrounded with shouts and cries, the mud infested with flies and the Pontiff's garments stained. A military helicopter mounted with machine-guns hovered overhead, and the Pontiff raised his arms. A nun near the medical tent went to take a picture, then came forward a few paces to make use of the sunlight. Beside the nun, a woman, her right cheek gone and her head-covering having dropped to the ground, knelt on that head-covering and began to pray. The camera showed the ravaged cheek very well.

He moved to the bedroom window. He stared down at the picnic table —just below him. At various pieces of flesh and refuse. Tin foil glittered.

At chunks of discarded pig flesh that had been bitten into. The closet door was opened. An old suit of his father's hung on a wire hanger—the jacket sleeves like stovepipes, the pant-legs like deflated sausages, the black shoes just beneath them, except the right shoe was placed below the left leg, and so you had the idea that someone would be walking backwards—or in opposite directions at the same time. The closet itself emitting a quiet stench of pressed board and mothballs, wire hangers ruefully naked and silent. An old dress of his mother's that Lois had worn to a Hallowe'en party lay on top of a cardboard box filled with broken chips of tile. Beth's underwear and nightgown, and her jars of ultra-sheer moisturizer, her Nivea cream, sat or lay in various attitudes.

"Old Popey," Georgie said, for some reason. "Old popey," he said, and he felt a well of self-pity come over him and he began to cry. "Ole pope," he said.

George was crying. And through this he suddenly saw what they were doing. Lester Murphy's foreman Russell Peterson, who they called Rumpy, was draining off Lester's tank of diesel gasoline—and five or six men and women, by the way they dressed, by the way they were silhouetted against the ghostly warehouse, women and men who'd moved here recently—those with their children who'd moved from central Canada and up from the States, were bargaining for his diesel gasoline. He could just make out the bargaining process, the hands holding canisters reaching for the spout on the diesel barrel—and Russell in the darkness, looking toward Lester's house and rubbing his hands over his mouth, was selling it to them. The men too looked furtive and sly in the darkness and seemed to want to show how well they conned Russell or bartered for a price. And all this was in a moment's shadow at the back of a warehouse. And then there was laughter from somewhere across the water. It was one of the women laughing at a man who had dropped his canister of diesel fuel into the dirt. Then he saw those people moving off with their contraband and Russell with his profit leaving also. And even though George still had the opportunity to get the police—why get the police?

The thoughts were, too, dismally associated with the way he'd tried to dress and act like Lester Murphy after the war years—when Murphy come back had already assimilated truck and lumber dealings. And hadn't he tried to wear what Lester Murphy did? Didn't he try also to sell hats and coats, and certain fire-sale furniture. But by then it was already too late. Murphy had gone on into apartment buildings and fishing camps. And then Ceril Brown rose up to occupy the vacuum Murphy had left. There was something sly about them. Though Georgie credited himself with often acting as sly as Lester Murphy—or even slyer. Georgie always credited himself with being one of the slyest people around the place. "As sly as anyone," or, "Oh am I sly!" No, no, no. The noise hurt his head. You weren't really that sly, truly you weren't any more sly than Russell Peterson who just sold those canisters of gasoline to the young men and women. You weren't any more sly than Kenny Ward who promised to pick-axe you in the years when you added three cents extra for mustard in Georgie's Hamburger Palace and went with Ceril Brown wheeling and dealing with members of the Conservative Party—the Conservative Party being the party on the river not locked up tight and therefore open to anyone who knew that the feeble talk of politics swam in the loins—the essential talk of the partisan mob is interlaced with smugness and smut. (And it came down to trying to wear the same type of coat as Lester—saying a certain phrase or two like Ceril Brown. Too, Lester had saved his life by dragging him into a ditch in Holland and had taken a bullet in the thigh for his trouble. Nor could he ever look as good in a raccoon coat as Lester did. Lester could wear a raccoon coat and high steel-toed black boots and could and would be comfortable anywhere—the Hilton in Calcutta, say or over in Kenya. So there you go. George tried a raccoon coat on once—actually Elizabeth got him to try it on—and looked like nothing more than a big raccoon.)

The odious smell of his own sweat came to him, and he could taste the odour from his mouth like the odour out of infected swollen gums—almost a comforting taste. The beer was somewhere across the room. But the memories were present as in all women/men on the river. Present. As was the realization of the whore of night (so many nights), the grey noises, the painful ideas, the faces of people amassing before him—like the old woman with her string shopping-bag, breathing in and out. The tranquil water the Americans fished. The professor of theology having taken a four-pound grilse out of Terri's pool in the dying moments of the evening. The elongated worms stretching their pores in puddles. The death of Little Simon.

Means, the idea of Father Barry was still there—hiking with the children to Cold Stream, the cub camp in one of those greying sad fields, polluted with the scent of toxin and squashed mosquitoes and the lime-coated waste of children. But he must realize that Father Barry was the adults' spiritual and cultural ambassador to their children, and that he'd set up the rules of the soccer match, and taking three of the better children to his side played with that sort of aggressive balance becoming a priest playing soccer in his black religious pants. But there must have come a moment when he could no longer pretend it was a game—when the children backed away timidly, except Little Simon, who still plagued him at his feet—

Means one thinks of the swank health and absolute incompetence of a man washing the sweat away from his burning shoulders with those buckets of water collected by the sixers after the match, the *mea culpa* in the mass tent later, sunlight fading on the Host and silver chalice—means, it easily erased itself from Georgie's mind, as did the sound and some of the terror of his own brutish life—means it was done now. Means: "A host of angels guides thee upward to mine light."

The memorial on the slab Lois had picked out for him. Buried not in a suit because he never wore one, but in the clothes that always seemed to substantiate some of the dark genius that ran in his blood—ran a little bit crookedly if it was genius, a little bit crookedly if you asked George.

"An where's Packet?" George said suddenly. "Where's Packet eh—" He stopped speaking.

A discoloration had appeared on George. There was a splotch on his hand. Quite orange. Another splotch—orange as anything—had by now covered his chest and was spreading. But George took no notice. They appeared whenever he drank too much wine and no-one knew what to make of them. The best thing was to keep drinking wine. The splotches wouldn't go away—so one might as well get enough splotches on his body and then in one terrific drunk unite them all, so that one would be totally orange. And no-one would say anything. Once, he'd remembered, before he went to detox, he'd walked about the house quite orange for three days—and the water he passed was pink—like—

He stopped speaking. *Torso* was the book Dale was reading, and it was a good book. And George thought that he would like the book back immediately—

George heard the car drive into the yard and shook his head nervously. Leona was crying—it was awful to hear such a crying from an exhausted child. Terrible feelings of rage ran through him, and he was exhausted also. He sneezed, *Achoo* twice. And walked back to the television.

"Atlantic Salmon Centre of the World."

Hallowe'en

(It was not Father Murtree then. It was Father Barry coming in, with his thick red fingers, reading prayers for the sick and then kissing the cross on his robe. Old Simon looked about, nodding in peculiar abstraction, because he'd forgotten and thought it would be Father Murtree. In the half-dark the bedpan looked like an earthenware jug. There was the smell of leaves. Then there were sounds of people leaving him—all going away.)

He woke, lifted himself up in the bed, moving the toes of his left foot; the toes on his right foot were numb again, white, with dead growth of skin at the bottom of his foot. They were sending him to Saint John. The blankets were damp with the smell of gauze the nurses had applied. Well, he thought clearly, that meant his leg. And of course after the leg the hip, and then the whole bit. He thought this and scratched his nose. Of course they'd said they were sending him to Saint John because they weren't sure. Weren't sure of what was the question. Twice now in the nights he'd been shuddering violently; he'd heard people leaving (walking going away in a hurry). He spat over the edge of the bed and leaned his head back against the pillow. He looked about the room, light shone glibly from the corridor, its gauze patterns in the corners. In the other bed, across and to the right, was Rance. Rance was from down-river. He was 24 years old and had blown his stomach.

"Wine," Rance had said laughing. "Too much wine." Sounds came from Rance's body—and Rance kept saying "Excuse me—excuse me" when they did. He didn't mind the sounds or the smell or the glib gauze patterns of light, with people moving but what he did mind was the "Excuse me.'

He hadn't always been angry here but the last few days the nurses hated the boys visiting him and had complained to the doctors so he stopped speaking to them, wouldn't let them wash him or he spit over the edge of the bed. The boys—his grandsons, Packet (Patrick) and Little Simon (his godson, named after him). They came in, Little Simon half drunk and swearing and they always offered him a drink. And Rance eventually buttered up to them for one. The nurses got angry and Little Simon would say: "What da fuck's wrong with yous?" and then they'd go to the doctors. Little Simon would look about, his dark eyes fretful and shining. Packet would sit in a chair. The old fellow thought, once Packet had bitten a man's right ear off in a fight. And he'd been interviewed on tele-

54

vision because he was a poacher. But when Simon watched the program in the Senior Citizens' home, the Colonel became angry. The old Colonel, with his pants held up by suspenders, got up out of his chair, tapped his cane and left the common room. "That's what they expect of us up there —act like monkeys for them—that's what they want of your grandson." And watching the television he became aware that this was so, and he became angry and then indifferent to the goings-on.

He wasn't tired. His hair was white with a pink spot on the top, and clustered hair grew out of his nostrils. His frame was gaunt and yellow, the skin clung darkly to the bones. This showed in his hands, forearms and bent elbows where his shoulder-blades jutted against his Johnnie-shirt. And now it was night. He tried to make himself more comfortable by moving his right leg slightly. It was all in shadow, all black and white, people moving in the corridor.

He was 82 years old—he'd spent 60 consecutive winters in the woods and now he was lying on a bed with thin white bedsheets, aware of a medicinal scent, the smell of gauze. He searched absently with his fingers for the bag of candy on the night table. He heard the boy sighing in the next bed.

"Rance," he said. "You 'wake?"

"How can you get any sleep in this fuckin place?" Rance said.

"That's right," he said. "That's right."

He looked about. He saw that Rance was awake now and watching him in the semi-darkness. Through the window the hospital stack sent grey smoke in the darkness. During the daytime children went to school and then they crossed the lot and the field above and at 2.35 there was a train and he'd listen to that. And from 3.30 until 4 the children would walk back. Rance was watching him and he moved his hands slowly upward, whisked a bit of saliva from his thin lips and then searched the bedclothes again, folded the sheet against his chest. Sometimes Rance would tease him during the daytime. He had noticed this for a week now, but had said nothing. Rance didn't even know he was doing it—it was just that way. The girls at the Senior Citizen home had done it also. At the parties in the common room an old woman started to cry once and the party broke up and he saw the staff looking at each other—and they all went back to their rooms. And you weren't allowed to smoke anywhere but the common room. As far as it went the Colonel was right when he said there were spies, because how did they know he was smoking in his room? The Colonel made his bed every morning and wouldn't be satisfied unless he could bounce a quarter off it. He had an old quarter made in 1901 with a

55

picture of Queen Victoria—her face, though oxidized, was still visible with faded red traces on the outline. The home was one storey tall and four stories long, curved with four corridors with rooms in every corridor, left and right, and the common room in the middle like the hub of a wheel. It was made of brick, with stucco walls, aluminum windows and a variety of plants and stuffed chairs, with the picture of a doctor and his wife who was in charge of things. Bordered by flowers, bordered by hedges, filled with dusty house-plants, with sunlight on the white linen, the smell at nine o'clock. They were supposed to clap their hands to songs also, and everyone would get concerned if you didn't do that. When the MC came every second Saturday night from the radio station. Everyone called him the Music Man. He was a man of 50 who was always happy, always getting people to clap their hands. That wasn't right, Simon shouted at them once—if a person didn't want to clap her hands, he said. But they were clapping their hands, and moving to and fro with the others. So they were an unbroken line of people moving, clapping their hands: "Those lazy hazy crazy days of sum-mer," they sang. No, if you didn't clap and sing along—even if you didn't know the song. Simon didn't know the songs. He didn't know many songs—except songs about the river.

He coughed, swallowed.

"Have ya ever been to Saint John?" he asked Rance. The room was warm, the stack blew outward—the night was black and pebbles stuck solidly in the rotted mud, mud and weeds stank in the ditches. Down the corridor at any time now the son of a whore would start yelling: "Be quiet." "Be quiet," he'd yell. "Be quiet," and that would go on until others started yelling, "Be quiet." He'd just come here, and right away he'd started yelling, "Be quiet."

"Oh I've been down there enough—too much," Rance said. "I worked for Irving too long down there." He said all this shaking his head in the darkness. It was a strange thing. A man, Lazarus Masey, once came up to Simon telling him that he knew his son was going to be killed. "I tol him —I warned the son of a bitch," he'd said, sharply, as a matter of logic, his eyes terrified and soot on both sides of his nostrils, his hair cropped short, dirty and brown and his skinny frame with the pulse-beat in his wrists. And the man kept flicking black-flies away with his thin right hand. And as a matter of logic the man kept saying: "Ya, well I tol the son of a bitch, Simon I tol the poor son of a bitch—eh," and then he laughed. He laughed and shook his head. And the man's wife kept shaking her head, though slower—and she kept fingering the buttons on her dress.

"What's it like down there—in Saint John?" he asked, sucking in his cheeks.

"It's a hole," Rance said, and then he thought for a moment. "It's completely different than up here—takes some getting used to—it's right on the bay—foggy as hell, there's a lot going on down there—lots of places eh—lots of pussy, eh Simon?" Simon looked over at him, the boy seemed to be grinning.

"What bay is that?" he asked.

"What bay is that?" Rance said laughing quickly, and then again he seemed to think for a moment. "Bay of Fundy—where Fundy Park is—on the Bay of Fundy."

"Oh yes," he said. "I see, I see—big as our bay?"

"Ten times the size," Rance said.

Simon said, "I've never been there—guess I'm goin though, tomorrow or the next day." And he smoothed the blankets down in an unhurried fashion, and looked one way and then the other. "Wanta chocolate candy?"

Rance began telling him how much he earned down there—that he earned $8.50 an hour. And Rance told him about some fights he got into down there. He said: "You wouldn't believe" and "I took holda the cocksucker and drove him," he said. Simon's eyes blinked and he felt lonely. He kept looking over at the boy.

"Look, you wouldn't believe what goes on," Rance said now, thrusting his face out in the darkness. "Anyways I had her in the back seat—like I was saying, and four of them—remember, the lad I was tellin ya about—called Sludge—"

"Oh yes."

"Well he's with them this time—now you'd never meet a meaner son of a whore than him."

"Anyway—I scoot out the back door and leave her—and the next day I hear they're looking for me with machine-guns—not your ordinary rifle, but machine-guns—oh they're a wicked son of a bitch that crew," Rance said. "Machine-guns," he said. "Machine-guns—anyway I was all buzzed out—she told me her husband was in jail—I was all buzzed out."

Rance laughed and reached over his head and snapped on the light. There was a pan on his night-table and the bed wasn't raised. Simon's bed was raised at the front. He'd wanted to walk about the corridor in the afternoons but they'd refused so he wouldn't eat his supper, and the nurse whose name was Gabrielle kept an extra eye on him because of his grandchildren. She was skinny, she was the one Little Simon had teased and had pinched her bum. He kept moving his fingers now unconsciously.

At first he didn't mind Rance talking—but the boy mentioned the features of women's bodies, talked about their panties. They'd started talking and they must continue talking. Now the boy wouldn't stop talking about panties and skirts and every time a nurse went by Rance would click his tongue and then stick it out, or move his middle right finger through his cupped left hand.

"Oh she's bad enough though," Rance yawned. Rance's forehead stuck out prominently, and his eyes were deep set. There came a sound, like his stomach was churning. "Excuse me," he said. "You know what, Simon?"

"What's that?" Simon said.

"Tomorrow night's Hallowe'en," Rance said. "That's a time fer a tear."

"I've never been to a city," he said.

"Oh well ya haven't missed much," Rance said. "Cept the women—how long did you say you stayed in the woods?"

"60 year 'bout—give or take a year ya know—in the winters."

"You wouldn't catch me doing that," Rance said.

"Oh no—it wasn't bad," he said. "It was a good livin—we hadda do it," he said.

"I suppose," Rance said.

"Did I tell ya the story about shootin the bears?" Simon said, sitting up and smiling.

"About all the bears being shot—you told me that one," Rance said. Simon looked at him, nervously tapped his fingers.

"Did I tell ya about the bear stealing the pork barrel?" he said, louder.

"Ya—that one too—that one too."

"Goo-nite now," he said. He lay down.

Rance turned out the light. It was dark again and too warm but he heard wind raging against the window. He grabbed the sides of the bed with his hands and tried bending the mattress. There was always some clicking noise now, someone moving now, someone talking just down the hall. The faint medicinal odour at twilight, with the scent of sheets, alcohol and disinfectant. Rance would read the paper every day and then offer it to him and he'd say "No, No" and mention something else because he didn't want Rance to know he couldn't read. But the only information he got out of the paper was what Rance thought important enough to read aloud. He found out that *Deep Throat* was playing at the theatre, and that two girls had been raped at a camp on the main sou'west. He'd asked what *Deep Throat* was about and Rance had told him it was about a girl who stuffed cocks in her mouth.

"Be quiet," the man yelled. "Be quiet there."

They said they had to take him to Saint John because there was a machine to scan his leg and his back. What type of machine he didn't know. But they said when the machine was available he'd be sent down.

"Rance," he said.

"What?"

"You in the hospital down there?"

"Never was, no," Rance said.

"Oh I just thought ya mighta been in the hospital down there," he said, and then cleared his throat. Rance jumped up a second later and rushed to the flush. The patch of gauze light stark now, white.

"Jesus Christ," he said, the Johnnie shirt only half covering his white hairy flesh.

When his grand-daughter, Lois, brought him a new pair of pyjamas and a basket of fruit, and seeing him sitting with Connie Simpson, who was reading him the newspaper with the Colonel smoking his pipe and staring out the window, she said, "I hope I'm not disturbin yous lovebirds, eh?"

He'd felt stupid and got angry and he thought then: "It's better to be in the goddamn woods." When the Minister of Health made a visit to the place a man started to complain about the staff and said there was a draft in his room—and asked what she was going to do about it. And he thought with the man looking around at everyone angrily, as if he had the only draft in the goddamn place, "Christ it's better ta be home." And tonight. He'd thought it for a long time.

"Be quiet or I'm goin home," the man yelled.

He might have stayed with his grandchildren Packet and Little Simon, or their sister Lois—no, maybe not Lois—but he wasn't 50 years old any longer. They bootlegged and sold marijuana; they had bottles all over the kitchen. They had fights over hockey games. If he was 50 years old he'd take it. But now he became nervous because he knew what they were going to do, what they'd be up to. Lois had always been nice to him—she brought him fruit and striped pyjamas. She'd had three children by three different men; she lived in a trailer with a woodshed on the back and you could hear her yelling at her kids all the time.

From where he was he could see the stockings of one of the nurses. He could see the metal legs of the desk, but beyond that there was darkness. He could just stare at the legs of the metal desk and see the shoes and stockings of the nurse.

Even if he had gone to his grandsons' how would he be able to get in

59

or out of the house—not only with the bottles all over the kitchen floor but more than once Little Simon had taken the doorknobs off every door. He never understood why but he'd done it. Anyway, George, his son, was home again and living at Packet's.

In the morning here they'd brought him soft milky eggs. In the woods he would never eat too much, never ate sweets, never took sugar, drank black tea.

Rance came back to bed and started punching the small pillow with his fist. Now and then the man yelled, "Be quiet" down the hall, but it did no good. "Wanta chocolate candy Rance?" he said.

"Listen to that fucker," Rance said. He didn't answer. He was rolled a little on one side and he could see Rance. When the man stopped yelling the whole place was quiet.

At times Rance stuck his tongue out, pretending to lick the nurses, and at times put his middle right finger through his cupped left hand. Rance said: "I don't give a fuck fer nothin—never did, never will." And Simon would say nothing. He'd spit over the side of the bed.

Now Rance was popping the pillows with his fist and adjusting himself for the night. He'd had a drink of rum from Little Simon yesterday and vomited, blackly.

The old man didn't feel sore—he didn't know why they were interested in his back. When he walked his leg became numb and pain rushed to his spine. But he could still walk. *Then if he missed a leg it'd be the hip and then the whole bit.* When he'd told the Colonel about his leg the Colonel had told him about Private Walsh who fought at Vimy Ridge with advanced gangrene. "Didn't bother him," he'd said, and then he'd said, "The North Shore Regiment advanced the farthest and fought the longest of any Canadian regiment in the first war—you know why?"

"I didn't get to the war because my elbows are crocked all ta hell," he said.

"There were a lot of crocked elbows in them days," the Colonel said, and then he looked at the floor, pulled at his pants. Simon said nothing. "Anyways—why we advanced the farthest is because they didn't think we could fight together, they didn't think we were fit or trained to carry on as a fighting unit and so they dissected us, after we'd been together and had trained as a fighting unit—and they put my men all over hell—with units from Ontario and Winnipeg, fought alongside the British and Australians —and in that way we fought in every major engagement in the war— every one. We showed them, we showed them—" he said. And then he went over and made his bed and bounced his quarter on it. "And the wood on this river," he said angrily. "Lookit how they're using our wood—where's the reforestation—where is it?"

"Are you asleep?" Rance said.

"Are you boy?" Simon asked.

"Sure," Rance said. They were silent.

In the afternoons he was tired and before he fell asleep he could hear the train and when it rained the steeple of the church was grey, and cars moved slowly on the hill with the children with their book-bags walking forward. The nurses bathed him every morning. In the morning a nurse would come in and close the limp white curtain around his bed and she'd have a white uniform with white stockings, and he'd say: "Got a boyfriend yet?" He'd blink and stare at the limp curtains.

"There you go, Mr. Terri, all fresh again."

"Me legs feels pretty good there now."

"You look much stronger today."

"Me leg feels good," he'd said. "When I was a young boy—yer age—I walked 40 mile on snowshoes." And he'd look about.

"Is that right?"

"40 mile—bind me own snowshoes."

"Is that right?"

"In them days."

"Well now you're going to have your breakfast."

"Is the doctor around today—can I see the darn doctor today?" As if he had something he wanted to tell the doctor.

"Oh yes—he'll be in."

The nurse stripped off the blankets and began to bathe him where his hip bones showed and his thighs were, and she clipped the mucus from his hairy nostrils with a tweezer. But the nurse took no notice of this. So he'd tell the nurse about something 50, 60 years ago and the body had nothing to do with either him or the nurse. And that same nurse, with the scratching noise of her stockings rubbing together, threw a cloth over the bedpan and took it away.

And when he told the nurse things, she said: "Is that right?"

He began spitting over the edge of the bed. It was better that he spit and he hated than talked to as a child and learn to like it. Every time he spat over the bed Rance laughed as if it was a great joke.

He'd thought yesterday when the nurse came in again he'd tell her something, but when she came in he couldn't bring himself to talk. He said: "You know that Packet?"

"Who's that now?"

"Me grandson there—the big one."

"Oh him," she said.

"Well, he's not so bad," Simon said. "He grabbed a hold a bull one time gettin in on his cows, took it by the horns and thrust it up against a fence —the fence had electricity and he said, 'That'll teach ya ya son of a whore!'"

"Is that so?" the nurse said, flinching a little. And he thought he should not tell her stories anymore.

The doctor would come in, scratch his face quickly and look at the right leg—which didn't look any different from the other one. The doctor would say that it wasn't a blood clot—this he would mention to the nurse while Simon nodded his head. The doctor said this morning: "You're going to Saint John—have you ever flown?"

"No never did."

"Well we're going to fly you out on a helicopter from CFB."

The nurse said, "You'll like that Mr. Terri." Then he felt a hollowness and looked away spitting. One afternoon the boys came in; Gabrielle got angry and Simon called her over to the bed while the boys were there.

"Can the boys bring me up my chainsaw—I'd like ta do some work on it."

"Of course not," Gabrielle said.

"I wouldn't start her up—I just wanna sharpen the chain and tighten it fer somethin ta do."

"I'll bring it up," Packet said.

"Of course not," the nurse said. "No you won't," she said to Packet.

Little Simon started giggling.

Simon couldn't help cursing everything about the hospital, the nurses, the doctor scratching his face—the nurse when he refused the enema— the boys giggling because they thought he was just joking and taking out rum in front of the nurse to make her mad. He lifted his left hand, the one with the missing finger, missing right at the knuckle, and waved irritably. Little Simon took this as a sign to pinch her bottom when she started to walk away and she turned around, yelling at them. In the evening with the taint of cold darkened houses, Lois would stand near him, holding his hand. "It's all right Papa, it's all right."

Why did Packet now wear skin-tight pink or golden shirts with his chest bare and a medallion on—and why didn't he wear boots any longer but loafers and pleated, flared pants. Why did Little Simon drive around in a car with Oliver Brown—an Eldorado—what was wrong? And when Oliver said: "Do you know what's wrong with this goddamn province?"

62

Little Simon would say: "Do you know what's wrong with this goddamn province?" And Little Simon selling marijuana and wild mushrooms, why did the old man fear this? "It's all right Papa—it's all right." . .

"You know I was married once," Rance said. His head rolled back suddenly.

"When were ya married?" he asked.

"I was married—I know the one thing that'd make a man drink is a wife—is that right or not?"

Simon didn't answer.

"Anyways—I got rid of her."

Simon shook his head.

"Yes," Rance sniffed. "Rid a that bitch—she was an undertaker's daughter—won't tell ya which one."

"I don' know—my wife an I were married fer 55 year maybe."

"Yes," Rance laughed. "But that's not the way she is today Simon—maybe you hadda stay together—but people today don't have to stay together."

He thought for a moment, smiled. "Well, I don' think we hadda stay together—we were married 55 years about."

"Maybe," Rance said. "But I knew from the moment we were married that I was gonna have a good time, what dya say—right or wrong?" Rance said.

Simon didn't answer.

"Anyway," Rance said. "I'll tell you something—to extract the blood out of your body they make a slit under your armpits and legs—and have you strapped up on a board. Then the old blood gushes. I found out a few things—when we drained the blood out of a girl—say fifteen or whatever —nice pussy and everything, eh—the old man would bend over her and examine her, and then he'd pump her tits to get the blood out. It's true," Rance said. "Every word of it." He whistled.

"An the only time they were happy was when they had bodies in the house—so I acted awful bad right from the start, stole their hearse. They weren't gonna get me in that business."

Rance laughed and then he started coughing. He coughed and you could hear him rolling on the bed coughing. Wind lashed the windows and then they heard rain. Rain over the dark streets, the leaves in the stinking gutters and ditches and dead strewn cat-tails—the row of houses across the field on shale foundations, all the same sheeting, the smell of foundations, the great empty church. He rolled over on his side. He moved his mouth together and wiped spittle from his lips.

"Excuse me," Rance said. "Jesus, excuse me Simon."

Then Rance lay very still, Simon was almost asleep. When the nurse came in she looked at Rance and called the head nurse. Simon heard them talking, and he heard them scuttling about and talking quietly. And then they gave Rance a transfusion. "Tomorrow's Hallowe'en," Rance had said. "*That's a time for a tear.*"

He didn't know he was old now, he just became old. And he could no longer shovel himself out to the road. The easiest thing to do was to use the rope bridge that crossed onto Lester Murphy's property. But he didn't do this. Simon felt that it was his job to shovel himself out to the far road. And he had sat in his house day after day staring out the window or sometimes he'd walk down to his shed and sit there or go into the shed and chop some wood.

He was as friendly with Murphy as anyone. And once, no twice, he'd been into the tavern and had drunk beer with him. You'd see cars drive into Murphy's tavern and men go into the back room. You heard that property Lester Murphy had, he was selling, and that American camps were going up. "Atlantic Salmon Centre of the World." And again cars would drive up and men go into the tavern. And Simon would sit on his porch across the river. Then you heard that Lester Murphy had financed the building of a tennis-court for the local kids. And when there was trouble from the provincial government about closing the regional school and bussing the children to town Lester Murphy and a few others in the area got together to block it.

Ceril Brown, who owned a junk-yard and bottle-exchange and sold scrap, one day drove up, got out of his car and talked to Lester Murphy. And Lester began to yell at him—you heard them out in the yard. And a year later Brown had a discothèque and the children wore medallions and chains on their throats. And after that no-one went to Murphy's tavern.

Oliver Brown came back from university and married Sandy Simms. And Oliver began to run the discothèque, and fixed the place up to look like a discothèque he'd seen in Montreal. And Simon heard Ceril Brown was now loaning kids money and cashing their unemployment cheques at the bar and having happy hours. And the kids wore medallions and crosses on their throats. Little Simon, who'd no interest in Oliver Brown before, now got along with him, and Oliver Brown bought Little Simon drinks, and Little Simon became a bouncer at the discothèque—and the music, "Dancing, keep on dancing."

Then it was heard that Little Simon beat up some Indians that came to the discothèque and threw them out on the pavement. Lester tried to get a petition going to get the discothèque shut, but nothing happened. Simon sat on his porch and watched, as Lester built a wall around his property and stuck up no-trespassing signs.

Simon would not cross the span. People died, and he sucked in his cheeks and looked down the river. In the spring the Americans came to fish black salmon.

He could see the discothèque lights across the river at night and people broke wine bottles over the road. Ramsey Taylor coming up to visit Lester Murphy, would sometimes walk across the rope bridge and into Simon's yard. When Simon saw him coming it was important he pretended to be doing something. Ramsey Taylor would scratch his yellowed hair. And Simon would say:

"How's Lester?"

"Oh well—he's getting by." Ramsey would shrug and Simon would bend over and pick up a piece of bark and taking this bark he'd put it into the barrel at the side of the house. On his clothesline there'd be a dish-cloth and a pair of socks and the wind would blow them about the clothes-line. "I hear yer brother died," he'd say.

"Carl's dead," Ramsey would say.

"Too bad that," Simon would say. "I hear Lester is losing everything to Ceril Brown—I heard."

"I don' know too much about it—"

"Too bad that," Simon would say.

Simon would suck in his cheeks and nod. And he'd watch. Lester Murphy in the morning directing men where he wanted the brick wall built. Lester Murphy in the evening coming from the apartment building he owned and striding across his back field toward his warehouse with a tin box in one hand and a birch stick in the other.

Now he'd tulips everywhere and you'd see him out digging at his tulips. *When kids one Hallowe'en came into his yard and dug up all those beds and put tar on his door-knobs, Lester came out of the house with a birch stick and began to beat at them, and they all ran away.*

"Goddamn you, goddamn you," he yelled and Donnie stood at the door. Donnie, his son, had suffered spinal meningitis as a baby.

"What's wrong there Lester boy, what's wrong there, excuse me."

"Goddamn you, goddamn you," Lester Murphy yelled.

"Go fuck yerself," the kids yelled.

"I'll phone the police, I'll police," Lester Murphy yelled.

"Go fuck yerself," the kids yelled. And Lester Murphy shook his head and went back into the house, pushing Donnie out of the way.

"Boys oh boys, what's wrong there Lester dear—excuse me."

"Rich ole bastard—rich shit," the kids yelled.

He stood on one side of the river and looked over at the other.. His grandchildren came to see him now and then and Lois asked him for money. On his eightieth birthday they honoured him in the church basement. And when he said anything they smiled at him—as he remembered smiling at old people when he was a young man—without the slightest attempt to hide that you were smiling fondly. When he said the government was terrible and didn't have an ounce of gumption—"Not an ounce of gumption"—they looked at him and smiled. When he said, "In them days—" they all nodded. And when seven o'clock rolled around he looked distractedly about.

"Oh Papa you're tired dear—you're tired," Lois said.

"Yes," he said. "I'm goddamn tired."

Lois came over and borrowed money off him that he kept in a coffee can. He'd go to the coffee can and take out the money and give her more than she asked for because she always wanted to "get to town." But she was kind to him. But he felt that if Packet and Little Simon had to come during the cold days and sit with him then he was nothing but a nuisance. The river was frozen, banks of snow topped the windows and you could walk on the crust. Lester Murphy walked about his property with his beaver hat pinched over his ears and his raccoon coat opened, hitting the side of his house with a stick.

Rance slept with a branch line sticking out of his arm, his head resting on one side of the small hard pillow. In the morning hopefully he'd be all right. Hopefully in the morning he'd be able to stick his tongue out at the nurses. He talked in four-letter words all the time. He said *cunt* at least 50 times a day. "Cunt," he'd say. "There's good cunt, eh Simon?" "Lookit the cunt on that, eh Simon?" in a raspy singsong voice, the same voice he had for all his problems.

It was raining hard now and he knew by the sound it would turn to snow. There was the stink of burnt paper, the gorged mouth of the incinerator below.

He remembered the men coming out after the drive, in the summer, when they had dances at the schoolhouse. One night it was raining. "A whore's summer this is gonna be," Havlot Peterson said. He laughed when he said it and the men laughed with him. Two men were fiddling and there were roars from the crowd. "A whore's summer this is gonna be," Havlot said again and again, looking around and laughing. Then he went outside and fought with the Indians who looked through the windows. The Indians—the younger ones—came to the schoolhouse to watch the people inside dancing, to listen to the fiddle going, and they stood on piled planking and now and then you'd see them looking in on you as you danced. "Goddamn Indians," Havlot Peterson said. "Jus' the smell a thems enough ta make a man fall down an gag—all shiny red and stinkin, everyone a them." The men laughed at this. So Havlot said it again. Murphy looked at Simon and Simon said nothing. Then Havlot said that if he caught one of them looking at him while he danced, he wouldn't "Stand atal for that there." He went as close as he could to the largest window and started dancing. He kept dancing to the fiddler's music and swinging around and knocking against chairs. Then he came back and said that the Indians were making fun of him. Both Simon and Lester said nothing.

But Havlot shrugged and went back to the window and kept glancing through the window. When he'd sufficient evidence that the Indians had looked at him he went outside. Rain pattered over his white shirt and his hair was slickd back and rain came off the building and dripped over the planking and into the muddied ground. Peterson walked as if he alone had the gumption to set things straight.

Simon and Lester went out also. There was a young man, perhaps sixteen, that Havlot fought with and he looked up at all of them as he backed up against the building with a stick in his hand. The sound of a waltz scraped the darkness. The boy wasn't an Indian at all, but Lazarus Masey, who lived with his brother and his mother who had a crooked spine. The stick was half-rotted and would break but the boy didn't know this. Nor did he know that Lester and Simon had come out to break things up. When you looked at him you saw that his hair was dirty, that he'd a tweed coat and a sweater on—that the tweed coat had one pocket torn off, that his pants were above his ankles, and his shoes covered with mud. And there was an Indian girl with him who started talking in Micmac as soon as Peterson came out. And the girl wore a round hat but her hair wasn't tucked under it but hung down across her broad shoulders, with her tight skirt. The boy stared at them all, the girl clutching his shoulder behind him. The boy stared at them.

"Look, the son of a whore's got a stick in his han'," Peterson said. "Look there boy," and he laughed. The laugh wasn't even unpleasant.

When Havlot ran at the boy Simon put his arm out and held him back. Havlot cursed. And Simon did a strange thing. He became apologetic.

67

He told Havlot that he knew the boy was watching him and that the boy shouldn't be, that the boy was Lazarus and not an Indian, and Peterson kept screaming and his legs trembled. He said: "A whole mess a nice ones but one rotten one'll spoil them—spoil alla them—look a that one now —lookit dear lookit dear, lookit the slut there now—look dear she's all dressed up—coming to the dance were ya—comin to the dance?"

When Lester went forward he tried to talk to the boy, tell him to go home. The boy swung the stick and hit Lester over the head, and then fell flat on his back. The girl cried, talking in Micmac, with her hat lopsided and her earrings twisted.

"Hit him there," Havlot yelled. "Hit him, hit him." With the girl crying and looking around for the stick and speaking in Micmac.

"Hit him—hit him there Lester—for Christ's sake, look your head's bleedin—*kick the son of a whore*—let me go Simon. *Oh for Jesus Christ's sake hit him.*"

Lester Murphy ran around his house and tapped his stick and walked through the darkness to his warehouse with one star shining and went out to direct the men on how not to plough too close to his culvert.

"I don't mind you crossing the span"—Lester Murphy.

"Trespassing sign has nothing to do with you"—Mr. Lester Murphy.

And when they honoured him on his eightieth birthday they asked Ceril Brown, a discothèque owner, to be guest speaker, and they introduced him as a man who had known Simon all his life. And Simon kept looking about. And the only thing he could remember—or what he mainly remembered about Ceril Brown was the time Brown had gotten lost in the bog when he was a boy and when they found him he was covered with mosquito bites. But that day he said: "I'm honoured to have the privilege to speak to you about my friendship with Simon Terri."

Lois smiled and looked at him. He didn't know where this friendship had come from or for how long he and Ceril Brown had been friends, but he knew that Lois had asked Ceril Brown to be guest speaker, so he looked attentively at the man who said: "This is a man who spent 60 consecutive winters in the woods; this is the man who saved more than one man's life at the expense of his own safety." And Simon tried to think of something to do so he wouldn't be noticed, so he spread some peach jam on a roll and ate it. Except his teeth made a grating sound as he chewed.

"Cept I can't shovel my Jesus road too much longer," he said smiling. And then Ceril Brown and others began talking about it and they kept saying: "Don't you worry about that Mr. Terri—don't you worry about that." But when winter came it was him that was shovelling from pine marker to pine marker and a letter from Lester Murphy:

"Goddamn nonsense you goddamn fool—you use the goddamn span"
—Mr. Lester Murphy.

The nurse had left the metal desk now. The light shone cleanly through the door crack.

To be brought here to people who talked in whispers and looked at you, frightening you because they, in their 40 years, understood something very important about the nature of the universe that you had neglected to discover in 82. And what could you tell them? That you made 74¢ a day and had to walk 40 miles on snowshoes, and had built camps from cedar and skids with the bow ribs made from roots and had stayed up two months in the woods alone and could smell fourteen different kinds of snow?

"Cross the goddamn span"—Mr. Lester Murphy, ex-village councillor.

The damn thing about it was, Lester knew Simon couldn't read.

He tried not to think. Oh yes—the music again, the girls leaning against the side of the disco, and Ceril Brown lending them money, and cashing their unemployment cheques at the bar for 5¢ on the dollar and Lois bringing Leona over to him and saying: *"You mind yer manners with Papa now—I'll be a while."*

"Where you goin Momma—where you goin?"

"You little son of a bitch—I'm goin out—can't I go out and have a good time—I wanta go out and have a good time—everyone goes out and has a good time and aren't stuck with snotty noses—I'm always stuck with snotty noses—" Her hair was bleached and her large blue eyes shone as she smiled at him. He'd look here and there for a cigarette.

"Mind yer manners with Papa now."

The old man jerked up now. He could smell the gauze on his right foot. He jerked forward and touched his leg.

And then he heard that George was back—that was Packet's father—and that already there was a big row at Packet's place because George tried to take over the bootlegging and had scared some customers away. And Simon said to the cat: "Awful man that goddamn Georgie," and then Lois came to play a game of cribbage with him and he told her this too, and she started to cry: "Oh Papa Papa," she said. "What can I do—I just stay out of that nonsense—I try to live my life decently—I stay away from the rows over there, I don't want to see Dad or any of them Papa." She was wearing a light blue blouse without a brassière and the way her breasts lifted, the way her nipples pressed darkly against the material gave him a strange uncomfortable feeling and made him keep shifting his eyes. He could see the rose tattoo above her left breast.

He knew after the second game of cribbage that she was bored, so he said to her, "Promise me you won't go over there and get into any squabbles with them."

"I promise," she said. "I'm going into town anyway and have some fun."

"Promise." he said.

"I promise Papa," she said.

But he heard that not only had Lois gone over to Packet's for a drink of wine but she'd gotten into an argument with a girl George had brought in from town, and when George started talking about his wife with anger in his eyes over how she'd treated him, broadening his arms to show how much money he'd given her and pinching his fingers to show how much love she'd given him, and the girl from town said, "My God Georgie," Lois had jumped up and said, "You fuckin little slut—you say one word 'bout Mommy and I'll cut yer tits right off."

And Packet and Little Simon had laughed and George started to get angry and talked about *No respect*, and *what a thing to say to a visitor*. And within five minutes Lois was crying and told the girl she was sorry, and asked the girl to sit on her knee.

Lester Murphy walking toward his warehouse, with the tin box, the dogs in the deer-yard running down doe. Little Simon picking hallucinogenic mushrooms in the heat. It was the skidooers coming in on the deer-yards. And it was Packet—*always it came back to that face, the curly hair, the green eyes, the shoulders flinching once when he didn't like a conversation, twice when he was angry.*

And it always came over the fields, the trees being broken down by graders, the dust, the new houses on shale-beds with cement foundations —one after the other—on and on, children in cars, Lois going to the discothèque to drink zombies in a glass and toking with the boys in the back corner as they eyed her uplifted breasts and the beautiful slant of her belly. It was all the same. She came over to Simon and cried, "Papa— Papa," and he'd see her beautiful round eyes as the rain poured greyly against the window and the stove ticked—the space-heater in his room. And he'd get up out of his chair and give her money. And she'd leave Leona with him, with the top of Leona's lip blistered from cold and her nose running.

When Georgie came back he lived with his sons. He'd a large paunch and a bald head but he'd managed to bring the girl from town with him and they set up at Packet's. And he talked the boys into upping the price

70

on their beer and wine and he bought some bottles of rum. And by the time he was set up he was also drunk, and wanted people to drink with him and talk. He'd sit all afternoon on a metal kitchen chair by the metal kitchen table with empty beer-cases in the corner and he'd drink and talk. The room off the kitchen was Packet's, with Packet's stereo and Packet's bear rug and Packet's records and books—always books; no-one went in there. When the men from the mines came off a shift and stopped for beer George'd want to talk to them and he'd follow them out to the van and ask them questions about anything. If he was too drunk he'd start arguing over the price of the beer and haggle them for money all the way to the van. When he was too drunk he'd talk about Old Simon. "That son of a whore," he'd say. "That quiff—that—I could lose ten old mans and not mind, but when ya lose yer mother—when you lose your mother—" and sometimes he'd start to cry. And the girl got in fights with him and Little Simon, and then Packet would come home and tell them he was going to kick them out. And George would say: "Haven't I been a good father—haven't I been a Jesus good father?"

"You're the very best," Little Simon would say.

"Come on," Packet would say. "I'll put you to bed."

"I'm not going to bed—here, where's that quart of wine—come on let's have a party—ya know I never had a party with my ole man—never had a party with him. If you think I'm going up there—to see him."

George's wife was now living in Charlottetown. George and Tully grew up. George got into trouble and had to spend two months in jail for burning down a barn before the war. Then after the war a Ripley girl began swimming the river to see him because it was the Ripleys' barn he'd burned, and if her brothers ever caught him near her or on their property they'd shoot him. So whenever she could she'd hide her skirt and blouse under a rock and swim the river in her underwear. So she became pregnant on the shore in 1949 and Packet was born. And Tully worked in northern BC and sent his father and mother pictures of his family and money at Christmas. But now he wasn't proud of that. For when Tully came home to attend his mother's funeral he was embarrassed in front of his wife. So Simon went up the back stairs and into his room, and all during the wake he sat in his room not saying anything. Until Lester Murphy came across the bridge with his brother-in-law, Ramsey Taylor. And Tully's wife came up the stairs and said: "Papa—two old friends of yours are here." And she smiled at him, fondly, at an old man dressed in a dark suit with a tie too narrow to be fashionable, his broad callused hands in total antipathy to the white shirt cuffs, sitting on his wife's rocking-chair near the dresser.

He looked at her, her dress, the gold wedding-band and bracelet.

"Thank you ma'm—thank you," he said looking about.

"Come on Papa—I'll help you down the stairs," she said, her voice as if they were sharing a secret. "Come on Papa," she said softly, so that his mouth trembled. And standing up he looked about the quiet room strangely, picked up three bobby-pins off the dresser, put them in his wife's jar and then brushed the dresser needlessly with his hand and nodded.

"Here Papa—the stairs are steep, give me your arm," she said.

"Oh yes yes," he said, not understanding why she took his arm or why her face looked proud when she'd done so. And then later that night when he lay awake he heard them talking in their room. He heard her saying, "Poor old man—poor—" and then he heard her saying, "We have to leave him some money—"

"Of course—we don't have to discuss it."

"But we will discuss it," he heard her saying and then he heard: "How much do we have in traveller's cheques?" The wind blew the curtain lace and the dresser looked strange—animate in the darkness. "Just under $1500," he heard.

Well I think we should leave him $500 or $600, he heard.

Yes, of course, he heard, we don't have to discuss it.

Well, he heard her saying, the poor old fellow just hobbled along to-night as if he didn't understand what was happening—I had to help him down the stairs.

Yes he's getting on—he's getting on, he heard.

And for all her pleading and Tully's pleading he would not take the money, and the more they asked him to, the more he fumbled about saying, "Christ now, no no," and looking as if he'd done something wrong. And the night after the funeral when he started up the stairs and she said, "Tully help your father, goodness." He looked around and shook his head and removed Tully's arm gently from his.

But Georgie, who hadn't come home for his mother's funeral—a November funeral and frost in the soil, the men as they dug the grave and broke two spades in the cold earth—and dug in the wrong place, twice hitting the collapsed shells of two other coffins and saying: "How did Jimmy get way over here?" Georgie now said: "Ya can lose a pile a fathers—but if you lose your mother eh?"

Which might be true enough in a way.

It was a hospital for sure. Just outside the room and along the corridor was a booth where the nurses sat. Sometimes they talked about boyfriends and parties—and sometimes when their voices became low you knew they were talking about the patients they had to check up on. When they came back from their rounds they'd inevitably say something. They didn't like the son of a whore who yelled "Be quiet," but that was natural. He was always ringing the buzzer on them and complaining about everything. He told someone he was going to punch him in the mouth—and why couldn't he go home and die instead of bothering him—and that he was going to go home too after breakfast. He called the nurses names and they often had to restrain him.

The Colonel visited Simon three days ago during a senior citizens' outing. The Colonel was dressed, not in his balloon-sized pants but in a well cut suit with his thin white moustache and his face flushed from shaving. They talked for a while and laughed, and Rance made comments. Then the Colonel sat in a chair beside Simon Terri. The Colonel looked at him and said, "You should have seen the goings-on last Saturday when the music man came."

"Oh," Simon Terri said.

"The music man," Rance said. "Who the hell is the music man—eh?"

The Colonel looked over at the boy with his prominent jutting forehead and his deep-set eyes and clicked his tongue. Rance clicked his tongue also. The Colonel clicked his tongue again and looked back at Simon.

"We had quite a time—miserable bastards every one of them."

"What's that?" Simon Terri said.

"They threw a smoke-bomb through the window at us—the youngsters that hang around there thought it was a great joke. Everyone started choking except me," the Colonel said. "Mrs. Simpson fell down—fell right down—and the music man ran out the door—everyone started choking 'cept me—I guided them out *by myself*."

Simon looked about and didn't say anything. When he breathed the hairs moved in his nose and the top of his head showed up purple in the grey light. Rance laughed.

"Threw a bomb in the window—that's something I haven't heard in a while."

Simon Terri said nothing.

"Yes—everyone crying and screaming. Someone had to take charge, before they all screamed themselves into strokes. Dently started to cry—of course he's a ole man. I got them out." The Colonel looked at him and showed both plates of false teeth biting against each other—Simon didn't answer.

"Backhand them—miserable fuckers," he said. The Colonel nodded his head.

"Shoot the bastards," Rance said.

"The police got them," the Colonel said. "The police got them—I was the first to get to a telephone and get the police. They don't play games," he said, "with me."

"We used to put stink-bombs in our shop teacher's desk," Rance said. "I was kicked outta school because of that there."

The Colonel looked at him and Rance smiled.

"They don't play games with me," the Colonel said, and he stared at Rance. Rance smiled, let wind and said, "Oh Jesus Christ boys, excuse me."

"And now look at what they want me to do," the Colonel said. "We're supposed to have a Hallowe'en party—look at the mask they gave me," he said, taking a rubber mask from his pocket and showing it to Simon, a mask with a grin, a big nose and a wart. "Now is that anything for a man to do?" he said.

"Put er on," Rance said, "and see whatcha look like."

The Colonel took the mask and threw it on the table, "That's enough of that," he said. "They wanta take us to the United Church Centre and have a Hallowe'en party—but they won't get me to wear a mask," he said.

"I don't blame you at all," Rance said.

When Packet and Little Simon came in the Colonel looked at them, stopped talking, looked at the boy again, shook his head—said goodbye to Simon and walked abruptly to the door holding his cane upside down.

"Who's that now—ta give me such a mean look?" Little Simon said.

Rance laughed and slapped his leg.

It had stopped raining. In the darkness he could still make out the stack —still thought he could see the tube in Rance's arm with the white curtain half closed. In the morning Rance said to the nurse bathing him, "You just wanta see my pecker, that's all." The nurse would say, "Listen I've seen better than this," but that wouldn't deter Rance. "I bet you have," he'd say. "You know I'd a wife once—she'd buckteeth just like you and great big feet and bent-in toenails—caught her playing with herself one night," and then he'd begin for the day. No matter how much they told him to settle down, he'd jump out of bed and walk around, with the back of his Johnnie shirt opened showing the dark hair over his pimply buttocks. And now he'd done himself in and had a branch-line stuck out of him.

Georgie now was making inquiries about the will. He was walking around, with his dark shirt with the cigarette burns, with veins in his eyes

along the dirty, yellowed scelra, and he was asking what was *going on.*
When Lois brought Simon over fruit and pyjamas he'd send a *little
message.* Simon Terri would look about and shrug. "The thing is,"
Georgie said, "I don't want the goddamn place—but it's a shame to see
it empty—do you know how a place goes when it's empty?"

"How Georgie?" the girl would ask.

"Make me a sanwich," George would say.

"I don't have nothing to make you a sanwich," the girl would say.
"Packet put the meat in the cooler and locked his room."

"That son of a bitch—jus like his mother," George would say, going to
Packet's room and trying the door. He'd try the door and if it was locked
he'd jump back and kick it. Lightly. If the door wasn't locked he'd open
it, and stand on the threshold, and look in at the bear rug, the stereo with
all the records lined up between bricks and at the cooler. When he kicked
the door he was always off balance and he always hauled his pants over
his paunch after he'd done it. But he wouldn't go into the room. "That son
of a bitch," he'd mutter. "Some day I'm going to set all his records out in
the sun—see how he likes that there." And then he'd wipe his mouth and
come back to the table. "And my ole man," he'd say. "If his leg's botherin
him why doesn't he go into the hospital like anyone decent would do—
instead of hangin around over there—and make up his goddamn will, so
I'll know how to take care of his property for him—oh for sure he'd give
it to Tully—for sure, but he'll want me to take care of it fer him and make
all the decisions—make all the decisions, that's the only thing I'm good
for ta them—makin all the decisions."

"There's lettuce and tomato in the crisper," the girl would say. "I could
make ya a lettuce and tomato." She wore a lace beach-robe with a bikini
under it, with one shoulder-strap twisted and a smear of tar on her bikini
bottoms.

"I don't know if I like lettuce and tomato," he said.

"With mayonnaise—it's the very best."

"I don't know if I like the bastard."

"Well I'll make you one and you'll have a try," she said.

"S'pose," he said. "That Packet's jus like his mother—you shoulda seen
the rings I give her—every finger had at least two rings, and the perfume
I bought for her—and the birthday cakes I bought fer her, about a million
birthday cakes—and Packet, he'd still be sellin his beer fer a dollar a
bottle, knowin him—and then he goes and locks up his meat an acts like
the big show-all round the place—an Little Simon's jus as bad—an Lois,
jus like her mother—only thinks of herself." He would sniff and look

75

around and shake his head, smelling her suntan lotion in the enclosed heat of the dark kitchen, with flies buzzing on the ketchup bottle, and he'd slide his hand toward her: "You're not tanned there I see."

"Will you stop!" she'd say.

"Yer not tanned there," he'd say.

"Don't haul them off like that," she'd say.

"Makes ya horny does it?" he'd say. "Makes ya *wet*—hello."

"Would you stop!" she'd say. Her face was blotched with freckles, her hair was straight and flat and shoulder length, brown and parted in the middle. She was nineteen years old.

Packet's house had three bedrooms, two upstairs and Packet's room, but there were cots along the upstairs hallway, the upstairs ceiling slanting downward left and right. There was no basement, but a cellar—and it was damp all fall and spring and cold in the winters—it was also hot in the summer but Lois preferred it to her trailer, which had a tin roof, and when she came in the summer she slept in one of the bedrooms upstairs— and now that Georgie was home he and his girl had the other with Lois' children sleeping on the hallway cots, Leona and Bradley with their feet facing each other and Jeffrey in the far corner. Jeffrey was nine and his cot faced Georgie's room. Little Simon when he came home at night slept on the couch in the living-room. And Little Simon liked it when Lois came over because the children had to be fed and there was a good chance he'd get fed too. Little Simon slept in his clothes. Neither Packet nor Little Simon would say anything to the girl unless they were having an argu- ment—they felt she was their father's business, and they didn't know or care to know their mother anymore. Packet couldn't stand to talk about his mother and never did. Lois remembered her mother in Stedman's when she was four and Packet was six. Her mother brought them to Sted- man's, to a display of miniature turtles and told them to wait there and watch the turtles and she'd be back later. They watched the turtles and watched the turtles, and the blue-coloured stones in the off-coloured smelly water. There were also goldfish, and then a lady came up to them and told Packet to stop breathing on the glass and clouding it up—and where was their *parents* anyway? And then Packet looked at Lois, who'd on a sailor suit with a dirty white bib with her hair in a pony-tail in a big red ribbon and a bandage on each of her knees—and he put his arms around her shoulders and looked scared. Tears came to his eyes and he kept looking around, but Lois only smiled.

"What's wong Packet?" she said. "What's wong?" He'd always been called Pat or Patrick before she could talk—but she always pronounced his name Packet. She, to this day, never understood why he started to cry, and why he led her all over the store crying—not uttering a word but with his eyes looking frantic and holding on to her hand. She always thought her mother was beautiful. She always thought of the day going to Stedman's, when her mother put her hair in a pony-tail and twisted the blond curls at the top of her forehead, saying *"Well, you'll never be as pretty as your mother dear."* She'd always run errands for her mother and brought her beer bottles from the fridge. And it was she her mother taught to trick the baby-sitter by sneaking out into the kitchen when she was five and setting back the clock. "Tippy toes—tippy toes," her mother would say whispering in her ear, with her warm breath against her curls. And out she'd go to the kitchen when the sitter was in the living-room and she'd scamper up on the chair and set back the clock and if the sitter ever said who's up she'd run into the living-room, put her arms around her neck and give her a hug.

"Oh you little rascal—go to bed now dear," the sitter would say. *And then Georgie got in a fight with his wife—and it wasn't like the other fights* and he left, and Elizabeth Ripley Terri tried to get a court order for him because of desertion, and this went on and on and they moved into a trailer—and then she too, finally when the children were half-grown, left for a trail of cities that went nowhere. Then they began getting money from Tully and his wife—and Lois began getting letters from Tully's wife, marked personal, about hygiene and habits and boys—all which she thought very highly of, all which she kept, all which she wondered about—for a little while. And still today she'd get money from them but no longer with a letter marked personal.

When Little Simon burnt all the old tires in Lester Murphy's back field Lester Murphy ran around his house and tripped. He shouted one thing then another. There were shocks of withered grass, the tires burned, the gas exploded blackly into the sky, there was a taste of rubber on the still-dead water. Simon Terri watched from the riverbed and kept slapping the back of his head for some reason. And when he stood up he went into the house and had a dizzy spell—things didn't look the same or feel the same when he touched them. He looked about. The tires blazed across the river lighting up the north side of the house and Lester Murphy stood like a shadow in front of it, his hands waving. And Simon Terri went over and turned on the radio by the stair.

"This Hallowe'en," the announcer was saying, "this Hallowe'en's for you," and then the song "Shake your booties—shake your booties." And then the sirens—all along the road that night there were sirens, and he wanted to go to the phone and phone someone, but he couldn't think of anyone to talk to or remember any numbers. His head was pounding—and he heard voices. And he kept looking out his window. And then with lights flashing, and the whirr as the sirens settled, the RCMP pulled into Lester Murphy's yard with two constables getting out. And they turned the searchlight all along the river, across to Simon's house, along his front window and porch. And then down along the river toward the American camps, along the hollow and back to the field again. And it seemed once they'd done this they were satisfied with themselves, and by doing this they'd threatened just about everyone, so they turned the light off. And then Lester took them toward the water, along the path, and showed them his brick wall, with the pagoda lights. And Donnie stood in the background and kept nodding his head, and slapping the smaller constable on the back. The constables turned and went back to their squad-car, and relayed the message over the radio, sat in the car for a second and listened to Lester Murphy yelling and then drove away. Lester and Donnie went back into their darkened house, turned out the kitchen light after five minutes. And as soon as they'd turned out the kitchen light, the whizz-pit of a .22 broke the night air and the pagoda lights at each corner of the brick fence. And out came Lester again, hauling his pants over his woollen underwear with a shotgun in one hand and a flashlight in the other. Out came Donnie behind him, crying "Boys what's wrong Lester, what's wrong, excuse me." And Simon Terri looked across the river, saw in the far corner window of Murphy's house, the hollowed-out pumpkin with the absurd carved teeth—something that Lester always made for Donnie every Hallowe'en. Back came the RCMP, back came the sirens and the searchlight.

Lester Murphy built his house to look just like Hitchman Alewood's. Simon remembered how the story went, that Hitchman in the eighteen-eighties became infatuated with a young Indian girl named Emma Jane Ward. And he brought her to the house, gave her her own cedar chest, dresses. That she lived with him in the house. He was constantly out to town, to see how the sawmill was running, and coming back to the village he'd find her gone. Sometimes for a day or two. She'd be visiting her brother Tom Proud, she said—on the reserve. So Hitchman using influence (and what influence a man might have owning in 1880 almost everything on the road) got the Indian Council to ban her from the reserve. Emma Jane Ward lived in the house. Hitchman bought her trinkets, presents, hats and boots. And whenever he left for town she, putting on those hats, boots, dresses, carrying in her hand a purse with a golden-coloured string, would walk to the reserve and standing there, wait for Tom Proud or someone else.

"Well you know how a young squaw—how good they can look, same as now," they said.

Her mouth was broad, her nose with a rash of freckles, her eyes, her lifting cheekbones showing some French blood. Alewood was 59 years old when this was going on—she might have been sixteen.

Emma Jane Ward walked the roadway dressed in the latest fashion—her soft leather boots in the rutted earth.

And on the night of her birthday, Alewood left the house. She waited for him in the dining-room. But he never came back that evening. The next morning she was found strangled on the road, just below Alewood's house, where Lester Murphy's tennis-court was now. They said Tom Proud had come to the house, had taken her to Cold Stream for her birthday—a stream that ran miles through the hills—and there he'd strangled her, she clutching her bonnet, her purse in her hands, her hands adorned with buttoned gloves but her fingernails showing through. And carrying her out he left her on the road, undid her clothing , her white woman's boots. The next night he came at Alewood with an axe, while Alewood was going through her things, and gashed his left leg.

"Boys I could run them rapids," he said to the nurse.

"Is that right?" she said.

"In them days," he said. There was a dry taste in his mouth and his tongue was thick. Boys if you don't have water you'll die, went through his head.

"Merium ya know—now *she* kept everyone in line—better'n me—she never went drinkin or smokin in her life or to a circus—she said once she'd like ta have been to a circus."

"Is that right—well we're going to have your eggs here in a moment, Mr. Terri."

"In them days—you know the best way with eggs—well, in the woods we useta stir 'em up together—scramble them, and stir them—in the morning ya know—there was big eaters in the woods—great food too—pork and beef—I wasn't a very big eater—but there was some big eaters, et too much bread though. You're not s'poseta eat too much bread—can't do a day's work then."

"That's true isn't it?" the nurse said.

He'd look at her and she'd smile at him and he'd smooth the blankets.

"Ya know I'd still be at me own place right there now—except for the shovellin—and a course then they caught me." He'd chuckle and look at her, "They caught me—I'd light the damn fire there by day eh—but durin the night ya don't hardly need one—they caught me," he chuckled. "Oh there was a big racket over that. "Papa," Lois said, "Papa yer gointa catch pneumonia," he'd chuckle and the nurse would smile as she stepped away from the bed. You could see as she smiled the nerves working in her face. She was trying to move away. "No," he said louder. "No—it was my wood ya see—I didn't have no wood," he'd look at her and laugh, as she'd look at him and smile, nodding quickly.

"I mean, do ya see—I ain't had no wood," he'd laugh and his mouth would open and the hairs in his nostrils quiver. "And Lois saying, 'Oh Papa Papa yer gointa get pneumonia'—do ya see?"

"Oh yes," she'd say. "Well your eggs will be here Mr. Terri—you're looking much better today—"

"Merium, of course, could've gone to a circus—she'd opportunity enough to go to a circus—she was a bit stub-errn—a bit stub-errn." The nurse would be gone. "A bit stub-errn," he'd say. "A fine girl—but a bit stub-errn," he'd look about.

"Rance," he'd say.

"What?"

"When I was a young fella yer age—I mean ya could see hundreds and hundreds a salmon on the water in the spring—hundreds a them."

"I heard that," Rance would say. "It's not like that anymore though Simon."

"No no—they got'er about all now—"

"It's the goddamn Indians and French that got her," Rance would say.

"Did I tell ya 'bout the bears—"

"About all the bears being shot?"

"Yes," Simon would laugh sitting up by pushing on his hands.

'You told me that one," Rance would say. Then Rance would scratch his buttocks.

"You know, Simon," he'd say.

"What's that?"

"You got the funniest weirdest elbows I ever saw in me life."

Simon wouldn't answer. Rance would look at him a second.

"I mean they were probably good in the woods for ya though."

Simon would put his arms under the blankets.

"How didja ever come by elbows like that now?" Rance asked, slipping into an upriver accent.

"Oh I broke um boy—broke up a long time ago." And then he'd sit up again and be ready to tell Rance how he broke them, falling between

80

the runners of a sled when he was seven years old, and just when he was thinking about how he should approach this, to make it funny—for it seemed funny to him now, especially the way his father looked at his elbows after he'd pulled the horse to a halt. But as he was figuring this out, Pamela Dulse, one of the "big-shot" nurses as Rance called her, walked by and Rance said:

"Look at that Simon—she looks like she got a gaff 'tween her legs." And Simon would turn around quickly to see what he was talking about, upon which Rance would say:

"Boys yer a dirty ole man Simon—what dya say?"

When Lois packed him into her boyfriend's white Camaro with the stick-shift she smelled of lazy perfume and the interior of the car—with Leona and Brad and Jeffrey sitting in the back seat fighting each other and Lois saying: "Shut up or ya'll get no goddamn Kentucky fried chicken —goddamn it—look yer bother'n Papa—yer bother'n Papa—yer bother'n Papa." And then she'd grind the gears and think she was in reverse and letting the clutch out with the engine roaring she'd go toward the house, with Simon hanging onto the handstrap and the children looking around.

"Yer in first Mom," Jeffrey would say.

"I *know* I'm in first," she'd say. And again she'd tangle about with the gears and again she'd say: "If ya don't shut yer mouths ya'll get no Kentucky fried chicken from me boys."

"We're goin get Kentucky fried chicken," Leona would say. "Papa— are you comin to town to get Kentucky fried chicken?"

"No no girl—no no," Simon would say.

"Shut up, yer bother'n Papa," she'd say, and again she'd pop the clutch and lurch toward the house, getting closer and closer to the now discarded, foul woodpile and the pipe that ran to the meter. "Jesus Christ why did he buy a car like this here," she'd say.

"I could go some other day," Simon would say. "Tomorrow's dandy. Tomorrow's more than dandy."

"Oh Papa dear it isn't yer fault—I've a bunch a screaming maniacs in the back seat."

"I don' know," he'd say, hanging onto the handstrap, with the heat coming in through the window. "I sorta miss my own place ya know— already."

"Oh it'll always be yer own place Papa," she'd smile, with the front axle squeaking as she turned the tires as far as they would go on the back-yard grass.

"Well ya know that will I gotta get there—it'll be for all of ya—the

81

property I mean—the house too—I mean if sumpin should happen—I had it fer Merium—but it's fer all of ya—even fer Tully, though I don't think he'd want nothing."

"Oh Papa don't worry about that dear."

"No no—I'm not worrying about that," he'd say, chuckling and blinking with the two tiny moles under each lid. "I'm just saying," and he'd squeeze the handstrap.

"Mum do you want me to back this car up?" Jeffrey would say.

"Try it smarty arse—try it then," Lois would say. Simon would look out the window. The shadows would come down over the spruces and there'd be pine-needles on the floor of the forest—

The river. Its current rushed onward, onward.

"Jesus Christ," Old Simon said as he stared at Rance. Poor bastard Rance; his parents never once visited him—and the only visitor he had was one with the strapped eye, Orville MacDurmot. "Jesus Christ anyways," Old Simon said.

Little Simon said: "It's better ta go quick—ya know, and not hang around like Papa or Momma—but go real quick—ya know."

"How ya gonna go quick?" Lois asked.

"Figure on eatin a whole bunch a mushrooms—figure one good crack on the skull—with a hammer—but I'm not gonna hang around. Jesus look at Momma—she was like Mr. Magoo at the end of her, bumbling and stumblin—"

"Shhh, Papa's in the other room."

"Papa's in the other room?"

"Yes."

"Well why in fuck didn't ya tell me?"

When Lois became pregnant with her first child, Jeffrey, she'd sat with them talking and laughing. And then she started to cry.

And Merium had patted her head clumsily. *Let this be our secret—ours alone*, Merium had said. *Let this be only our secret*, Merium said to Simon when he left for the shore.

"It wouldn't be good to talk about it," Merium said to Simon when he left for the woods.

"It wouldn't be good to talk about it."

"No no—course not course not—no no," Simon would answer. Lois ran around and talked about it. They couldn't keep her in the house for talking about it. She talked about it to everyone—and as the months passed, winter with the snow against the boarded hedges and black

82

shingled shed, she talked to everyone. "I'm going to have a baby—and I mean, the doctor thinks everything will be fine. I mean—it'll sure be a hard birth—"

And then a total calmness, bordering on insolence after the baby came. "Well," Merium said. "She had a hard bringin up."

For the first years of Jeffrey Terri's life he lived with his great-grandparents almost all the time. And old Simon, because his hands got too cramped to roll a cigarette, taught his five-year-old great-grandchild how to roll them for him. And the boy would hand the cigarette up to him, grinning at the old fellow. "God bless—God bless—that's a fine rolled cig'rette there."

But when Jeffrey went home to Lois—to the trailer, in the heat, the sun glancing down across the tin roofing and onto the arid soil—Old Simon by sore practice had to learn again.

But it was as if Lois had found the prince of the church sitting in her living-room. For her son, five years old could roll better than she could—and she was tired of smoking marijuana in a pipe with tin-foil over the bowl. So she'd set him to rolling and there he'd be with his off-reddish hair, sporting freckles all over his face, with his bare dirty feet twisted so his toes touched and played against one another. And he'd roll her a toke and she'd go around the trailer singing "Auld lang syne" from the first of December onward. But then one thing followed another. Jeff seen at the playground. Jeff who had the run of the road since he came home to the trailer, seen at Denby Ripley's watching stag films for the price of two joints. The RCMP driving up to the elementary school and talking to the principal who not only ordered Jeffrey out of the playground but said "There's something gone wrong with society today" and fumbled with a grade-six geography book in his hands as if to prove it—a man who would succeed in becoming principal of the regional high school in four years and begin wearing a Toronto Blue Jays' cap, sporting a St. Francis Xavier graduation ring on his finger. And it was only the intervention of Packet who took all the marijuana off Jeffrey and hid it behind his record shelf and gave the boy two slaps and a talking to that prevented Jeffrey from being picked up.

"Oh Papa Papa—what can I do—I try to live my life decently, what can I do?"

"I know—I know," Simon Terri said.

What would become of Rance? It didn't matter. The man down the hall, Bowie they said his name was, "Be quiet or I'm goin home," and then he'd

83

try to beat someone up. Simon shrugged. The miserable pungent scent of gauze came over him.

His parents didn't once visit him—he must jump about, reeling this way and that to show his independence of the nurses who yelled at him and told the doctors. Sometimes during the day he'd look out into the corridor when a young woman went by and he'd start hitting his pillows. And Simon would watch quietly as the woman's footsteps receded, went, gone. Then Rance would scratch either his bum or his nose and shake his head and smile. Then he'd get out into the corridor and sneak a pop, and then he'd read the paper. But always he'd be looking at his watch to see what time it was, when visiting-hours were. When someone came through the door he'd light up, but it'd be visitors for Old Simon. Still though, Rance would be part of it—throw his comments about, and butter up to Little Simon for a drink. Only the young Orville MacDurmot would visit him. And Rance and he'd talk. In the evenings it'd be visiting-hours again. The sound of women in the corridor. Rance would pop his pillows —waiting for his wife, his ex-wife. Waiting with his bright eyes pressed into his neanderthalian head. He was waiting for his wife. Rance in his madness, in his terror of all things that weren't Rance because he hated himself as much as Simon might hate the chemical flush of the mills, and the manager—*from away*—(wherever that might be in Simon's mind) who flew around in a private Cessna 172, over the clearcut acreage and condemned men to layoff who'd worked twenty years driving the same road with the same type of tractor. And the men stood there—men who laughed at how the Indians were subservient when trying to sell you a fish, now being subservient to a head office that didn't know what a fish looked like: "You know what's wrong with this goddamn province," Little Simon said. "No, I don't know what's wrong with this goddamn province," Simon would say. "I just hope they leave me a piece—a scratch a ground ta lay in," and then he'd chuckle guiltily, and look around and wink.

Rance—it was as if he were a child waiting for someone along a corridor, seeing nothing but a dark room and the sides of a metal crib—in a house that not only had no books (except the salesman's copy of *Encyclopedia Britannica* beside the family Bible with names and dates of birth and death inscribed) but not a drink either. Neither book nor drink with the scanty afternoon light coming through the window. The bedevilled smugness of a thousand such rooms and corridors in a thousand such homes on one of the most violent rivers in the country.

Rance woke Old Simon one night and said he had a rash under his

testicles that was as itchy as hell.

Simon looked over. "Get the nurse."

"Fuck it," Rance said. "I scratched her till she bled."

"Get the nurse," Simon said.

"Fuck it," Rance said. "I wonder what it is."

Simon shrugged.

"Maybe jerkin off too much," Rance laughed.

Simon shrugged.

"Yes sir, maybe jerkin off—ya think?"

Simon didn't answer.

Then he paused, thought and said, "Canada's the stupidest jeesless country going."

"I know that," Simon said.

Rance said, "And ya know who they're lettin in now doncha?"

"Who are they lettin in?"

"All those Pakistanis and everyone else," Rance said. "Ya know what I'd do if I met a Pakistani bastard Simon—and ya know there's a bunch of them right around here—I mean there's a guy here ya can see walking to work every day—walks right past here in the morning and then walks back again in the evening—ya know what I'd do if I see the bastard?"

"What?"

"I'd grab holda the cocksucker by the scruff a the neck and rip his face off—that'd teach the bastard not ta be Canadian."

"I suppose it would," Simon Terri said.

I suppose it would Simon said. I must get back on the road, Simon Terri thought—I must get back.

The things I could tell you Rance said, she's different today.

He dressed and left the hospital, walked out, once the nurses left the desk, down the exit steps and into the grey night. Under the stack there was a porch-light, a door. The door was slightly ajar and he heard a man shouting drunkenly. It was now a detox centre.

From the detox centre he made his way to the front of the hospital. He looked toward the streets and houses, the smell of night, the towering cement edifice of the church to his right with spurts of steam from a dirty loose pipe at the side of the hospital, and water trickling into the grated manhole covers. Soon it'd be frozen, the town would be silent.

The town was quiet. The two long streets spread downward toward the water, the quiet secondary streets at right angles to them—and from Station Street on down, a haze settling over the earth. Now and then a car

85

drove up the hill, screeched to a halt and then roared off again to the laughter of youngsters. He walked to the court-house and sat there on the cement wall. Across the street was a barber-shop, boarded with a rain-wet rusted Brylcreem Charlie sign over the door, and he moved his hands along his right leg. He would walk again in a moment, go up across the tracks and hitch-hike home.

A van crossed, heading upward. It had a tiger painted on the door and a picture of palm trees on its side.

It didn't matter of course.

When they took him to the home they went down along the roadway, in the spring there was the pleasant smell of soil and earth. The white Camaro strained with its lifted rear-end with the oversize white-wall tires. Simon kept his hand on the handstrap and looked at the scenery. And Lois talking about the army, for her boyfriend had gone into basic training. And she said the word *civvies* the way Simon had heard her boyfriend do when he left her the car.

"We're gettin Kentucky fried chicken," Leona said.

"Yer not gettin any, just me and Jeffrey," Brad said.

"I am so," Leona said. "Eh Mummy—I'm gettin Kentucky fried chicken."

"Last time we went into town me and Jeffrey got a flag and you didn't."

"You shut up."

"We got a flag and you didn't, we got a flag and you didn't."

"You shut up."

"Cause yer a girl, cause yer a girl and we got a flag and you didn't."

"I did so. I did so."

"Raise yer hands up in the back seat who got a flag last time we went to town."

Shut up, yer bothering Papa—I'll kick all yer arses.

And they went along and the road curved and the frost heaves stuck up, the gorged-out patched roadway. And Lois smoked a cigarette. And Lois said, "Any of seven bases we could be attached to Papa." And the engine throttled past the mill, past the white houses, past the widening of the river.

"I love the goddamn river," he said.

"What's that Papa?—You kids shut up, me and Papa are havin a conversation."

"I'm gonna go to school Papa," Leona said.

"Ya know dear someday you'll be far prettier than yer mother—"

"I know all 'bout school—wait'll you gotta go ta school," Bradley said.

If ya know all about school why'dya flunk, ya little bugger.

They went down to the white-and-red building with the revolving bucket and a picture of Colonel Sanders.

"This is where Alewood's sawmill was now—years ago," he said.

"If I don't get it for them now Papa they'll be yelling all the way."

"No matter, no matter," Simon said and he looked at the building and the red-and-white uniforms of the girls inside, and Leona bounced up and down on the back seat and Brad kept wetting his finger with spit and trying to put it in her ear. And the windows of the building were plastered with advertisements for shirts and buttons and pins. And when Lois went to get out of the car Simon reached into his pocket. "I got some money here," he said.

"Oh nc Papa," she said.

"No it's my treat," he said, and he chuckled.

"No Papa."

"It's my Christless treat," he said becoming nervous and yelling. "It's my treat." And even with the engine shut off the car sat like a hulk of menacing power at this far end of the parking-lot and there was Alewood's smile and Packet's flinching body—taking married women into the field of a night and they crying to their husbands after, in the botched corner of the discothèque in the sad longing place. And he thought of Lester Murphy chopping Alewood's house (the first great house on the road) into apartments and a tavern—and he wondered what it was he was supposed to be doing. He didn't know what it was he was supposed to be doing.

What was important?

The last thing Merium said to him was "Don't worry—I'll see you at three o'clock," as he left the house and went down the path carrying his gun, and bird-shot in his pocket. He carried his sack with a piece of bread and butter and a container of tea and she wrapped three chocolate candies for him. The earth was hard under his boots and there was wind along the path, though the trees were still and frozen. When it's windy the birds are scarce but he saw five birds, nor did he shoot any. There was too much racket in the woods and he realized it was a holiday. He walked. When he reached the river he had to wade around a half-frozen swamp with yellowed nettles and rancid cat-tails. And he felt the icy water against him and saw frost on the rocks and the slivers of ice along the edge of the bank lik curdled milk now—the way the sun fell on it. He sat down on a log and opened his container to have tea—pouring the tea not into the cup that was the container's top but into a battered tin cup he always carried.

87

He looked about to see exactly where he was, and he guessed that he'd come out halfway between Lester Murphy's span and the main bridge. On the other side the main road ran close to shore. And he thought to himself. He'd walked quite a way and was tired, and this made him calm though the bottom of his legs were numb. In the distance he heard shots —one, three, five, seven, on and on.

He wondered if what was said about Packet out west was true, and then guessed that it was. And he thought of Packet. Packet was always alone—he didn't remember Packet with anyone very long. They said that when Packet was out west he'd caught a man stealing his oilers—he'd worked underground out there—and he lifted the man and hung him by his feet over an open stope 100 feet wide and 200 feet deep. And then he got in a fight in a bar in Calgary or somewhere—and a fight somewhere in Northern Ontario and then in the Gaspé where a man pulled a knife and Packet dared the man to stab him, with his arms opened, and the man threw the knife down and ran away.

And he remembered the times—all the times Packet and Little Simon had been a torment to the whole road. *But Packet was always alone.* He'd bring Merium over salmon and come in the door. He'd place the salmon, wrapped in a newspaper, on the table and leave again quickly. Again alone. In his old car with the Waylon Jennings music and the Jim Morrison and the Doors music blaring when he stepped out of it. In the night, his burly head and off-green eyes. And there were women too— married women. And he'd go home—alone. And now his stereo and records and bear rug from a sow he'd slaughtered, over the whole earth, and the stars in the sky. Alone. Perhaps the only one who could go into Packet's house any time day or night and be sure of a welcome (unless it was Old Simon himself) was Lois. He, the man in Lois' children's life; he, the advisor to Lois' boyfriends on cars and rapids, canoes and flies.

On the other side the main road ran close to shore. Along that road while Simon sipped at his tea came Donnie Murphy pulling his waggon filled with beer botles. Twice a week, Donnie left his house and went along the road pulling a child's waggon, collected the beer bottles that had been thrown from cars and took them to Ceril Brown's junk-and-bottle exchange. And there Ceril Brown would count his bottles for him, tell him how much they were worth and plant the money in his fist. Donnie didn't know anything about money. Then Donnie would smile and go home and set his money on the kitchen table and Lester would count it out for him and put it away for him. Donnie would wait three days, until enough bottles had been thrown from enough cars and out he'd go again, with the pipe planted in his mouth the same way Lester Murphy planted his. Simon watched him walk along. The trees were sparse and naked now, the houses and the roadway naked. Donnie had a chequered jacket and mittens on. Sometimes by accident he'd wander too far out into the roadway, a car would slow down, blow its horn and screech around him. Simon Terri saw a car screeching around Donnie and Donnie hurrying to the side of the road, looking about as the people shouted at him. Then the people roared at him again, laughed, and he waved to them. Simon heard the people in the car cursing, saw a bottle being smashed on the pavement. Donnie ran up to it and shook his head, looked around at the jiggling bottles he had in his waggon. The car roared out along the calm November roadway. Simon saw the car stop, roar backwards, fishtailing along the asphalt. Two men got out of the car.

"How she goin right there now?" one said. "Where d'ya steal them bottles?"

"Come on in Bennie," he heard a girl say from inside the car. Then the other man said something, and then Bennie said something else that Simon couldn't hear properly.

"C'mon in Bennie," he heard the girl say.

"Where d'ya steal them bottles?" Bennie said.

"I—I," Donnie said.

The men laughed.

"I—excuse me boys—it seems I found them," Donnie said smiling, looking about—to either side of the road.

"Them are my bottles I threw out the other night," the second man said.

"Get in this car," the girl said.

"Look," Bennie said. "Those are our Schooner bottles."

"And our Alpine bottles."

"And my Moosehead bottles."

"Get in this car right this minute," the girl said.

Bennie looked at her and made a gesture.

Donnie looked about, then put his head down. He clutched the wooden handle with both mittens and started to turn the waggon around.

"Those are our bottles—we were lookin for those bottles," the second man said. Donnie now stood with the waggon sideways on the road.

"I—it seems here I found these on the road—well ask Lester." The men laughed. Donnie looked about absurdly. Bennie bent over and began to jiggle the waggon.

"Leave him alone," the girl said.

89

The second man grabbed a bottle—Donnie tried to reach for it but he threw it. When Donnie let go of the waggon the man grabbed it and started to walk away, imitating how Donnie walked with a sluggish clumsy motion. Donnie turned first to one and then to the other. The man started to run in a clumsy circle with the waggon and Bennie threw a bottle up and caught it first in one hand and then in the other.

The men laughed. They laughed and exaggerated their gestures and yelled to each other, and the girl yelled at them.

"Excuse me," Donnie said. "Excuse me." The men laughed. There were sounds of shots along the perimeter of the trees.

"Excuse me—I found them," Donnie said, pointing into the ditches as if to explain something. "And ya—ya can get them on the road," he said, nodding quickly. "Ceril Brown—ya can go an get—it seems Ceril Brown'll tell ya—ya can get them."

"Sure ya can," the bullets came again.

"Sure ya can."

"Sure ya can," the rifles sounded.

"And how many people did you kill in the war?"

"Ya, how many people did you kill in the war?"

It was just after noon-hour. The bottles jiggled, the sound of shots, the men laughed and the girl yelled, with Donnie now running this way and that and trying to keep his pipe straight by touching it with his mittens.

"Hello," Simon Terri yelled. "Hello," he yelled.

Everyone looked at him. "Hello," he yelled. "Hello."

The men turned about. Bennie picked up the waggon and threw it, end over end. They laughed and ran to the car.

"Hello," Simon yelled. "Hello—hello," he yelled.

"Hello," the men yelled back. "Hello—hello there, hello."

"Oh hello there," the men yelled.

"Jees yer awful," the girl yelled.

"Hello there," they yelled.

"Yer just awful."

"Oh my soul, hello there," they yelled.

Donnie stood in the middle of the road a long time. Long time. He watched the car on the November road—as if metal and soil had become one now—with the tooting and jeering and aping along—where along the road the black front sign of Ceril Brown's junkyard, where soon, a little ways beyond that would be the red sign with studded buttons of the dischothèque with a picture of a twenty-year-old man in tight clothes swinging a twenty-year-old woman with a loose dress against her electrically lighted legs. He stood there and watched after the car and then he turned and looked at his waggon reeking of spilt beer and broken bottles and cardboard boxes that Lester gave him. When he looked to see the old man who'd yelled at them he couldn't see anyone. Simon had gone. He'd turned and gone into the sound of rifle fire.

In the evening Simon came to his property—a property built by Merlin Terri and inaccessible in 1909, the year Alewood died, from everything, but now with a drive to the secondary road and a span to Lester Murphy's. It wa sevening, almost dark, there was still the scent of fading dead leaves and apples, lingering with the new cracking of the frost. The road was rutted, the tree in the small orchard reaching outward to the sky, and he was thinking of this. He came into the kitchen and his grandchildren and great-grandchildren were there. He looked at them. He was thinking of the rifle shots.

"Merium's gone—Momma's gone," Lois said. He looked at her and her mouth was open, showing her healthy teeth.

"Gone where?" he said. "Where did she get off to now?"

"She's gone Papa—she's gone," Lois said. "She wanted to put up those drapes—she was up on the stool and she wanted to put up those drapes— you know those drapes?"

He looked about. Packet looked at him quietly—Little Simon turned away and grinned slightly. Brad was slugging Jeffrey.

"Where did she go—what drapes?" he said. Then he said, "Goddamn it—" and then he stopped speaking.

"Well what—," he said. "What—"

Then he said, "About her med'cine—she had her med'cine ya know, she did—we went up to the doctor and got the med'cine—what about her med'cine?"

And Georgie did not come home—nor could they get in touch with him. Nor did Elizabeth Ripley Terri know where he was—she herself sending a card. And the undertakers set up the casket and put down plastic and ran cords to light up the electric cross and Simon watched all this. And he asked them questions about it and nodded his head at everything they said. And then the undertaker, and the undertaker's assistant, a pimply-faced boy of sixteen, led the family in the Hail Mary, the Our Father— and then Mass cards came and wreaths. And Simon kept looking at the people as if they were supposed to tell him something important—and as if when they told him this important thing then everything would be all right. But the only important thing he was told was when Packet asked him aside and told him he should put on his suit. And the only feeling Simon Terri got was that he was in the people's way and he went outside. And overhearing the assistant saying while walking to the hearse, "Did you see her hands—what a hard life the old bitch had," Simon went up to them awkwardly saying, "She had a good life—ya know."

"Of course—of course," the undertaker said, staring furiously at the boy.

"Yes—she had a good life—I mean she didn't get to a circus, she had opportunity enough to get to a circus—but she was a bit stubborn—a bit stubborn." There was saliva at the corners of his mouth. Why he had to explain this to them he didn't know. And then he went into the house. "A bit stubborn—"

And it seemed grabbing onto this idea he was satisfied about something and he said to Lois, "Merium was always a bit stubborn," and nodded his head as if this put everything into perspective. Devoda and Tully flew home and Devoda took Lois into an upstairs bedroom and had a conversation and Tully kept asking Packet about his life—and Packet with a look around the room said, "My life's no different than anyone else's."

"Great then—you're getting along are you Patrick?"

"Getting by," Packet said, and he stared at Lois when she came down the stairs.

"Well they're getting along fine here," Tully said.

And Devoda smiled and Tully smiled, and Lois smiled—because they said she was getting along fine, they who sent her money. And then Devoda mentioning something about the reserve across the river and how she'd discovered the West Coast Indians to be much prouder than the East Coast Indians.

Packet got up. And Devoda mentioned the artwork of the West Coast Indians and Tully said that they'd some fine Indian artwork in their home, and Little Simon said, "Oh ya, the totem poles out there," and couldn't stop looking around and grinning.

"Simon you want a drink," Packet said addressing his grandfather who was sitting alone by the kitchen door, rolling a cigarette. And Packet went and got the old man a drink.

"Well you're a fine family—a wonderful family," Devoda said. And Lois smiled.

"That was Momma's help," Lois said.

"Has anyone gotten in touch with George?" Devoda said, when Packet brought in the bottle.

"We don't need him here," Packet said.

And then Tully said he must make plans to get down more often. And Packet drank at the end of the room with his eyes as sharp as they were when he watched Lois come down the stairs. And Old Simon felt all this —knew it by the way Little Simon grinned and the way Lois nodded every time her name was mentioned. By the way Devoda, whom Packet did not look at or speak to, kept saying, "I think Patrick's a bit of a rebel," and then said, "Our son's like you are Patrick—isn't he Tully?"

"Oh yes."

"Yes, both named Patrick—both *rebels*."

And Packet watched them from the corner of the room. The talk went on, people came in and out of the house, the old man stood by the door when someone came in and nodded to everyone. But he kept expecting someone to tell him something.

He saw all this and when people looked at him he said, "She had her med'cine ya know—she had her med'cine but she'd always lay her aside somewheres." And then he'd chuckle.

"Well she had her med'cine—but she'd lay it down and she was all excited over the last week or so—"

He saw it all—but there was a festive air to everything. And he noticed Tully, and Devoda kept saying, "You men—really," though Packet wouldn't look at her, and it was strange and sad how out of place she was and how she kept changing chairs to sit wherever Lois sat. When he looked at her he saw a woman, still in her forties, dressed in a black knee-length skirt with makeup and her hair dyed, the pink skin along her cheeks, smiling at anyone that looked at her. "Fuck it," Old Simon thought, and he went upstairs. "Well you're a fine family—a wonderful family."

Every now and then she'd mention something out of context and inopportune and look intently at them.

And she wanted to help Simon down the stairs, and give him money. And too, the afternoon of the funeral when the ground had been dug into —finally at the proper place, four and one half feet, the sky cold with leaden clouds that didn't move, she came up to him.

"Papa," she said, "I think you should have a moment alone—"

"Alone?" he said.

"With your wife," she said, smiling. And it seemed to him that this was a very intelligent thing and he must do it and when he nodded she looked gravely about and told the people in the living-room that Simon would like a moment alone. Little Simon looked about, nodded seriously and getting up off the sunken couch cushion, couldn't help grinning. Then she led Old Simon into the room over the plastic, the cards and wreaths and half-hidden cords for the electric cross. And she left him there. Simon looked through the half-drawn window drapes—the water was grey and still going mirror-like, it would freeze soon—the dead woman lay sunken into the cushions, her eyelids too white. He did not look at her but tried to think of what he was supposed to do. And then he nodded and left the room.

Simon cursed his leg. The numbness had left his leg long ago, and it was overactive. He could feel the blood in it, as if the blood in his right leg hadn't been bonded by anything more durable than water, now and then a spear against his spine.

"Bastard," he muttered. And on he walked—leaving the wall, the Catholic school with its orange lustreless brick and its large rectangular tired windows that had looked starkly and angrily over three generations at the three Protestant churches with their white clapboard that surrounded it. The street was shaded, the houses hidden and clandestine along the avenues. Now and then a car roared by and Simon would look up.

He'd learned about Packet out west from tales that had come back while he was still out there. He'd heard that Packet was lured into some place, made drunk and thrown out a two-storey window by two men in an attempt to kill him. He took seventeen stitches on his forehead and spent a month in the hospital. Little Simon telephoned him, asking him to come home. But Packet didn't come home until he'd dealt with the two men, cracking their skulls and breaking their legs with a baseball bat. When he came home he never mentioned it and no-one ever mentioned it to him. When he was expelled from school the teacher looked around for his parents—there weren't any so she went to see Merium.

"Of all people—Patrick shouldn't leave school."

Merium nodded.

The teacher said Packet could be a brilliant student if he wanted, and Simon went to talk to Packet—to ask him to wait out his two-weeks' suspension and go back. But Packet was gone—he'd walked to town on the old freight line and had hitch-hiked away. He telephoned Merium from Saint John and said that he'd found a job and that his mother was there—that he'd seen Elizabeth Ripley Terri in the company of a man, along some street one night.

"Are you going to see her—talk to her?" Merium said.

Packet was silent for a moment.

"Of course not," Packet said.

The old man crossed the tracks, the spine of the rails glimmering white below his feet from the switch-yard and trailing off into the distance. Two boxcars sat near the old bank vault—and there was water and soot in the night. Down below him now the hospital, dimly lighted with its giant stack and to the left of that the room where Rance slept. There wasn't a moon or stars to follow. The streetlights had a haze over them and scores of white houses sat with cement steps and proper gilded railings—each with some immaculate priority the old man disliked but didn't understand—as if all those houses had been beaten out by the same hammer for the same unsatisfying purpose, and the cars they rode in sat in the doorways. "Jesus Christ anyways," Old Simon thought.

The morning after they'd burned tires at Lester Murphy's, in came Little Simon reeking of soot and gasoline and sat in the living-room, and at eight o'clock turned on the TV hoping to see cartoons. Old Simon came down the stairs and looking at him for a moment went over and put on the kettle.

"Did your cat die?" he said.

"What?" Old Simon asked.

"Cat—did your cat die?"

"Oh yes—ole Tom, got in with a weasel couldn't handle it."

Then Old Simon said, "Do you know who was in on that las' night?"

"In on what?" Little Simon said.

"In on the burnin."

"What burnin was that?" Little Simon said, his face white except for a dab of soot on his nose and the corners of his mouth twitching, as if he were ready to gasp in amazement or smile. Little Simon who climbed down the drainpipe so often in grade nine that he finally broke it off and fell to the pavement below, getting a broken shoulder blade that made him look as if he'd a permanent chip on his shoulder.

"The burnin at Lester Murphy's," Old Simon said. "The burnin at Lester Murphy's—Christ," he said. He went over and began to shake Simon, his godson, grandchild who in spite of the smell of gasoline and dabs of soot kept looking about in shock. He looked incredulous at the old fellow—with his yellowed gaunt skin, shaking him, shaking him. His mouth opened and his head moved back and forth.

"Hold'er down now, hold'er down—don't get upset."

"I'd jus love to smell the barrel of yer .22," the old man said, growling. "I'd jus love to smell it—-you bring it over, I'd jus love to smell er—"

And Little Simon couldn't help saying, "Jesus Christ—that's a unusual hobby Sim" as he'd said to everyone—to Denby Ripley who now and then ran stag movies in his home at the price of $2 a show and bring your own booze—the conflagration of sweat and skin butting from a projector onto a screen—and Jeffrey Terri at five years old getting in on a joint and watching this as he now watched his grandfather George and the girl from town through the light slit under the door—and as Packet Terri his uncle had watched Elizabeth Ripley Terri years ago while his father was drunk at the Legion—being at more battles at the Legion than he ever was at in the war, spreading his arms to show the size of a shell that exploded next to him, pinching his fingers to show how close it came to killing him.

"Don't make that mistake again," Old Simon said, shaking him. "Don't make that mistake again."

"Jesus Christ Papa—get a holt of yourself, you'll have an attack or something."

"That's my brother yer foolin with remember that."

"Your brother—how, your brother?"

"Never mind—never mind."

"Les Murphy is your brother?"

"Never mind."

"Jesus—he never give us anything."

"Never mind—never mind," Old Simon said letting go of him.

"Jesus—he never give us anything," Little Simon said with the soot standing out on his nose.

"Never mind."

"He's one a the rich ole coots on the road—he never give us a thing."

"I don't want that mentioned," Old Simon said.

That morning after he stopped shaking Little Simon, Little Simon stood and began pacing the living-room from the old flue that was rusted at the elbow and a little slanted to the mesh-backed chair and with his hands behind his back began to say, looking out the window now and then at the still smouldering tires—"You know the way I figure it—it's those goddamn Indians—not satisfied with nothin Simon—"

"The Indians get blamed for everything."

"Well," Little Simon said, "they don't do dick—all except burn things down, and they get paid fer doin it."

"The Indians had nothin to do with this."

Little Simon looked out the window, and then at the snowy picture on the TV.

"Ya well, you should see them—takin every salmon outta the goddamn river they can—and then if they can't sell them throwin them in the dump

96

—paid for it too, all their education—the clothes on their back." He looked out the window, with a dab of soot on his nose—and when he saw Lester coming up to inspect the pagoda lights and Donnie with a shovel and a dustpan behind him, he laughed out loud. And then he calmed himself and said, "You should hear the statistics and all Ceril Brown has on how we feed and keep alive the average Indian—and then the first chance they get they go an do that ta Lester Murphy." He turned around and looked at Simon and he didn't know at that moment how he looked like Lester Murphy, his jaw and nose—how there was something of a delicacy about him. How Lester Murphy the night before had sat in the kitchen with the shotgun, with a red spot in the middle of his ribcage, like the permanent obscure circle on the face of Jupiter.

"Ceril Brown should shut his mouth about the Indian,' Simon Terri said. "He'd a died eatin his own shit if it weren't fer Daniel Ward, the time he got lost."

"It was you who found him."

"It was Daniel Ward—"

Little Simon yawned. He smelled of alcohol and gasoline.

"I've got nothing bad to say about the Indians," Little Simon said. Old Simon looked at his grandson.

"You want tea?"

"Sure," Little Simon said. "No sir, I've got nothin against yer average Indian."

For he was an old man—and hearing when he was fourteen about Alewood who lived at one time in the eighteen-eighties with a Micmac girl who was sixteen, until her brother brought her into the woods, strangled her and out of guilt brought her out and left her on the ground near the roadway—her tongue was sticking out and her lips were purple and she'd flesh under her nails, and her people came and took her away quickly—and there was a consensus in the small village and along the road that no matter how many priests came in to civilize the bastards they'd always been like that and always would be—but he'd *learned* that. He'd learned it all along the roadway. In the evenings the flies drummed in the bog, drumming and whining, and people said that the French who'd gone in there lived just like the Indians—that there were great clusters of them gone in farther than any cutting—and they interbred so that they had albino bloodless children. And he thought of sucking lice that his father complained about and he'd later found out about (that his father was not so much complaining about lice as giving them their proper due). But he knew about the French and how they'd gone inward after 1756—and he learned about the Indians and their reserve, which was a five-mile stretch of houses and boarded shacks. And he knew how Packet and Little Simon went down there and lifted nets and how the Indians wasted salmon. And he'd done it too—all of it. So it was no different.

So it was no different. And the Indians stood along the roadway and women looked through the curtains and locked their doors—a woman would lock her door and tell the children to get to bed, "Or the Indians'll get ya and cut ya up—cut off yer nose and ears and the squaws'll have them for breakfast." And the Indians stood along the roadway. And in the nineteen-twenties when the Indians walked along to the store—the girls with red hats—Havlot Peterson would wait for them, and he knew enough Micmac to say things to them—to tell them they were pretty—to say "It's all right—it's all right"—the girls with their wide faces looking back over their shoulders and their dresses in the style of Zelda's flappers. And Havlot raised money to pay the Indian girls to take off their underwear.

And he'd done it all too—all of it. And so he talked to Little Simon that morning and Little Simon kept scratching his hands. And then Little Simon had a talk with George a little while later, and George said all he'd had all his life was "Indian problems." Little Simon agreed. George said that Old Simon liked Daniel Ward because he was a buddy in the woods but that you couldn't take the woods out of an Indian—even in this day and age. Even in this day and age, George said.

"The West Coast Indians are a little bit prouder than the ones we got round here anyways," Little Simon said.

"A bit more accomplished," George said. "Got a Doobie."

From rumour and knowledge pretty much, on down. So when people said anything to him he usually thought of something else. But the one thing that many people didn't care about—or that he himself didn't know —is that when you start mentioning things to an old man, when you start mentioning how things come about, he might think of anything, of something far in the past but he still might look at you as if you were mad— stark raving lunatic, and not even know he's doing it. Or look guiltily, or look at his thumbnail before looking away.

He sat on his haunches near the gravestone. Behind him in the graveyard was the white statue of Jesus on the Cross looking down across the cold water. He could see his breath, and when he breathed he could feel his nostrils come together. And he felt his spine. It was no longer his leg, but the burning of the back of his hip and spine. As if the spine wasn't his spine but something else entirely—something with its own set of rules. If you thought about it. There was a train shunting now, and it had been a long time—there was the smell of sulphur in the air. In the morning the children would walk to school and in the afternoon they'd go home— they'd cross the fields below him. The younger ones would go along first with their bookbags strapped to their backs and then the older ones. In the afternoon the hospital grounds-keeper burned leaves outside in a barrel—when the air was blue and the smoke curled white up out of the barrel Simon believed he could smell it, taste it you see, and he watched it. He watched the grounds-keeper whose name was Robert and who had an *HMS Bonaventure* tattoo on his arm, steadily dumping boxes of leaves into the incinerator, with some of the leaves getting caught in the drift of smoke.

He squatted on his haunches and leaned leftward against the grave-stone. There were revellers across the street and he watched them, coming out of a small house with a peak over the front door. The night was dark but he could see grey clouds of sulphur moving along, from the south-west, where the largest of the three mills sat. For a long time he'd not minded the mills and then he saw a rinse in the water—and parr floating belly-up (like they did when someone blew a pool with dynamite)— and then he minded it. And then, now, he didn't mind it anymore.

He sat on his haunches and watched the people coming out of the house, drunk, in Hallowe'en costumes. There was a bit of snow coming now.

"Let's make snowballs," one said.

"It's getting cold enough," another said.

"Oh Mike let's make snowballs."

"Let's make goddamn snowballs," the girl yelled.

"Shhh, you'll wake the children."

"Give them my love," the girl yelled.

"Shhh, you'll wake the children."

"Give them my love."

Simon Terri looked through his clothes for snuff. He knew the girl who was saying "Let's make snowballs," and "Give them my love," was Lois. She had a witch's hat on and she carried a great old straw broom (that she must have taken from the shed) but he could not see her face. But he knew it was her by her upriver accent, by the way she walked from the door, and especially because she answered the woman back every time the woman said, "Shhh, you'll wake the children." The woman finally closed the door.

"I've been at healthier wakes," Lois said.

"Shhh," Mike said.

"Not only that," Lois said. "I'm looking for a man tonight." The men laughed; Lois turned to them, took off her witch's hat and put it back on. "And if any of you fuckers happen to see a man—let me know will ya."

"Are you takin her home?" someone said to Mike.

"I'm not takin her home, she's got her car, I'll go home with you."

"Where's she from?"

"Not where I'm from," Mike said.

Simon Terri sat in the graveyard and leaning against the gravestone watched them: his hip, his spine, was like a sharp metal plug had been extracted from it—like the extraction of a tooth—but metal. He did not wince. When he heard the Bowie yelling, "Be quiet or I'm goin home," when he heard Rance going on and on about women and politics—Rance in his madness, in his terror of all things that weren't Rance, he thought: "It's better ta be in the woods than this here" and he thought of his wife. He thought of a lot of things. Rance talked about women. Lois kept twirling her hat around, throwing it in the air and trying to get it to land on her head. When it fell to the ground she cursed playfully. The men and women kept moving away from her as she stood outside the house with its peaked front door and laughed and cursed. Simon Terri watched her, and thought of Leona getting Kentucky fried chicken as the sulphur swept across the houses along the shore and Bradley kept trying to stick his finger in her ear. The sulphur clung to the houses and people couldn't hang out their washing. If people lived on the southwest they couldn't hang out their clothing with a northeast wind and the other way around. In the centre of town there were great numbers of cars in the car-lots, and there was a smell of rubble and dust from the liquor store they were expanding, and the sound of jackhammers too. And Leona kept looking out the window and waiting for her mother to bring her fried chicken, bouncing up and down on the seat and kicking the back of the seat with her red sandals. But she only ate half a piece of chicken and Jeffrey kept trying to force coleslaw down her throat until she spilled her pop on her dress and started to cry and then Jeffrey said, "Geehovus, ya big baby."

And Lois said, "Shut yer goddamn mouths—jus give me goddamn time fer me and Papa ta eat our chicken—Papa you want some chicken?"

"No."

"Well there's plenty a chicken."

"No."

And as he sat there listening to them eat, with Lois turning around and spitting on a napkin wiping off Leona's dress saying, "My, my dear some day now ya'll be far prettier than yer mother," he thought of this. He thought of Daniel Ward—how they took Randolf Alewood hunting moose. They came up on a bull and the bull turned toward them. And as the cow started bawling—that tremendous eerie bawling—the bull strode toward them. Neither Ward nor Simon had guns. Alewood had a rifle and he turned and began running. But they went back to the camp that night and the next afternoon there was a calf, which the man shot. He put eight bullets into it. And with his hands covered with blood he began laughing—and as Daniel Ward began to cut the calf, with its snout that was ugly enough to be human, and flies in the dry air, he began to laugh too, and Alewood couldn't stay away from it and couldn't stop putting his hands in the calf's blood.

"See the shot I made—that first shot—"

"That was a good shot," Daniel Ward said. And Simon hated them both and turned away. And he couldn't stand the soft Micmac tones of Daniel Ward nor the shimmering happiness of Randolf Alewood, his pants were breached with clotted blood.

"That was a good shot." He'd hit the calf in the left hind leg with the first shot and belly-shot it three times—running right behind it screaming as the calf ran frantically along the streamway. The calf bled and there was blood in the turned weeds and puddles and blood in the calf's hoof-prints. And the man began telling Daniel Ward about the organs—pointing out the white intestinal tract and the liver and Ward, hunting moose since he was ten, kept saying, "Oh das it," and Simon thought, *The fucker wants a drink.*

And the calf, at the last, backed into a corner alder where two roads joined, turned to face her adversaries, made a threatening gesture with her head and went down and Alewood put four more shots into it.

And Alewood kept talking about why the calf bled so much—the reason for it the blood system and glands.

"Oh yes dere."

The fucker wants a drink.

Lois threw the hat and caught it on her head, and she yelled as the hat came down. The light in the doorway came on and the woman came out again. "Listen we didn't invite you here," the woman said. "We don't know you—and we don't have to have you yelling and screaming around here."

"Am I yelling and screaming?" Lois said, yelling.

"Please go away," the woman said.

"Don't screw around with me," Lois said screaming.

"Just please go home," the woman said. "You'll wake my children."

"Give the buggers my love," Lois said. But the woman slammed the door again. Lois tipped her hat back and shook her head. The cars started up, the people drove away, their lights falling on her and on the soil and on the black pavement. As the cars passed Lois ran out in front of them and made the gestures of a matador, and then bowed when the cars went around her. The snow was starting to come now.

"I've been at healthier wakes—" Lois shouted. "I've been at healthier wakes."

But they had left her. She watched the cars drive off and the lights in the house turn off. She shouted something loud and indistinct. Down across the tracks the cars drove. She shouted something again, the train signals began to clang. Then she put the broom between her legs and began hopping around and laughing. When she turned again Simon Terri was standing beside her.

She looked at him and stepped back and then her mouth twitched. She wore an old black dress of Merium's that she must have taken from the attic and she had buttoned it wrong and the arms puffed out on it. She'd put dabs of blue and red cosmetics on her face and had drawn a wart on her chin, with the word *wart* written under it—but Simon Terri could only guess what the word was.

"Hello girl," Simon Terri said. He smiled and his right hand fumbled.

"Papa," Lois said, "where are you—I didn't know they let you out of the hospital."

The night was cold now. This night had come down so that their voices and the clanging of the track signals were lost within it. He looked at his grand-daughter, as she held the broom with her witch hat pressed into the folds of her hair, and he looked about. A used package of cigarettes, its tinfoil gleaming in the puddles.

"I need a lift home," he said.

"Well when did they let you out—home?" she said.

"I need a lift home—I wanta lift home," he said.

She looked at him. "Oh," she said.

"Are you gonna give me a lift home?" he said.

"Oh," she said. "But don't you think you should be at the hospital?"

"No need."

"Papa."

"No need, no need," he said. He began walking.

"Where are you going?"

"Home."

"Well get in the car Papa."

"No need," he said walking away with his legs bowed outward.

"Get in the car Papa—please Papa."

A man came to the door and snapped on the light.

"Listen you silly bitch," he said. "I'll phone the police."

"You shut yer goddamn mouth and have some manners—I got my grandfather here," Lois screamed.

"You'll spend the night in jail, I'm tellin ya."

"I've got Papa here," Lois screamed. "I've got Papa here—you understand."

And Daniel Ward did all the work. In the camp it was Daniel who got the fire going and carried the water from the spring, and laid out the man's bed. And not only the man's bed, but Simon's also. And the night they got the calf Randolf Alewood kept drinking and talking. He looked at Daniel Ward and he kept explaining things to him—he kept talking of the Indian to Daniel Ward, and of all the trouble on the reserve and how he was sorry about it. He kept mentioning the incident where a woman left her baby in scalding water and he shook his head and kept reaching over and clutching Daniel's shoulder.

"Oh dere's some bastars there," Daniel kept saying.

"What do you think can be done about it?" Randolf said.

'Oh dere's some times dere I don' know," Daniel kept saying. And Randolf clutched his shoulder and looked at him. And Daniel did everything for the man—the man wanted his potato baked and how good a baked potato was with sour cream and fried bacon-fat and Daniel nodded. Randolf didn't happen to know or didn't keep it in his head that the Indian girl who'd dropped her baby into scalding water was Ward's cousin. And later Ward took off his clothes and lay in his underwear on the old mattress and there was a field-mouse running along the beams up and down the old pressboard walls. The fire cooled through the cracks in the stove and they could hear cinders cracking. Randolf snored in his sleep. There was the eerie bellowing of a cow moose in the cedar swamp and Simon Terri lay next to the stove with his hands behind his head. Far into the night he lay awake in the bed Daniel had prepared for him. There wasn't a sound from Daniel Ward but he knew Ward was awake also.

Daniel Ward's mouth curved down, yet the bottom lip was puffed and hard. His cheekbones made his face wide and his nose was blunted and his hair fell over the left side of his face and was shaved up the back of his head. He spoke little except when he was drinking, and he drank too much. When he drank he'd buy things for his children—miniature toys and cars and hockey-sticks, and he'd tape the hockey-sticks himself when he was drinking. And he'd bring these things home and give them to his children, who sat on the cot in the kitchen, and give them french fries and ketchup in a paper carton. Then he'd go into the yard and start to drink and then he'd ask Simon Terri for money for his children.

"Thin' of my little girl dere, she'd got nothin," and Simon would look at him. Simon would say: "Dan—I don't want to talk to you when you're drunk—come back in two or three days when yer sobered up and ask me the same thing agin."

"Remember when we saw the panther," Dan would say.

"Yes—I remember."

"No-one beleace we saw it."

"Well we saw it—we came up on it—we saw it, no matter."

"Ole Simon Terri—ole Simon Terri."

"Come back when yer sober."

"We see it by Cold Stream, remember?"

"Yes I remember."

"Remember Alewood, who shot the calf in the gut?"

"That's something I don't want to remember."

"Remember Alewood gut-shot the calf?" They brought the calf out and Daniel got very drunk in the night—the next night—and then Randolf said, "Indians can't handle liquor—it's in their blood—there's something in Indians' blood—I've heard stories about Indians strangling their own sisters—it's in their blood all right—they can't handle that at all—that calf went 400 pounds didn't it Simon?"

"Yes."

"You know it's the first time I've hunted moose—"

"I'm feelin just fine," Daniel said, walking back to the barn on Alewood's property where Simon, with a lantern strapped on each side of an improvised beam, in the pleasant smell of hay and straw, had broken the pelvis bone and was scraping the hide, with blood spots against his beard. "Mr. Alewood, you have a drink, Mr. Alewood and Simon, eh Simon?"

"When did you shoot your first moose Simon?" Randolf asked, poking his finger, nubbing it into the left hind wound and blinking because of the lanterns, while stripping away the hide showed the exposed perforation of shot, bluish, fleshlike in the subdued and yet somehow fierce carcass.

"Oh—while ago."

"Don' talk moose, talk women," Daniel said.,

"Well this is the first I've ever shot—I hope that picture turns out."

Daniel went back outside. The sky covered with stars and there was a smell of frost in the air, and it left a full scent in the hay and drowsy flies nubbed and squandered with white curved lines on the front of their heads, and Daniel sang outside. Randolf said, "God, you try to help them you know," and removed his finger and a film of blood from the left hind wound. The pelvis bone was stark and bloody under the lanterns and Alewood, his face resembling his grandfather's in all but the lips which gave him a sensual look, stood by the upside-down calf with its eyes indignant and its teeth biting its frozen tongue, "Like tonight I gave him a little more money than I gave you—I mean I know you won't mind."

"I don't mind."

And Daniel sang outside. Daniel sang. Then he came in again. Simon worked carefully. Daniel put his hand on Randolf's shoulder and smiled and nodded.

"I don' know sometimes dere about dose guys were sayin las night."

"Oh yes," Randolf said. Randolf went around to the other side of the carcass and helped Simon pull down the hide so there was an instant smell of rich and overpowering hung weight and Daniel weaved back and forth and smiled and nodded. Then Daniel went over to a stall and lifting the coarse rope from its bent spike entered the stall. You could hear him urinating and singing.

Randolf looked at Simon and smiled. His hands were again thick with blood, and Simon with deft silent movements scraped the hide away from the fat as Alewood pulled it down. When Daniel came back he saw Alewood struggling with the hide so he sat on his haunches and took it himself. But he was very drunk and fell down. He said, "In hot water—the little girl, but she diddin know dat woman—she sorry—she diddin know," and then he crawled into the corner and fell asleep.

"What's the date today?" Alewood said, as if he was angry.

"The 24th."

"Good," Alewood said, as if he was put out.

Daniel slept in the corner beyond the glare of the lanterns. Simon lit a cigarette as he worked. Alewood said, "May I have a cigarette?" And Simon rolled him one and wetted the paper himself with his tongue and Alewood put it quietly aside. And Simon felt guilty over this and worked more fiercely.

The moose with a full rack turned in the dusk and the wet yellow weeds and came toward him—the filter of the dusk like sad powder. They were at the upper end of Cold Stream. Alewood's sawmill was gone, though the store was still operating at the corner of two village streets, its greyish-white cement wall with the sign: ANYONE CAUGHT LURKING OR LOITERING HERE WILL BE PROSECUTED.

That was knowledge, as Simon Terri worked with the moose, as Simon Terri presently drove in the car with his grand-daughter. You could say nothing—you were always a little suspicious and in awe of people like that. The Americans in the evenings with their first feed of salmon, and he drinking bourbon from their leather-covered flasks with a delicacy that prevented him from touching the flask with his lips. The Alewoods and Bryans who owned camps and cottages that were more finished and had more amenities than Simon and Merium Terri's place ever had. The distinct impression you got when you walked into those camps, cottages? That this was not you nor ever could be. But what did all these lights and radios and telephones—and latterly televisions and swimming-pools in cottages and camps—mean when you walked into them? And Simon Terri stripped the moose naked, the shot-filled, somehow still-living flesh, and didn't understand this or anything else. And Randolf Alewood asked him to take his knife and dig a bullet from under the ribcage that was lodged in a clot of blood. Daniel struggled in his alcohol. And the next day Simon went to visit Daniel and Daniel lay on the kitchen cot and stared at the ceiling a long time. A long time.

And Randolf Alewood smiled that night. The fields were brown with frost. Lester Murphy came in and stood in the barn, in the smell of the hay, and Daniel Ward began to throw up his alcohol and Randolf Alewood said, "What time is it I wonder?" And Murphy and Terri helped Ward to his feet so he wouldn't rest in his spew out of the light of the smoking lanterns, the dazed bitten tongue of the calf moose.

"I get a little too much—Mr. Alewood—Mr. Alewood I get a little too much."

"What do you think of this moose?" Randolf said. He looked at Lester and held the nubbed bullet in his hand, the carcass stripped; the dislodged head lay in the straw-dirt.

Lester Murphy said, "Come on Dan, we'll go home now."

"Dat was a good shot dere Mr. Alewood—boy you miss something Lester—you didden see Mr. Alewood—"

Randolf kept flipping the bullet that falling in front of the lantern was like a cold burnt-out meteor in the light of the sun. The faces strangely excited and subdued and Daniel with the heavy motions of a drunkard kept rubbing vomit from his coat, and nodding his head as if he approved.

In the morning he would lie on the kitchen cot and stare at the blank kitchen ceiling a long time. Simon would go to him, Simon would say, "How are you?"

Daniel would look at him and look away.

"Firs time."

"First time what."

Daniel would speak.

"Don't speak Micmac."

Daniel would say nothing.

"He's a good man Mr. Alewood—he give me plenty of money—" Daniel stared at the ceiling with hardened vomit on his chin.

"Do you want me to scrounge you a drink?" Simon said.

"Wouldn't be too bad," Daniel said. "Very good idea."

Simon stood.

"You tink the calf was spring calf," Daniel said.

"Oh yes," Simon said.

The car drove on; the passenger train snaked its way past the creamery where an odd tree stood bleached and barkless; a hanging tree they said, because a youngster had hanged himself there a decade ago, his glasses broken, his hands tied behind his back—so he must have had some help in the matter Old Simon thought. The tree's warped branches catching the cold snowfall now. The old man felt the metal plug of distracting pain. Rance.

Old Simon stared at the hospital tag around his wrist and his mouth chewed unconsciously. So Lester Murphy now, he'd heard, was helping to bring in a family of refugees. Boat-people. And they were to live in the village and become attached to jobs and homes and ties there. People with swollen bodies lay in various corners of the earth—so Anne Murray told him on television, people with their skins wracked with sores, or hungry—and he'd seen on television Begin and Sadat too, and the Palestinians—and children with flies crawling over their body, as he'd seen them crawl over Daniel Ward's children in Daniel Ward's house—and Daniel Ward's and Burton Crow's children had various itches and couldn't sleep, and everyone fought over jam and things.

He stared at the hospital tag with its ink markings. They would pass now, houses and barns, and the brown crooked trees would rise up.

"I know where you should be—Papa, Papa, I know where you should be—you should be back in the hospital, where you should be," Lois said.

The old man didn't bother to answer any more. A group of children raced across the road in front of them. The old man stared out the window as the youngest one fell and Lois screamed and slammed on the brakes. She rolled the window down, as the youngster scrambled to his feet and took off in the direction of two small shanties. Across the dirt ditch other children waited for him, where they had piled and hidden tires to burn tomorrow evening.

"You damn little Jeesers," Lois yelled. "Who in hell do you think you are anyways?" Her voice was shaking, her hands clutched the fur-covered steering wheel. Another car swerved past them. The youngsters picked up rocks from the ditch. The rocks whirled through the air, the dark. "Who in hell you think you are, hitting my car with rocks," Lois yelled. And squealing the tires in both first and second, old Simon's head trembling and jerking back and forth, they went down into a narrow gully, over a bridge crossing a furious black stream, half-covered by ash-coloured alders.

"Member that man fed Packet all the chocolate-coated Exlax?" he said.

"I was too young ta member that," Lois said. "Mummy was sure mad."

"Member that man?" he said again. A great long car with tail-fins came off a sideroad and roared off in front of them.

"Goddamn it," Lois said.

"Burton Crow choked himself to death on a chicken bone—I tried ta help him out—chicken bone, can you imagine?"

"Papa, you start talking about these old guys I don't know nothin in the world about—"

He didn't answer.

"But go ahead Papa—talk if you want to."

He didn't answer.

"Oh me and my big mouth, Papa—I don't care if ya talk—if ya wanta talk."

"That Nobel Simms is a nice youngster—he wanted to marry you," Old Simon chuckled. She didn't answer.

"When you were at the convent there—after yer mum left he useta go out ta town ta see ya—and then come back and meet me and talk about ya," he chuckled.

She didn't answer.

"Why didn'tcha ever have a shine on him—?" he asked and then he said, "There Lois."

"Because I ain't marrying a barber—I'm not marrying a barber in a barbershop."

"Oh well."

"I'm not marrying a old barber in a barbershop, Papa."

"No—I s'pose not," the old fellow said. "I s'pose not."

The car drove on with its scent of imitation pine. The radio blared, and the lights shone along the road—with the houses right and left, as if the houses themselves were transient. The whining of the jacked-up rear end and the radio. The old man sat. Not bothering to say anything any more. (The smell of blow-flies and blood as Randolf Alewood, blood-covered, stood facing the windfalls, and the leaves in a patch of woods that now was gorged and pitted.

Lois did not look at him. She had followed him along while he walked, his old legs bowed out. She had said, "Papa Papa." "No need, leave me alone—no need," he had said. Over the clanging, the switch-yard, the smell of tar and the dresses of Hallowe'en-suited people, the man yelling he'd call the police. And then he'd jumped into the car quickly and had said nothing. So now he was going home.)

The Indians drove around in cars now much like Lois' boyfriend, and they went to the Real Thing disco. They went to the disco—and though they were allowed to take salmon for themselves, they had the river that ran along the five-mile stretch of reserve houses, where Indian children played and skipped rope next to the white, bare Catholic church, well fenced-off. Then they'd take the fish to the cottagers. The cottagers, the Bryans and others, and they'd try to sell them. The cottagers were always at the Indians to get them a fish—or a poacher like Little Simon. Sometimes the Indians would get too many and throw the salmon in the dump —along with worn-out tricycles and battered toys and rotted tires, in the stench of dump-smoke and the flapping of decomposing cloth, garments the wind blew into the trees like old potato sacks. And the dead salmon lay there covered with flies, their globular eyes half disengaged from the head, their scales translucent in the sun. The Indians would say, "No money no more, pertty bad." Their chests would heave stubbornly when the cottagers called out to them. "$3 a pound now—tink of my family, we got nutting."

They passed now, he and Lois, houses that had corridors and hallways and light fixtures and loved-ones' pictures, with cars and mopeds and motorcycles covered in tarps, and skidoos in the outer barn—with the sons/daughters of those houses riding around in the cars and racing around on the motorcycles, the younger ones putting about on the mopeds, and the whole family roaring over the desolate tracks of snow in the forest into the deer yards in the grey evenings on skidoos, the old trails shocked with treads and the sterile smell of metal—and the laughter as the stars winked out in the half-dead sky, back to those houses where the earned money was accounted for and spent and the children sat five to a couch and watched programs from southside on TV, in the long splintering cold nights, and the atmosphere of aerosol as their pictures sat on the unused bookshelf with an unused Bible and a copy of Jacqueline Susann, and the noiseless second-hand of the clock on the kitchen wall with the children watching.

And the freezers full of contraband moose and deer—the moose having been snared—a snare being a barrel, a drum, buried on a moose trail, the tin cut into pie-shaped wedges, and the moose running, his right or left fore-hoof sinking into the barrel through the cut pie-shaped wedges so there is no way it can get free, dying of loss of blood and shock, after maybe a two- or three-day struggle—struggling, struggling and grunting in rage and complete bafflement—and the men coming onto the moose and disembowelling it and hacking the hind quarters and slicing the pelvic bone, and the profitless guts of the disembowelled creature filling the quiet light under the snow-covered spruces, the frozen rock where Hudson Kopochus lay with a bear on his journey to kill a man in 1825, and the children catching the bus for school the next day, the dark-faced displaced French, the stubborn self-destructive Irish, the celtic blood on one of the most violent rivers in the country, "Fuck ya, fuck ya," for "I love you, I love you" or "Help me, help me," the passionless day in the schools where nothing was said or learned, the poor teachers with baseball caps on their heads, their university rings polished on their fingers, looking at the fifteen- and sixteen-year-old girls, and the docile never-be-taught Indians, some pregnant, sitting at the back with their heads on the desks, some knife-scarred along their bellies in the rites of drunken manhood, as day by day the afternoon winter months played on resolute, determined—like the lanterns in the camps he remembered of 50 years ago, the electric lights beaming out over the grey ice, the purple ridges, this roadway, as if not giving up one ounce of human commitment—commitment for what is the question, commitment for what—and Begin and Sadat came over on the radio in the houses, in the imitation pine scent of the cars, with frozen cinder-packed snow at the back of their wheels, and Levesque says something and says something else and Trudeau says something too and the Premier goes to a meeting and sits with the mill manager from away (wherever that might be in Simon's mind, wherever they managed to make people like that) who says the company needs more money—this province, the north of this province having to bring people in to set up businesses and having to pay them to make them stay, until the trees are gone, thousands of acres downed and nothing planted and the men working in the same part of the mill for ten years, driving the same type of tractor over the frozen roads with their faces freezing and transmission oil over their strong hands, the pulse-beat in them beating out over the fields and wires and ridges and swirling gusts of wind, looking around in absolute bafflement and going home to their wives and sitting on the edge of their beds in the half-lit room, and the wives who've done the accounts and taken care of the house, the money, the input/output of all the families' lives listening as their husbands talk, and then saying, "You're drinking too much."

And the mill with its pipes and jarring smoke, with the washed-down liquor flushed into the river and the boilers washed out with sulphuric acid and washed into the river—and those same children, the displaced French, the wild angry Irish and Scotch swimming in the provincial park not a mile away from the mill and coming out in the twilight as the salmon struggled on upstream into the vast network, little boys and girls sitting on the porch steps. "We aren't going there anymore—"

"The river hurt Debby, she got a burn—"

"We aren't going there anymore, eh Debby?"

"Show where you got the burn Debby—"

"She got the burn on her bum—"

"I did not—"

"You did so, you got the burn on your bum—"

"I did not—you got a burn too—"

"My burn's a lot bigger than yers is anyways."

"It is not—it is not—I got a burn just as big as yous."

"I'll give you a quarter to see yer burn."

"You don't have a quarter—"

"A nickel's got a beaver and a quarter's got a moose—and I got a moose, so there—and you show me yer burn and I give ya a moose—so there."

"She got her burn on her bum—and if she takes down her pants I'm tellin Mum so there."

"Chicken—"

"I'm not as much chicken as you—so there."

"I seen lots a girls' bums before—doncha think I haven't" in the heat with the new houses going up, new foundations on the shale and trailers with their tin roofs gleaming and the dusty tea-sized marijuana plants under the sun at the edge of the field, and Little Simon picking hallucinogenic mushrooms in the heat—through the summer onward into fall, into winter, into spring again, where in March the dogs, following a massive bitch along the deer-yards running down doe, and at Easter, Indian, French and English walking the roadway to church.

They passed those houses, an old man bundled in his woods' jacket and his boots, with his legs bowed out, and his grand-daughter dressed in his wife's ancient dress with a witch hat on the top of her head and her long fingernails painted purple. And what was it?

Through the sons of this century and another. From Alewood's Indian wife Emma Jane Ward, to Alewood's son Daniel lying in his vomit while Alewood's grandson Randolf nubbed a bullet in his bloodied fingers.

"I suppose ya wanta know why I was in town tonight Papa?"

"No no—"

"I mean I was gonna put Momma's dress back after—"

"Oh yes yes—that's all right, no need no need—"

"I mean Harry's comin home next month and we're pretty set—I don't wantcha ta think—"

"No no—no need, no need girl."

"I mean I just don't want ya to have a bad opinion of me Papa?"

"What—"

"I jus don't wantcha ta have a bad opinion of me—"

"Of course not."

"I couldn't stand it if you went around having bad opinions of me Papa—"

"Of course not—of course not—no need, don't talk no need—Don't get upset, no need."

He didn't look at her. He stared out the window. There was the smell of her perfume and the smell of pine, there was a Virgin Mary on the dashboard in gold and blue and the steadily decreasing lights of the houses.

And down through, past that, onto the second war—with Georgie and men from the towns and villages and outlying areas—Indian and French and Irish and Welsh who called themselves Canadians—in a country that didn't even know about them joining the North Shore Regiment—pulp-cutters and fishermen and businessmen and professionals and shopkeepers, and pampered boys and middle-aged men, leaning on their dufflebags in the dirt where the picture was taken, joining other boys and men, and chaplains and medics from farther north, and swinging onto the train from the wooden platform in a way only rookies do and smiling through the windows, with stark Canadian uniforms in the summer dust—going over, from Lester Murphy who became a captain to Georgie who was a private to the seventeen-year-old boys who carried equipment onto the beaches in June 1944—until you saw pictures of them taken, with sharpened eyes and hardened faces, in some northern European village on a dirt roadway beside their buddies—a picture of them in Holland on the steps of what might have been a court-house or town hall—and as always in those pictures the face a little too stubborn, remote.

And then George when he came back—through the dead heat of the fifties with Georgie and his wife Elizabeth Ripley Terri and their children, Packet, Lois, Little Simon.

And George with schemes and ideas for building up some sort of dynasty, coming home excited about each new way to earn it—to set himself up as he said. From selling watches, fan-belts and tackle to bringing in pinball machines with Ceril Brown—the first venture Ceril Brown ever had, the (at that time) twenty-year-old Ceril Brown, who it was rumoured could win up to $200 in one night playing poker against young men with fiercely sad/happy faces, the games being played in the shed of his parents—Loel and Mina Brown. And the boys sat in the shed as the snow came out of the sky. And George older than Ceril Brown by fifteen years setting up the poker table and standing by the shed door, the shed with furniture and broken vases and rotted mats and lamps from the nineteen-thirties—the dead smell of it. The boys with broad chests and opened shirts to the cold and drooping solid shoulders coming in and sitting in the shed, with their imitation talk and clothes, losing their quarters and dollars to Ceril Brown and feeling not only happy but obliged to do so—because of the absolute smartness, the cunning of Ceril Brown they felt intimidated if they happened to win. Add to that the fact that it was Ceril Brown who managed to get them Canadian rye whisky and Scotch and bootleg it to them with George talking about pinball machines, and pool-halls and saying, "Come back 'gain now boys"—as if he himself had prearranged everything. In this part of the province in the fifties where there was still not even a tavern to go to—where boys drank behind barns and sheds on lobster boats or in the back of cars and drove back and forth past the regional high school watching the girls walk home. The taverns being closed from the summer of 1917 until the summer of 1963—that presbyterian madness of the law—out of the fifties with children staring from metal cribs into the long dark empty corridors with the sparse winter light coming through the grey venetian blinds—in a house that had not only no drink but not a book either, with vases and imitation fruit on the dusted furniture and the smell of linoleum along the hallway and the sad cardboard light-shades in the living-rooms which no-one entered until the priest/minister was invited for Sunday dinner and the children were dressed and washed and the table arranged and religion and town-council affairs discussed and parish duties discussed and business/banking and local charities discussed. Until the one thought in a child's mind was how fortunate you were to live here in a nice community without drink or books either, except the encyclopedia—until out of that, out of it all it would take an imbecile or a lunatic not to become a drunk before he was twenty. A thousand such hallways and rooms and lampshades on one of the most violent rivers in the country.

This that and the next thing Georgie came home with. They brought their pinball machines in and set them up in a barn—Ceril and he—until the dampness affected them, so they removed them to a drier building near Alewood's general store—and it was there the RCMP caught them —or not them really but George, for Ceril Brown, who wasn't there at the time, said it wasn't his place and he didn't know what was going on— that liquor was being sold and that men were gambling against the house on pinball machines. And George said, "I'm no goddamn squealer," and George said, "We learned how not ta squeal in the army—"

And George with new schemes and new ideas after he'd paid a $250 fine—with as much laughter over it as possible, and a big drunk in which he beat up Daniel Ward's son Kenneth, and then Kenneth and the Ginnish man came at him with a butcher knife on a dark street.

Simon spat. George and Ceril Brown with schemes on how to create their dynasty, playing music for a dance and advertising on the sly about beer (all those dreary colourless little rooms with the chairs stacked in the corner where George and Ceril planned out strategy—strategies for such a vast array of projects—all now seeming quaint and lost and frittered away) and sadly enough Georgie buying coats and hats and shoes wholesale, "getting into the market," as he called it, and trying to sell them—so that cheap pointed leather shoes filled one closet of his house, and flawed coats with the seams breaking filled a box; and the house, unfinished, with the plenum smell of the furnace, looked empty and desolate unless there were fifteen hats lying around. While across the river Lester Murphy had already built his warehouse. "Well anyway—imagine being ashamed of your own son," George said. "I'm glad Elizabeth and I aren't like that— if we never have money—if we never have money—of course Donnie's stupid—my God he's stupid—stupid as hell all round—but still though ya pretty well have to admit to him—even if he didn't admit to the Irish one he knocked up—pretty sickly business weren't it? I 'member one time when we tried to get Donnie to eat his own shit—or it might have been dog-shit—don't remember—perhaps it was dog-shit, boys Lester was mad over that—I remember we got Donnie to carry all that lumber when they were building the new part onto the house, and we got him to carry about a million square feet a lumber about a mile, and hide it on his old man. Lester roarin and screamin that someone stole his lumber—*that's* how stupid Donnie is—"

"He was always after me calling me Mummy," Elizabeth Ripley Terri said. "Can you imagine—he wanted to kiss me—can you imagine!"

"Some stupid," George said. "Got any more a them green beans Momma?"

"I was frightened of him really and truly—he tried to grab onto me and kiss me—slobbering on me, calling me Mummy," Elizabeth Ripley Terri said. "And I have my doubts about Lester also—grave doubts."

"Some bad," George said looking at the bacon and pondering which pieces to take. "A few years ago now—oh about twenty years ago—they woulda gelded a boy like that—"

"Georgie—" Merium said.

"Truth's the truth Momma—"

"Georgie!"

"It's true Merium—I know we don't want to think of those things—but it's true," Elizabeth said.

"I mean I just don't want to think of things like that," Elizabeth said.

Until George, with a loan from Old Simon, finally set up the *Hamburger Palace* in 1954, a stand halfway between Lester Murphy's span and the bridge. There Georgie and Elizabeth sold hamburgers and fish and chips, hot dogs and pop—the overripe smell of food along the roadway—a little clapboard stand with Georgie's Hamburger Palace in red block letters, which became known as Georgie's Place or the Palace—and there they eked out a living—with Packet and Lois and Little Simon the baby being fed pop and fries, with Elizabeth working from eight in the evening until two in the morning—and George, as proprietor, tried to make the right decisions and talked about a restaurant and how they might be able to swing a restaurant—with Elizabeth working and holding the money and taking care of the children. And the children sat outside on the steps or played in the gravel until all hours—Lois in Packet's T-shirt, Packet in a pair of grey shorts without a top, and Little Simon in a cloth diaper that both Packet and Lois filled with gravel more nights than enough. And the smell of food rose out over the ditches and over the wildflowers and onto the road, mingling with the smell of gas, and the empty barns and buildings with their dark virginal quality, and the

houses with their lights on for the evening. And under her greased apron Elizabeth Ripley Terri held her full body firmly, and leaned against the counter to talk to the teenagers, while Packet sat on his haunches and made carry-out trays, and the smell from the steamed buns and the hot dogs and the mustard, and coffee dripped into the coffee-pot. The mines opened again for iron ore and men came from the southwest and down-river to stay at the mining camps, and the overflow went into the apartments Lester Murphy built—and those men, bachelors or young married men, walked in the evening along the roadway and went over to Georgie's Hamburger Palace. Elizabeth Ripley Terri leaned over the counter. She laughed with them as they leaned forward and whispered to her, and made jokes about the hot dogs, and the size of the wieners—as Packet looked on from pouring mustard or ketchup into their containers. He looked at them. Elizabeth Ripley Terri was pulled this way and that by the men, and it was all in fun—she laughed and leaned against one's shoulder and laughed.

"Yes and what's the size of your wiener," she'd say, and laugh and lean against a man. And then the men would go in through the screen door and coax her out into the parking-lot and she'd laugh with them against the warm building or in the farther shadows where the trees played in the night. His mother would laugh and the men would laugh—and then there'd be no laugh for a while—in the husk of breath from the lilacs and the wooded ground. Lois, in a T-shirt with her legs uncovered, saying, "What's wong Packet, what's wong?"

And Packet would listen. Then his mother would laugh again for it was all a joke. His hands would be shaking against the carton. She'd come back and press her apron down, and smile at him and pour a coffee. And Little Simon would fall asleep on Packet's knee in the late hours, and Elizabeth smoking cigarettes in the darkness, the now-deserted parking-lot—

"Yer sorta religious or what Simon?" Rance said.

"Oh boy—I don't think so—very much."

"Well I jus thought all the stories ya told me—about the bears, and running the river—always ended up with 'God bless,' " Rance smiled and looked about.

Simon chuckled.

"I don' know sometimes. Once I bopped a man right over the head for no reason—no-one knows why—I don't know why—but there it is—that's what I'm like."

"Well I'm not going to bother you about it," Rance said. "Anyway if you knew what I knew about Saint John and things—I mean she's different today—in this day and age ya haveta watch yerself—I never in my life met a meaner son of a whore then Sludge—and I was just thinkin, if you were religious, I mean upriver religious, like the pennycostals up that way—thick as flies up there, I was just thinking, maybe ya didn't know about—well, what I know about—" he paused. "About *it*."

Simon said nothing.

"Some different today," Rance said.

Then Rance had a dream that night, about being lost, alive, in his own coffin as men with masks over their faces and rubber gloves on their hands, calmly in and out of the shadows of the white clinical room began to drain blood from his body. The dream went on, and Simon rang the buzzer—Rance whimpered, his pale face and his eyelids fluttering—lost.

For the first time, as the car moved on, Old Simon felt that he was blind; felt that he could no longer see as much as the headlights of passing cars, only hearing the pale wind now and then, the echoing, cajoling vortex. He would try not to think any more about Rance; some disastrous baby boom come to manliness in main offices of Avco Finance, come to adulthood in the back of vans coloured and painted primeval, the thick bloodrose carpet, the antiquated adolescent noise. He had smelled Rance's lukewarm blood and had seen in his face, and features, in his deep-set eyes, the look of a child—magnificent, sold for trinkets, commercials on defecation or the lack of it. (The American man feeding Packet the chocolate-covered Exlax? Ha ha—what ha).

He'd seen Denby Ripley too long, driving home in his Buick perhaps —as if he'd strived for and finally attained what it was that he had wanted. Or in the evening in front of the drugstore, the cardboard Santa Claus toppled by a snow-plough, as Kevin Dulse and his wife hurried away, Denby to stop Clarence Simms on the street and to have the bad taste to ask him, "How was your Christmas—I've spent mine well." Clarence who spent his Christmas—as he'd spent them previously. This Denby Ripley coming from his job as manager of Avco Finance, wearing the white winter jacket that looked like a space-suit with various air pockets, in the cold air the smell of Brut—Denby who had the good fortune to realize that life held more than drinking with Little Simon, held more than chasing young girls—children who might or mightn't have children of their own—girls who were known by name and circumstance in this small town/village, ridiculed and gossiped about not only by the young wives in prefab houses who somehow knew everything but by the very boys who'd made them pregnant in the back seats of cars that smelled of high-school jocularity—Denby realizing at age eighteen that there was more to life than all that Packet, Lois or Little Simon could offer, matriculated and trained, now an officer amongst those groups of officers (wearing the same three-piece world-acknowledged business suit as they) who dealt solely in possessions. And stopping Clarence on the street that evening (so many evenings), Clarence coming from somewhere—all faces anon, all glasses tipped back and emptied—where he'd sat in a bar drinking with town youngsters, wearing, even in January, their cut-off denim motorcycle colours, the white twilight fading into the spotted beerglasses, the tables cluttered with cooled tobacco ashes, on the seat beside him the album *Dead Babies,* as one youngster perpetually snickers. Means: Clarence then might have believed he was in the best place possible, as he kept patting a fellow on the back saying—

"Oh oh ho—I know your father—ask your father if he knows Clarence Simms—I cut his hair—"

Or they buy him beer then, and he laughs, turns about and nods at someone he knows, frowns quickly and then shakes his head. And stopping Clarence in the street that evening, staring at the cracked coldsore on his lip and having the bad timing to ask, "How was your Christmas."

We might as well set down the table. For Rhonda, the Colonel's granddaughter, who worked in the store owned and operated by Ceril Brown, who wore those brown sexless $60 Wallabies—at all hours of the night she worked there now, as Ceril talked to her over the counter-top—and she to be whisked onward to somewhere in Quebec to some room where the illegal abortion will be performed—that personal and private decision of a woman, the sad warm privacy of bodies:

"Now you might feel some discomfort," Ceril said, like all men who feel rejuvenated in middle age taking on the expressions and mannerisms, donning the clothes and hats of some socially conscious idiot. "Now you might feel some discomfort—"

One must not overlook the possibility that new freedoms are attained. And this D&C process, whether curetage or suction was performed—that is, whether the foetus was scraped or sucked away—or whether a salt solution was introduced into the amniotic sac—

And Rhonda, wearing for her trip the knee-length Arctic fox fur that had been bought for her—the diamond heart for her left breast, the ruby knee-length dress with the superficial slits—"Now you might feel some discomfort."

George to put down the book, *Torso,* under its plastic wrapping—

Clarence, who would introduce Villon to Packet and who would try to direct at the regional high school one other play besides *Riders to the Sea* —yes, the smell of Dustbane over the Legion steps when he fell and hit his head, the white nightmarish January afternoon—so many afternoons. How in God's name can you blame Lester for not wanting him around any longer, because even before a man begins to piss and shit himself he has the walk and smell—until Clarence found himself in the unenviable position of playing tiresome fool to a man who was supposed to be his partner, so that he must finally, to save some sort of pride, take a barbering course in one of those schools in the south of the province, and live in some sort of scorn not only of riches, but in the end, of cleanliness and order. Who would at times be seen fixing Lester Murphy's storm windows, sprinkler, or porch door for $10, while Liberal colleagues from the capital sat in the living-room—"Atlantic Salmon Centre of the World."

A hedge rose up in Simon's eyes; had he been asleep? The snow scowled now. Lois was still sitting beside him. They were going home. The car turned, the hedge was gone and a mailbox on a slanted log passed them and suddenly he saw various rock heaps in the middle of the river and there was a plane droning above them; the river was uniformly silent, lights from various street poles winked out upon it. In the morning at the hospital various small silvery pipes several feet from the base of the brick stack gave a steady stream of cold white smoke. And in the old folks' home he'd been interviewed by the local paper. They called it a human-interest story and the woman who interviewed him said, "Yes— I understand—I understand." Then the Colonel didn't talk to him for three days, nor play checkers either. Saying to Mrs. Sampson: "I've been in two world wars—second war I was an advisor to a whole regiment, had to decide on logistics with other commanders—one thing. I never wanted to be interviewed. Oh they wanted me to be interviewed. But why be interviewed? You do what you do, you don't have to be interviewed about it. So when they asked me to be interviewed—well I laughed it off, laughed it off."

Simon never got to see the paper he was interviewed in.

"I was a teamster when I was seventeen," Simon had said.

"Oh yes—" the woman had said.

"Ya see there ma'm—horses was always quite friendly with me," and he'd chuckled and choked, his face turned red, the Colonel shook his head.

"But I'd some bad times with horses—one got drownded on me, froze my fingers awful bad one time. Ma'm, Father Murtree, he bathed me hands and saved them, ma'm." The woman smiled.

"I'm not ma'm," she said.

"Oh no no no," Simon had said.

"*Ms*," the woman said. She stared at him.

"Yes Miss," Simon said, smiling—wishing he'd put in his teeth, staring at the woman's thin legs with the little veins near the ankles. "Wanta cup a tea?"

"An then I walked—I walked an I walked, ya know—and got the men goin, and checked the jams, and sorted lumber in the booms fer Alewoods—on the trucks, and scaled too—" He stopped speaking, looked at the floor at the pinches of dust—and at his black-and-white ankle-high sneakers with great big bows that Lois had bought for him.

He jerked forward in the car seat, the unplugged nerve in his spine, and grabbed the handstrap unwillingly.

"How's Clarence Simms?" he said.

Lois, trying to light a cigarette without taking her eyes from the potholes in the road, swerving to one side of the centre line and the other, said, "He's drunk—when he gets drunk now, he buys about seven pints of whisky, hides them all over the house—he won't eat, so he's been away for malnutrition in Moncton—but he's home again, and I think he's drunk again—cause it's Nobel now that's cutting hair—I took Bradley in—"

Simon said nothing.

"And that's just what I mean about those Simms—why did Clarence ever give up such a job with Lester Murphy anyway? What's the ins of that Papa?"

"Oh nothing—nothing. They didn't get 'long—"

"Is that all? People say Lester didn't want him around the house."

"Nothin is all, nothing is all."

"Now I'm not tryin ta upset ya Papa—goddamn it—I'm not trying to upset you—he'd such a job is all, a beautiful job—gorgeous job—but I'm not going to upset ya. Then he quits—and goes to the barbershop. What's the ins of that Papa? As if I'd try to upset ya."

In the hospital he lay in bed, and at first they'd put a furry boot on his right foot to keep his heel up. But the doctor said he didn't need it. Of course the nurses, not the doctor took care of him, enticed him to eat—listened to him—called him *dear*. And when he had a fever he talked to people both living and dead, and once in the middle of the night someone was sitting on the edge of the bed talking to him. And perhaps it was Merlin Terri telling him about Tom Proud—about how Emma Jane Ward teased him; how he'd come around the house and Hitchman would chase him away, and then when Hitchman went to town Tom Proud would come back. How Emma Jane ordered him out of the house for using the indoor toilet: "Ha ha ha Tom—la la la—you think you can use it Tom—you can't use it, go outside Tom—la la la."

How the men laughed at that! And Emma Jane Ward shook her head as if she was fed up with people using her indoor toilet. How she sat on the buckboard or carriage with golden-coloured spokes with Hitchman, their backs both straight, the chests stuck out. How Tom Proud would run behind the waggon, wearing the lace tie, the pants Emma Jane had stolen for him. Running behind the waggon after them.

"He don't look much Proud to me, girl," Alewood said. Or: "What does he want?"

"Money, Hishman—he wants $3."

"Money is it—tell him the only way he'll ever get money is if he prays for it, girl—eh?"

And in his fever perhaps he saw Tom Proud running—behind the waggon, falling down, and the men standing there laughing. With Emma Jane Ward, her back straight, her chest out (already going fat on childbirth and chocolates and probably not discriminating between one and the other) with the corners of her mouth curled.

"I am not a squaw—I am an Indian woman."

"Yes."

"Pretty—in Micmac—is that how you say pretty?"

"I am not a squaw, I am a Indian woman."

"Yes."

Tom Proud going up to the house after Alewood left, his lace tie, his white shirt and pants she'd stolen for him torn at the buttocks. He trembled there, and knocked on the door.

"Get out of here Tom," Emma saying.

"Listen to her Thomas—get out, get out," the men saying. "Listen to Mrs. Alewood—eh Emma?"

"Yes," Emma saying. "Listen to me—listen to Mrs. Alewood—listen to me."

"Listen to Mrs. Alewood—eh Emma?" the men saying.

Tom stared at them, his hands trembling, his eyes puffed like a boxer's mouse at 22 years of age. Emma Jane's breasts heaving, her face corrupted with imported cosmetics in the drivelling sunlight.

"I am not a squaw, I am a Indian woman."

"Ha ha ha Tom—la la la—Hishman—Mr. Hishman will hit you 'gain Tom—like las time—you run from Mr. Hishman Tom—I see you

—run run run—ho ho ho."

"You want to use the toilet Tom?" Emma saying. Thomas looking
with fevered eyes at them, his lace bow-tie.

"If you want to use the toilet Tom—you pray—pray to me Tom. Pray
to me."

Tom staring at them terrified. The men laughing.

"Pray to me Tom—and then you can do it—you can use it—pray to
me." Then Tom laughing, his eyes closed. "Pray to me Tom—on your
knees—and then you can use it—pray Tom, dats it—pray to me."

But it was his fever and the nurses (for it is always the nurses and never
the doctor) had him on antibiotics. The serum seeped into his blood.
Begin and Sadat sat on the edge of his bed, arguing over who owned the
span. And Anne Murray kept wagging her finger at him, telling him of
the bodies overseas.

The car now, with Lois in it. She was sitting there, her back hunched
forward a little. Yes. The plane that had droned by was now fading.
There was a cement plant to their right with thousands of cement blocks
piled row upon cold row—under one cold naked light, and the building
stood up corpulent and dirty. He wondered if Lois—if she had married
Nobel Simms and had become a nurse, and had worked at the hospital,
had gone to university, as Sandra Simms and others of her friends had
managed to do. Could there then, could there perhaps then not be the
lame cowardice of discothèques and drink? Her mature nipples under her
blue blouse buttoned up, the day she played cribbage. No, they sent her
to the convent after her mother left—where she bought and sneaked into
the convent *True Romances*, where she finally tore a cross from a nun's
bib and was expelled.

His head trembled. He was cold suddenly.

"Ya know—I liked Rocket Richard," he said.

"What's that Papa?"

Funky town
Take me down
To Funky town

came on the radio.

"Rocket Richard—liked him—the whole Forum got in a rebellion
over him—"

"Oh the hockey player—"

Lois smiled.

122

He cleared his throat, and pressed his thumbs down on his knees.

"Packet, Little Simon and their friends useta have some awful great tussles over hockey—"

"A lot of bloody noses and broken teeth over it—at one time."

For some reason they both laughed.

He'd seen them too, the youngsters who hung about the old folks' home and bothered the seniors when they went for walks. Ah, they had nothing—not as much as the price of a Friday-night movie in their pockets. Their clothes were thin, soiled—and would be all winter. Their eyes were cowardly, cunning and dangerous. He'd known men who would beat men senseless for no reason—and women with narrow souls who would laugh and ridicule the beaten men. These youngsters were no different. Their women would be no different.

Susie Masey came to mind just as suddenly. And he was about to ask Lois if she'd heard of her lately, but somehow she prevented him—Susie's mother would walk a carriage to Ceril Brown's junkyard and bottle-exchange. The carriage filled with bottles, covered with a blanket. There she would take her bottles. There Ceril Brown would sell her a few quarts of beer for the price of the bottles and she would return home to Lazarus Masey. Inevitably there'd be a great deal of talk about the smell of her—and what it was like to. Susie had her first period in class, had no idea of what was happening to her. Then the teacher would never leave her alone, telling her in front of everyone to get to the washroom—talk about water being free. The teacher kept saying, "You should get married—what are you doing here?—you should be married." Susie was married when she was fifteen.

"She's in the hands of social services now," her teacher sighed. "God helps the social services—"

(Lois had also a tattoo of a tiny rose on her left breast. In the summer wearing a bikini with the straps down, sunning herself, this tiny rose signified something pure and life-giving about her, exuded from her a quality of love, though she said she'd gotten the rose tattoo on a $20 bet with a man, she said, who couldn't hold his own piss.

"I suppose not," Old Simon said.

"What's that Papa?"

Men who would beat men senseless? "Yes dear," the nurses would say. "You try to get some sleep now, Mr. Terri, there there."

"There there and over there and there," Rance would say, rolling his eyes and sucking his teeth.

He pressed his huge thumbs against his knees and felt the top of his bones, the movement of his joints when he moved his legs outward. The Virgin Mary glowed from her metal pedestal on the fox-fur dash.

Lazarus Masey was the boy Havlot went out after that night at the dance. The Indian girl with him clutching the back of his coat looked about for someone to protect them.

"I have to stop for gas Papa," Lois said.

The urgency of the power-lines, as if they were crosses of missionaries, thrusting above the trees, right through the swampy area and the snow already melting on the poles they graced, and the small lights above the gas-tank in Calvin Simms' Irving station, with two junked cars near the white-washed cement siding, just beyond the men's washroom with the broken door—Old Simon lifted his head. So Lois and he had not been speaking for some time now. It was better. Nor did he forget that at this garage they once had a monkey chained by the leg near the men's wash-room—and it roamed about its wire cage. Then when Oliver Brown tried to feed it by hand and had his thumb cut for five stitches they destroyed the animal. It was a wild thing, and used to rattle its chain against its dish for food. Another plane, by the sound a Voodoo, screamed above them. And then another. Where they would travel across the sky to the coast of Newfoundland and there fly on either side of Russian cargo planes bound for Cuba. The Russians would wave to them.

In the service-station the van was stopped—the one he'd seen at the court-house corner. A girl got out laughing and a boy roared at her. Everyone seemed to be drinking in that van. "Just hang onto yer pecker," the girl answered the boy. "I'm comin back." "I'm hangin onto it," the boy said. "Don't worry—"

Then there was some confusion. The girl started running and someone screamed. The side door opened and the boy sitting on the carpeted floor with his boots jutting outside began to get out. He was holding onto some-thing; there was laughter, and someone screamed again. The boy came out of the van. He held in his hands—so that its body and especially its head looked petrified—a four-foot-long snake. Only when the boy turned quickly, pretending he was going to throw the thing, did its body coil about the boy's arm and its head move slightly. Everyone was laughing. The boy relaxed his arm and the creature became passive again. There was something remarkable about the van, the boy with the snake. The moist and primitive tropics—?

"How d'ya like the size of me plaything?" the boy said. He was looking at Lois, who still had on her witch hat, and was looking intently at the snake's head. There were fumes from the gas-tank. It was cold when she

124

rolled down the window.

"What do you feed it?" Lois said. "Looka that Papa—looka that."

"White mice," the boy said. "Where's Little Simon?"

"I don't know," Lois said.

"Tell him I have a new deal for him," the boy said. "Tell him Dale has a deal for him."

Then he stared into the car at Simon and smiled slightly, showing under the light of the gas-tank red raw gums and tiny white teeth. Old Simon looked away.

The girl stood in front of Lois' headlights lighting a cigarette. Perhaps she was fifteen; the match flared and seemed to reflect against the snake's body. The boy hung the snake about his neck and started to walk back and forth with his hands in his pockets, singing. The snake remained motionless, with its large head, with brown and yellow stripes about the eyes, resting on the boy's dirty jacket sleeve. The girl dragged on the cigarette. "White mice," the boy said.

"You can see them being sucked down by his muscles—head first, their feet and then their tails slipping in—pretty neat the way he does it—" the boy said. "The mouse always teases him—always."

"It might be a female anyway," the girl said. "How can you tell if its male or female, tell me that—"

"I don't like the buggers whatever they are," Calvin said.

And with that Calvin sniffed and spat. The snake looked very private upon the boy's arm, as if it was on some dark forest trunk, its eyes staring toward the cement wall. Inside there were chips and cheesies behind the counter.

The boy laughed, patted the snake's head gently.

I wanta get back on the road now, Old Simon said to himself. I mus' get back on the road an have a say with Packet. The boy's hair was short, and the lights of the service-station seemed to glow on his head.

"Are you goin home Simon?" Calvin said.

"Oh yes—home—yes."

"What was wrong with yer leg then?"

"Nonsense—all nonsense—there's a Bowie man in there real sick, should take care of the Bowie man—he's sick—"

The scuds of snow were still again. There was an oil barrel with a black greasy tarp over it, tied tight with wire, just beyond the light of the service-station window, and someone from inside the service-station started a motorcycle. Then the garage door rolled up with a clatter, and amid two-stroke gas-and-oil fumes a Suzuki rolled away slowly, and then torqued gear after gear, the man driving it wearing no helmet, the tail-light broken and the driver lifting his feet now and then away from the spinning slush. Then the motorcycle came back again and stalled. The driver fell against Lois' car. Everyone was laughing at him—he was obviously as drunk as a lord. He was also, as Simon could see, Russell Peterson. His left hand rested against the hood of the car like a snowshoe.

"Binded me own snowshoes? In them days? Oh we all had to do it in them days," Simon remembered himself saying at one time to the lady who interviewed him, and at one time to the nurse. How conceited and drivelling that had sounded. Russell Peterson worked for Lester Murphy as a night watchman. He'd walk about the warehouse once or twice and then fall asleep on the sacks of feed. When friends of his came to syphon diesel gas from the barrels for their tractors, he always managed to be sleeping.

Now Russell got off the motorcycle and left it resting against the car. Lois paid for the gas, but couldn't continue with the motorcycle resting there. "I have some pain here," Simon said, before he could stop himself or even understand what it was he was saying.

"What's that Papa?" Lois said. "What's that?"

But Lois was watching Russell—because Russell had staggered toward the boy and with one motion had whacked the snake to the ground. The snake lifted its head and opened its mouth. Dale jumped away. "What in hell ya doin Rumpy," he said to Russell, "wit me snake?"

"I wanta wrestle it Dale," Russell said looking about. The snake lying on the cold asphalt seemed disorganized as if it suddenly found itself some 10,000 miles from the night trunk upon which it was resting. It started to crawl away from the beam of the lights toward the dark crevice near the men's washroom.

Russell Peterson jumped on his motorcycle and started it again. The motor screamed plaintively—like tin screaming, and backing the bike with his feet and then clunking it in first gear he began to chase the animal.

"Leave it alone Rumpy," the boy yelled.

"Ahhh-whoo," Russell yelled. "Who ho—" he yelled. And he made passes at the snake, and each time coming toward it he'd kick at it with his boot, almost upsetting the machine. The snake lifted its body and watched the bike and made a series of melancholy retreats toward the darkness. Russell's boots had seen better days. There was a small shoelace in each boot, the boots were bent and Russell was wearing no socks.

"Ha ha—aha," Russell yelled. The snake now retreated, now lay still.

The machine turned. Each time Russell came closer to the snake, and each time as he booted at it the machine's tires slid from under him. Russell yelled.

"Come on Russell," Calvin shouted. Lois watched. Suddenly the animal turned. Its eyes with their brown and yellow stripes.

"Come on yous," Russell said to it, taunting it. "C'mon you snake," he said. Across the sky again those Voodoos raced, the earth trembled. The snake in confusion lifted its head. The ground vibrated. The snake lifted its head in confusion. And at that moment the machine whined toward it again, Dale tried to grab it away and Russell Peterson ran across its head with the bike. Turned and ran over the snake again. The bike stalled and Russell fell off it. Lying flat on the ground for a moment, he giggled. His left boot had come off and two of his toes started bleeding. The snake's body twisted once, twice the whole length of its back, and even with its head crushed seemed to want to slide away. Perhaps into some thicket or swamp.

"Ya killed my snake," Dale said. "Rumpy you son of a bitch—"

"I didn't mean ta kill it—it wouldn't get outta the way—"

"Ya killed my goddamn snake," the boy said, kicking the snake to make sure it was dead.

"It wouldn't get out of the *way*," Russell giggled. "I was just playin with it—it wouldn't get out of the *way*," he giggled again.

"$150 down the cocksuckin drain," the boy said. "$150 for a snake down the drain," the boy said. Russell stood up, hopped on his right boot, lifted the bike and set it on its stand. Then he hopped over to the snake, the blood from his toes dripping onto the cooling stones. The night was quiet again.

"$150 down the drain," the boy said. "C'mon Rumpy—help me throw the cocksucker in the river."

Rumpy giggled, turned and hopped back to get his other boot.

The car drove on.

"Dale," Lois said. "His name is Dale Masey—he's inta all sorts of things, he gets his money," Lois said. "Lazarus' boy—you know."

"Oh yes—grows snakes does he?" Old Simon said. He stopped, cleared his throat. He looked at the dress she was wearing. And just then Lester Murphy passed them in his International Scout on the way somewhere. Old Simon pretended not to notice.

"There goes ol' Murph," Lois said. The car rounded a bend, over five scraggly potholes filled with water. She sighed, lighted a cigarette, her breasts lifted once. The Virgin glowed, its aura ebbing away from him.

There were tears in his eyes. Nonsense. He wiped them away quickly, tried to smile.

"Well I'm a joker, I'm a smoker, I'm a midnight toker," came the music. Lois' thighs twitched slightly, lovingly to the music. She geared down quickly.

"Because I'm right here at home—" came the music. Nonsense.

"Oh Papa, yer cryin dear, yer cryin," Lois said. Lois said, "Oh Papa dear, yer cryin."

Nonsense.

"Well you're the cutest thing I ever did see. I really love your peaches, let me shake your tree," came the music.

"Papa," Lois said. "Papa dear," quietly: "Papa."

Sleep, to sleep an hour? The car was now human, the sound of its engine, the throes of human—? You would think anyways—?

Lois sang to the song: "I'm being followed by a moon shadow, moon shadow, moon shadow—"

The song was over. And the announcer said, "Bolivia—" and static drove in black electric currents about him, and he thought of how good rum tasted in the evening, or beer when he'd redone Bryan's old homestead for them.

Again the announcer was saying, "Bolivia—in conjunction—"

"Goddamn radio," Lois said. "Sure as dog's got a tail it'd stay clear for 'Back to the Bible.' " Her lips were pursed, formed a dry curse word. Then, switching the dial, she found the provincial capital, and Buck Owens and his Buckeroos.

"I'd like to crash this car right inta the side of a barn sometimes," Lois said. "I really would—right inta the side of old Hitchman Alewood's— that'd teach it," Lois said.

In the flare of the light Lois looked quite beautiful—the match that smelled of sulphur in her hand, her left leg moving with the clutch. How old was she? He tried to remember. Strange to think this. To think that Elizabeth would always say, "Tch Lois—ya'll get yer arse in trouble, tch, yer clothes are always so tight."

He was shaking now, and afraid—he did not wish to admit that fear had come over him—

"Hold on Papa—I'm goin over a bump."

He felt himself being hauled somewhere and he tried to hang on—to what? To the handstrap. You must hang onto the handstrap. Suddenly, the flashing ambulance lights, with the word *ambulance* inverted, raced out of the back reserve road, through the slush, turned straight toward his

128

side of the car, and veered dangerously away, "Eeeeh eeeh." He could see clearly the driver and the heads of two ambulance attendants.

"Jesus oh fuck," Lois said. "Crazies wanta kill everyone—son of a bitch."

"Sorry for swearin now Papa."

"Sorry for swearin."

"I should shake my head for swearin Papa."

"Shake my head."

She sneezed. It sounded quite comfortable.

What did Alewood say, when coming back to the Maritimes from Boston in 1865, with his American, semi-aristocratic wife: "Long-legged Amanda," they were to call her on the roadway. "Bloodsuckers," he said. "They'll ruin us," he said, learning of the Charlottetown conference. "Trickery and a moment's sentimentality," he said, while all about him others called him traitor—when he said in 1867: "we're part of the stew now, and it's their recipe gentlemen."

Tom Proud walked the roadway. Though he had no year of the tiger, no year of the monkey, nor understood a calendar of stone or paper, he looked somehow (like his sister Emma Jane Ward) oriental—if not Chinese then Mongolian, his eyes like a boxer's mouse at 22 years of age. Born in 1867. He came out of a reserve and tried to emulate the only man he considered worth the trouble. Alewood himself. And so in a way in the eighteen-eighties he somewhat resembled an unsmiling Chinese Tong. He walked the roadway and stood near the house watching his sister.

"Oh Thomas, there you are—there you are—come here," Emma Jane would say.

"No."

"Are you frightened of me—you scared a me—you scared a me Tom—ho ho, Tom's scared a me."

"No."

"You are too Tom, you scared a me—la la la Tom, ho ho ho."

"No."

"It's my birthday Tom."

"I thought it was your birthday las week."

"It's my birthday every week—you don't know."

"I do, you said it was your birthday las week."

"Tom—it was, and this week too—you don't know how many birthdays I have—Mrs. Alewood has."

"No."

"I am not a squaw. I'm an Indian woman."

"No."

"La la la Tom la la la." "What does Tom want?" "He wants $3 Hishman, he wants $3."

"Hishman had a white woman—in town."

"So—you tink I care—you ever tink I care?"

"No."

"Hishman says, I don't want him sitting on my toilit, is what he's say, he's say, I don't want his bones sitting on my bones, is what he's say, his bone on my bones—"

Tom says nothing.

"Pray to me Tom—to me—I'll let you do it—to me Tom to me." (Ho ho ho.)

The clouds parted, the moon shone down along the fringe of the fields, old fence-posts and stretches of spruce and small gullies and empty houses with vacant windows and doorways and barns with pulp and sprags supporting the struggling remnants. Shadows like benefactors from one end to the other. In the dark shadows the snow flurried now, and the snow flurried onto the windshield of the car.

"Yes yes," he said for no reason at all. He looked at her—an old man with a tooth on the right side of his mouth and a tooth on his left side— her soft features under the absurd dress and smiled.

"A course it's a dern shame I won't live ta see what happens."

"Happens when Papa?" He grinned.

"Happens happens," he said, grinning.

"Well I know right now where you should be is in the hospital," Lois said.

He didn't answer. In the winter the snow made you calm—the more violently it came the more calm, and now the snow flurried for the first time this year along the potted roadway and came at the window and melted—and there was no longer the smell of pine, of her lingering perfume. He was calm now and said nothing, and the white face of the Virgin was somehow glowing. And why be angry with her? She'd done nothing. At twelve years of age she was still running about in swollen bloomers and a running nose and raiding Murphy's garden with the boys —when she was sixteen she quit school because everyone did, because she'd been taught more or less, and she smoked cigarettes at thirteen. Run away from the convent they'd sent her to and she'd gotten a job for a while at Zeller's—until she thought that the floor manager was picking on a young boy who worked there and she told the manager to fuck off in front of the customers. And on her first day of work she came home with a plaque with the poem "What is a Mother?" by Helen Steiner Rice and she gave it to Merium—and at seventeen she was pregnant with Jeffrey. But why be angry with her? She sat George's girl on her knee and stroked her hair and moved her fingers along the girl's shoulders, with tears in her eyes—and she hoarded things, like a chipmunk might. Her trailer was filled with things of no value, but she kept them as mementoes. And she didn't know what to do with her children—and she was always going to get married to the *right* man. And every Christmas her trailer would be smacked with lights from one end to the other, lights would shine up the crude icy walk-wall and glow from the windows, the windows adorned with artificial snow—and there'd be a great giant plastic Santa Claus on the doorstep, and she'd buy the children all sorts of toys that were usually broken the next day, dolls and horses and spacemen and trucks—and she'd sing "Jingle Bells" to them—"In a one-horse open sleigh"—and dress them and take them to midnight Mass—and the kids would gorge on candy.

He'd seen Elizabeth Ripley Terri fighting over a chocolate bar with Little Simon—when he saw her near the lawn-chair by the trailer that day with Lois screaming and Little Simon crying he turned away, and went over the hill to the stream. And he was carrying a sack of new potatoes for her and he dumped the potatoes out and kicked them away. And her face came to him, and sadly enough the grass blew like strands of hair. And later when he crossed over the hill to the trailer again she was sunning herself and the September day was bright and cool, and Lois sat on the porch steps without any underwear on, crying. George had left her and she was alone; the hamburger palace had been torn down—where they'd painted and scraped and made menus listing all the things they were going to sell—and how all their friends and relatives would always come there—with Packet having the job of filling the ketchup bottles and making carry-out trays, and how they were going to build on this and have a restaurant because Georgie knew people—you see Georgie always knew people. And she was alone, eating an Oh Henry chocolate bar and sunning herself and lifting her head from the lawn-chair to take a bite while sucking the chocolate from her fingernails. She did not notice him. She said, "You fucking little Jeeser—that was my chocolate bar you stole —and yer goin ta bed early tonight, the whole goddamn bunch a ya— and Lois you get in the house and put some panties on—now, go on, now."

And he did not intrude.

Because she was enticed to go farther and farther from the hamburger stand by the men who teased her. And when Georgie came in one evening with Ceril Brown—Packet wouldn't say where she was—but Packet wouldn't look toward the apartment. And George with Ceril Brown went up the fire-escape heavy with the undulations of frost and through the half-open door. She lay on the cot, without even her apron off, her skirt pushed up. Perhaps that was where the awful tragedy lay. The evening silenced by the frost in the heavy-limbed trees, and the stones of the empty parking-lot below where one weak yellow light flickered over Georgie's Hamburger Palace. When George opened the door Lester looked at him. There was a silly bemused look on Ceril Brown's face. In a room on the third floor with a cot, with an army blanket, the hot plate on the cupboard and the yellow electric lights. Her red panties crumpled up on the floor. Lester looked at them, suddenly shrugging.

Georgie turned around and left the room, not even stopping to notice the look on Ceril Brown's face, the mouth that twitched, or Packet leaning against the wooden railing with his arms folded across his brown chest and ketchup stains down the side of his throat, with Elizabeth yelling obscenities one moment and crying the next.

Packet left that night. He heard his mother yelling obscenities and crying—and then holding onto Ceril Brown and asking him questions, "I demand to know, I demand to know," with Lester Murphy crossing the room with his boots in his hand and going to the door. Packet went down the fire-escape. The gravel stuck under his feet, black at the ankles. He saw the tail-lights of George's car heading toward town, and he heard the radio from inside the hamburger palace. He wore shorts without a top and the night was cooling and he could hear the soft voices of Micmac along the water. It was one of those September nights that let you know summer has ended—and the grass and water suddenly does not look or feel the same. There were voices of Micmac, and the cedar canoes were beached and turned over. The sounds of the rapids were very quiet now. When he lay down under a canoe and tucked his legs up and held them with his arms he could hear the water and the sound of his heart. He remembered Little Simon and Lois alone in the hamburger stand—and remembered Little Simon crying. He worried about that a long time, hearing the sound of his heart.

Cold days followed. Packet rounded the roadway, still in his shorts and bared feet while the hamburger stand was boarded and closed. Kenneth Ward stopped him and asked him where his father was. "I don't know," Packet said.

Another Indian spoke—they with their hair greased and combed, both sat in cheap suit-jackets and the inside of the car was stained with grease and dirt and blood. Kenneth Ward said, "I don want lettle fish—I want big fish."

The other Indian spoke. Packet stared at them.

"Do you have anything to eat?" Packet said.

They looked at him incredulously. He looked at them calmly, and for the first time (and how many times after that—how many days and times and years would it happen?) he felt his eyes grow stony and cold and there was a taste of salt and lead in his mouth. The bright day played down on them—at the spot where Thomas Proud carried his sister Emma Jane Ward and laid her down and folded her arms in 1889—with Alewood who lived in the house above staring out the doorway. Thomas folding the girl's arms and smoothing her dress and unlacing her white woman's boots while the smoke rose from Alewood's yard. Thomas looked up and stared at Alewood and Alewood stared at him. Then her people came and carried her away. Then that night Thomas Proud came at Alewood with an axe as Alewood was packing Emma Jane Ward's trunk and gouged his left leg.

Packet stared at the two Indian men—with their dark faces, and lifting cheekbones. The smell of men's perfume and Brylcreem in the slicked-back hair that made their temples look narrow and cruel. Their pointed shoes, and suit-pants with the tight worn look at the knees and thighs. The round red balls that jiggled over the car windshield. The rank smell of blood from jacked animals emanating from the trunk. Packet stared at them. Where Alewood had stared at Thomas Proud whose face was scratched across the cheek, and there was flesh under Emma Ward's broken nails and her tongue was bitten.

"I want something to eat—" Packet said. "That's all."

The Indians looked at him. Kenneth Ward laughed. He laughed and looked at the other Indian—who not only imitated the white man's perfume and slicked hair but somehow also imitated Kenneth Ward.

"Tell yer father I kill him purty soon," Kenneth said.

Packet stared at them. The car with its ticking valves and heat lingering like an aura upon the bluish-green hood. Then Kenneth looked at the boy and grabbed a quart of Moosehead from between his legs and handed it to him with the rinsed suds foaming in the green bottle.

"Jus beer," he said.

And Packet took the beer and drank it, and it ran down both sides of his mouth. He didn't taste it but he drank and kept on drinking. Kenneth looked at the boy and looked at the other Indian, who had a tattoo on his left hand.

"Sorry I got no food dere Mr. Terri," Kenneth said. "Tell yer fadder I kill him dere purty soon—any day now."

The car drove off in a cloud of pebbles and dust with the rear end fishtailing and the rusted muffler droning and sputtering for a long time. Packet went into the field near Lester Murphy's barn—away from the apartments and road—and he lay near the barn and stared at the sky. It seemed so deep and he was far into the sky—past those little scuds of pale clouds—far into the sky. And his head was moving. When he woke he was shivering and he found it hard to walk. But he went into the woods through the gully where the moss was wet on the trees and twilight lingered. He came up out of the ditch and walked toward his house. There was no-one at the house at all—the doors were locked so he broke a screen window and got in. And he made himself a bologna sandwich and stared here and there—at the walls, at Georgie's hats and coats and the upturned furniture—the couch broken. He sat in the corner near the register a long time.

When George found Elizabeth and Lester together, and Ceril Brown was there, and Packet—in bare feet coming up behind them to lean against the wooden railing—Lester rolled off the bed cot. Elizabeth sat up with her apron and dress pushed up over her waist and she faced them. She looked for a moment at the floor, and she picked up her red panties and put one leg into them and then the other and stood to haul the panties up. And for one second, she was completely absorbed in this and nothing else mattered. And George went out and got very drunk and listened to Hank Williams over and over and found Mammie's shack and went to bed with her.

He took Mammie's clothes off and his clothes off but he couldn't do anything. He tried but he couldn't. So he drank wine and broke the windows out of Mammie's shack. "You promised me a good time, you promised me a good time," Mammie said.

"Fuck you you ole whore—jus like me fuckin wife—think I care?" And he began to tear the wallpaper off the walls and then he took the Virgin Mary and tried to do something to Mammie with it. The town police were called by neighbours farther up the lane who heard Mammie screaming. So the police came and took George away. They went into the cell and beat him and threw his head against the bars and the next morning George woke, and Simon got Ramsey Taylor and they went down to bail him out. George would not look at his father. There was a cut on his forehead but George said, "I had better cuts" and said he couldn't remember what happened.

They signed a bail release, and they found out George had ten charges against him. The constable kept shaking his head. George who was still drunk kept talking about D-Day and how they'd advanced to the road and met up with A Company. He thought the constable was interested in this. The constable kept nodding and shaking his head and George looked at Ramsey Taylor helplessly. "Well—yes, but I guess you know what these charges mean," the policeman said, and he looked at the list of charges again and his jaw tightened. It was cold outside and children were going back to school. George was still drunk—George did not remember that it was this man who had hit him with the billy and when George swung back and had knocked his hat off the constable had drawn a gun from the desk drawer and put it to George's head, until his fellow-officer said, "Jesus Christ now," at which he put it away abruptly, keeping his thick hand opened. Ramsey Taylor asked the questions, the policeman nodded.

They went out to Ramsey's truck, to drive George home. The police had his car impounded.

George sat in the middle and looked in the rearview mirror. "I had better cuts than this," he said.

"He seems like a nice 'nough lad that policeman," Simon said.

Ramsey cleared his throat.

Packet hid those nights under a canoe and in back of an oil-drum, near the line that ran the iron ore out to the ships in town (ore-boats as the people called them)—or he didn't hide really but simply stayed away from everyone. The oil-drum had a tarp over it and he hauled the tarp off and rolled up in it. The oil-drum had the letter S circling it and the tarp had an unsafe feeling and smell to it. He tried to think of pleasant things. He thought of the circus and how everyone went to the circus and his mother ate cotton-candy and it got stuck all over her lipstick, and there was a trained bear that just lay there and the trainer was very angry with it and wanted to show the people that he was angry with it, so they'd know that the bear wasn't usually like this. And there was a Spaniard with a monkey and you could have your picture taken with the monkey. The Spaniard would put the monkey's left arm around your shoulders and you'd put your right arm around the monkey's and then he'd take the picture for $2.

The monkey's face was wizened and its mouth turned down. It kept looking around at the trainer and everyone was laughing, and the trainer kept putting cigarettes in its mouth and trying to get it to blow rings. Everyone laughed at the monkey (it was said the monkey at times did dirty tricks for you—that the trainer could get it to pull on its penis any time he wanted, and gesture around with its paws on its penis and Ceril Brown said he'd pay ten bucks to get the monkey to do that, but the trainer who spoke fine English said he didn't understand, "No comprenda— grazie," and everyone laughed). Then the trainer loaded the monkey's mouth with cigarettes. The trainer wore tight black pants and his shoes were flat, pointed and shiny, but scuffed with dust and there was the smell of hide and dung just opposite in the field. Everyone wanted to get their picture taken but Elizabeth said she wouldn't touch it. She tried to touch it and then she ran back and said, "Ohhh ohhh" and pulled her hands up as if she were about to breathe on them and Ceril Brown hugged her and said it was okay. Packet didn't want to get his picture taken with the monkey.

"What's wong Packet, what's wong?" Lois said, and then the trainer got a toy gun and pointed it at the monkey's head and the monkey raised its arms and then did a double somersault and everyone laughed. The monkey thought it was over then—because that was supposed to be the last trick and it started to go back to the trainer but the trainer was making money and kept giving the monkey things to do. The monkey looked around at everyone with its eyes wide and its mouth turned down. It kept looking in one direction and then the other and everyone laughed. But Packet wouldn't get his picture taken. "Don't be a damn sissy," George said. "That monkey isn't going to hurt you." And then they all got candy-apples and went home. Lois and he sat on the porch steps smelling the rich smell of the garbage, eating their candy-apples. The taffy stuck all over Lois' mouth just as the cotton-candy had stuck all over his mother's.

After that night—being alone like that, the strange and important-looking meteors colliding in the darkness, Packet thought that he'd be able to take care of himself. Although that night as the meteors guttered and withered he lay flat on his back, with the tarp over him, smelling his own fear (like the smell of his own blood). He knew the next afternoon when Kenneth Ward talked to him that the rail-line met nothing and the tarp was rotted and what stirred off in the gravel was mouse or weasel. And when later Merium, Simon and Ramsey Taylor saw smoke coming from George Terri's chimney—they found Packet sitting in the corner over the register on his haunches, alone.

"Where's Lois and Little Simon?" he said.

"Where are they—who's got them?" Patrick said. There was still a streak of ketchup on his neck.

"Elizabeth has them at your granny's house," Merium said.

Packet said nothing. He looked at the broken dishes, the upset couch, the list at the top of the door for all the things Georgie's Hamburger Palace needed, salt and pepper and oil and napkins (the napkins Packet folded deliberately and calmly). Merium kept trying to smile. Ramsey cleared his throat. Packet said nothing.

Then Georgie had to go to court—all the charges except two, disturbing the peace and resisting arrest, having been dropped. And George sat there listless and depressed the day before the appearance. He was sitting with his arms on the couch in an old torn-away T-shirt with a St. Christopher medal on. He didn't even feel like listening to Hank Williams. When he looked both his wrists were blue and swollen.

When he began to remember he remembered Mammie's smile and how he lay down with her. Then the wallpaper—he remembered standing in wallpaper shouting at her that the wallpaper was old and waterlogged anyway. Then he didn't remember anything until he was inside the police station. Yes, the constable. And then they took him into the cell. Then they handcuffed his hands between the bars and two of them began to beat him. He kept trying to kick at them of course but they were using their feet also and he was kicked in the shins and knees and punched in the kidneys. George was a strong man then and he remembered having kicked one of them pretty good but they got the better of him. He stared at his swollen wrists and then rubbed the St. Christopher medal. Then he remembered the constable saying that there was an RCMP officer coming in and they uncuffed him quickly and left the cell. His lawyer, Mr. Bryan, told him to plead guilty and get off with a fine because the judge would be consulted about the circumstances and the town police had him cold. Mr. Bryan's face jerked. George was depressed and didn't even feel like drinking or listening to Hank Williams. Then Elizabeth came in and tried to make him supper and he threw her outside on the ground. All the time he was carrying her to the door to throw her he was really hoping that she'd make him supper and that they'd forget it all. Then he went back inside and locked the door.

So Elizabeth had the children after he left her and, "in her own way" as Merium said, she tried.

The village now had street-lights, and paved streets, with elms lining the drives, and it had modern stores—it had three churches and those three churches sat on those sidestreets and their bells chimed on Sunday. From a haphazard road it had changed (slowly conditioned by time), to become like all villages with streets and elms and churches. And there was talk of a new mall with a K Mart and there was talk of a McDonald's fast-food hamburger restaurant. They said that there were great deposits of iron ore under the earth—so that even if over the next decade the mills shut down there was iron ore. And the children and their children, and the children of those children, by man's expedience to do what they had to do would go into the future. When the woods were gone the river'd be gone, but there'd be iron ore, and when that was gone there was uranium also.

You could see the village lights as you drove along Cortes Road by those clustered French houses, with the bright rainbow colours. There were brick houses now along Cortes Road and during the summer months the families from town visited their camps and cottages along the river, named after TV programs, "Green Acres" and "The Ponderosa," and had no-trespassing signs and private-property signs set up along the fences of their properties. Above there was a fish-tagging trap where the number of salmon and grilse were tagged after coming out of the reserve waters, and there were waters above and below that were leased to American sportsmen.

More than one sportsman said they were sad about the condition of the great river, and they remembered when the salmon were large and abundant. But now they were sad about how the village and town flushed sewage into the river and they were sad that the old guides were dying—men like Simon Terri who worked in the winter for a lumber company and guided fishermen in the summer—and would walk up to 30 miles a day and prepare bedding for his sport and take them into the better pools at the right time of year. But now there was too much poaching and shots being fired at the wardens who patrolled the branches. And Simon Terri thought about this. There was pain from his right hip to his left shoulder-blade cutting across his spine and there was no sensation in his right leg.

The road was solidly paved now and the snow flurried darkly upon it.

He was shaking again, sporadically. The fires in the winter, the cool cool fires beyond the ice, the lake ice with those trapped air bubbles—"Father —Father."

(Ha ha—what-ha.)

We may as well lay down the table: what of it? Was Lois saying something? She was again telling him of Dale Masey, that Little Simon dealt in drugs with him—that Little Simon himself did not seem to be well (eyes flitting in a sort of sporadic darkness). Was she telling him other things, oh the boat-people had landed—and they were all given a Canadian flag at the airport—everyone was nice to them—everyone went out of their way to help them adjust—and now they were already guaranteed jobs by Ceril Brown himself—a man who had already written a long letter to the paper welcoming them.

"But," Lois was saying, "will they be happy here Papa? Don't ask me."

There was a sad face in front of him and that sad face was the Colonel's: "We never ran," the Colonel was saying. "They don't play games with me."

There was a whirring noise in his ears, something like the noise a man might have when things aren't quite as lucid as they should be—but this was not the case; or at least things flitted in and out of his mind, perfect shapes were formed—instances so clearly remembered as to be painful. When he was a young boy for instance, in 1909—he had to keep care of Hitchman Alewood, bathe him and feed him; and he was strong enough to carry him back and forth to his room, let him look out the window. One day Bunny Peterson, Havlot Peterson's father, came in to visit Hitchman Alewood—and Hitchman Alewood made fun of the boy caring for him.

He kept saying: "Look at me now—bein kept on by a useless sprag of a lad," and he laughed, and Bunny kept thumbing the brim of his hat and shaking his head. Hitchman looked at the boy, as if he knew exactly what the boy was thinking, not only of him, but of Bunny Peterson, grinning and thumbing the brim of his hat. Simon remembered this. Alewood's new shoes were twisted in opposite directions; he had a crinkled bow-tie on, and his throat went cluck-cluck—and then his throat went cluck-cluck again and a bit of phlegm came into his mouth which he wiped hurriedly—and Simon felt embarrassed and sad for some reason. And then Hitchman Alewood fumbled in a large leather wallet to pay him.

"Tomorrow now when ya come—I want you to lop off that maple branch for me—so I can see the river out of this window—I asked Burton Crow to do it this spring—he said he would when he had time—"

"I can do it now," Simon said, jumping up.

"I said tomorrow—can't you hear?" Hitchman Alewood yelled. "Tomorrow," he said, "when you come again—so you'll have to come again," and he chuckled.

"Now I'm not trying to upset ya Papa—goddamn it—I'm not trying to upset ya."

Oh yes, Lois was saying Lester Murphy was about to do something big with his tavern—you could ask anyone—something big was going to happen.

"God knows what that'll be," Lois laughed.

"Bolivia—in conjunction—troops—"

"Dale—well Papa if you knew Lazarus ya'd know why he's mixed up —havin a father that opens and closes the door for the people going to the Glad Tidings Tabernacle—he says that's all he's worth—standing about with his head bowed, two tufts of hair sticking up out of his head, opening or closing the door for people—or going into Ceril Brown's bookstore last Saturday and seeing—findin out who's buying the dirty books so he can tell Brother Dudley—and then Brother Dudley telephones the parents about the dirty books—no wonder Dale's not wired quite right—Lazarus raised from the dead all right—eh Papa—raised from the dead—is it true he took a two-by-four and smacked his wife, what's the ins of that Papa? You'd know all about that wouldn't ya Papa —about Lazarus smackin his wife with a two-by-four—"

The sign by the broken door of the men's washroom at Calvin Simms' Irving garage—was that still the same sign or, as they called it, one sheet about the movie, *Erotica* to be shown at the drive-in theatre for the graduates; *Erotica* and *The Story of O*, the aging one-sheets still showing scenes of women and men their eyes betraying our corrupt use of social intelligence—the snake trying to retreat toward, or was that a different one-sheet—had these months already passed? And so there would be new graduates in the months to come—

Where will you do your shopping today?
What will you get and what will you pay?
If you want to do better
Check out the difference at Sobey's—
Check out, check out
Check out the difference at Sobey's!

came the commercial. Simon found himself snapping his thumbs.

George to set down the book, *Torso*, under plastic wrapping. Or Daniel Ward staring at him. That night they were going to the whore-house to stop George from selling Daniel's grand-daughters—one of the ventures for profit entered into by George and Ceril Brown, Ceril Brown and George bickering for profit in the small Knights of Columbus room with the chairs packed against the back wall, after hours—or after George had gone over the dissolution of his marriage, the vague and anxious thoughts of Lester Murphy saving his life by pulling him into a ditch in Holland, making him feel in some way, somehow sub-human.

Daniel wore old steel-toed rubber boots from the mines, and held them together with curious red laces. Or even more curious, the young puppy he carried under his cigarette-burned sweater. The puppy having a small oddly shaped head, Daniel looking like a man about to apologize for an injury he'd received—like a man who is beaten might say, "You beat me good," and put out his hand in friendship to the man who'd beaten him —as if to defend verbally that man's God-given right to beat him—

They went to the whore-house then. And how hot it was that evening —how inescapably hot, and the puppy whimpered to be under the sweater, its joyless queer-shaped head sticking up now and then to witness the breathless sloping roadway—where Alewood's store sat, its cellar windows grated and painted over black, and boarded doors with names scrawled across the boards and endless dateless graffiti written up on the cement. Where in the formless parking-lot, a broken ladder-backed chair had lain in the dust and a ball of wire creaked an inch or two forward.

Daniel went in behind him. The corridor was half-lighted, electric candles flickered on the brown wallpaper. Blond grass grew over one of the windowsills (you remember strange things). Oh yes, also those stringed pea-shaped beads. Simon turned and walked through those beads. The Indian girls were sitting in pink frilled nightwear, with their breasts showing and their legs bare. Daniel stood behind the beads with his arms holding the pup he'd found. One man put a candy in his mouth. (In Micmac—is that how you say—pretty?)

It was all rather nervous—one man tapping his fingers on the coffee table as if bored, but that record-player playing Elvis Presley—on the floor in front of them, just catching the twilight through their naked armpits, the motions of two girls jiving, their flesh having the peculiar lonely and rude scent of children and you could tell by their soaking garments how they were suffering from the heat. A dish of mints sticking together.

In an attitude that was artificial and terrible a young boy in Texas-styled boots was pacing back and forth in front of George (this was taking place in a room that Hitchman Alewood had once kept as his office) demanding his money back. His head made a shadow against a white sheet—and the silhouette of his head, especially how his ears stuck out, made one think that no-one believed in evolution.

"Come on," George was saying. "Don't be a jeesless sissy, go in and try it again."

"No way—I want my money back," the bay was saying. "You give me my money back—"

"You can't stick it in that's not my problem," George was saying.

(This conversation then, being carried forward as if it were a matter of principle, which in a way one might suppose it was—and yet the awesome feeling of the woman lying behind the sheet.)

"Not into her—"

"She's not dirty," George was saying.

The heat, and that awful humidity. The movement of the woman beyond the sheet. The boy whispered and said he'd paid good money—and a kind of rage moved across his features. Perhaps the boy was sixteen—perhaps he'd wanted to back away from the whole adventure—

"It's not my money," the boy whispered. "I stole it from home."

George absent-mindedly kept sticking a toothpick into his gum, and when he turned around to laugh Daniel was staring at him.

Daniel kept talking in Micmac.

They left the building. George stood at the door. George said: "What's wrong with it—everyone has a good time—what's wrong?"

Daniel kept talking in Micmac.

"What's wrong with it?" George said. "Damn it—Simon come here—I want to talk to ya."

Georgie said: "You think you're too good for your own—you always did—didn't you though?" George shouted. "And you Daniel—you—drunk and coming here—so come here I want to talk to you!"

"Oh," the boy said. "All I need—oh?"

"What's wrong with it," George shouted. "There's good money in it."

"Who are they?" the boy said. "Will they tell?"

The woman, the mother of those girls jiving, laughed and cursed him in Micmac.

"There's good money in it," George had said. He remembered a man who took people hunting to shoot bobcat said the same thing. So Simon and he slaughtered many a bobcat for money; there was snow in their fur and terribly alive eyes. Simon never hunted much after that.

"Some bastards dere," Daniel said. "Sometimes dere I just don know—"

Daniel left him at the road to the covered bridge. He walked away. Then turning he said: "Dat one who gutshot the calf—did they kill him in the war?"

"Oh yes," Simon said.

"I didn't see him around heres too much anyways," Daniel said.

When Ramsey and Simon found Daniel Ward by the high school the year before they drove him home, he kept patting them on the back. "Ole Simon," he kept saying, "Ole Ramsey—member that time we saw the panther at Cold Stream—no-one blease us—"

And they took him home. He asked them to come in and drink. And then he got angry at his daughter because she didn't have dinner made for them. Ramsey sat in a chair and Simon stood by the sink. When Daniel's cousin came in—a fat woman in greasy black slacks—Daniel tried to get her to sit on Ramsey's knee. "Ole bashelor—ole bashelor," he kept saying. The woman wouldn't speak English to them. When they left Daniel got angry with his daughter and cursed at his cousin and kept asking them to stay— (Everyone said that Lazarus Masey had a plywood plank he took to his wife's head, but if it was true Simon didn't know. He only knew that the village helped them. And Father Murtree organized a benefit for them the year Billy Masey was lost—and was later found by Packet Terri and Denby Ripley, who hauled the body from a cesspool in the back of Hitchman Alewood's store. Everyone said that Lazarus Masey kept a plywood plank to discipline his wife's head—if this were true or not Simon didn't know—

They went searching for Billy Masey. Lazarus sat in Simon's house, his wife sat beside him with the baby, Dale, on her lap. Mrs. Masey kept fingering the buttons of her sweater—made for a man—and Lazarus sat in the chair beside her with a dirty white shirt on, with greying hairs growing along his throat. It was also obvious that certain people kept a watch to see if there were any marks on the children or upon Mrs. Masey. Some (perhaps most) would take delight if they could see these marks of abuse. Simon never saw any—nor ever cared to. Bobby Simms was always looking for and forever seeing signs of such violence, and would remark about it to the women—

They went searching for the boy. Mr. Masey said,

"I wants pay you boys now for this."

"Don't be ridiculous," the women said.

"No no now," the men said.

"Well I can go make sandwiches," the wife said.

"Don't be silly," the women said. "We've everythin here."

The men were out all day and night. They came into Simon Terri's and Mr. Masey would be sitting there. He no longer went into the woods with them because he'd gone screaming and yelling along the ridge at Cold Stream and had fallen over the fifteen-foot precipice and had broken his left wrist. Then Ramsey Taylor took him aside and said, "Maybe ya'd better go back now—and we'll get the boy for ya."

"Poor little Billy," Lois said.

"Poor little Billy Masey," Lois said dancing around the room, with her arms flying up above her head.

143

"That's enough now—you go to bed," Merium said.

Mrs. Masey would smile. Lois would see Mrs. Masey smile.

"Oh poor little Billy," Lois said, dancing with Packet's shirt on, her legs red from the light of the stove, with her hands up over her head clapping.

"That's enough, that's enough," Merium said.

"Oh I don't care if we get money," George said.

"I'll pay yas all—I'll pay yas all ta find him," Masey answering brashly, looking about terrified.

"No no now," Ramsey Taylor saying.

Simon Terri clearing his throat.

"No no now," Ramsey Taylor saying, and looking at Simon who looked away.

"Shit I don't want money very much anyways," George saying.

The next afternoon Masey stood by the fence. George came back through the path old Simon had always taken into the woods and talked with him. He told Mr. Masey that Ceril Brown was lost and that Simon had found him, and that now Ceril Brown was "one of the richest men around here."

"One thing though," George said, "I don't think they're handlin her right atal—I think I'd better track out ta Brice Pool this afternoon and look around—"

"Brice Pool?"

"Oh he coulda went in that direction—they don't even consider that—I think I'll have to get out there and see."

Then Lazarus took his leather wallet out, and took a $20 bill from it—the only bill he had in his wallet—and he handed it to George. It was an immaculately crisp new bill, and Lazarus hesitated, rubbed his fingers over it to make it snap and handed it to George.

"No, no," George said.

"Ya know I want you to take it—you're all helping me and Shirley so much there."

George spat and looked back over his shoulder. Then he nodded angrily and took the money.

Then when he crossed the fence he saw Daniel Ward looking at him. Daniel Ward was drinking wine and staring through the pine at him—

"Let's get goin," George said to Daniel Ward. "Let's get goin—now we've a boy to find—come on now—come on, let's get going—how many Micmacs you have in here anyway—how many?"

They went searching for the boy and Father Murtree went with them.

There was still snow in the woods then and Father Murtree wore his long black coat. Father Murtree said, "They're the poorest family I've ever met—and this always happens to the likes of them." He said, "You can smell poverty from the poor—they're like ghosts really." He was an old priest who'd worked here for 40 years. "You can smell poverty no matter how much she washes her clothes and sews them up—can't you?" he said. "Can't you?"

The men said nothing.

"Pe-ew Father, pe-ew," George said, looking around with his mouth opened and laughing. Father Murtree picked up a stick and swinging it at nothing kept on walking. George searched for three hours and then went out to town to get a water-pump for his car.)

When Lois helped the old man out of the car he didn't tell her he couldn't see her. He could see far-distant shadows—

"He said me darn leg's no problem anyways," Old Simon said.

"Who did?" Lois said.

"The doctor—the darn doctor there—said it's no different, and it's all a big fuss over nothin," Simon said. He chuckled. When she helped him up he leaned against her and pressed his hands on her shoulders. Then he saw her staring at him again, with a witch hat on, with *wart* written under the chin, and he remembered. He remembered that he'd walked all the way from the hospital to the tracks, and that he'd met her at the house there and that she was playing with a broom tucked between her legs—that the tree, which they called the hanging tree, stood bleached and barkless in the field beyond the crucifixion—

"What's wrong?" he said.

"What Papa?"

"What's wrong?"

"Oh don't be silly Papa—everything's fine—you just get some sleep tonight."

"What's wrong?" he said.

"Well George has moved in here," she said, "and his girlfriend."

"Who?"

"George has moved in here Papa," she said. "No-one thought you'd mind."

How beautiful she was he thought—how like her grandmother, and George was like who? And Packet—who were they like?

"Are we home?" he said.

"Yes," she said. "Of course Papa."

She took his arm in hers. "Come on Papa now—you'll go to bed now," she said.

"What's wrong here—what's wrong?" he said.

When they went inside George was sitting at the table with his girlfriend. The house smelled of grilled bacon and the leftover savoury fat from french fries. The wall behind the stove was marked with a new scent of grease. Underwear was draped over a line to dry in the far corner, but it in itself must now have been permeated with the scent of bacon rind. Old Simon blinked his eyes, staring in a vague distracted way at the shadows, the ceiling, the picture of a Pichard draft-horse, and his father on a log drive in 1889. A pair of the young girl's panties, the elastic torn, the colour of white skin, fell silently to the floor when George tipped his chair.

"Hello Father," George said. "Listen I got a bunch of wood for ya—it's comin in tomorrow, Ceril Brown got it for me at next to nothing—Dale Masey there eh—they know a few tricks about getting wood—"

Simon nodded.

"So what d'ya think Papa?" George said.

"What?" Simon said.

"About all the wood I got for you," Georgie said. "A really good deal."

"Fine fine," Simon said. "Where's Packet?"

"Oh God—I don't know," Georgie said. "Said he was going away."

"We haven't seen him in a while," the girl said.

Simon sat in the chair near the door, staring at them. Georgie winked at him and smiled. Georgie tipped his chair back, shook his large head and winked. One of his depressed tits showed through his torn T-shirt. Ah, and what complemented the smell of grease, of slow-drying clothes, if it wasn't human sweat?

"I'm going to make up your bed Papa—and then you can lie down," Lois said. He reached his hand out and smiled. He didn't see George looking at his girl or his girl looking at Lois. He didn't see Lois blowing her nose and looking at George. He didn't see, beyond the clothes, that Georgie had Simon's great map of where and when the salmon hit the pools over the years, on the far side of the kitchen wall, and since graduation had been taking salmon to the cottagers. He didn't see that George had a big note written out to Lois which said, "Hospital wants him back, lickety split—lickety split—" and that note lay on the kitchen table and that's what George was doing as soon as he heard the car, asking his girl how to spell *lickety split*.

"I'm going to make up yer bed now Papa," Lois said. "Do you want some tea?"

"Some what?"

"Some tea," Lois said.

"Oh no," Simon said, scratching his pants. "This is fine—no no—this is fine."

"Oh Papa—yer tired dear—yer tired," Lois said.

Simon Terri woke. The early-morning wind was blowing. He heard the wind blowing and felt his leg paining and his breath was short. It took him a long while to be able to open his eyes. He lifted himself up and sat sideways on the bed, hunched like an old beaten/unbeaten fighter with his shoulder-blades jutting out in the cool early-morning air, and the dresser and mirror still. Lois had brought the cot upstairs and had set it up in the corner and was sleeping there, the man's pyjama tops she wore loose-fitting and the shafts of light against her and one bared brownish leg outside the blankets with her toes painted. There was no noise besides the wind. When he looked out the window the sky was clearing. The snow covered the field in a thin layer and the river ran slowly, full-bodied like some slow-blooded thing.

"There's something wrong here," he thought. Across the field Lester Murphy's house sat, and beyond that the old Alewood house, which he could no longer see clearly, and three or four cars sat in the dooryard there. When they started up their cars in the morning the fumes lingered in the foul mud ruts, and their bumpers were caked with mud. In the air on these mornings the crows would sit high on the naked trees stabbing methodically at their feathers, the sky white and cold and the pebbled streams losing ice and gleaming in the three or four hours of steady sunshine. The partridge would cluster together at five or six to a brood. The shots would ring out, and the crows would soar above their resting-spots only to land again. And he thought: that they would all go down this night—that there'd be one more night of burning tires and the foul smoke in the purple sky. Lester Murphy'd run out with his birch stick again, with Donnie behind him running round and round—as it had gone on in the past and there'd be the shots of a .22 across the way, over the hollow and the American camps—and the broken bottles on the roadway, with the cars, with the blood of jacked animals emanating from their trunks and with the young coming drunk from Ceril Brown's—dressed and masqueraded as chickens and rabbits—cute rabbits with floppy ears, and cats—there'd be cats with tails and cats with whiskers—they'd come out into the road as they did last year and the year before. And Little Simon would say, "Hello fer a fuck of a time," as he did last year and the year before, and then he'd say, "May's well quit drinkin—what ya say?" And there'd be Martians and robots moving along the roadway in strangely cold motions, as the sky heaved with the smoke, and the old man across the river beat about his tire warehouse, with his 30-year-old raccoon coat sagging and his woollen pants tucked into his boots. "Bastards," he'd yell. "Bastards."

"What's wrong Lester—Lester dear, boys oh boys excuse me what's wrong there?" Donnie would shout (as if Lester at that instant told Donnie that nothing was wrong or that nothing would ever be wrong Donnie would clap, raise his hands and dance about as Lois had done when she was a child). But there'd be the strangely comical and hideous dress of the Hallowe'en party—of skirts and dresses out of age and fashion and rouge implanted on the cheeks of girls, and the stony smell of alcohol, sweat and crêpe in the night. There'd be fights along the river also this night—maybe a dozen sets of dishes would be broken, there'd be men and women in the bars, and a barrel thrown through this window and that—but before that the youngsters, dressed as ghosts and Superman and witches—would be walking the roadway in the ash-like twilight. They'd go from door to door (Leona, Brad and Jeffrey) to collect chocolates and raisins and kisses and apples (throwing the apples away—or at one another), some with a delirious sense of mischief and achievement, others with a total sense of boredom and duty, not even wanting the candy they went out for. There'd be the police sirens—the thousand and one rooms not giving up one ounce of human commitment until morning, with fog in the hollows—the bottles and sacks and masks in the ditches.

Lois slept with her brown leg visible to the thigh in some remote place far across the room—and Packet, where was Packet? He coughed lightly and there was a twinge in his spine that made his shoulders thrust forward quickly, that he had no control over.

The shots would ring out—all this day and until November 19th. The shots would ring out—the power-lines hum. Above them in the twilight the stars winking out softly in the sky.

He leaned hunched against the window like an old beaten/unbeaten fighter—an odd antipathy to himself in the dim early-morning smell of dresser and mattress, the cool dust. He'd heard the soft sound in the night under that register in the upstairs hallway after they'd laid him down. He'd heard them too, talking on the telephone. Then Lois came up and it was quiet, and then George said, "Don't wake him up now."

"Of course not."

George said, "Move that cot carefully about in there, don't squeak it around."

"Of course not—shut yer goddamn mouth."

"He might haveta be in oxygen tamorrow an everythin—"

"I know that."

"I don't know what got inta his poor old little head," George said. "I just don't know—odd, odd man—always was."

He went into the woods in the early morning. It was warm, so the snow would melt, and he found a nice quiet place and sitting on a cedar fell rolled a cigarette. When he dragged on the cigarette he unconsciously looked about him for tea—but he'd brought none with him and the smoke was vague and white in his eyes.

"Do you remember yer mother?" Merlin asked.

"I remember sitting on her lap," Simon said.

"That's the way things go," Merlin said. "She'd have a fit if she saw us drinking here now."

"But don't you think that was a bad thing?" Simon asked. "As far as it goes?"

"Oh yes—a bad thing, as far as it goes," Merlin said. "Emma Jane Ward all dressed up in new hat and dress and boots and walking right back with him to Cold Stream, and waiting there while he scratched his nose and looked around for something to kill her with—a bad thing, as far as it goes."

Simon nodded.

"She wore a bonnet and white boots and she used to parade back and forth in them, all day long you know, in front of us. She carried a purse and had her own trunk with things in it—money and stuff that she kept," Merlin Terri said. "Ya never know about those things anyways—never do, do ya? She was always gigglin, that's one thing I remember. She was always talkin—an you know how a young squaw, how good they can look —I mean same as now eh? He was in his fifties an sillier than her. It was bad in that way—that neither a them knew what they were doing— hangin around the roadway that led up to the houses in her new clothes and talkin back to everyone. Then she had a kid by him—Daniel—an still hangin around though. Then going to Cold Stream and waitin around—while Tom Proud looked for somethin ta kill her with anyways —and then when he started to strangle her it was too late, an all she could do was scratch his face—"

Simon stared at his drink, shrugged.

"Anyways," Merlin said, "ya never know about those things—with them anyways—an even at the last of her, scratching his face she mighta thought it was all a joke—because even then she wouldn't let go a her goddamn silly purse."

"Yep," Merlin said smiling, bringing his glass down. "It's pretty bad when you're being strangled and you won't let go of your purse."

Old Simon butted the cigarette beneath his boot and it sank, curled and died in the soft bark and snow. It was wet and the trees were quiet. It was melting. There were moosebirds bobbing in frantic excitement a little way into the grey melting, and there were the sounds of harvesters cutting and men. He felt, sensed Alewood's body as he carried him with clumsy unconsciousnss into his chair or out of it.

When the shots started, after the sun came through—the shotguns for partridge, they were only intermittent against the rumbling of the harvesters, the warmth of mud and gasoline. The old man shrugged. He was no longer sitting on the cedar fell, but leaning against it. He rolled another cigarette carefully and lit it and tried to look around.

"Oh yes—tea," he thought looking around, and then knew he hadn't brought any.

"What happened to Thomas Proud?" Simon said.

"He went after Alewood with a axe," Merlin said. "As you know—and then me and Bunny Peterson caught him an took him inta town—anyways I don't like to talk about it."

"Why's that?"

"Because we hadda tie him and beat him ta get him in there."

Simon said nothing.

"And how he wanted us ta beat him ta death—"

"Oh," Simon said.

"An how we did," Merlin said. "An how we did—ya know, beat him to death there accidentally."

Simon said nothing.

Old Simon moved his right arm along his right leg and swallowed. He'd no woollen shirt on, just a jacket over his woollen underwear, opened at the neck. His neck was red and coarse. He'd hear the men in the afternoon, the harvesters shut down. "He'd hear, "Oh Papa—Papa, Papa," coming closer and then getting farther and farther away.

Graduation

Sound came from the television. He stepped away from the window.

"What's wrong Lester—excuse me Lester dear, boys oh boys what's wrong?"

The red spot expanded outward from his breastbone. The Americans had come up from the pools for the evening, the hollow lay still.

"Atlantic Salmon Centre of the World."

There was laughter from youngsters on the roadway. "Jesus Dale," said a girl, who may or may not have been fifteen. It had been hot all day. The window was open. A swarm of bugs under the pagoda lights. The little Vietnamese girl wearing her McDonald's uniform walked by, looked quickly toward the house.

He stood in his room and heard the lingering music. Soon too Begin and Sadat would be on the television. The girls walked in twos and threes. He could see the discothèque's circular outside lights shining upon the pavement.

The radio played now, songs of New York and California. He listened to Donnie laughing. Donnie watched television. He'd put the pipe in his mouth and look contemplative and he'd take his pipe out and laugh whenever the audience laughed. Then he'd put his pipe back in his mouth and re-light it. The window was open, a lay of broken bottles in the whispering June grasses. The Professor of Theology, as Donnie said, "That Professor or so of Theology," showed him the four-pound grilse he'd taken from Terri's pool—a pool named after Simon Terri—as sunlight paled in the trees—in a place below Ripley's where in 1949 an eighteen-year-old Ripley girl hid her clothes under a rock and swam the river in her underwear. He'd smiled at the professor, the professor smiled back— "Atlantic Salmon Centre of the World."

"Daley," the girl said. They were standing by his closed gate with the spears sticking up and silhouetted. There was a boy standing beside her and Dale in a van. There was more laughter and talking. Upriver—the white flat rock Hudson Kopochus lay upon on his journey to kill a man in 1825, the rock that lay in the middle of the last great tributary, immersed now in sullen waves and night dust.

The boy with the girl scampered onto his wall, putting his right hand on the last spear on the left side of his oval-shaped gate, and the girl leaned against the van which had a picture of a tiger painted on the door and had fur (bobcat, coyote?) on the door-knob. Donnie laughed gruffly in the other room. He heard. The van throttled in the quickening, heart-beating silence.

He drank, the lime having discoloured the gin slightly. The van throttled.

Donnie laughed at the Love Boat up from southside in the other room.

"Fuck," Dale said, the van with the carpet, the cassette, the 30 gadgets to make life, if not bearable, at least pleasurable.

He thought of an unpleasant memory. His eyes grew cold and then shrugging he lit his pipe and glanced at the picture on the wall of the fire which, in the autumn of 1825, destroyed 8000 square miles in ten hours. The water nearest the shore had begun to boil and a three-masted schooner was sinking, its masts aflame, yet people were trying to crawl upon it. There was a pregnant woman at Strawberry Marsh with a bundle of dishes in her arms, and the flame had begun to crawl up her skirt, just at the point she was beginning labour—

When they first settled here they settled at the enclosure where the first graveyard was, which boys and girls now used as a place of romantic interlude; but did they know that some of those people buried there had died of nothing more than infected mouth and rotting teeth? Had died in the struggle of procreation also—procreation being always more serious than mere recreation. But now he supposed that van with the coyote/bobcat fur on the door-handle—he supposed now, Dale with wine and cannabis and matching rear speakers for the cassette recorder, had driven over those gravesites with their decayed quarry stone, and had stopped there among those pioneers who'd come from Scotland/Ireland with leprous settlers in the holds of their ships, reserving an island at the mouth of the bay for the lepers. And the lepers receiving lepers, watching the ships move on, beyond the bend to the place that was to become Ireland on one side, Scotland on the other, with priests, ministers, tobacco merchants, rum merchants who brought in 18,000 gallons a year. In the intervening years the misplaced Acadians moving back (a story, no less true because it was a story, of a man hiring himself out in Louisiana for a coat and a pair of boots and without reporting for work turning north and walking—home, back to the river, returning to the same soil, piece of stubble, defying the laws of a country that didn't know him. The French moving inward even to the swamp and marshy areas of this forest, so the sons of their sons and the daughters of their daughters would be looked upon as raving lunatics by sons/daughters of the English, Scottish, Irish and Welsh—would be looked upon not as descendants of Brittany, Marseilles, Avignon or Paris itself but as malfunctioning creatures who for some unknown reason preferred a mud bank beside a ditch to the river, a mosquito swamp to the bay).

The red mark on his chest grew outward. The boy sitting upon his wall and Dale in the van were arguing and laughing. The girl leaned against the van and stroked the fur, and looked at the boy on top of his wall. "Spending the night together—oh oh oh oh," came the song. The bulbs along the brick wall were encrusted with bugs, flicking and writhing. Dale passed a joint to the girl, and looked toward Lester Murphy's house, and to his window where he stood. Their eyes met for a second.

The Vietnamese boy strolled by. Also in his McDonald's uniform.

The girl looked at him, turned quickly, put her head through the van's opened window and giggled.

Along the roadway the Indian girls walked in the summer with sweaters over their shoulders, with sandals, made with Taiwan leather strapped up their brown ankles, their tight shorts, their purses (and as things might be, purses which weren't very different from the purse that girl Emma Jane Ward carried, her bonnet, her boots. And Thomas Proud wearing what he'd gotten her to steal from Alewood—convinced that if he wore pants that were five years old, boots that had no heels but a shirt that was given to him just the week before, he'd too be appropriate).

(The Americans, which he used to call "my Americans," must think it's unusual at best to find across from their wilderness camp, up from a river of struggling currents, beyond the fish trap that recorded the life adventures of salmon in this last great dying tributary, a discothèque owned by Ceril Brown, modelled, with its revolving lights, its Jack/Jill washroom, its sound system that cost thousands of dollars, its carpeted stairway that led up to an exclusive room with leather chairs and sofa and a picture of the premier on the wall shaking Ceril Brown's hand, and knicknacks and antiques taken from the properties around. They must find it strange that the girls/boys here were no different in their furious dancing, the men with their fierce sad/happy faces, with their brooding fun-loving, somewhat violent eyes. The Americans must think it strange to get up in the morning and walk up the road to McDonald's hamburger and fast food, which was now situated where Alewood's store once was— strange they must think that their guide while cooking their first feed of salmon had friends of his deliver a Big Mac with onions and pickles.)

He drank down his gin. What road where? What did it matter? Or did it matter that old Simon Terri, with that bedevilled stubbornness, left the hospital—the boy Rance who at 24 had tubes sticking out of his arm, and being discharged from the hospital, in a matter of days became drunk again, loitering about those musty taverns in the early hours after opening, with men sitting quietly in the corners talking about the First World War, old men drinking draft at ten o'clock, quiet and dignified in their chairs, with cigarettes burning in the ashtrays and the sound of the kettle boiling water for the waiter's coffee, as day after day the ore-ships came in with Spanish, German and Russian sailors, the stevedores waiting on the dock as the ship manœuvred. The Spanish, German and Russian sailors looking at the stevedores, the stevedores looking back, the bow cable handed over. Nor did it matter that the morning Simon Terri was making his way toward Cold Stream, Lester Murphy and Ramsey Taylor had gone to visit him. There perched on the bed with a grin on his face was Rance talking back to a nurse.

"Hello boys," Rance said. "How's she goin right there now—" affecting an upriver manner of speaking with his downriver Irish Catholic accent and then rubbing his nose. "The little old fella took off," he said.

"Took off where?" Ramsey said.

"God knows," Rance said. "They were sending him to Saint John taday—awful son of a whore of a place, so I imagine he lit out."

Ramsey's face took on an expression of burden and weight. Lester grunted, "I knew it."

"Oh I knew it too," Rance said. "Are you guys his brothers?" suddenly looking burdened—and disturbed also. Ramsey fidgeted with his hands, his longish bent yellowed fingernails. Lester said nothing.

"Poor ole fella," Rance said.

"You were talking," the nurse said, "about the undertaker—and how you drained blood out of a body—" the nurse said. She looked at Ramsey and then looked at the bed.

"I was not—I never said anything like that," Rance said.

"And you're not getting up today," the nurse said.

"Getting up—God no—get up no—I'm a sick boy," Rance said, winking his obsessively lonely eyes in his somewhat Neanderthalian head. "One thing 'bout Simon though—he had visitors, visitors day in and day out—if I reach 82 I hope someone remembers me," Rance said. His lips twitched, his face was white. He moved his hands over his blankets. The room was warm. Outside the ash came from the stack, the children with bookbags and binders had walked to the school, the pitiless day, the spire of the Catholic church rose up in a pale sky, over the graveyard, bones, metal-case coffins of the Catholic dead. Two ships lifted dry out of the water waiting to be loaded with the ore that the men rooted out of the earth—where they worked, spring winter spring again, the nattering of lights from their safety helmets along the wooden railings of open stopes, glowing feebly as if not to give up one ounce of human commitment.

Down those Canadian shafts in metal cages, crowded at each level with laughter and cursing, down into the earth, the dark head-frame, the smell of ore and snow, and the giant Kenworths that hauled it, the yelling of foremen to the workers, the yelling of senior workers to juniors, the smell of dynamite. So that if the trees were gone, so'd be the river but there was iron ore. There was iron ore here, and gold also, so man in his necessity and his sons and daughters and the daughters and sons of those would go on into the next century, the cacophonic sound of machines. There was, they said, uranium also.

Out of the hospital stack, with a long greasy wire settled against it, came the ash. There was an inch of melting snow in the parking-lot, the stones like rudimentary polished weapons. Rance sat up straighter. He began talking to them. Lester didn't listen. Outside Clarence Simms and his wife Ida were in an argument, Ida dressed in an attempt to show her respectability, Clarence with one shirt-sleeve out, the other tucked in. She wore a poppy on the lapel of her coat, her hair tucked up under her hat. Clarence wore no poppy, no hat. He kept coughing. Perhaps she'd given him his last drink that morning and perhaps as he drank it he assumed it'd be nothing to go again to the detox centre. Lester's lips twitched. The taxi-driver pulled away, stopped. Clarence began cursing. Ida tried to pretend she wasn't with him. They were both utterly alone, it seemed. When Clarence tried to get into the taxi again, the taxi bolted away and a bit of purple gas rose quietly in the air. Ida smiled when two orderlies came out. She stood there, with large black coat-buttons, her poppy and hat. The taxi waited for her—conspiring angel—by the stop sign. Clarence kept trying to kiss her hand. Rance was talking and he'd put on a mask—he said he was going to wear it most of the day, because it was Hallowe'en, that he was going to fool his friends when they visited him. Lester didn't listen.

"Are you his brother?" Rance said, talking behind the mask with a big nose, a silly grin and a wart. Lester moved—his boots with the steel eyelets, his blue eyes, both seemed to glitter. Sulphur would rise in the sky almost lovingly, from the broad mill stacks it would cling to the houses, the scent of ammonia. The train tracks would run across the country in opposite directions. On the radio there'd be the news from Quebec, news from Ottawa, and a woman would give the closing figures on the stock exchange, some important takeover perhaps.

"Are you his brother?" Rance said. "Are you—both of you—his brother?"

Lester put his arm under Ramsey's to help him, because Ramsey's legs were arthritic.

"Jesus," the girl said. "Are you comin in the van with Dale or not?"

"C'mon in the van and see me new snake," Dale said. "Me new one—eats mice."

"Leave me the fuck alone," the boy said. "Go with him if you want to."

"Yer so jealous," the girl said.

"Go with him," the boy yelled. "Go on."

Dale looked at the window again; they stared at each other.

The snake also was visible. The snake's head lay pressed against the side-door window—like some cat's head (one might think anyway), when a cat sleeps with its ears disappearing. The snake looked very private upon the boy's arm this afternoon, when he had it out and was showing it to the Terri children, Brad and Jeffrey and Leona, who'd just come back from town with her mother. Dale laid the snake around his neck and it rested its head against his arm. The words on Dale's T-shirt read: "Boogie till you puke." The sun played down upon this but Dale did a rather fine imitation of a chicken, and Leona's bright little eyes watched it all. Dale did a remarkable job of imitating a chicken—the van's doors were opened—and seemed to be impressed with suffering human bodies —nights spent. The children themselves were mesmerized by the animal. Dale, still swishing his feet like a chicken, took the cage from the van and set it on the ground. Laying the snake in it again he produced a mouse. Half the mouse's tail, after it was eaten, lay out of the side of the snake's mouth for a second and then seemed to slip away.

"Jesus—some snake," Jeffrey said.

"I knew it could do that," Bradley said.

Bradley was eating a bag of gumdrops. He had his mouth stuffed with gumdrops, and when he saw Leona looking at him he hesitated and gave her one—took it back quickly, produced another one of a different colour and handed it to her. She looked at him as he put five or six more in his mouth, then turning completely away from her, he chewed and swallowed self-righteously, his head bandage quivering. Dale smiled, patted his snake on the head once more—

He poured the gin from the bottle and squeezed some lime into the glass, and walked across the room. In a dusty row of books, a small 1940 hardbound edition of *Fathers and Sons*.

The disco had signs pasted on the outside walls of young girls in thigh-slit skirts, of John Travolta with one arm raised and one hand clutching his side like an over-confident matador. And they had rock 'n roll revival nights too, end-of-the-school-year nights, Victoria Day and July 1st nights.

"Oh Papa Papa," Lois had yelled last Hallowe'en after he and Ramsey had come back from the hospital. "Papa Papa," she screamed, her skin still faintly brown from summer, her stance, somehow in some way like her mother's. At darkness she came back to sit on the shore. It was snowing faintly and she sat with her feet stretched out, almost touching the water, and her arms folded as if praying. In Old Simon's house there was music, there was a group of cars on the backyard grasses, the throbbing of their engines. There were people in costumes and tinsel. One dressed as a robot. Lois sat on the shore crying. George said, "Strange—strange little man— always was odd as a duck." He sweated, his eyes almost closed. "He'll probably be back though—knowin him—hey—betcha twenty bucks." He set up a pumpkin with its hideous carved grin on the stump outside, and lit a candle. Leona danced around the candle in a trance. Brad and Jeffrey ran errands for men and women, opening their bottles for them. Onward the river ran, onward with jackets and vests and pump-action shotguns the men from south of the province moved in from the highway to the secondary road, over the bridge, into the stubble and density. After a while cars raced on the roadway and across the road Alewood's old house, his apartment building and tavern went up in flames.

"Amazing," one of the men said. "There was no loss of life here— amazing—"

"Indians—by the jumpins—excuse me—I tell no secrets," Donnie said. And cars stopped and the roadway stood still, and people came out of their houses and stood still. The fire started tragically enough with dirty undershorts soaked in oil and stuffed into a closet filled with yellowed copies of the local paper. Cautiously enough the men, women, girls and boys stood motionless, watching it, dressed like characters from some sad comedy.

He sat in his chair. Inside Donnie's room the television advertisement came on for Stay-free minipads, or Stay-free maxipads, he didn't know which it was, and he drank. Crepitant paper blew in the breeze, beyond the ditch. He drank again, trembled slightly.

"Beautiful people eh—beautiful people eh," he'd said to Donnie.

"Ohh oh oh beautiful," Donnie had said. "Some's awful dirty when they're drinking though."

How could anyone talk to a six-foot child who weighed 235 pounds, who when the men tricked him into carrying away over a thousand pounds of lumber put over 200 pounds of broad sheeting on his back and said, "It seems—how many miles do I have ta go with this—"

And then going to Denby Ripley—taking his beer-bottle money, and getting in to watch those stag films (possibly not even watching them—but wanting to be there, because the young men were there. When the young men laughed Donnie laughed. When they spat he spat. And it was when he was a small boy Elizabeth Ripley Terri had asked him to take off his clothes and he had. And then he'd had to walk home three miles naked, with Havlot Peterson sitting out on Alewood's steps saying, "I've seen some sights—I've seen some sights, I been alive long time I've seen some sights." Elizabeth Ripley Terri saying "Ttch—I didn't do anything —he's always after me to kiss me—can you imagine?" And whenever Lester tried to explain to Donnie good things and bad things, for a month Donnie would go around the house saying, "Boys oh boys, there's some good things—there's some bad things—boys oh boys."

Yesterday he'd said, "I think the goddamn law's unjust—did they come here when they broke into my warehouse—did they get whoever did that —did they investigate Ceril Brown—Donnie—did they?"

"No—no did they?"

"No they didn't."

"No—I didn't think they didn't—I mean they didn't."

"Of course they didn't—but now for a few dollars' pocket-money an old building, they'd just love to see me in jail—wouldn't they—wouldn't this road just love to see me in jail?"

"I don't know Lester."

"Of course they would."

"Sure they would."

Lester laughed. Unpleasantly.

Donnie laughed. Unpleasantly.

"I'm glad Simon Terri's not alive to see this—Ceril Brown's world now."

"It sure is," Donnie said.

"Jesus Christ—" He chuckled unpleasantly.

"Oh oh," Donnie chuckled, lifting himself up on his toes and staring out the window, where at Simon Terri's George was standing talking to some men and passing a bottle of wine back and forth. A brand-new car sat in the driveway, a new but damaged car was up on blocks in the back yard. Lois had won on Atlantic Loto—he didn't know how much, though he thought it was $50,000. Now men came up to George and George

158

would get drunk with them, point over to Lester's house. They'd all laugh and shake their heads. Men too, a new man was with Lois every day. Little Simon was dead now. Packet, where was Packet?

There was the faint sound from the disco. He drank his gin.

The tennis-court he'd built for the children, used predominantly by the cottagers in the summer, or for road-hockey matches, his hands shaking slightly, palsied, didn't the grumblers know not only the worth of the tennis-court—because tennis now was ravishing North America—but the cost?

Fathers and Sons he'd never read, though he'd picked it up once or twice. See a man coming home one evening with a book and going into his room tearing the paper bag away and opening the book—beginning with the first chapter (actually the only thing he remembered about the book was that someone—a servant—wore an ear-ring) in hopes that it was some study—rules of some kind. Once or twice after that time he'd picked the book up, reading a line or two. He'd nod to himself reading a line or two—and then he'd put the book away.

He stood in the bathroom, near the sink. From the bathroom window he saw the lights of the roadway, looking warm, heard the sound of the water in the evening air against the screen. He'd clipped his beard down now, and was shaving himself with the razor. His new three-piece suit sat in the room on the bed, so precise it sat there, looking as if someone deflatable was in it. His new shoes with the air-holes.

The bathroom had green tile walls with brass soap-fixtures and a large old-fashioned bath with brass legs that sat, dominant and important along the far wall. Philodendrons once grew here, but they had died, though he always managed to keep one flower or plant—creeping or not creeping about. A large golden-coloured wooden clothes-hamper sat behind the door. Once a week a woman would come in to do the clothes, and clean what needed to be cleaned in the house. She had her own ideas about the place and had already rearranged some of the furniture.

He lathered his face again and stared in the mirror. The water sullen and filled with bits of lather, the lather brush smelling faintly of dead facial hair. His chest was somewhat sunken, the skin over his breasts withered and brown about the concaved mammaries, the shoulder-blades and collar-bones where sparse hairs grew white and long. Each firm stroke of the razor showed more of his jaw, coloured the colour of ash in the bottom of a wood-stove at daylight. Light glanced from the mirror into his eyes, played in the scuds of sullen water.

The gash was not long. Amazingly he didn't realize he'd cut himself. For a number of seconds there wasn't any blood.

"I really love your peaches, let me shake your tree," came the music. A pearl of blood dribbled along his cheek. The moon now was out over the trees. In the hollow—in the hollow there were the lights of the American camps, the stone fireplaces, the ancient muzzle-loaded hammer-muskets that went along with it—that had nothing really to do either with the river or the men on the river, having more to do perhaps with some Sioux chief in the land of Frederic Remington but which gave the places their atmosphere.

He kept tamping his cheek with a Q-tip. The blood oozed out, the smell of lather peculiar. Ceril Brown now wore a full-length fox-fur coat, with high leather boots and a fox-fur hat in the winter. As the wind blew the fox hair moved. The water dribbled into the sink. There was a roar of laughter across the water at Terri's. He went over to the window and peered out with his shoulders hunched. In an odd stance, unbeaten, with his arms hanging down. When the red spot on his chest touched the windowsill there was a burning sensation. Across at Terri's there were men in black shadows walking to and fro about a pit fire. They were laughing. The night was warm and sweet-scented. Their shadows moved to and fro the fire in strange solitary motions. He could make out George sitting on the stump with his girl leaning over, in a beach-robe, basting the pig upon the spit, head and all. They'd built the fire with charcoal and rocks. George turned the spit with one hand lackadaisically. The girl said something to him. He said something to the girl, the pig revolved, its legs turning to the creak of the rod upon the splayed birches—somehow as determined as the men to have itself cooked and eaten. The stars lingered palely. George laughed and wiped his mouth. Out of the house came Bradley with a quart of liquor, and stood looking at the pig and then at the men who were all talking. The smoke rose. The men talked.

"I'm a joker—I'm a smoker,

I'm a midnight toker—" —the song.

(The wind came up through the cold empty hay-less barn, through the cracks and fissures of the boards. The shadows of men near the 60-watt light-bulbs as they scalded the hair-bristles from a pig, moving to and fro in the sparse light with the sound of Don Messer and his Islanders on the radio or the sound of Hayshaker's Hoedown on the radio, in the fall twi-light afternoons at six o'clock butting their cigarettes into their empty Coke bottles with the weight of the hung pig and the scalding water. The old matted dogs who lay under porches came out to sniff the blood of their cousins, and then took a leisurely stroll along the highway, turning now and then to bite their infested fur.)

Bradley had stolen a canoe from the hollow and had paddled upriver to the giant flat rock there and, practising some boyhood game, had fallen, hitting his head against it. He'd lain, bleeding on the rock for an hour until a sportsman seeing him had canoed over and carried him back. Now he had a bandage wrapped around his head, pinned with a safety-pin at the front—looking with his serious white face like a lost soldier in one of the vast lost campaigns in any one of our pitiless centuries. Somehow he enjoyed that—being bandaged about the head like he was. He stared at the pig quizzically. Leona stood beside him, with a paper plate in her hand, watching the men walk around her, pat her head—Jeffrey, where was Jeffrey? The men talked loutishly, unconfined. Leona screamed suddenly. Lois came out of the house. "Bradley get over here—come on, get your arse over here."

"I'm not doin nothin."

"I saw you—"

"I ain't doin nothin—"

"You pulled her ear."

"I didn't pull her ear."

"Ya did—ya pulled her Jeesless ear—get the Jesus over here."

"All right then—I'll run away—I'll run away—I will."

"Get over an lissen ta yer mother," George said. "Eh Lois?"

The pig turned, Leona stood with the paper plate and napkin, quizzically watching the basted legs turning, creak upon creak.

Farther along the road the tennis-court with its mesh fence surrounding it. And farther still McDonald's (a $100,000-franchise run by Bobby Simms and backed and financed by Ceril Brown). Tonight too there'd be a party—graduation for the regional high school. The prom, the girls dressed in long gowns, with bouquets, the boys in three-piece suits not unlike the suit he would wear to court. The music from England and America, the local band in glittering outfits, the sound of amplifiers and the peculiar scent of the sanded gymnasium, the metal locker doors smelling faintly of sweat, with the wooden chairs placed against them. The outdated staging and props for *Riders to the Sea*.

And then, after, they would come out. Changing into street-clothes they would go to various parties in various camps and cottages, upon the shore the girls and boys would sit, in absolute pent-up freedom, or what for a time must be considered freedom, staring at the water, at the treeline in the distance. There to drink and dance and rage about an open fire, the passing of joints and liquor—the sand-gnats circling.

Now only the cement steps of Alewood's store remained, seven steps into nothing. There was still rubble here and there, a pipe sticking up out of the rubble, and the lights from McDonald's shone upon it. Wild yellow grasses, as sharp as primitive spears, grew up about it; in the summer it had the smell of piss. "Anyone caught lurking or loitering here will be prosecuted." How that sign read. From that day to this—or the day Packet Terri was fed chocolate-covered Exlax by a man who thought it was a joke to see the child gobble them up. "I told him—I told him," Elizabeth Ripley Terri said. "Makin a pig a himself—I told him—huh—get himself in trouble."

The Real Thing disco lights went on with a final permanent flash. In the other room he heard Donnie coughing. Donnie would take an orange and cut it in two with his jack-knife and set it on the table before him. Throughout the night he'd suck on it. Before he went to bed he'd have a glass of porter—which was Moosehead premium ale. Lester kept combing his hair with fingers that were thicker than most men's thumbs. His wrists seemed to vibrate. The roadway had the soft closeness of before a storm—

They went to war, and George fought bravely. There was a town, and because of the communiqué they were ambushed. Boys in uniforms, something peculiarly Canadian about them, fell startled at their wounds, stood up once before they died. "Kanada," the German prisoner said. "Ferry bad—Kanada—" He'd a turned-up nose and one side of his face was covered with dust. You could see his Adam's apple under his helmet-strap when he swallowed. He complained of a cinder in his eye, and George kept dropping water into it and moving the eye-sac with his fingers, probing it, looking into it and shaking his head.

The van now was parked across the road and he could see Dale yawning, glancing toward the house.

"What am I Donald?"

"What?"

"What did I tell you yesterday that I was?"

Donald lowered his eyes, became sheepish, a bubble of spit at the corner of his lip. Oh the people teased him. He'd a great white cat and they called it Charlie. And Charlie was always out on the roadway mating. It also sat on the rock at times. It swam the river too, which showed that not only was it an intelligent cat but one with its own particularly fearless nature. Anyway somebody got hold of the cat and killed it, and attached it to the clothesline that stretched from the back porch to a pole in the centre of the back lawn. And when Donald was bringing in the sheets he brought the dead cat in with them. Somebody must have gotten a laugh over it. And then after Lester had taken and thrown the thing in the dump, Bobby Simms told Donnie that all cats should be buried with a cross or they wouldn't get into heaven. Then Lester got another cat for him, and Donnie called it Charlie and showed the little female to everyone and kept it under his coat when he went out for his bottles. And sometimes Lester'd get angry and say, "You're no son of mine," and Donnie would puff on his pipe and refuse to eat his supper. So there you go.

"What did I tell you—eh?"

"I—I don't remember."

"When I spoke ta Beaverbrook what did he tell me—eh?"

"I don't remember—I'm thinking," Donnie said.

"Jesus Christ man—love to see me in jail—wouldn't they love it?"

"I don't know Lesser—"

"Sure they would."

"Of course they would," Donnie said smiling. "Yes surely—sure they would."

"I'd love to see them try."

"I would too."

"Jesus Christ," Lester said, sticking his pipe in his mouth. Donnie put his pipe in his mouth.

"Wanta light Lester?"

"No."

"Oh I though ya might—I mean excuse me, wanta smoke yer pipe—now that it's in yer mouth?"

"Well I don't."

"I—I see."

"No you don't see nothin—nothin at all is what you don't see. What did I do for the bastards, eh? Who got them their tennis-court eh?" He was trembling.

"You did Lesser.."

"Of course I did. What did Ceril Brown ever do for them? Who got them their skating-rink—is that a crime?" he yelled.

"What?"

"Jesus Christ," he said, suddenly smiling.

Lester scratched his mouth. Donnie scratched his ear. Smoke furled giddily, the tick of the clock.

Donnie, making a squelching sound trying to get the last bit of pulp from his first half of orange, reclined in the lazy-boy chair in his sock feet, his toes impressed. His tobacco and pipe sat on the table beside him. Three young women, talking over their love-affairs on television. The audience laughed. Donnie chuckled.

Lester, from this room which had a large bay window, stared at the van. He stabbed at his pipe, filled the bowl half full, and lighted it—inhaling strongly, the smoke furled here and there. On TV a girl was explaining to a woman that her father was going through a crisis, his "change of life"—his "menopause," the girl said in exasperation. The audience laughed. The little actress, conscious of her grown-up joke, smiled slightly. The camera faded back. Lester stared at the van. Was it or was it not a tiger imprinted upon the door? He could see Dale's feet—his legs.

Ceril Brown now wore felt sweaters. He'd given up his first wife and had been seen about the village with Rhonda, both dressed in fur in the winter, sweat-pants in the summer when they jogged or bicycled—

The cottagers were already moving in. The camps, the cottages with names like the Ponderosa, Green Acres, Little House on the Prairie, the names inscribed on huge rocks at the front of those shadowed, pebbled driveways. Leading down to the cedar cottage, with bar, television and swimming-pool. The girls walked in white tennis-shorts onto the court, the balls thwacked across the net. Bradley and Jeffrey would begin selling things to them, Kool-Aid and blueberries and half-pound trout that they jigged out of the pools. They'd go to the men/women sitting in the shade, with the smell of wind, the scudding gusts across the fresh-water swimming pools. The smell of suntan lotion, of lemon and ointment. The smell of human waste in the river. *Torso* was the name of the book Dale was reading now, a splotch of egg on the cover—the cover showing the hillside at Hamilton where the murder took place.

So he'd gone into his camp, stared at the out-of-date posters on the walls of young girls on ponies, advertisements for bread and milk and cheese, the wholesome ten-year-old Caucasian female on a pony with a golden mane, dressed in a cow-girl's outfit she sat, assuming perhaps that she was a cow-girl, the pony with its embroidered bridle, the grass and field pocked with flowers so colourful it made you lonely—out of date now. The dark river spined with rocks glowed in the evening. Not once did he cast his fly-rod or even look at his collection of flies.

So he'd gone back to Malcolm Bryan, in an office that reminded one of a clinic, with large plants looking like plastic, and two or three paintings. Neither Old Simon nor Ramsey Taylor would take a cent from him, even when Taylor was fired from his job as warden. He'd lay money down, and Taylor would shove it aside. He'd given Old Simon money. Old Simon would hand it back to him. He'd lay the money down again. Write a cheque, the bastards would tear it up. What was wrong with his money anyway? He'd asked Donnie, "What's wrong with my money?" "Nothin." "Then why won't they take it?"

Yet Bobby Simms coming over, dressed in his Knights of Columbus uniform, with the plumed hat, with the plumed hat on his head, his hands sporting three rings each—and now he was secretary for the Knights of Columbus and wore a sabre and a uniform, and plumes on his hat. A 57-year-old man wearing plumes on his hat and talking about the Knights of Columbus so he could get an expense-paid trip to New Orleans or London, England—coming over then, and asking Lester why he'd helped Clarence Simms buy a car. "But you won't help me buy a car—will you— you'll help Clarence. We're all relations you know—I suppose you didn't know we're all relations?"

"No you fucker, I wouldn't help you buy a car—if I had the biggest car dealership east of Windsor, Ontario you wouldn't see me giving you a spark-plug—"

But Bobby went back to Clarence, and asked Clarence to intercede for him, and tormented Clarence for two weeks to intercede for him. Which infuriated Lester but made him do the strangest thing ever. He took Bobby Simms into town, Bobby Simms and his daughter Sandra, and he took them to a car dealership—and instead of buying him a medium-sized car with a few luxuries he couldn't help feeling positively justified in buying him the biggest car he could find. The one they displayed in the picture window—the Lincoln Continental, with *everything*. And he kept saying to Bobby Simms, "This here rig has everything—everythin—" and Bobby shrugged when he looked at it, and then nodded, and Sandra with a wave of her head turned in another direction.

"Clarence said I could get a car, he did, Clarence did."

"Of course he did—of course," Lester said.

Bobby nodded his head as if he were the angriest son of a bitch on two legs, and when he sat behind the wheel he looked as if he'd been born there.

"Can I take it home right now?"

"Well," the dealer said, "it should all be checked over."

"But I want to drive it home," Bobby said. "Sandra came with me so we could drive it home—"

"Sure, sure," Lester said. "Drive it home now—take your wife there, lovely woman, out tonight, drive it home—drive it all around—over hill over dale (heh heh) over hill over dale, as they say—eh?"

The clock downstairs struck once. It was quarter after nine. Along the street a boy in a baseball uniform red and green, the same colour as his house. The hat lay lightly upon his head, his tousled black hair—he had a wide pudgy face. He strode along, saw the van and went over to Dale. He leaned against the van and talked, nodding.

The boy in the baseball uniform kept slapping the flies away with his arm, Dale, still leaning back with his sneakers sticking out of the opened doors, passed over a joint. And then a bottle of beer. So the night would begin.

On television now there was an advertisement for *Fantasy Island* which Donnie always watched because he liked the way Tattoo talked. There was a slight rumbling again. His whole chest pained suddenly, as if he had indigestion. Once, a month ago, when he urinated he'd passed out. He still remembered his hand groping to clutch the curtain-rod, Donnie running in, picking him up and crying.

He looked at Donnie. Donnie laughed and picked up the second half of his orange, and he always wore an orange moustache after that, and had a seed or two on his shirt. God—why did they do that? Why did Denby Ripley invite him in to watch the faces of men and women, their eyes showing the corrupt use of our social intelligence. It was Packet who went over after Jeffrey had been let in for the price of two joints, and picked up the projector and threw it at the screen, cut the films to bits with his knife, while Denby Ripley stood there watching him. Packet not saying a word. Packet who broke into the principal's office and then left school, to follow his mother about the Maritimes—one deadened conservative *bloodless* city after another.

"Holy oh Jesus fuckhole," the girl said, leaning against the van.

He turned, Donnie looked around at him quickly. He smiled slightly, with his lips pressed together.

"What's wrong Lester—are, excuse me, those young fellas paa-aintin our wall or something—"

"No no," Lester said. For a second, almost two seconds, he wanted to talk to his son—tell him something.

"Watch where ya squish that orange," he said. "If yer Uncle Ramsey hadda seen ya leavin those orange peels around—" His head trembled. He left the room.

He took the bottle of Tanqueray with him out to the porch. He opened the screen-door quietly and sat in the chair on the right. The moon lingered faintly against the roof of his warehouse. There was an old broken flower-pot oddly shaped, where no plant had been for years. The pig was black above the red pit. The people moved to and fro. After Lois won the money on the Atlantic Loto draw, she bought a microwave oven and a new car. George began having champagne breakfasts. He had about eleven champagne breakfasts, and the worst row in the country sat on his doorsteps in the morning and drank champagne. Lois would drive back and forth in her new car, with Leona, Brad and Jeffrey. The girl (Georgie's girl) invited her parents up for a champagne breakfast.

So you sit on one side of the river and stare at the other. Lester Murphy did that. Lois came and went (and Packet who would not take money from her, but from working up north managed to save enough to buy the land behind his house, buy his ploughs and a second-hand tractor). Packet now and then dropped over to see why his father was celebrating. His father would go out to him, stumbling along. "Packet," he'd yell, "Packet—what's wrong—what's wrong Packet?" Then he'd look around and smile. He'd point over to Lester Murphy's and laugh. The men with him would laugh. Then one day they all got their picture taken with Lois' new camera. "I don't know how this fuckin thing works," she said, and one of the men said he had one just like it and tried to help her. Then she got angry with him and George told him he'd kick him out of the yard. One day the girl got angry with all of them, and packed her suitcase; she came out of the house screaming and Lois crying coaxed her back inside.

In the spring the sound of men cutting. In the summer there'd be the smell of the spray-planes, the distant sound of cutting—

There was the faint smell of pig. Leona stood with paper plate and napkin. Bradley, like some lost soldier, about a bivouac. There was the sputtering of smoke. He would drink again, and then walk to Simms' to get his hair cut. He trembled slightly. And Jeffrey—where was Jeffrey?

Bad girl—talkin bout bad bad girl
You see them on the street—

Outside now they'd set up a floodlight. Four men stood at various distances from one another, but all in close proximity to Lois. Lois with her hair in small curlers, with a see-through pale blue blouse and her breasts uplifted, the sad beauty of her small beer paunch, her hips lilting in some profound woman accomplishment. The car up on blocks was the one Jeffrey had sneaked the keys to, and had rammed it into the side of the house, and then run away for two days. When he came back, Lois cuffed

167

him across the back of the head. "You red-headed little Jeesler," she said. But then she bought him a moped—a whiny gaseous little mechanism that sputtered at all hours of the day and night.

Mad Dash came the television advertisement: *two couples compete for cash and prizes as host Pierre Lalonde presides over the fun.*

He took a sip of Tanqueray. The floodlight glowed over the yard, across the water, a thousand malicious bugs scavenged. George rubbed his arms. The pig with its stern grinning face turned over twice. The evening was pale, you could see Ursa Major. In the very shadows the dying sunlight had struck a gauze pattern against the thick leaves of wild rhubarb with their curious white veins.

(So you must remember how they came up out of it: Elizabeth Ripley Terri with her brood, Packet, Lois, Little Simon—in the evenings at eight o'clock, when she sat behind the house, the country gone savage—with the sound of a thousand squabbles, unused materials, wasted lands, the flapping of decomposing cloth in the fuming dump, where the Indians threw their unsaleable salmon, female salmon with dying roe, with batteries, acid-corroded, and commodities that were bought broken and thrown away, the stench of metal. It was then, in the evenings, after fumbling about the house, that you drove out to visit her. In the evenings, you lay about on the bed—seeing George's suit in the closet, his socks, shoes (the sock hanging out of the left shoe) lying there.

One of the men had a cleaver. They had lifted the pig off the splayed birches and carried it to the waiting picnic table.

Volare, Volare—woa oh woa woa, came the television. The screen-door smelled of night now. There was a sense of night about him, like an aura. The distant cottages, Bryan's doberman barked, the fawn-coloured bitch with the pure-breed papers they wanted to mate with a quality sire. High-strung, it barked in its wire-mesh kennel; down farther came the answer from the Reserve dogs who lay about the porches of the Indian houses—the fruitless adventures of new houses on shale foundations, new television stations playing, new cars and stereos boughten. He could hear crickets in the grass. The Indians walked the roadway, yes—and during that time he was visiting Elizabeth, the Ginnish man with the tattoo on his hand of a snake around the cross of Jesus, with "Born to lose" written just above his knuckle, and looking closely you saw Jesus winking, and Kenneth Ward searched the road for George Terri (who, knowing George overseas, probably could have killed the both of them). Then too they took their out-of-season game to Ceril Brown who ushered them into the junkyard, with used tires and cars on blocks, in through the back way—and there paid them, and then sold the meat off again to another buyer for 150% profit. (You might envy a man like that—who then drove a two-tone Pontiac with copies of the *North Shore Leader* on the floor as mud-catchers—and sometimes took the Terri children for drives and bought them ice cream so they all loved him, saying that he could live anywhere but telling the children that any man with *connections* usually lived in a hotel—with room-service; so they loved him even more, perhaps thinking of a Clark Gable movie.)

Mad Dash: two couples compete for cash and prizes as host Pierre Lalonde presides over the fun.

Half of the pig loin was scorched. George said something about this to his girl, his girl came back with a retort. Bradley began to dance around with his finger over the mouth of a Coke bottle, and suddenly he let it go and began spraying everyone. "Jesus Christ," one of the men said. "Lois, you teach yer kid some manners."

"What are you sayin bout Bradley?"

"Nothin."

"What?"

"Nothin."

"You keep yer trap shut about Bradley—"

"He just ruint my new sweater—"

"He did not."

"I didn't," Bradley said.

"You shut yer mouth ya little maniac," Lois said.

("K-anada—ferry ferry bad," the German soldier said, and the bastard started running—why in God's name did he run? George had been trying to get the cinder out of his eye. There were other Germans there—so why did he run—and down main street. The Germans shouting at him, the Maritimers shouting at him—he running, with his legs spread far apart, as if each foot wanted to go in an opposite direction, his torso not moving at all. And then George shot him, through the pelvic girdle. And then a supremely stupid expression on all their faces. The Germans screaming at George, George screaming at the Germans. An upturned nose, and an exasperated look on his face when George couldn't get the cinder out of his eye—)

"Har har," George said, grabbing one of the men by the hair and shaking him. "This is the very choicest pig—I think it's my night ta howl. Hey, thanks Lois."

"Don't haveta thank me," Lois said.

"Thanks Lois though," George said.

"Let go a me Jesus hair," the man said.

They were all except Leona standing about the picnic table—Leona being seated upon the steps with her paper plate and napkin tucked into her dress, sitting quite ladylike, with perhaps half a pound of pig on her plate, her hair tied in bows, and a glass of Coca-Cola beside her. The night moved him into thinking of the quiet flowers, the lawns and backyards of those houses (in town) where families of four and five generations lived, the shop-keepers, merchants, businessmen—the men who with Alewood once had lumbering contracts—their sons and daughters and the daughters and sons of those now sitting out on their porches, in their yards the sound of lawn-mowers silenced at last, the rippling of the sprinklers, the quiet shaded avenues, and the men and women, 18 to 24 home from university, who would work for the summer at the mills or the mines or play golf or tennis no better than fairly.

When he came back home one night Ramsey Taylor was there. They sat outside. He said, "I been seeing a woman there—ya know, Elizabeth Terri there, everyone knows—so I figure you know," and then suddenly he smiled.

Ramsey didn't look at him, but Lester could not stop smiling—the lips pressed tightly together. He tapped his feet.

They sat on the lawn-chairs.

"I suppose there but she's married—there," Ramsey said at last.

"Oh yes so she is (heh heh)," he said. Ramsey sat in the chair beside him, fidgeting and looking guilty. "So she is," he said happily. He snuffed and spat, all things he did when he was with men. He wore no socks, only slippers, and his ankle-bones stuck out with white hairs on them.

"Anyway—everyone knows—Georgie probably knows himself—probably," he said, angrily. Why was he so angry? Why suddenly did he want to hit someone?

Ramsey said nothing. He looked across the water, scratching his knuckles. The span looked black and lonely in the twilight and might have been any one of a thousand bridges, or hundred thousand, and you might link all those bridges forever—and across the way Simon Terri and his wife were doing one more row of shingles on their barn. Merium could carry fifty pounds of shingles in each hand and work all day without chalk-line and marker. He watched them for a while working. "I'll get us another drink," he said standing quickly. Ramsey looked at him, seeming apologetic. Lester laughed and felt empty. Why in hell did he laugh? The whore of night. The cars on the highway with their plumes of exhaust. Georgie's Hamburger Palace. Georgie's and Elizabeth's house smelled of disinfectant, and when he went to the flush one night he smelled its pungent masking scent. On the bathroom shelf was an illustrated manual on sex. He stared at its cover blankly and at Georgie's socks over the towel-rack, dripping a bit of red dye against the bathroom tile. Behind the illustrated manual on sex, in the shelf's upper nook was a box of prophylactics, the plastic curtains fumbled in the wind. Beneath the rack was a pair of yellow panties that he'd stepped on accidentally. Too, that night she asked him for a loan so she could go to Montreal to see Frank Sinatra—

George had fenced his place off now, had put up "No Trespassing" signs on the lane by the secondary road, had ripped up Old Simon's pine markers, and had yarded the (maybe) hundred cords of wood that signified Simon and Merium Terri's property, had sold the outside three acres to the mines, who were going to use it to build a camp for their executive who flew in twice a year from New York. He'd taken the money from the cords of wood and from the sale of property and had bought himself various things. And right upon this came Lois' winning ticket. Lester was woken one morning—the morning he was formally charged with fraud —by shotgun fire. Looking out the bathroom window he saw George, firing a twelve-gauge pump-action shotgun, standing in his long underwear, dirt over his hands and face, yelling.

Now George walked about his yard, looked across the river to Lester's, shook his head as if he was sadly displeased about something, and wanted to show, not Lester (the arsonist) that he was sadly displeased, but Jesus Christ, the Virgin Mary and God himself, who were hanging around just above the chimney. After he shook his head he'd go back inside. Later he'd come out with a plate filled with pancakes and eat them at the picnic table, with a bottle of champagne.

Then he'd pull out a book from his back pocket, wipe his face off and open it. The book, Zane Grey or Louis L'Amour—he always had one, and he'd begin to read and sip on his bottle. Now and then as he turned the page he'd look across the river, or down into the hollow—or farther across to the gutted apartment building, the sunken-in barn, where Simon Terri and Daniel Ward had scraped the moosehide down for Randolf Alewood—

The Indian woman who fixed appliances would be getting a drive along the road by her son. The early-morning landscape, even with the dust blowing up, or the smell of slack water. Then his girl would come out—take his plate away, the day begin.

The men would arrive. Each of them would have something to tell

171

him. They'd laugh and talk. George, if he wanted to drink that day, would be filling their glasses. Some glasses he'd fill and some he wouldn't. The men's glasses he didn't fill would pretend they weren't being snubbed and didn't want a drink anyway. The men whose glasses he did fill wouldn't notice this discrepancy. Then George would begin to tell a story. He'd say:

"Remember Larry—when you and I got that bloody barn ta burn—with just one match—one match eh?" Larry would sip his champagne.

"That wasn't Larry—that was me," one of the men would say, a man who didn't have his glass filled.

George would look at him—stare right through him. The man would look away and shrug.

"Remember that Larry?" George would say.

"Well," Larry would say.

"Remember—we both spent two months in jail."

"Lookit," the man would say. "It was me who spent the two goddamn months in jail with ya Georgie—I member every goddamn meal I had."

George would shake his head.

"Member that Larry?" he'd say.

"Well—I mean—"

"Who lit the match Larry—me or you?"

"I think it was you, wasn't it George?"

"Georgie—I lit the match," the man would say.

"Now there's where yer wrong," Larry would say, "cause Georgie lit the match."

Then George would offer all of them a drink, except that man. Then they'd all tell stories, about this and that. Once or twice the man would agree with them to show he was there also. Then George would wave them all inside and say, "C'mon boys—see ya later Butch."

"Ya, see ya later Butch."

Butch would watch them going inside. "Catch ya later, Butch," Larry would say.

The next day George would say, "Butch I knew it was you all along who lit that fuckin match—but on my order—"

"Well it was yer order—but I lit the match."

"A course ya did—but I wanted ta prove somethin right there and then —yesterday eh—I wanted ta prove how much a liar that bastard Larry is, an how ya can't trust him—"

"I knew that."

"So the next time he comes here I'm kickin him outta my yard."

"Well."

"The next thing ya know he'll be tryin to steal my money."

Hank Williams dream is Canada's dream, came the advertisement on the television faintly down the stairs and through the purple screen.

That night he brought Ramsey out another drink; he laughed and slapped Ramsey's leg. Ramsey sat there, staring at Simon Terri's orange kitchen light, in the kitchen Merium walking back and forth, their old mongrel lying outside. Lester kept talking on and on, about his conversation with the Minister of Education—the Minister saying it was only a matter of time before the regional high school would be closed, the children bussed into town. "Over my dead body," Lester kept saying. Ramsey, sipping on his drink, kept nodding.

"Yes over my dead body," Lester said, spitting and looking about. He covered his mouth and cleared his throat. There was a spot of yellowish phlegm. He looked at Ramsey Taylor. Ramsey looked away embarrassed. "Understand Ramsey?" "Oh—yes yes yes."

The dark windows of the regional high school were still in his mind. The children for 30 years coming and going from the building, with its oblique structure, its gravelled front yard—all those faces—degrees from St. Thomas and St. Francis Xavier, with men and women who used the strap frequently, kept the procedure of learning that they had been taught going—he remembered too the Minister of Education, a man with a swarthy complexion, who had collar marks along his rashed throat, somehow a smell of dead skin, chuckling. Teachers took summer courses to get more credits, more money. They sitting in the university, classes on sociology, anthropology, or European history, complaining to the professor of their study load—becoming students again, cribbing notes.

"It's very important to me Ramsey—it's important," he said, clinking his ice, and yawning—both deliberately.

"I can see there," Ramsey said. "I can see there ya—you always do right by the village here—" Ramsey stared at Lester's slippers, his pointed ankle-bones. Lester snickered, grabbed Ramsey by the elbow. "We'll get those bastards—we'll get them all," he said.

They were all except Leona standing about the picnic table. He stared at the little girl, had been for some time without his eyes focused. The light they had set up gave the surrounding yard a strange whiteness. George had a piece of blackened pork in his hand. Lester poured a gin at the same moment George was pouring a drink. Lois had taken some of her money

—had set up a small craft shop in the new mall—selling watches and trinkets, and disco shirts and medallions that showed the signs of the zodiac—she had rented floor space there. But within a month she had a 50%-off sale and then a "down-to-earth" 50%-off sale and then a going-out-of-business sale.

He himself had bought $5 worth of incense, cradled in a small basket. There was something about the men who hung around George and her now, like nattering inoffensive old maids who sat about in a distant cousin's household to cause intrigue. All of them broke into song. Lois sat down beside Georgie's girl who all month had been looking pregnant, and suddenly began stroking her hair. Off in the distance there was a rumbling again. He stood, finished his drink and turned away.

"Leona—you get in that house and change yer dress, yer spillin goddamn pop all over it—go on—get in yer room and change—now—go on, now—"

"Lissen ta yer mother," one of the men said. "Eh Lois?"

So you remember how they came up, from one year to the next—Packet, Lois and Little Simon. "What's wong Packet—what's wong?" As if, at the moment she stood in Georgie's Hamburger Palace, a place that smelled of fried food, in Packet's soiled T-shirt, her bared legs, husky and pink, the smell of oil, as if—if Packet would tell her what was wrong, explain it to her she'd dance, laugh and clap her hands together—never again to worry. To collect her winter-carnival pins and her exhibition and circus stuffed toys from that time on throughout her history. Lois in her jarring beauty, who even at fourteen gave the men sly winks that weakened them as they sat in the apartment building and scratched their angry arms.

Disco, disco duck came the song, a smell of rain in the wind that had just blown up while he walked. He'd changed into his suit, a London fog coat, his soft leather shoes with air-holes. You could see the stars beyond the brooding, gathering clouds from the northeast. He walked on—an old man passed the double track, where the ore-cars ran out to town, to where those girdled ships sat in slack oily water—the Russians, Spanish and German sailors, the stevedores in the morning, with ships bearing Greek or German registration. The myriad lights winking from the ships, the shore lights answering, the sound of whining booms, and the mill whistles at seven o'clock, their boilers washed down with sulphuric acid. He walked slowly along the road, passed his fifteen-tier brick wall. There was a little moss in the cracking mortar. Across the road, up the hill, the wind made a penitent sound through the windows of the gutted building, its tarpaper flattened. He could hear the van idling somewhere in the darkness behind him, laughter. Here he walked, here now was the hollow, and here too, cut out of the broad soil, just beyond Alewood's old house, sat the tennis-court, enclosed in a fence, its net stiffened.

Of course now, Packet looked amazingly, with his long sloping shoulders, his powerful arms, like Merlin Terri—there was a picture of Merlin Terri, standing beside Alewood, the four draught-horses with their manes falling about their large intelligent eyes. Alewood in a long tweed coat, with half-cloak and a white furious-looking beard. Merlin Terri posed staunchly, almost religiously for the picture (circa 1889). Down farther, at a point where they used to hold tent meetings, there were dozens of late-model, fashionable cars and vans sitting in the parking-lot of the new Glad Tidings Tabernacle. Two ministers ran things there, brought in guest speakers. *How everyone can have a wholesome life with a good income. How to be happy*—The oblong spire of the tabernacle rose up, the windows looked guarded. From there too at a reasonable distance you could hear guitars and singing. The ministers with their wives, with pleasant brooches pinned on their bosoms, had a talk-show every Thursday and Sunday on the local TV station entitled *Exploring Reality*, where they compared today's world with the Book of Revelations. The late-model vans and cars sat there, two-tone and rust-proofed against the north-of-the-world extremities. Inside with electronic equipment, with guitars, bass and rhythm—the tallest minister, a man who broke away from the Pentecostals and with his wife and daughter first drove the roadways, stopping at no fixed point to preach, the girl with large bones, thin, his wife with an absolutely timid expression; they had a cake with pink icing and a jug of Kool-Ade that they steadfastly handed out to the faithful.

Later he'd heard that the man, setting up his travelling church in the wrong area, was beaten almost senseless by Russell Peterson—trying to crawl away. Russell laughing—it was said the minister tried to play possum, his wife's face kept twitching—

When Daniel Ward was drunk he fell down, in front of the school. His hat blew away. The children tried to wake him up, they nudged him with their boots, and then began kicking him, and when he opened his eyes he had dead eyes—and then Ramsey Taylor drove him home.

"They're pretty tricky, those goddamn clutches and brakes an everythin else," Little Simon said, the night he drove his mother's boyfriend's car into a wall. He was seven.

Little Simon said: "Ya know—we done a awful thing—but it's Packet who had the bad dreams about er," Little Simon said.

"About what?" Lois asked.

"Well we useta tease Billy Masey all the time—but he's deader than a nit now—ya know, about his mother and father," Little Simon said. *"But Packet, he's the one that found Billy Masey dead—ya understand?"*

"Yes."

"An we useta do all sorts a stuff ta him—take off his clothes in the winter an stuff, an tell him ta go call his mother a quiff and we'd give him a quarter—and out he'd come runnin with his father behind him givin him a cuff across the side of the head—an then we'd pelt his father from the bushes with rocks and he'd yell, 'Okay I'm running away—I'm leavin er, I didn't *do nothin—I'm getting outta here.' Packet has some dreams about er."*

"Do you have dreams about that?" Lois asked.

"Not very likely," Little Simon said. And then he said, "Oh I've the odd bad dream but nothin like Pack—I saw him grabbin holt a his head."

"Ya always tease people," she said.

"I don't tease people," he said.

"Ya goddamn well do—all the time—"

"Am fuckin not."

"You and Denby Ripley are always teasin Calvin Simms."

"Am not."

"Tied him to his seat an let go with firecrackers—whipped him with branches, took him out on the raft when he couldn't swim—and threw him in."

"That was jus kiddin," Little Simon said. *He was ten years old.*

He walked by the tennis-court. It was here Tom Proud carried his sister Emma Jane Ward. She wearing white woman's clothes and hat and boots and powdering her face with white powder. Carrying with her her cloth purse. She got Alewood to buy her a cedar chest. And Alewood went to town to visit the mill—the mill at a place where the Kentucky Fried Chicken was now, with its bright bucket revolving, the sulphurous skyline, amazing, the jackhammer going, the litter billowing in the wind across the naked lot.

Now and then a firefly glimmered in the field—the field where Lois and Denby Ripley pressed their bodies together, that fall afternoon, cold and cloudy. And coming up to them, almost tripping over them as they lay in the rigid earth, came Little Simon, who had skipped school and was making his way back home. They jumped up startled. Little Simon jumped back startled. Then Denby grabbed onto him, began swinging him around, the air a tumult of angry winterish clouds, the grass grey and

176

dead, the night descending, and in the forest the smell of powder, of shot.

"Jesus Christ get a holt of yerself Denby," Little Simon said, as he always said, as he said to Calvin Simms time and again, after he'd teased him to distraction—when at Calvin Simms' wedding he went into the church and kept putting a stocking-cap on Clarence's head, and pulling it off quickly so that his hair stuck up electrically—and then, as soon as Clarence turned around again, on would go the cap and off it would come. Until Clarence finally said, "Are you crazy are somethin boy?" and pushed him a little. Then Little Simon grabbed him and began to wrestle with him out in the aisle. Clarence, with a desperate look on his face kept trying to protect his carnation. And later at the reception Little Simon took a garden hose and watered all the guests. "I—I I I was gonna kill him," Calvin said. The bride was reduced to tears. "For Jesus sake," Lois yelling, "have some manners Little Simon—it's their *very special* day." (I never met a man like it, Denby Ripley said, who could be sober, and be barred from a tavern he was never inta before in his life, without orderin a drink.)

"Jesus Christ, get a holt a yerself Denby Ripley," Little Simon said, as he was swung around. "I come dizzy awful easy," as the sky was under him, with snow clouds. Lois trying to adjust her bloomers, her red slacks.

"Guess what happened today," Denby said. "Guess what happened there today—now," Denby said. Lois looked at him. His whole body was trembling, as it had trembled strangely upon her, the smell of heat and moisture. They'd pressed their bodies together—they'd wrestled. Always they would wrestle in the trailer. They would wrestle on the couch and roll onto the floor, just wrestling. Until Little Simon said, "Get outta the trailer—there Lois if ya can't get along and are forever attackin Denby Ripley." But today they'd come into the field, and it was the sad smell of November. They lay down together, just wrestling.

"Guess what happened there today," Denby said. (The sounds of frozen earth, the Indians walking the roadway from time to time laughing, carrying their beer bottles to Ceril Brown's, the dark brown bottles like the earth itself, and in the houses the smell of meat, a jar of milk and a loaf of bread caught under the 60-watt kitchen lightbulbs at five o'clock.)

"What—" Little Simon said. "What what—"

Lois looked at Denby Ripley and tried to fix her bloomers. It was awful wearing bloomers—a sense of shame overpowered her because he'd touched these bloomers with his hand.

"They killed President Kennedy," he shouted. And turning toward the road he kept shouting, "They killed President Kennedy—he did a lot fer

Canada too—don't you think he didn't—he did a lot," suddenly becoming angry—

When they left Denby she remembered his breath and the feel of his hand. Her underwear was bunched up and so it wasn't comfortable. She walked on over the field to the roaway, with Little Simon behind her. She thought of the man looking at her through the window of the apartment, with the plastic curtains and the light against him, in the lingering twilight. She thought of Elizabeth Ripley Terri and her boyfriend, Bennie, how her mother lay in her girdle on the bed in the morning, with her ear-rings still on, and her slip in the corner, the used pads stark against the dresser. Listening in the evenings, with her dark nipples pressed against her slip, to Perry Como: "I love Perry Como."

"Tell me this now," Little Simon said. "I got somethin I wanta ask ya." She turned around.

"What," she said. Her hair smelled of ice, and wood-smoke and the river. The impossible love/violence of the river flowed in her veins.

"Well tell me this," Little Simon said, stooping suddenly to take a rock out of his shoe, "who's this President Kennedy?"

A child passed him, and farther along where the dust smelled like mortar a boy perhaps fourteen with something under his shirt wrapped in a thin brown paper bag—hidden, a book of some notoriety from Ceril Brown's bookshop. A taste of cinder and ash like a compost heap came to him, where eggshells, tea-bags and the multifistulous entrails of chickens lay in cold and hardened stove deposits. The boy passed him; the book, hymen moved by imaginary kisses—the boy with rubber-soled shoes and thin blue socks passing him, skittering left and right, and slouching—not unlike a criminal who was escaping for one evening.

The gong of the Glad Tiding Tabernacle bell.

There were too, many memories of lights in offices. The youngster looked at him as he passed, held to the far side of the road, twisted his hand farther about the book. Lester nodded at him. The boy seemed startled at this. His rubber shoes thick and black (and somehow even physically demeaning to the boy). Or was Lester at this moment thinking of Little Simon? Little Simon knew how to skitter left and right and slouch not unlike a criminal. Mr. Walsh who'd lost his legs to gangrene in the first war and who ended his life selling gumdrops to youngsters in a candy store, loved to have Little Simon push him along in his wheelchair:

"All ashore that's goin ashore," Little Simon would yell and he'd start pumping his legs, and then: "Better grab hold of yer toes there Mr.

Walsh—we're ready ta move—"

"Step aside step aside—Little Simon's comin through," Walsh would yell. At the end of the day, Little Simon would be exhausted, his teeth quite black from gumdrops. It is not inconceivable to think that Father Barry (with the bland health and absolute incompetence of a man who would wash himself down at five in the morning with a cold hose—and rouse the cub-scouts out of their sleeping-bags to witness this) hated Little Simon for that reason. "Did I hurt you?" Father Barry would say that year at cub camp to him. "You were standing in my way—"

"Well that's the game ain't it?"

"Pardon?"

"The opposition is supposed to stand in yer way—" Little Simon looking up at him.

There were enough alleyways for Little Simon to slouch like a criminal, when the police were after him in the nineteen-sixties—or worse, perhaps there weren't enough—yet too—

Of Packet, Lois and Little Simon.

Or last April when people were watching Clarence Simms in front of the liquor store, and Clarence was singing for them, they were all laughing. Clarence singing:

Jimmy crack corn and I don't care
Jimmy crack corn and I don't care—
For my master's gone away

and the man with him said, "Stop singing or we won't get any money."

"Jimmy crack corn and I don't care," Clarence sang, screeched, stamping his feet, singing, "Because my master's gone away," and the man with him said:

"Yer ruinin it—we'll get no money—yer ruinin it."

"Gone fishin," Clarence yelled.

"Stop it—"

"Gone fishin—mackerel—mackerel," Clarence yelled, screeched.

And Lester put a $10 bill in his hand. Clarence stood in the slush by the liquor store. He looked at Lester—their eyes met, Lester smiled. Clarence spat away the cold sore's opening, put the money in his pocket.

"I thought ya ruint it—shoutin mackerel—" the man whispered, his lips already gone sugary. "I was sure ya were gonna ruin it shoutin mackerel." The man now seemed to want to touch Clarence, touch him and pat him. Lester looked away.

But when he came back that April day—hadn't Packet arrived from out west, and wasn't Elizabeth Ripley Terri wearing the new necklace, the ear-rings Lois had bought her, for her trip back to Charlottetown?

"Mummy wait—I wanta take yer picture—"

"My picture—really Lois—"

"Just one—with your new necklace—"

"I'm not much at having my picture—here I'll hold Mincy too—all right Lois—" The dog with the manicured furballs yapped at everyone—

"Mincy," Elizabeth said, "stop it—whatever am I going to do? Stopit."

"Atlantic Salmon Centre of the World."

"Once I had a secret love," Elizabeth sang, after the meeting for concerned parents that night, when Lester Murphy, being a member of the village council, sat at the head table.

"Once I had a secret love," Elizabeth sang.

Let's go to the hop, let's go to the hop.

Bennie would sit in his suit inside the trailer. He'd fight with Elizabeth Ripley Terri over the money they spent going to the exhibition, and sometimes, when he was in a particularly good mood, he'd haul out his teeth at the supper-table and lick them.

"Oh Bennie," Elizabeth would laugh, "really and truly Bennie."

Bennie was 23.

"Well you'll never be quite as pretty as your mother dear—turn around, tch—yer clothes are always so tight on you—Packet, well Packet'll end up in jail or hung the rate he's goin—some day now you'll get your arse in trouble."

When her mother went to town, in those days she was "looking for a job," Lois would come home from school and make Little Simon and her supper.

At supper she and Little Simon ate alone. Simon would look at the clock and then stab at his bologna. She kept looking out the window for the taxi to bring her mother home.

"What'd ya do, fry up yer rubber arse?" Little Simon would say, and then he'd pick up the bologna and do various tricks with it to make her laugh. One night they ran out of oil and didn't know what to do so they got all the blankets out and covered the pipes.

One night Little Simon got into a fight out on the street with an older boy. It was in June. They were playing baseball and the boy had tried to take a lead to third base—thinking the pitcher had the ball, but Little Simon had the ball tucked in his pants. Simon tagged him out.

"I'm safe at second fuckhead," the boy said.

"Ya might have been safe at second fuckhead—but ya aren't safe now."

"Ya were cheatin—hiding the ball."

"Yer cheatin—get off me goddamn bag."

"Can't even play baseball without cheatin."

The boy went to the bag and stood there. Little Simon thought for a moment, stepped back and threw the ball at him, hitting him on the head. Then since the boy was a good twenty pounds heavier than he, he as he said later, "ran ta beat fuck." But the boy caught him on the street, grabbed him by the back of the jacket and hauled him to the ground, into the mud and loose pebbles, the drain off and the silent sweet-smelling ditches. Lois happened to be looking out and when she saw the older bigger boy attacking her brother she became weak. Never before had she seen Little Simon as she saw him then, lying on the ground, his jacket too big for him—as it always would be (as he always, in later years when he could afford them, afford the jackets and shoes and clothes he wanted, would he wear coats too big for him, buoyed up by sweaters to look larger than he was, so would he let his scruffy beard grow to hide his delicate intelligent features)—and one of his shoes, a hand-me-down of Packet's lying just at the corner of the shale ditch in the shadow of the culvert. She watched as the boy beat him with his fists, and as Little Simon put up a valiant hopeless resistance, with his face puffing every time he took a punch—the smoke coming from leaves burning and the sky white. Lois looked at this, saw her brother struggling and for a moment cursed Packet for not being at home. Then swinging the trailer door open she went out, down the short rockway, picking up a rock along the way. She came down with the rock across the boy's head, saw blood gush from the dark wound. The boy yelled, grabbed his head and rolled over. She turned and ran back to the trailer. Slammed the door, went into the broom-closet and hid. Forever would she remember that broom-closet, the enclosed scent of darkness, the smell of polish and brushes and straw, a small cardboard box filled with odd tops of pickle-jars. She sank down in it, and because of its size she wasn't able to move.

Then she heard that the boy's sisters were planning to get her in the girls' washroom at school. Little Simon walked about the trailer for three days, his face still swollen.

He said, "Well I don't know what sounded funnier. I don't know. It was pretty funny when I hit him with the baseball—right on the back of his head—it sorta went pop and the ball bounced too, *pop*, and then the ball bounced off his head—that was pretty good. But when you smucked him with the rock—I never heard a sound like that bafore—" and then he smiled. But they didn't go out of the trailer for a week, unless Packet was with them.

She grew up. Out of that odd arena of time and events, of men and women with their hot-bloodedness and nefarious backbiting. Along the road and waterway, the sounds of Micmac when they crossed to Ceril Brown's junkyard with bottles in the evening, their dogs beside them. The Ripleys, Terris and Simms, the cottagers in the summer. The men working, looking at her from apartment windows.

"It's just terrible—it's absolutely disgusting how those men look at me—leer at me—really and truly—" Elizabeth would say.

She saw her mother putting eye-shadow on, leaving her bathing-suit inside-out in the corner of the bathroom floor.

"Less go up ta Murphy's and spook the drawers off the retard," Little Simon would say.

Sometimes a man would drive into the yard, and Elizabeth would lean against the car and laugh. Little Simon would stand behind her scratching his nose. The man would look at Little Simon and then look back at Elizabeth Ripley Terri. The man would be dressed in a blue suit and a narrow brown tie with a tie-clip that glittered. The car radiator would tick and you'd smell it, and you'd smell the brown lug of hornets that mashed against the grille. The fish-tailing cars on the highway.

"Get outta here," Elizabeth would say to her son, taking a swipe at him, which Little Simon dodged. "Murderer," she'd say.

"I'm not a murderer," he'd say.

"Well ya will be some day—hanging people now that don't need a be hung."

Because coming from a Randolf Scott movie one afternoon, he and some cottage boys tried to hang Calvin Simms. They'd put cheesecloth around his eyes and tied his hands behind his back.

"That was just kiddin," he'd say.

"Hoisted him up," she'd say.

"Well okay—I asked him—I said 'Calvin you wanta be hung—' and he just giggled and hiccupped, and couldn't stop gigglin," Little Simon would say. "So we hung him—but we asked him 'fore we did."

"Huh," Elizabeth would say. "Murderer—"

"I am not a murderer—I am not—we cut him down an everything—"

"Go on," she'd say. "Get outta here now—go play."

"I'll go in and have a go at a bologna sandwich." Little Simon would start to walk away. She'd grab him by the hair and pull it. "Now ya already had a sandwich—yer not havin anythin more—"

Then she'd turn back to the man, smile slightly, her face white. "They're so saucy—they're all going to get their arse in trouble, without a *man* around—George, pity before you laugh I always say."

The man would nod his head. "Coming for a drive then," he'd say, "or what?"

"I don't trust you—yer such a devil—you make me feel just like a *devil*," Elizabeth would say.

God knows where Packet stayed. God knew his coming and going—sometimes the younger men poaching, with flashlights and kerosene lanterns, over the sides of their dories, in the open water, their faces jubilant, bold and spattered with mud, their pants soaking and their rubber boots filled with water, and in the midst of them (and of that increasingly furious occupation) Packet sat with them, shared their catches with them, mended and set the nets better than they, knew in what time and what pools the salmon would be—and fought off the cold and the rain wherever he stayed. He grew taller, stronger, his forearms and neck thickened, his face looking unnervingly like a photo of his great-grandfather, Merlin Terri, on a log-drive in the spring of 1889. The photo now in some buried archives in some metal filing-cabinet in a back room on one of the side streets in the provincial capital.

Lois met him coming from the dark side building of Alewood's store, and he looked at her, drawing into himself, his eyes callous.

He swept on past her as she turned. He was gone. He was gone down to the men, who sat out nightly against the moon, the water lapping faintly, the stars winking out patiently, to drink wine and rum with them, with Indian girls in the smelt-sheds strewn with coarse grass, with the corroding serial-marked engine-parts, the smell of food and oil lanterns, the acrid scent of wood.

And Packet was seen again, in the company of Kenneth Ward's widow, in the company of the Ginnish man who'd a tattoo on his left hand, who everyone said had bad eyes.

"Ha ha," Elizabeth said. "He'll end up in prison—always in trouble—remember when the RCMP came—member that?" She stared straight out at the roadway, curling her painted toes around two dandelions, her chin pampered with oil and her bared shoulders showing the strap-marks of her brassière, her black panties outlined against her white shorts.

"I know what I'll do—I'll go to church and pray for him," Lois said.

"Listen," Elizabeth Ripley Terri said. "Listen," she said.

"What?"

"Now with all you blabbin I missed it—why do you always have to ruin everything?"

"What?"

"I won at bingo—my name was s'pose to be mentioned on the radio—I missed it, I missed it."

"You didden tell me you won," Lois said.

"Go get changed—sitting round in that wet bathing-suit, go get changed, what? And don't look at me like that either—do you think for one moment, little bitch, that *your* name will ever be on the radio?" she said. "Your bathing-suit is so tight around the arse—tch."

Her mother read about a Spanish captain who seduced a young English lady (of young girls in manors becoming spellbound by rakes and captains of a foreign country, and being saved by rakes and captains of their own). And her mother had a picture of St. Veronica of Milan, praying in a peasant dress. The halo on her head was like sunlight—like shooting stars. Her mother said, "Those Spaniards—those Spaniards."

Packet was seen in the company of Ken Ward's widow. At the funeral of Kenneth Ward and his children the pallbearers found that they had to go over the snowdrifts, and that there was no walkway shovelled to the graves. Rosie Ward wheeled her infant's coffin toward the graveyard, but they told her it had to be lifted and carried. Rosie Ward hadn't cried at all in church. Her face had looked dead, like her children and her husband's. When they told her the baby's coffin had to be lifted over the snowdrifts she looked about at the white posts sticking up, and here and there smoke puffs in the glassy sky. Turning, she wheeled the coffin a few paces in one direction, came back, turned and walked away again. She began talking to herself, and the more she looked for a path—even as the men were lifting the infant over solemnly—the more frantic her movements became, her mouth jerking. She kept going back to the carriage even after the child was at the gravesite—the nightmarishly white cemetery with its smooth gravestones. All the time talking and jerking her mouth, staring wide-eyed, the new black boots she'd bought herself with their rabbit-fur tops.

Packet stayed away from the trailer. Elizabeth Ripley Terri came back from town with Bennie. Sometimes Bennie brought a taxi. They brought things from town and she and Bennie would come in. Elizabeth would say, "I don't want you or Little Simon touchin a sniff a this—Bennie bought it for me and him."

Little Simon played in the taxi when they weren't looking and one day he called over the two-way radio, "Yer taxi driver jus hit a moose and went off the road."

"Who is this?"

"I'm jus a little lad," he said. "But I'll tell ya right now yer taxi driver jus hit the biggest moose I ever saw—"

"Yes—now where are you—is that Bennie?"

"It mighta been Bennie—coulda been Bennie—mighta been—but no-one's really sure—ya'd better get the ambulance."

"Is that Ben?" the woman at the office shouted.

"Lissen—I gotta go—get a ambulance up the norwes' road here."

Which they did, with RCMP squad-cars and sirens and people coming out of their houses. They spotted the taxi in the driveway and came to the door. Bennie was sitting at the table eating strawberries and cream.

Little Simon had run into the woods and hid at a distance, where he could see the commotion, the lights flickering, the RCMP officers walking around. And then he came back later with his hair soaking wet. "I been swimmin—I been swimmin," he said when his mother grabbed him by the scruff of the neck. "Holy oh frig, ya can't even go swimmin around here no more can ya?" he said, rubbin his neck. "Jumpins."

Packet they'd heard had gotten into a fight with a man because of Rosie Ward. They'd been eating at the man's house. The man had taken Rosie Ward's money after she was drunk. When Rosie sat with them she started feeling Packet's dark hair. She said it was nice hair. Packet sat with his shirt off, leaning on his arms. The man laughed, the money in his shirt-pocket. He laughed. "Don't laugh again, she can rub my hair if she chooses," Packet said. The man laughed and turned to another man, rolling his eyes. Packet jumped over the table and kicked the man's head with his knee. The man's nose bled viciously and Rosie looked simple-mindedly at them, her eyes still with the death car inexorably in them. Packet shivered looking at her. He picked up his shirt and left the house walking.

"Don't trust a Terri—don't ever trust a Terri," the second man said.

"He'll get his," the first man said.

"I 'ope he does too," Rosie said. "I don' like dat Packet Terri very mush —I don' like him—I like you—I—"

She said, "I lick you—do you lick me—I like you—I don' like dat Packet Terri for sure." She smiled at them and began searching through her purse.

Mixed up with squaws now—isn't there enough bucks around for her, without getting mixed up with my son?

Elizabeth Ripley Terri told her she was going to get her arse in trouble and she and Bennie ate fresh strawberries and cream, and listened to Perry

185

Como. Bennie said Elizabeth was old-fashioned listening to Perry Como
—Bennie was 23 years old. When her mother went to change the album
Bennie slapped Lois on the inside of the thigh. Then in the night he and
Elizabeth got into a fight—you could hear her mother—and then you
could hear Bennie. Then her mother said something. She said, "I heard
yer wife screwed every goddamn sailor on every goddamn boat that came
up this river—Bennie—I hear ya useta find her in the pulp—Bennie
Bennie." And then there was a wailing sound; it came from Bennie's
throat—not rage or hurt or anything but a lost sound. Then he was beating her mother. He slapped her mother and slapped her. Elizabeth said,
"Bennie I'm sorry Bennie, I'm sorry dear, Bennie—please." She thought
of her mother's full hips in her white shorts, her thighs that still touched
when she opened her legs to put lotion on, and the way she slapped under
her chin with the top of her hand.

The next morning her mother had a towel over her eye. Bennie said he
had a sore shoulder and her mother said she could massage his shoulder.
She pressed herself up against his shoulder and he grabbed her. "Bennie,"
she said, "have some manners—some *manners*." He grabbed her inside
her tight legs.

They whispered all that day. Bennie lay on the lawn-chair with his
shoes still on and his shirt still on. There was a smell of perfume on him,
like the perfume on the top of the toilet, and the dried-out pimple where
he'd cut himself shaving. And Bennie did card tricks for Lois and Little
Simon, and showed them how to always deal themselves aces. Elizabeth
made them Kool-Ade. They whispered together. Elizabeth Ripley Terri
lay up against him, in her bathing-suit with the flowers, damp-smelling,
and the clothesline twisted about in the twilight, with the sharp yellow
grass and the clothes-pins like burnt shadows. Bennie had false teeth and
he took them out and licked them after he ate, and made a sucking sound.

Lois stayed in her room, against the shadows, and the smell of summer
through the window-sashes. The late summer, the clothesline twisted.

Those men who walked up and down the roadway and drove in cars,
the cottage women who played bridge and said "Really and truly—really
and truly" when they talked. And the women said "Really and truly" and
then drank their gin and gingers, and Lois sat with Malcolm Bryan on the
hammock that day, thought these cottage women were the finest people
she'd ever seen—their hands and faces and features so stern and delicate.
She wanted to smell them. She wanted them to like her. She kept trying
to walk near the table. "Who is this little girl?" Mrs. Bryan said. "Martha
—that's not Gerald Camp's daughter is it?"

"No no—that's a Terri girl—from here."

"Terris—Terris—oh yes—yes," she said, looking at her delicately and sternly and then looking at the others. They smiled at her (and she remembered them long after, how she'd tried to smell them and touch them, how she smiled and wanted them to like her, to say *oh really and truly, what a lovely girl, what a fine girl, what a fine mother. "Do you know her mother?" Oh yes Elizabeth, what a fine mother, what a fine girl —and then she'd laugh with them. They'd say, "Go and telephone your mother—we are all going to the beach after, what a fine day."* And when she remembered them long after, their sternness, their buttocks sunk into the canvas chairs, their laughter, to sit, their buttocks pressed against the canvas in assumed positions. Their hair was caught dowdily in the sunlight like the brick barbecue, with the scent of grass and charcoal over the spruces. And they talked and perhaps their children would be part of the school play, one of those productions of *Riders to the Sea* and perhaps too they'd graduate with good marks but they were all "little devils").

"Terris—oh yes—yes yes," they said. And they talked and drank their gin and gingers. They talked about the Rosie Ward who yesterday went at her dead husband's girlfriend with a pan of scalding water. They said, "My God—isn't that terrible—how some people live."

"It's really frightening—"

And they smiled at her. It was good to be smiled at by them. She wanted to be nice. She wanted to sit prettily for them. And when she drank Pepsi and had to burp she wanted to say "Excuse me" for them. They would ask her if she was ever in a production of *Riders to the Sea*.

She thought too of the man with *HMS Bonaventure* on his arm, the man in the tallow evenings looking at her from the apartment window, carefully surveying her over and over as she walked by him now. Packet came from the corner of Alewood's store, his eyes looking. And then he was gone.

She said, "Mum, do you want me to knit you a sweater? I can knit you a sweater—I have a pattern—it's a nice pattern—I can make you a dress too—you should see the pattern."

"If you want to go to the exhibition let's get going," Bennie said to Elizabeth.

"You should see the pattern for the dress—I can cut it out tonight."

"Why's your voice so loud? Don't yell like that Lois," Elizabeth Ripley Terri said.

"Huh—I'm not yellin—but if you want that dress you have to help me with it, right—you have to help me with it."

187

"Okay okay dear—my God what have you got over your face?"

"Lipstick."

Bennie laughed.

The Indian girls came and went along the roadway. She was warned about the squaws, and getting mixed up with them. They walked in the evenings, with their sweaters over their shoulders, in the soft night, the graceful movement of women, the graceful land, the white rock and the shoreline opposite.

Elizabeth Ripley Terri sang, "Catch a falling star and put it in your pocket, save it for a rainy day," and left her bathing-suit turned inside-out on the bathroom floor, the used pads that were next to her, the motes of light caught against the dresser and chairs, the scent of dried blood and the disordered bathrobe. The old men sat out in the cool August evenings, the houses white and green with a cold, distant, foreign look.

Havlot Peterson sat on Alewood's steps. He sat there with burn smells in his clothes, and his face was clean shaven. He told her stories. He said, "Do you know little girl—that you and I are related?"

"No."

"Well I'm your great-uncle," he said.

"An what's so great about him I wanta know," Little Simon said.

He was a sad old man. He watched this Indian girl or that Indian girl walking by him, holding on to their used 5¢ Pepsi bottles. And hearing the cars, the sound of pebble-filled mufflers shocking his old age. He said, "We used to bring them in—in the spring—" He was talking about the sports. And he said, "Simon—yer grandad useta wade up to his neck for them. And I remember Simon had a man comin in and he went to prepare the camp—you know, and he found out he'd no Black Dose on him. Now Black Dose was a fly that man particularly liked so yer old grandad walked eighteen miles back out to get him some, and then come in and got the canoe fer him—ya know, and took him to the pools, ya know, and landed his fish for him, and got him squared away, with a meal and a bit of rum. And then made sure everything was ready for the mornin—oh yes, and then got ta bed hisself." And he laughed. When he laughed he didn't make a sound. He just opened his mouth. "I figured I'd make some money off them horses—but I didn't. No, we worked a lot, but we didn't make too much." He watched the Indian girls. His old eyes were wide, lustreless, with yellowed splotches of blood. He said, "There was a Indian girl now a long time ago—her brother took her into the woods there." He looked at Lois. Lois looked at him. Havlot smiled. He smiled and his false teeth had yellowish plaque on them, and besides, when he smiled there was something unnerving. Even though he was a sad old man, he seemed to enjoy making people uncomfortable. He liked to tell them things that he'd heard about them—pretending he didn't know it was about them—and whistle. The worst thing he knew about them was, the easier he'd tell it and the more he'd pretend he didn't know it was about the person he was talking to. And he'd whistle. He'd whistle and pick up dust off Alewood's old, worn-down, ruined steps, and he'd let this dust fall out of his cupped hand, the sunlight would make the dust warm and they'd taste it in the air, with evergreen—and the memory of a vacant parking-lot where the cars drove in and out, and where the dust was smooth.

"There was this Indian squaw a long time ago," he said. "Her brother took her into the woods where Col Stream is—you know Col Stream?"

"Yes," Lois said. "When I was alive?"

"No no no no—a long time ago," Havlot said. "And ya know what he did to her in them woods?" Lois' heart was beating. It was beating and wouldn't stop growing out of her, and Havlot looked at her, with his old, deceitful, blood-yellow eyes. His deceitful eyes looked out at her merrily. "He strangled er," he said, moving his arms, in a jerking arthritic fashion and laughing when Lois jumped. "Ha ha," he said, and then he laughed without making a sound. He stared at Lois, and then he began to whistle. It was as if he knew something about her, and she racked her brain trying to think of what evil thing about her he'd know, in relation to a man strangling his sister, in some dead run of years.

"He strangled her up," Havlot said. "Her name was Emma Jane Ward —took her minutes ta die there—thumbprints on her—and then he carried her out to the road here, and dumped her, ya know, right near the white people. And that's why white men an Indians never got along since —but can you magine," he said.

"No," Lois said.

"Oh yes," he said. "You ask Old Simon about er—see if he knows anything about er more than I do—that's why I always don't trust a Indian," Havlot said, smiling merrily, his eyes burning into her, somehow like he knew an evil deceitful thing. Then he whistled. "But that Tom Proud wanted ta show off—he was just a show-off, understand, an so he dumped her out near the white people—if he just left her where she was, well, no-one would've found out and he woulda been the very best— but he was a show-off and he unlaced her boots there and musta wanted to sell them. But just as he was unlacing her boots—gonna run away and sell them, you know, out comes Hitchman Alewood—who useta own this here building, and he sees Alewood and runs away. Boys," he said, "if ya can't go into them woods with yer own brother for fear of being strangled up then something's wrong—eh Lois?" He looked at her, smiled. "I don't think one Indian girl on the reserve ever dared go into the woods with her brother since then."

Lois shivered. She looked away. The old man laughed without making a sound. In the village the Indian girls walked, carrying their empty 5¢-on-the-return Pepsi bottles. Over and over again the women would play bridge at the cottages. They would talk, filled with the same endless topics, the discussions of this and that, the disasters of life. On and on. Lois smelled their perfume and the patio smelling of charcoal and oil; when they looked at her they smiled sternly.

"Oh yes—Terri—oh yes—well, how are you?"

"Fine," she'd say.

Their children sat with terry towels over their thin shoulders. They would have wiener-roasts in the evening, the women with their inevitable talk about society and justice, after the swim, when their children are in bed, and they're sitting on their high-backed $1800 chesterfields, with the cottage door opened listening to the river.

And she would come up to these verandahs, stare in at that wealth (for it was that middle-class wealth, so ordinary and so desperate—the boys and girls will go to college, they'll rebel, acquiesce and in the end become lawyers or teachers—that wealth that could be seen in hundreds and thousands of homes, the lampshades, the corridors, the staid porches with potted plants, the spotless windows, the living-rooms and lampshades, their children returning from junior golf tournaments, neither winning nor losing) and staring in at them she'd say, "Is Malcolm in?"

They'd look at her. The cool air of evening, night, the stars in the sky. "My soul, who's there?"

"It's Lois."

"Lois—the Terri girl—oh well, do you know what time it is?" The woman would come to the door. She'd open the screen-door and Lois would smell that comfort, the coziness, the fireplace, the model sailboat on the fireplace mantel, the glowing electric candles at either end of the mantel. The smell of the verandah, the dusty cots where the Bryan children had played Monopoly in the afternoon—the Monopoly game now carefully put away—and yet Lois stayed nearby—hoping to be liked by them, to smile, to paint shells with them, with watercolours. The chesterfield, the old knitted rugs, the oak pantry with the door slightly ajar and the cereal boxes, the cereal bowls.

"They've all been in bed now for an hour—you come back tomorrow, okay?"

"Okay," Lois saying. The woman, smiling again, staring at her, at the frayed blouse, the shorts too tight over her hips, thighs.

"Don't you have shoes on?" the woman saying, "or sandals?"

"Nope," Lois saying, looking at her.

"Come back tomorrow dear, okay?"

"Okay."

And she'd leave. The woman would go back to her company. Looking at each other they'd make that desperate expression of understanding, but the conversation would go on, the clock would tick. The conversation (the talk that Lois heard in the drowsy afternoons that filled her with a bewildered sense of awe at how lovely and brilliant and special these people were, who had their own maids to take the youngsters for walks). Her bitten fingernails, her painted toes, her tough black skin at the bottom of her feet. The somehow fetid smell of her too-tight shorts in the long summer days, when fourteen-year-old Malcolm Bryan would look at her, grow weak and become silly.

The cottages were built, the patios put in, the flowers planted. The women were all "one big family" and their children came and went in and out of the cottages because they were the children. But this wasn't how they felt, nor how they'd act once they went back to town. There was a good deal of drinking. But they didn't drink like Lois' father. Nor did they drink like the men who worked on the back of the trucks, or the women who went to the Legion, who danced and clapped their hands and sweated under the arms. Nor did you ever see one drinking alone (no doubt they did drink alone at times). Nor did you ever hear one fighting with their husband or yelling at their children (no doubt—even to Lois that year who loved them as sort of goddesses—they did have fights with their husbands and they did get angry with their children). But Lois had seen in her fourteen years some fairly basic fights between men and women. She had seen her friends and her enemies being paddled with a stick across the arse up the street—herself also. This would not happen here—nor could she imagine it happening.

"Once I had a secret love," Elizabeth Ripley Terri sang.

Lois walking along the road. From the apartment building men watching her.

Lois went along the roadway. Robert had just driven into his yard. He was a thin man with sinewy power and the HMS Bonaventure tattoo was faded and covered with dark arm-hair. He was hauling his lunch-bucket out of the car and he looked at her. The men in the apartments smelled of oil. Some had tried to make their places, those rooms, comfortable so they'd set up plaques and pictures, oven-mitts and oilcloth on the table. But they worked and lived alone, and like all men living alone their places had that masculine disorganization, because what was important to them sooner or later took the forefront of those dusty lime-green rooms. That is, a case of beer found its way to the centre of the floor, an open can of beans, the beans eaten cold and in a hurry in the morning sat upon the table—and perhaps would sit upon the table for three or four days—a week maybe. Their boots were beside the cot—their clothes piled here and there, and the closets empty save for the suit they never wore. When they went home on the weekends they might take the suit, but this was unlikely. A small line was rigged for washing out their socks, the window opened with a hardbound book, and cowboy books and *Playboy* magazines were under the bed, along with a sheet of tin they'd used to patch their car. If you happened to open their cupboards you might find a used set of spark-plugs, a pair of scratched safety-goggles. Still they set up their photos of wife and children, or a picture of some stream—a salmon taking the fly, a picture of a downed buck in the dazzled gloom of a wood road, *November 1954* scrawled under it. The radio sitting near the hot-plate next the cupboard, the smell of burned toast. And those oven-mitts and oilcloth, slippers—given to them by their wives, a pillowcase given to them by their wives only brought home their aloneness.

"Hey—how are you?" he said to her. He said it with a soft French accent. He was not from here—the accent was not the same.

She went up to him, the men sat on the upstairs verandah; he pretended that he hadn't noticed she'd walked up to him. She had on white shorts, with the behind grey and tar-streaked from swimming.

He said, "Picking any berries this year?"

"No," she said and laughed. She laughed—as if she were far too old to pick berries, and she tried to laugh—like in the taxi Elizabeth Ripley Terri laughed, she said: "Of course not," and she took a package of cigarettes out from under her shorts and opened the package. Her hands shook when she lit a cigarette, but she inhaled it and offered him one.

"You don't smoke," he said. His skin was leathery and dark, his eyes blue. His voice was soft. Perhaps he was 35. She didn't really know about how old men were. They were older men.

"I'm trying to quit," she said. "I been tryin and tryin to quit."

He looked at her and smiled. She looked away. Across the river now the twittering of birds, and she saw Old Simon walking from his shed. She talked to him for a moment and then she left. There was nowhere to go now except back to the trailer.

But as she walked along the roadway the cars passed her and she kept glancing around. Then she saw his car turn from the apartment and swing in her direction.

He'd changed his shirt but he still wore the same pants, boots streaked with yellowish mud. The inside of the car was warm, and smelled of earth. His hair was quite short. It was night now. The roadway had that lasting August air, the fleck of bugs and the quiet homey sound of the river.

"I'm goin to the hexibition," he said softly. "Do you want to come this time?"

She smiled and opened the door.

It was late at night. The man no longer looked at her as he drove Cortes Road and he no longer talked to her about her friends. She'd been telling him about her friends all night.

So they'd come home again. And then he'd turned off on a sideroad. "I'd better get home," she said.

"Why?" he said. "We ave a drink here."

"Oh I don't drink very offen atal," she said. "Once in a while ya know," and she stared at the windshield. She'd combed her hair and put on lipstick and brought with her a purse with a makeup kit. Her feet were tucked up under her. Her blouse and her shorts were too small for her. Robert looked at her. He had a strange weak look about him.

"You have a drink now and we go to the hexibition tomorrow night—again."

He was alone here, he said. He said that he'd been all around the world —England and everyplace—and that he'd go again. He smelled of the aftershave that the men wore, and as he scratched his arms she saw the tattoo—the second tattoo on his right arm, a tattoo of a strange name. He took out a quart of wine and opened it, and lifting his head she saw the scratch marks where he'd shaved, the rough tight skin of his throat, with small reddish pimples.

"What about that girl—Sandy Simms?" he said laughing. "She seems awful silly that one."

"Oh she's just a little arse," Lois said. "But she's still my best friend most of the time—her father Bobbie Simms—no-one likes him, he ran for the Mayor and no-one voted for him—two votes somethin like that —Mum says she could run an everyone'd vote for her."

She took a drink of wine. There was a smell of pine scent on their white sweat. He drank, and then he'd give her the bottle, and he turned on the dash light and took out pictures of the ships he was on. He showed them to her and she drank the wine. She drank the wine. She became very excited and began talking too fast. She began using curse words and he laughed at them. When he laughed, she laughed at them and used them again. She didn't try to think of them, the words she'd heard all her life just came out, and when she spilled wine on the crotch of her shorts she used them, she said, "Oh fuck me ole hole," and she leaned her head back and laughed giddily.

"Pretty good wine there Lois," Robert said. His hair was short and sweat glistened from the ends of it, they stuck out over his entire head.

The wine he had was Loganberry, a sweet wine that youngsters drink behind the theatres and warehouses and sheds and become drunk on for the first time. That is why she thought it tasted like pop. And because she'd never drunk before she wasn't accustomed to any degree of taste. So she drank and he began to tell her stories. They were stories of women and men, of boys and girls. She laughed, and then became silent, and broodily watched the window. They were stories of boys and girls and women and men in some of the long-deadened cities where he'd been, in the stark platforms of metal and ice, in and about the Canadian years he'd travelled. They were all "very rich—very good people" and these "very good people" had these urges—urges, is that how you say urges, but they are very rich very good people—"As rich as old Murph," she said, burping suddenly and laughing.

His hair glistened; he was sitting close against her and he was talking of how silly it was to try and hide these urges. And when he looked at her, with the red scar-pimples on his throat, with his hair glistening, she became filled with a strange sensation that frightened her. She stared at his watch-strap and the dial, the ticking in the darkness. She felt lightheaded. And then frightened. Then she knew she was going to be sick. He was sweating so there was a slick on his forehead.

The rest of the night. There was mud on the ground and gouged tractor marks that had cooled. Her hair fell over her face and he kept holding her hair back while she was being sick, and when she fell sideways the stars were growing and receding, going round and round, they were determined obsessive things. She wanted to go home. Robert had a paper towel and was wiping her mouth, and she felt mud on her legs. He was laughing, and every time he laughed it was terrible to hear—to think of. She crouched on the road and then tried to stand up. Then he took her back to the car, and laid her in the back seat. She saw the ceiling light, and a bug caught in it—a small bug like a blackfly. "Here we are," he kept saying.

"You'll be all right this time—here now." His voice was very soft. He wasn't laughing. "Here," he said. "I'm helping you—here this time," he said.

"Help me go home," she said. "Help me go home—where's the purse, where's Mum's purse?" she said.

"I am helping you go home—I am helping you right now," he said.

"I have to fin' the purse an go home," she said.

It was as if an event was being played out, again and again—as if what was happening would continue to happen in some long stairway in some drizzling back shed, in some unkempt room. That he had no compassion for her soiled shorts, her soiled undergarments strewn on the car floor, her legs with the scratch-marks from the shale rocks along her thighs, the tiny blue veins of her wrists, and the tough blackened feet. She stared not at him, not at his unusually thick thighs covered with dark mats of hair, not at his eyes which were distant, not at his hands. She stared out, wide-eyed, with her teeth clenched.

She said, "I want to go home now—okay okay huh?" And Old Simon walked from the shed. How horrible that was, that he walked from the shed, the smell of musk between her widened legs, and the smell of sperm, man's lotion and sweat, again and again. His weight like the weight of a thousand occasions when humans laid their bodies together, when men came home at night covered with transmission oil in the startled February cold and the wives who'd accounted for every penny in their lives watched *The Price is Right* on television,

"It hurts you know—eh you know, what do you think, it doesn't hurt eh—you don't know," she said.

Mucus came from her nose and spit from her mouth. She stared out. If she moved her head in a certain way he might think he was hurting. He was hurting. Why wouldn't he stop? Because if you're hurting someone then you stop—okay?

She lay in the back seat now. He sat in the front with both hands on the steering-wheel, staring out into the darkness of spruce and maple. She lay curled up with her hands between her legs, staring wide-eyed at the back of the seat. She could hear him lighting a cigarette and blowing the smoke out angrily. She stared at the back of the seat where the seat-cover straps were twisted, where the back-seat ashtray glittered in the fouled rut smell of the car.

"I'm going to be sick again—so there," she said after a long time. She heard him lighting another cigarette. "So there," she said. "I'm going to be sick again too."

She waited. She heard the cigarette smoke blowing out angrily and confused, like his eyes were confused and transient, how they seemed to dart within their sockets at nothing. There was vomit on her brassière and blouse. They lay beneath her, rumpled with her shorts and a soiled sock. She still had one sock on, a pink sock, with the toe and heel faded. She said, "Hey you—" She waited.

He stared out in front of him, as he must have stared on watch on one of those ships that travelled the North Atlantic lanes.

"You get dress," he said. He said it as if he was disgusted with her. She stared at the back of the seat. From the patient sky the stars were calm, and the moon lingered. She did not know that she was in shock and that the shock came and went. She lifted her hands and sat up. There was blood on her hands and on the seat and on the inside of her thighs. She sat there for a long time.

"Take me home," she said.

"You get dress—an stop swearing," he said.

"I'm not swearin—you take me home."

"Swearin all night—a girl like you," he said. "You get me so mad," he said.

He turned on the dash-light now and looked at her and when he saw the blood he turned away, the muscles at the back of his neck seemed to run like two cords. And she stared at her clothes.

She dressed, tucking her blouse into her shorts carefully.

"I'm goin to sit in the back seat," she said. He turned the dash-light off and started the car. He was shaking, the car drove on, she sitting on the passenger side of the back seat.

"Swearin all night long—a girl like you," he said. He threw the purse into the back seat, so that the makeup kit and the tube of lipstick fell out. He threw it.

"I didn't do anything—and I didn't swear all night—" she said. He was shaking.

The next day she hid her clothes under a rock and came into the trailer. She was sitting there quite calmly. Then she stood and went into her room. She lay in bed for three days. Little Simon made her soup, and made fun of her in a way he always had to make her laugh. Elizabeth Ripley Terri sat on the edge of her bed. She said, "What's wrong with you Lois?" Lois didn't answer.

"Is it yer period—are you havin yer period?"

She didn't answer.

"Do you know what a period is?"

"Yes I know—I know what a damn period is," she said. Her mother's flesh smelled of the white grub of 34 years of living. She said to Little Simon: "Would you ever buy a girl presents?"

"Never would no," Little Simon said. "I'd butcher-knife a girl before I bought her presents," Little Simon said, scratching his bum and looking at her. She jumped out of bed and came at him with both fists. He stared at her in dumb amazement. She was stark naked and she screamed a desperate-animal scream and came at him, she scratched his face and kicked at him. He stared at her in transfixed amazement and then he ran out of the room, closing the door behind him as she tried to come through the door. "Get a holt of yerself—holy oh fuck Lois," he said, running as she chased him. "Get a holt of yerself—there's something wrong with you—ya aren't wired right atal," he said. Bennie sat in the chair. He stared at her as she came through the door and down the hallway. She fell down crying. Bennie stared at her. Little Simon looked at Bennie. His mother wasn't there. Bennie looked at Lois. Little Simon said, "Turn yer fuckin head around," and ran up to him, his teeth biting his bottom lip.

"What's wrong with her?" Bennie said. "What's wrong with little Lois?"

"It's none a yer tripe," Little Simon said. And he went into the room and grabbed a sheet and covered her.

She sat up in bed with the sheet around her. When the door closed, she stared at the door. In the late evening Little Simon knocked on the door and came in. He saw her staring at him unblinking, with the jigsaw puzzle she had out on the floor, the pieces scattered upside down. She watched him as he approached her sideways. It was as if she'd taken the jigsaw puzzle out with grim determination to do something and then, as soon as she felt the pieces in her hand—the actual touch of those cardboard cutouts, her determination faded and she sank away from them as if to retreat from everything. He came up to her and squatted on his haunches (Little Simon squatting on his haunches was like Old Simon walking from the shed, was like the men on Alewood's steps, old men their time come and gone like one rush of current along some white scalding wire now ebbing through some grizzled transformer—but his eyes, his face, his delicate hands had the beauty of an exquisitely alive child).

"How are ya now?" he said.

"I'm okay," she said. She didn't look at him really, but stared past him.

"Well anyway—here ya go," he said. He laid the present on the bed beside her. Her toes stuck out under the sheet and her bared arms were wrapped about her knees.

"What's this?" she said.

"Well you'll have to open it and find out," he said, staring at it and blinking quickly.

He picked the present up again, looked at the miserable bow he'd tied about the wrapping-paper, shrugged quickly and handed it to her. Lois looked at him. Little Simon smiled. He was twelve.

Bennie liked to give orders and he felt that he could give them. And he set himself up in the trailer. He'd tell the worst stories he could think of, about the cottagers and various people on the river he felt had stole what they got. He'd say, "Don't think I don't know about them," or "They have parties on their sailboat—swimmin naked, she runs around on him—little money." But he was one of those people who comes into a house, looks over his position, sees that he can be kingpin and so becomes kingpin. He talked nonsense, which Elizabeth Ripley Terri laughed at and thought was great stuff. He was always "gettin this one back" or "takin nothing off of him—" He was uneducated, ignorant and stupid. So he had a wealth of stories about "the educated people—a little education's a dangerous thing." "That's so true," Elizabeth Ripley Terri would say. He remained untanned throughout the summer; he didn't like to walk but would always drive from the trailer to the corner store. There he'd buy ice-cream cones for him and Elizabeth Ripley Terri. He'd lie in his suit out on the lawn-chair with his girlfriend—taking off his shoes and his socks, he'd roll up his pants. His legs had pimples and brown hair, his left toes were curled in one direction, his right toes were curled in another, and his feet were, as Little Simon said, "the skinniest feet I ever saw." They were also white and wrinkled. He didn't mind picking his nose at the table, hauling mucus out on his finger and looking at it or taking out his teeth and licking them. The more ignorant and stupid he was, the more he talked about being here or there, Toronto, Montreal, Halifax. He didn't like Halifax because "it's gettin just like the States—so much niggers." He didn't like Montreal because there were "so many Frogs—ya walk into any place up there ya see a whole bunch." This is what he talked about. This is what Elizabeth Ripley Terri agreed with and thought was great stuff. This is what the children were exposed to. They were also exposed to his and their mother's fights. Fights over money and who paid for rides at the exhibition, and "You owe me $1.25" and "I don't want the kids touchin a sniff of that—I bought them for me and you." He was also, unlike George, a terrible physical coward. When he looked at Lois naked Little Simon saw his eyes bulging and his mouth working and went up to him. Not only did he look away, but he left the trailer, got into the car and drove away. He talked nastily about Packet before he ever met him and he was going to give him a talking to and "cuff some sense into him." Elizabeth appreciated this. But when he met Packet later that week—he looked at him, nodded at what the boy said and offered him a cigarette. This offering of a cigarette was a ritual with him. He would always offer a cigarette to one person and pretend not even to notice or care if another person was around. He'd light his cigarette—a lighter with a picture of a naked girl (when you held the lighter upside down the girl would open her legs, he'd show this lighter to boys, laugh, shake his head and put the lighter away, as if this in itself was some tremendous accomplishment)— and the cigarette of the other person and with a great deal of posturing he'd exhale and blow the smoke away, while the second person, who wasn't offered a cigarette, would pretend not to notice and try to get into the conversation. These were not men he was dealing with but boys twelve, thirteen or fourteen who lived nearby. The boy he'd given the cigarette to would try to smoke it and keep nervously flicking it and staring at the roadway in case relatives of his walked by. Then he'd show the boy a picture of a woman in such an obscene position that not only was it beneath eroticism it was beneath common lust. On one occasion Elizabeth Ripley Terri told him he had to sleep with Little Simon. Little Simon had taken over Packet's room. When he got into bed with Little Simon he curled up and kept putting his legs over Little Simon's waist and kicking his chest. Little Simon stayed awake all that night, and though he didn't know what bothered him so much he couldn't stand Bennie after that, a deep physical repulsion overcame him when he smelled his hair lotion and underarm deodorant.

So this is how they grew up. She sat on her bed. In the evening the children played. They called for her. Sandy Simms said, "Where's Lois these days Mrs. Terri?" "I don't know what's wrong with her—I think she needs a good talking-to—I think she does." Lois sat with her feet tucked under her, staring at the objects in her room—objects she'd hoarded away from the time she was nine years old, as Old Simon was to reflect years later, "like a chipmunk." When she heard a car she'd put a pillow over her head. And whenever she heard a car in the yard she'd get scared. Perhaps Robert was coming back to tell her mother. On the fourth night she heard her mother in the kitchen. Bennie was talking to her, they'd just come back from town where Elizabeth Ripley Terri had spent her bingo money on a new hairdo and skirt. She dressed and went into the kitchen. It was a warm late August night. The radio was playing "Love love me do—you know I love you."

She went into the kitchen and sat at the table and picked up a plastic apple and squeezed it. Darkness had just come over the roadway. Bennie and her mother had been drinking and they were laughing. When they laughed she laughed also.

"With a skirt like that you better watch it—ya might get raped—someone might rape ya," Bennie said. "Ha ha."

"Tch," Elizabeth Ripley Terri went. "Tch," and she laughed. She laughed. Bennie laughed. Elizabeth told the story of Donnie Murphy—how he was so stupid and how he tried to kiss her when she walked home from school. "He was always after me to kiss me." She laughed and laughed and kept tapping her chin with the bottom of her hand, leaning on one leg, so that her hips and behind posed in the skirt in some sad, profound woman accomplishment.

Lois stared at her, then at Bennie, and nervously clawed the plastic apple. Everyone was laughing. Elizabeth said, "Rape Bennie—my soul don't talk about rape—I have my little girl here."

"She a little girl no longer," Bennie said with authority—as if he could decide when little girls stopped being little girls, as if his saying this should please mother and daughter.

"Well my soul Bennie—we don't have to talk about *rape*," she said shaking her head.

"It's just a part of life—" Bennie said, trying to chew gum with his false teeth and it continually snapping. His gold watch-strap glittered under the kitchen light, there was the hum of the fridge. He smelled of dead facial hair. Her mother said, "Bennie Bennie Bennie."

Bennie snapped his gum. Sometimes if he was in a particularly good mood he'd offer you a stick. He was in a particularly good mood tonight. He lit an Export cigarette and began to talk about the movie he and Elizabeth had seen. It was an educational movie about the conception and birth of a child. Bennie said the movie wasn't much. Elizabeth Ripley Terri said, "I don't know why they showed women naked but didn't show men—they only showed one man's rear end."

"The only time they showed her naked was when she was having the kid—and before that a bit of hair—that's no snatch," Bennie said. Then he took out his lighter and wiggled it. They laughed, everyone laughed. Lois laughed. She laughed and laughed.

"What are you doing Lois? What are you doing? You ruined that apple —you put your fingernails right through that apple—what are you doing?"

"I din't mean to," Lois said. "I didn't I didn't."

"What are you yelling for, what are you yelling for?"

"I'm not yelling," Lois said. "I'm not yelling." Bennie was looking at her. To his mind he was making her excited by the talk, and by wiggling the lighter. He'd drunk just enough to have this thought in his mind, also the thought of her young body naked on the floor, her breasts with the mature darkened nipples. He snapped his gum, his gold watch-band glittered, his cufflinks. The fridge hummed. He reached out and put his arm around her in a fatherly fashion, which she shrank from, jumped up and ran back to her room.

The next day she grabbed her rosary and went to church. She kept thinking that if Father Murtree were alive she'd be able to talk to him, because Father Murtree would know how to help her know what to do. Father Barry, the new priest she had never talked to. When she went into the church she saw the side basement door opened, and heard someone downstairs. She thought that Father Barry would help her, that she'd go to confession. She went down the cement steps through the windowless hallway and up the steps to the Knights of Columbus room. She would kneel right in front of him and go to confession—she would tell everything, not caring that he knew who she was, but tell him that she'd drunk wine and what the man had done. She was thinking this with such determination that she was into the room before realizing it. And in the room with his back turned to her was Father Barry. He had his shirt off and he was piling old army tents that the boy-scouts used into cardboard boxes. He was working and hadn't noticed her. She stopped and looked at him. His broad red hands were shoving a tent into a box and there was sweat trickling down the middle of his back and hair on his jutting shoulder-blades. She looked at him, her mouth worked. She thought of Father Murtree, how gentle his eyes were and how he'd patted her absent-mindedly when he gave her a rosary. And now, in this dull dusty room, with dust in the piled chairs, was this man packing boxes. When she got outside she ran. It was raining.

Four Indian women had taken over the Band office, widows, unwed or separated or divorced mothers. They locked and barricaded the doors and got in touch with an Indian Affairs representative. They told him how the monies was allotted for new houses, and work done on the upkeep of houses—how the chief decided what work was done, what monies went where and who got what. The chief had all these practical things to decide. If Barnaby's house burned down, if the man and woman had ten children they'd go to the chief and ask for money. The Band had money allotted to it by the federal government for just this type of crisis. But the chief must consider; the Barnabys were having a feud with the Francises—there were people cut with bottles over it, and the feud showed no signs of letting up. The Francises were the chief's greatest supporters. If he gave money to the Barnabys who in the last election visibly supported someone else he would lose the support of the Francises. So there was no money for the Barnabys. In this and a thousand other ways the Band council showed itself to be no better and no worse than any other council or government.

The women barricaded themselves inside. Other women came to throw bottles and stones at the door and there were threats of shotgun fire. The women stayed huddled with their children, and had pushed the filing-cabinets against the windows. But other women on the pretence of joining the group—supporting them got inside on the third night. Then they opened the door and let the men in. There were foul cries. The women fought against the women and their husbands as the children huddled in the corner. Two women grabbed one of the protesters by the head and hauled her through the door as she screamed and tried to bite them. The sky lit up against the overturned filing-cabinets and the ruined screams of men and women. That night there was a party at the Bryans' cottage. It was their yearly last-of-August party and Mr. Bryan had hired two men from the fire department to set off fireworks. The partyers sat outside with their children and watched the fireworks go up, the rockets exploding and showering the sky as the children clapped their hands.

There was a constant shower, and the missile-like rockets trailed with cords of yellow sulphur.

Mrs. Bryan said it reminded her of a scene from a movie, but for all she was worth she couldn't remember which one.

Lester walked. There was suddenly a hellish noise of people coming and going. The Glad Tiding Tabernacle, built at a place where they used to have circuses with monkeys and bears—the monkey to do tricks for you, play dead, smoke a cigarette—the tabernacle with its sign in bold block letters, "Do you want real joy? Wishing won't work—meet the original pentecostals," was damned hellish itself.

There Lazarus with bowed head now opened, now closed the door that led into an inner sanctum. Lazarus could embarrass them it seemed—as they walked past him. One man for instance—the fat minister with tiny shoes—seemed to step sideways quickly so as not to touch him. Lazarus smiled, as if he knew something and had understood something about this man, with his tiny shoes, with his appetite for flesh and his insatiable illiteracy—to move now by Lazarus (known as a reformed wife-beater: wife known as an unreformed and never-to-be-reformed Catholic.

When Packet and Denby Ripley pulled Billy Masey out of the cesspool everyone had run to look. It was in the evening and the sun lay over the swift water, the subdued faces, the Americans with their fly-rods coming up out of the water. Lazarus stood with the other men and said to them: "I tol him—I tol him again and again, stay away from Hitchman's, she's all a sunken in—and what about the wife eh—what about the wife— someone has to go tell the wife—what about that," and he kept brushing tears away from his eyes and looking about proudly, his white face set and rigid, the hairs along his throat. The Americans holding their fly-boxes saying nothing, while their guides squatted on their haunches and the dark flies sucked.

"I swear on the palm of me hand I told him!"

The flies swarmed in the pines, their needles headily filling the evening air, and the distant ridges of Cold Stream, the grey roof of Alewood's store, the wall with his faded sign: *Anyone caught lurking or loitering here will be prosecuted!*

The adults stood talking in twos and threes and the children stood together; Lois scratching the fly-bites on her legs with the back of her dress buttoned wrongly. And Lester drove up in his car, and for some reason Mr. Masey kept wanting to shake his hand.

Up out of the sixties they came then: Lois, Packet, Little Simon.

Lois who now had a poem on her trailer wall—who even after she'd won on Atlantic Loto didn't think of moving, and the men came and went, and came again, and the poem read:

Begin the day with friendliness,
keep friendly all day long,
keep in your soul a friendly thought,
in your heart a friendly song.
Have in your mind a word of cheer
for all who come your way
and they will greet you too, in turn
and wish you a happy day!

Up out of the sixties they came, one year to the next. Packet stayed in a ranger station. Little Simon was caught poaching.

"He's in trouble," Lois said. "He was caught poaching—an he bit a warden on the nose—he almost bit the nose right off, Packet."

"I know," Packet said.

She looked at him. It was a cold night. He was staying at a ranger station, a small white building. He had his own box of supplies and his lantern. The stove glowed and smoke came off the flue. He sat there unconcerned with her—he was reading. He'd come back from some city or other, where he'd seen Elizabeth in the company of some man or other, leaving a bar, along a grey street with the snow blowing about the parking meters, their minute-tags buried under the zero-minute mark, and a man in a Salvation Army uniform, who looked to be simple-minded, standing there, the grey venetian blinds of second-storey windows. He looked at Lois. She wore makeup and ear-rings—her hair was bleached. He went over to the cot where the lantern light was better and lay down. There he read from his book, the place smelled of the warm scent of meat.

"Do you know who buys that meat? Ceril Brown buys that meat off them, and sells it at a big profit."

Packet said nothing. In the evening there'd be the deer, the fawns and does lying down. You had to be smart about it. You must know where to shoot them, where to take them out of the woods, and where to hang them in what sheds. You had to have it perfected. The whole ritual of skinning and hiding, the debowelling. And if you knew this, and could out-con other poachers, and the wardens also, then you were good at what you did, as Little Simon was.

Lois looked at Packet. He stared at her.

"Are you coming home?" she asked.

"No."

"Well I'm not walking out of here alone," she said.

"Who gave you those ear-rings?"

"What ear-rings?"

He shrugged.

"A friend," she said.

Tonight a friend had driven her round and round. They told jokes. She told him a joke about Moby's dick. He laughed and laughed.

She lay down beside Packet. After the stove went out she listened to his breathing and then she took off her ear-rings. It was a fine jewelry store where she'd picked them out. They weren't expensive but so much else there was. There was a grey blanket they lay on, a sleeping-bag over them. On the corner shelf that had been made for canned vegetables and meats was a row of books, most of them stolen from the local library. There was also a cross, an old brass one, and a picture of Dali's maelstrom above the books. She thought, when she stared at it, of the steel girders and beams piled on eighteen-wheelers, with vacuums of snow blowing up from the rear axles. When she woke in the morning Packet was sitting on the edge of the cot, a yellow bruise on his back where he'd been punched boxing. He was throwing bits of bread to the mice. He'd laugh as they sneaked up bravely to gather it, and then scurried away, with others waiting behind the stove; marauders to sabotage their whole venture.

Little Simon was sent by the social workers through a committee to a brick house in town, where the flush ran constantly in the night and the woman complained of necessities—

The rain came down, rushing across the sky. The gusts blew. The tabernacle, with its black spire thrust upward, its aluminum-framed windows looking guarded. The smell of wet pieces of fresh mortar.

Lester turned left and walked along a village street. Across the field there was the river, the rock where Hudson Kopochus lay upon his journey to kill a man in 1825—and where Bradley playing at some sport fell and blood sprinkled on the rock. From where Lester stood he could see the yellow McDonald's M wink out. The van turned down the road and headed toward it.

"Hooga hooga hooga," went its horn. The van's tail-lights twinkled through the dirty air. At Clarence Simms' barber-shop there was a rusted Brylcreem Charlie sign over the door, and next to that, on the verandah door, was the circular Alcoholics Anonymous sign, with the words *Service —Recovery,* faded—

When Little Simon stayed in town he roomed with a boy called Blinky. Little Simon didn't know that Blinky had been given tranquilizers since he was five years old, that he'd wet the bed until he was ten. Blinky liked him and stuck to him.

So when they came into the house after school they'd smell the dinner cooking: in October it smelled one way, in November another, and in December it was different still. The house drew into itself. The same dinner/supper. The same hours kept, the same talk transpired between husband and wife. The lights went on, their halo glowed over the asphalt, the street, the ground hard, secreting its last warmth, the snow driving against the mercury-vapour lights, the wires covered with ice. The houses on the block. The upstairs got cold and then colder. The square brick, ugly house, squared as if by some geometrician interested not in the shades or subtlety of lines and motion but in their stark conformity, in their powerless inability to move or to breathe. And so nothing moved or breathed, nothing transpired—the ugly sink and washtubs and pots and pans, the couch with its plastic covering, the black-and-white television that blurred when the wind blew. *Teens and Twenties* on the kitchen radio at four o'clock. The four bedrooms upstairs, the master bedroom downstairs with its locked door.

Little Simon found it unbearable. They were all fed regularly and yet all of them were hungry and hoarded food, snitched crackers and dry cereal, slices of bread—and when lucky, cookies. They guarded this food from each other, but the stash was always on the windowsill in their rooms, so everyone pilfered. They stole candies out of the five-and-ten. There were exact times for eating and not eating—so that at nine o'clock when he was in bed Little Simon couldn't think, "Well I guess I'll get up and have a go at a bologna samwrich." With his stash on the windowsill he could say, "I've four crackers an a pawfull of Rice Krispies," and he could stare into the darkness, while the wind withered about the house, the creosote, the station, out over the blackness.

The woman fed them because she knew she detested him. The man talked to them, asked them about the Toronto Maple Leafs and the Montreal Canadiens—asked them if they wanted to join the Boy Scouts of Canada. He asked them this because his wife insisted. So he called them in one at a time. He said:

"Do you want to join the Boy Scouts of Canada?"

"No."

He'd long legs and when he sat down in his chair he'd never any place to put them.

"Do you want to join the Boy Scouts of Canada, Blinky?"

"Do you want me to Mr. Dalton?"

"I'm not talkin if it's up to me—I'm askin you," he growled.

The snow came down over the earth. It made the alders wet and black, and lingered on the rust-coloured foliage. Little Simon would get up at 8.30 in the morning and walk to the junior high school. He rarely had time for breakfast—and he had to be told when to take a bath. And the house, with its dismal Canadian (a peculiar type) of emptiness, preyed upon him. He became more and more gloomy. In the evenings when you came home through the town streets already darkened, with a scatter of snowflurries over the sidewalks and the men and women now hanging out their Christmas ornaments, and the town hanging out theirs—their Santa Clauses and paper bells against the buildings, and stringing the lights from one end of the square to the other. With countless people milling about on the street from store to store, and he detested going through those doors, he detested putting his boots right-foot left-foot against the wall and looking at the duty-roster to see what chore he had to do that evening—scrubbing the toilet out with cleanser was put up on a duty-roster for them weeks in advance. (This chore along with others was supposed to instil in them a sense of social responsibility.) This physical pain of loneliness drove into him, and fights became more frequent and quarrels, and snitching each other's food—and Little Simon's habit of stealing other people's socks—because he always liked to wear at least two and sometimes three pairs. He was caught stealing cookies. The woman called him in front of the other boys, told him that when he stole he stole not from her but from the other boys. And she looked at the others and shook her head. He was standing behind her and stared at her broad ass and her slip which showed and her scuffed brown shoes. He remembered how one night when she was watching TV she took out a pack of doublemint gum, "The most borin gum God ever created," opened the stick carefully, tore a quarter off, wrapped the rest away and began to chew. And he'd watched how she'd chewed that bit of gum, putting the rest in her pocket, so that you could still see tinfoil sticking out. The night she caught him stealing cookies she told him he had no pride. "No pride," she said. No pride—like a little animal—not an ounce of pride." And he winked at everyone, his large eyes and thin face, his slender fingers with the nails long and dirty.

He stared out the window. The snow came down on the brick ledge. He sat in a white room and stared at the white earth. The local jail was beside the school. In the daytime the prisoners got outside for exercise, chopped wood. There was a smell of wood-smoke. They called to the girls: "Hello there cutie—hello there hot stuff—where'djer mother find you?" They walked along the top of the rickety fence and got youngsters to run errands for them. Then they'd be taken in again, they'd go to the cell windows and their girlfriends would stand talking to them. They'd curse back and forth at each other and their girlfriends would look around, as if everyone should laugh.

"I'm gonna kill the fucker."

"Oh don't say that Lionel."

"That fuckin cop—beat me—two of them—can't prove it, but they did—gutless bastards—I'm gonna kill the fucker."

"Did you hear what Lionel said? Don't say that Lionel."

"Lionel will too—if I know Lionel."

"Well I know Lionel Walsh bettern you—an I know he will."

"Well I'm goin ta."

"Don't say that Lionel."

"Lionel has a awful temper."

"Don't get me mad—that's the first sacred rule right there—an they got me mad."

"I know they gotcha mad Lionel—I know they did."

"Well they did."

"I know they did Lionel—I know they gotcha mad."

"One thing about Lionel—he's the best man in the world, in the world but don't get him mad."

"I don't hurt anyone—less they made me mad."

Little Simon would walk by. He'd say: "Did they getcha mad Lionel?"

Lionel would look out at him, stare at him. His hair would be slicked back and greasy down the back of his neck. The girls would be in jeans, with orange or yellow jackets, with the hood-string all bitten. Their hair was shoulder-length, split into a thousand ends, their faces painted and flushed with the cold air. The freight-cars would shunt.

"Who's that?" Lionel would say.

"Oh I don't know who he is Lionel—just a fuckin little punk—go jerk off ya punk," the girl would yell.

"Yes," the other girl would say. "Go back to Momma."

"He'd better not mess with me," Lionel would say.

"Think I'll go way downtown an have a big scoop of french fries," Little Simon would say. "Wanta come Lionel?"

Lionel would stare out at him, Little Simon's loneliness would diminish. He'd stand by the fence and grub at his nose. Lionel would stare at him. You could smell the hard rubber of the truck, the booms of the rigs, the metal ice and the thousand blocks of the cemented structure with its high windows, its broad rooms, its green blinds—called a school, where the children came and went, and the buses turned in the yardway.

"He'd better not mess with me," Lionel would say.

Little Simon would shove his hands in his pockets. The girls would look at him, their fat transfused faces, their Levis struggling, the rise of their bellies.

"Scoop of french fries—plop some gravy onta her—big Orange Crush," Little Simon would say. He'd yawn and look back over his shoulder. Lionel would stare at him. Stare. Lionel would say (sadly),

"I suppose he doesn't know I knifed a man, does he?"

"You don't know that—do ya?" the girl would say. "Ya fuckin little jerk-off—ya'd better not get Lionel mad."

"Ha ha," Lionel would laugh. "He don't know me—he don't know what I'm capable of."

"Go out to the show—John Wayne an a bunch a Indians."

"Tell him to get off my back," Lionel would say.

"Get off his back," the girl would say, picking up a block of ice. "Get off his back."

"Great ta be Christmassy," Little Simon would say. "Great ta be Christmassy Lionel." And then he'd go, crossing the parking-lot where the wind hit him and the powdered snow froze to the sides of the buildings, down the front step, past those wooden houses, all the same size, with their thrusting eaves, their two front windows on either side of the front door, each door with the little knocker—houses built in the late forties, all catching snow on the exact same point of their roofing—a little more, a little less. The air cold with a white haze rising over the street. *Teens and Twenties* on the kitchen radio at four o'clock.

The woman and man argued about what to them was necessary—the changing of his shirt or underwear, his brown shoes for his black, his hair cut, his shave, his after-shave lotion—the side of the bed he slept on, the quarters he spent on his cigarettes.

"Did you change your socks?"

"Yes," he'd say. "I did."

"Yes—I know you did—you put on those woollen socks again."

"I like woollen socks."

"Let me see them."

"Not now—I've them on."

"Take off your shoes and I'll show you the hole in them."

"Only a little hole—they're comfortable."

He'd take off his shoes.

"The hole'll jus get bigger—take them off—put these on."

"I don't like those skinny socks, they'll ruin my feet—and these shoes pinch my heels."

All this at 8.30 in the morning. And not only did he obey her—he seemed to know when he hadn't dressed properly.

"What's wrong?"

"That shirt."

"What about it?"

"It doesn't go—who ever heard of a plaid shirt with suit-pants?"

"I like it—"

"Go change it."

And in he'd go, changing it.

"Did you clean your razor?"

"Yes."

"Did you leave hairs in the sink?"

"No—let me think—no I don't believe I did."

Nor did she tell him what to wear—only to change once he'd something on. Nor did he (and this must have been happening for 30 years) fight back—backed into that corner as he was he became unbearably weak and guilty looking—over socks, over a shirt, over a piece of underwear. And when she had him dressed the way she wanted, scented the way he should be scented—with his only protest a slight grumble (or sometimes triumphantly he'd come from the bedroom saying, "I thought ya told me to wear my brown shirt—well it's in the dirty clothes." "Oh yes—I forgot it's in the dirty clothes—well, well just put that blue shirt on and wear the V-neck with it." "Yes—yes—I knew that brown shirt was in the dirty clothes—I coulda tolja that," when she had him pruned to her satisfaction then he'd open the porch door, bring in the morning paper, go into the living-room and sit in his favourite chair. He read the paper from the back to the front, reading her horoscope out loud to her.

"Guess what it says for you today?"

"What's that?"

"Lunar cycle high—correspondence, you receive praise from one in authority—Number 8—whatever that is."

He'd pull at his pants, his long legs lifting upward and outward, and he'd light his first cigarette. At noon when you came home he'd still be in the chair, or if he wasn't in the chair, the paper folded over the chair's arm, he'd be sitting on the chesterfield, in his V-neck sweater and blue shirt. Twice a month he'd receive his pension and then he'd work on his ledger. He also counted his cigarettes to keep an eye on himself about smoking. He'd smoke one, and count how many he had left on that side. Then before he had another one he'd count them again to make sure. And every night he'd tell her how many cigarettes he'd gone through that day. But he cheated on this. Never did he tell her he smoked over 15 cigarettes in one day but Little Simon knew that on his pension days he smoked over a pack. Whenever he could tell her that he'd kept it to nine cigarettes he'd look at her for approval and say that he should give them up altogether. He walked with his knees bent a little but his back was very straight. His hair was shaved all the way around his head, smooth on the crown but white and fuzzy at the front. At two in the afternoon—every afternoon except Sunday—he'd walk downtown and visit the merchants, the stores. He was a great buddy with a man who owned a shoe-store. "He's got money coming out of his shoes," he said once a week. Every second Thursday he'd come home smelling of Brylcreem and after-shave lotion.

So Little Simon went on, etching on the plank at the bottom of the bed, how many days and weeks he'd spent there—how many duties he performed in that time, the duties that would make a monk grapple with the terms of his existence—or paid two bottles a day make a wino go back on the street. You'd hear the flush of the toilet in the morning and realize it was your day to clean out the bowl, or as the woman put it "our bowl." You heard the clattering of dishes and you knew you had to scour them for everyone after supper—the boredom of a ritual that became obsessive, the shoes along the porch, right foot left foot—a thousand rooms and corridors, and lampshades and smoky vases and porcelain women in eighteenth-century dress.

On the day he came back from teasing Lionel Walsh Little Simon went up to his room, looked over his shirts and socks, his two pairs of pants, one corduroy, and wondered how much money he could get for it if he took it to Ceril Brown. Ceril Brown had by now gone into bigger and better things than ever. He bought truckloads of antique furniture and would haul all there was to Ontario and hold auctions on it. He also knew when land was coming up for sale, how much he could buy it for and the price he could sell it for within six or eight months to the Americans. He knew many things. He made money. He had a new split-level house of brown brick with a double garage, two cars, a motorcycle for his son, two skidoos. The house had modern furniture, a big bar in the basement with mirrors and plaques that had poems about being hungover on them, a picture of a dog pissing against a tree that everyone laughed at—Irish sayings on the wall that Ceril became melancholy over. He'd invite in friends and show them the house; they'd drink scotches and talk local politics, and fry up great moose steaks at four in the morning, with mushrooms and onions and HP sauce. Sometimes he'd invite local teenagers in and treat them.

Little Simon counted up his clothing, thought that he might get $25 for it, maybe a little more. And he would find Packet and live with him. It was all very simple. In fact, look what Ceril Brown had done—not a day went by unless one saw those rickety $\frac{3}{4}$-tons moving along the highways, with those ancient settees and vanities strapped to the back, the cold and humourless driver geared for the long drive to somewhere, the furniture itself, by its very immobility impartial to the journey, and just as humourless; a scud of grey water under the bridge, a scud of grey cloud above, apropros. Little Simon already a part-time thief—and a good one; already knowing, for instance, where the keys to the creamery trucks were, and which keys fitted which trucks (and knowing this it was a very simple task to break into the creamery office through the roof, steal these keys and have a jolly time driving the trucks about the warehouse on those lonely winter Sundays—ah what entertainment—even when the fresh wind smelled of cinder, the numb woollens freezing and forgotten on backyard lines—there it is; also the cooler he'd been into; perhaps he knew his way about that creamery as well as any employee and more fondly), knowing the trains; that is the freights—stay away from the caboose; where the flares were, the blasting caps, and now and then things of more hellish importance—liquor, which is how he came to know certain people. And people he knew, from Sky Town, from Skunk Ridge, from Indjun town and the rocks—yelling and waving at them as well as anyone; as he was also part-time rink-rat (to the end of his life the smell of the compressor was in his nose), part-time janitor's helper at school (on Tuesdays and Thursdays, cleaning out the basement garbage-bin)—

"Hello."

"Hello Little Simon—hello—"

And having his clothes laid out upon the bed, he turned about and saw Blinky. How old and shrivelled-up Blinky looked, with that blink of his and his clean, pressed shirt buttoned to the last button, and his pathetic smile when he realized he'd caught Little Simon unawares. Little Simon turned away, took his clothes and threw them into a paper bag. The wind came up and scowled against the window. The clock burred. It was cold in the room, perhaps no more than 50 degrees and in the mornings it was always freezing. Outside there was a northwest field and new blackened telephone poles lying in the snow (to Little Simon the town had a continual ungodly glut of poles and virgin wood). There were sparrows that fluttered in the eaves and fed on crusts of bread thrown from the back porches. There were red maples, and in the yard across the street a weeping willow, its branches bent, the extremities of its branches caught in the snowdrifts and frozen. The snow was hard yet most of the streets were still bare; bare and black and silent, with snow now and then scudding across them like northern apparitions. The smell of fresh bread from the bakery in the mornings at eight o'clock.

It all ran through his mind. How Blinky always stuck next to him, one pant-leg tucked in and one out. How Blinky played road-hockey without any co-ordination, and how he must always be on Little Simon's team, and how Little Simon always picked him, even though he knew with Blinky on the team you might just as well go inside and put your stick up forever. How Blinky was checked and fell on his stick and went inside crying. How Little Simon had to share his stolen chocolate-bars with him because Blinky couldn't bring himself to steal any; and his crackers and

Rice Krispies. How at the theatre one night with a good monster movie on Little Simon held the exit door open for two minutes with Blinky's pale face, pale body at the edge of the door, scared to get caught, while across the street men were loading barrels of stinking fish onto a truck, and the fish-stinking wind blew the exit curtain wide apart, so that the ticket-taker started to walk down the aisle with a flashlight. And when Simon had to shut the door Blinky jumped away. But that evening Blinky was waiting for him on the steps that smelled of the lingering vapours of the town. And Blinky jumped up, smiled and said: "It's after our curfew, its after our old curfew."

And smiled and seemed happy that he was going to be caught and reprimanded with Little Simon. Little Simon walked home while Blinky walked along behind him, not more than three feet—or no more than one rectangle on the sidewalk.

Until everyone became so used to seeing them together in the house and around the block that there was a rhyme about them.

—And Blinky knew nothing of cars, while Little Simon could already get under a hood and tear a car apart (although as yet he couldn't exactly put one all back together again)—how he knew nothing of those things which seemed absolutely necessary to know.

"What ya doin right there now Little Simon?" he said. (And that was another thing—he was using Little Simon's upriver sayings, and stealing his jokes.)

"Nothin."

"Ya can tell me."

"I can't neither," Little Simon said.

"Ya got yer drawer all cleaned out," Blinky said, drawing a breath. Little Simon had his back to him.

"So," he said. "What's it to ya?"

"I was just wondering but you can tell me—we're bes friends ain't (*ain't* instead of *aren't*, intentionally) we—like brothers."

Little Simon turned to him, raging and pushed him back. Back he went over his bed, hitting his head against the wall.

"I'm not yer goddamn brother," Little Simon said. "I've one brother— one—one's all I have—he's my brother, yer not," he said. Blinky looked at him. Little Simon had both his fists clenched, his silhouette against the night-table against the dim light, the iron darkness of the window. He looked at Blinky's shoes, his pressed shirt, buttoned to the topmost button (as if in some way he must do things right). Fisherman's report on the radio at five o'clock. The evening train above them, above the town, the streets, the doorways smelling of rubber boots, socks and woollen lining —the mothers, children and fathers sitting inside for supper. Blinky began to rub his head: "Ohh-ohh," he said his face flushed with blood, his pencil/pen scribbler and science book on his side of the night-table.

"I'm gettin the fuck outta here," Little Simon said, whispering harshly —as if to whisper that way showed no remorse or turning back and you must be hardened to it and readied.

"I hurt my head," Blinky said. You could already see the blue bump on the side of his forehead where he pressed his hand, where on his wrist he wore a cheap Timex watch given to him for his birthday, where he was constantly looking at the time and checking it with the clock in the kitchen before he went to bed, so he could get up in the morning and set the upstairs clock by his watch before Mrs. Dalton rose. Because he never went to bed before unplugging the clock, saying its humming kept him awake. That he always took off his watch before he played road-hockey so as not to break it and Little Simon had to tell him not to take it off and put it in his pocket but take it off and put it in the house.

"Let't see—put a face-cloth next to it."

"No," Blinky said.

"Is it bleedin? Let's see."

"No," Blinky said. He sat up, rubbing his head and couldn't look at Little Simon.

Little Simon went and sat on the chair, stared at the creatures, gargoyles of ice, smelled the ice through the windowpane. He would leave tonight and he would go. They'd catch him and bring him back, and again he'd go. They'd take him across river, where he'd fight with everyone, again and again and again he'd go. He'd go back. Back to his part of the river. Again and again. That night it was his turn to scrub the pots, pans and dishes, and since the duty-roster had the same implacable never-be-varied-in-a-dead-blue-moon schedule as the menu, he had to scrub the same fat from the same roast pan, the same scraps from the dishes. Blinky didn't stay in the kitchen with him.

He left that night, as soon as he could feel lateness, as soon as it came over him. Perhaps Blinky was awake. He thought of Mrs. Dalton and how she chewed her gum, two quick big chews and stop, two quick big chews and stop, with the tin foil sticking up out of the top of her pocket—and at the supper-table everyone had "one cookie—no more." He thought of Mr. Dalton counting his cigarettes, over and over.

"Guilt," Little Simon said, "is always with ya—can't go a day without sneezin in the wrong Kleenex—"

Her mother wrote: "a heart of gold is better than a hand of gold." Her mother wrote: "I got myself a Mustang—some nice."

Packet was away. Little Simon began to hang around with the town boys. You'd see him leaning against the side of a store, in a back lane, in March when it was warm; everyone was going about without jackets. His hair grown longer and dirty, his eyes wide, his left foot resting against a small pipe that ran along the building. There he'd stand watching the mail-trucks backing into the doors of the Post Office, the men working. There on the embankment in the night the whores would be sitting with the sailors. Little Simon knew them all, and it was said they treated him just like their child (or most likely better than their own) and that he drank wine with Emmerson Morrison who was gassed in the First World War, and lived with Emmerson Morrison for a while. It was said that he helped with the bodies at a local undertaker's and that he teased the man he was working with for having to get drunk to handle it. Putting the body on the board and strapping it in, lifting the board horizontally. The room was white, with white enamel basins for the blood. You sliced under the armpits and behind the legs. Little Simon drove around in cars with the town boys. The town boys would take their cars—their Mustangs, Volkswagens and half-ton trucks, their Chevrolets with wing-tails and pointed hoods—in the winter out across the river—the main branch, the northwest and southwest—and driving them at 70, 80, 90 miles an hour slam on the brakes and go into spins—out across the blue ice, almost to the open channel. He and Andrew Turcotte and John Delano going along the northwest branch, travelling so far up it that the RCMP chasing them turned back, knowing the danger of the swift water, the airholes and the shifting ice. Little Simon sitting in the front seat with his boots up on the dash drinking Hermit wine and chasing it with beer. His large brown eyes inward, suspicious and tormented. Then too, corresponding with his brother, learning of his brother's stint at university, his brother being thrown out a window in Calgary—all coming back to him, his brother working in the northern camps, the stark head-frames and steel structures, the row of small trailers where the men stayed, where they slept, rose in the darkness and went out, the huge open pits of waste the line of trees, the stereos playing on and on with Eskimo women from the village wearing perfume and makeup and denims with high fur-lined Texas-style boots, where they lay on the cots, where the men had names for them like "tons of fun" and "plenty good fuck" and "come right now" and the yelping cries and arguments between them and the men, throwing them out of the rooms and the women coming back clawing and scratching abuse at the doors, the four winds blowing across the worn earth, the sunlight for one bleak instant on the grey skyline.

Little Simon too, making money off trafficking—at first only now and then, at first only to friends when in those days you could get hash for almost nothing and you sold it to youngsters in the pool-halls or outside the taverns and it was all very secretive and dangerous.

He was thin and slight and strong, his face, his delicate hands growing to manhood, showed something dark and lovely in the blood.

Nobel Simms looked at the old man's hair, held delicately the mount of skull between his fingers. The squall had stopped. Dead hair-balls lay about the floor, grey-black or colourless.

On the radio came a southern song:

I got my mo-jo workin babe
but it jus don't woo-rk on you—

The old man kept staring straight into the mirror, where on the shelf was the ointment, the powder, the razor and brushes and towels, where pinned on the walls in various profiles were the pictures of men, aged 19 to 26. Nobel had left the door open after the rain. He could see the van turn into McDonald's, and the cars owned by people gone to the Tabernacle were parked on both sides of the street.

Now and then a hair-ball floated across the floor, and if there was sunlight it would come through the rectangular windowpanes, Nobel was thinking—on warm summer evenings, the smell of hair and skin-bracer, and the thin smoke from homemade cigarettes, the long-sat-upon varnished benches. The shuffle of men on Saturday evenings in spring, thin smoke from homemade cigarettes, and now and then a pipe or cigar, the pink naked skins of children wrapped in cotton towels, the smell of grey lukewarm water in the tubs—the somehow satisfying smell of dirty water draining away.

"Goin down to Louisi-anna babe," came the music.

Lester Murphy's mouth was turned down, Nobel was thinking, and his bottom lip was cracked. With the towel tied about his neck he looked like a thousand other little old men Liberal Party or not. There were brown spots on his hands, and his feet were pointed in opposite directions on the metal footrest. Not only that, but his feet squished when he walked, because he'd been caught out in the rain.

It didn't matter. They were all dancing tonight. At the disco the lights would whirl like small planets. The Real Thing Disco was having a wet T-shirt contest later with the first 50 people to come receiving a free drink. Packet now, back from up north, had bought his tractor and plough, and he and Emma Jane had finished working on his house. George was walking about, rich. Lois had won her money.

Lois who they'd sent to a convent after her mother left. The convent, like all convents you might suppose. For who became nuns, but seventeen-year-old girls who had been seduced—yes *seduced*, Nobel supposed. So they bade Lois do penance, restricted her movement. He went out to town to see her on Friday nights, she sneaking out the side door with the mediaeval arch. The smell of spices and tomatoes from the kitchen. Perhaps that arch, her hand? They had their spies out, of course, after six o'clock to see what Lois and the other girls did—who leaned with their boyfriends against the dirty cement wall, with red splashes of paint—across from the graveyard that rose steadily toward the hills. Their convent uniforms, ah, even their lips, had a lonely enlightened scent easily associated with stringency. In evening walk the aged nuns to vespers.

Anyway, Lois wanted nothing much to do with this Nobel Simms. She teased him, patting him under the chin. He wrote her poems, perhaps a little like Edgar Allan Poe if he thought about it. She still had them probably—probably as she'd kept and hoarded everything, she'd kept and hidden them, somewhere. Then, in an argument with a nun, ripping the cross from the nun's bib. How could they hold her anyway—a job at Zeller's and then back to her own part of the river. He even (if *even* can be used) asked her to marry him during two of her pregnancies.. It was all so distant now. Her sad glib answers to him on those occasions. Ah though! He'd heard about her and certain women. What difference? How she sat them on her knee and stroked their shoulders.

"Nobel—I just can't see myself married to a barber in a barbershop"—

"Well—if you were a woman Nobel—could you see yourself married to a barber in a barbershop?"

"Now I'm not trying to upset you Nobel—goddamnit I'm not trying to upset you—"

The van was parked across the street at McDonald's. The inside light was on, and Dale was taping something to the bottom of the dash. The young girl had her feet up, with a pint of Alpine in her hand. The old man fidgeted slightly, with the striped bib over him. There was the touch of the metal razor against his skull, and it gave his skull a peculiar hollow sensation.

The van gave Lester the strange sensation, as the razor whined along his skull, of things impressed with perfected toiletries and human bodies, and a whole generation swank in alcohol and banishment, with fuck-you-perpetuating T-shirts. Of the Dustbane over the disco steps. The smell of Dustbane from the corridors and concrete stairways and buildings where men and women trod.

Lester sighed.

Upstairs from the darkness came the song.

"Jimmy crack corn and I don't care."

"Shhh," he heard Ida saying.

"Jimmy crack corn and I don't care—"

"Shhhh."

Nobel said nothing.

"For my master's gone away" came the song. The razor attached to its electrical cord in a room that smelled of crisp hairstyles. There was the flare of a match when Dale lit a cigarette, and you could see him smiling at something the girl said. The day Lester and Ramsey left the hospital they found themselves by mistake in a room, dark and silent with blue lights shining on the ribcage of a certain x-ray. He'd taken Ramsey by the arm because Ramsey's legs were arthritic. The warm rib bones, bluish, seemed to say:

(ha ha what, ha)

"For my master's gone away—gone away now, gone away"

Lester fidgeted in his chair.

Christ. Nobel stared down at the old man, staring abstractly here and there, and remembered that at the preliminary hearing Lester kept taking notes and handing them to Malcolm and smiling at the prosecution. The court clerk kept falling asleep, his head bobbing. A long time ago Clarence came home drunk from a Liberal meeting, where he'd taken a great deal of notes because Lester asked him to, and then Lester drove off with Mr. Bryan, his head bobbing back and forth and Clarence running after them holding up the notes with ink marks on his fingers. Perhaps Nobel was thinking this.

Of course it wasn't right to think that or hold it against an old man. Lester's lips seemed to gum against each other. Even Ida couldn't help fawning over him those times when he came for supper. Whenever he said anything Clarence would nod, or Ida would laugh—the children would be happy because Clarence was nodding and Ida was laughing. Perhaps it wasn't right to hold that against him either. "I can understand —I can understand that," Clarence would say. "One thing I want you to do," Lester would say, "I want you to run over to Fredericton for me tomorrow Clarence—I need to clear something up with the liquor board, and I think you can do it for me—"

"Sure—what are partners for," Clarence saying, smiling, patting Ida's hand. Lester had remarkable blue eyes.

This went through Nobel's mind. The morning in the courthouse; with the old man taking notes and trying to look stern, with the clerk asleep; and then looking bewildered when the prosecutor introduced the tape of his telephone conversation with Ramsey Taylor—when he told Ramsey that either Ceril Brown was going out of business or he was—or maybe both.

As the tape played Lester kept hunching his shoulders. Seeing Nobel Simms he nodded quickly, smiled and then looked away. Malcolm tapped his pencil, and the lead broke.

"Great Expectations Hair Salon, for the man with the means to move in the groove" came the commercial on the radio. And hadn't they named the new mall the MicMac Mall?

The roasting-pan Bobby Simms carried, the ludicrously happy oven-mitts, the scent of warm meat that day Bobby's daughter Sandra married Oliver Brown! Bobby's eyes naked with the thought of money he might receive; pigeon-holing George Terri and asking him why in the world was it he avoided the Knights of Columbus. The blue patio and the walkway with blue stones shone under the floodlights at nine o'clock; when Karen was patient enough to let Bobby swirl with her; and Bobby snapped his fingers one-snap-two and kept swirling about until his wife told him they had to go home; and Karen said, "Well thank God I didn't have to meet that awful George Terri—"

And Bobby kept snapping his fingers, whose moons were tremendously white—

Didn't she realize that Georgie had at least had the good manners to give her son a present of $100, even though he might have had the bad taste to say that he'd earned it that afternoon by selling the coat he'd worn to the wedding.

Lester fidgeted in his chair. Nobel put the chair in a reclining position. They stared at each other for a second, and then Nobel took hot lather and put it against the stubble the old man had missed.

Dale now was onto something. That is, Dale stood outside the van— that machine that had idled in the dooryard all day. Dale was practising a sort of chicken-dance, with the snake around his neck. The headlights shone upon him—

"Gone away—gone away," came Clarence from upstairs. (The circular

Alcoholics Anonymous sign with the words *Service—Recovery,* faded.)

Lester fidgeted in his chair. Nobel wrapped a towel over his face so just the nose was showing.

Dale was now dancing about happily, the snake with its patient darting tongue. The girl said: "Dale—Dale."

The boogie-till-you-puke sign on his T-shirt glistened, stained with body moisture.

"Imagine there's no heaven," Dale was singing—to the little boys and girls gathering outside the tabernacle doors, where Lazarus kept his head lowered. Lazarus kept his head bowed as if waiting for the great godawful axe of small-mindedness to accuse him of breeding Dale—who now danced, now swirled in the air in front of the dirty headlights.

"Jesus Christ, Dale," the girl said.

"Jesus Christ has nothing to do with it," Dale came back. The girl laughed. Freddie Silver and the whole crusade team up from somewhere in West Virginia.

What was Lester trembling for? Nobel had turned the chair around so it faced the darkness outside. The McDonald's M winked out, yet you could still hear, from the inner sanctum of the tabernacle, the faint droning of voices.

"Pope John Paul II made an unplanned visit earlier today to the principal leper colony—" came the radio.

(Really Lester was thinking of the night Clarence got mixed up in a fight. A group of men crowded about. There were sounds and headlights turning off and on in the cars. There was no use begging for mercy—but somehow Clarence did, because he kept lifting his hands that had been cut on the blue ice and the headlights shone upon his hands. And the blood might have made Clarence think of some saint's blood liquefying. Well at least that's how your own blood moves you. And wasn't there compassion in compulsive violence?

"There's blood here—now there's blood here," he remembered Clarence saying.

"Dale stop that—leave him alone," Lois yelled.

And then Lois was biting, shouting and clawing to protect Clarence, her cursing as vulgar as Dale's, who was backing away.

"Jesus Lois," Dale said. "I've no tangle with you—"

"C'mon now Lois—me and Little Simon—me and Little Simon—"

Lois with her coat off, lying on a patch of ice; a black sky, certain machinations and headlights shining. Clarence stood and brushed off his coat. Jesus, as if that was important. And Clarence did what he always did, what Lester Murphy always remembered him doing—he tried to look offended. He began showing the blood on one of his coat-buttons to anyone who would look at it, and kept shaking his head. Not remembering what had happened. That at first he'd kept falling against a table. Then he'd carried a chair over to sit with the people there. Then he began to tell them his life-story. But why did he take the shuffleboard rock off the table and pocket it? That's when Dale came at him—that's what happened. He'd kept looking through his pockets to show them something—calling a young girl's attention to the fact that he had no money.

Lester's lips trembled. Charred paper like pins drifted in the air, their edges orange with sparks.

Praying, they were all praying. His mother and his half-brothers Bobby and Clarence. It was Lent. Every day his mother would bring them into the living-room. Clarence stared at their mother in her housedress. She was praying. Bobby was saying the words aloud, praying.

He remembers that now and it is savage. It is savage. Bobby is fighting over a piece of cake, the cake rests on a plate in the kitchen and Bobby is screaming: "I only want my share—Mummy Mummy—I only want my share." Bobby is crying. Clarence stands silently behind them—to the left, horror on his face. That constant whispering, "Hail Mary full of grace, the Lord is with thee," in the March light that batters the windows, comes through on the cold plate holding the chocolate cake.

His mother is screaming, hitting Bobby with the spatula. "I'll board you out at the Indian's," she is saying. "I'll board you out at the Indian's," she is saying. Tink tink tink over the frozen years—the light battering the windows, the upstairs of the house cold and still at twilight, smelling of starched linen, of tiny spots and shadows.

"Don't let me catch you—don't let me catch you," his mother saying. "Oh Mummy Mummy," Bobby saying.

There is an old truck, men with black shoes walking. His stepfather is dead. And he can see his stepfather's nose shaped like a little egg. He can smell the grave in the house, through the boards, the men in black shoes. Havlot Peterson is laughing outside with some men—they are telling him they know what star is shining and Havlot is betting them they don't. One man knows emphatically what star it is that's shining. Havlot is laughing.

"No stars are bigger than our sun," he says.

"I tell you there are stars ten times the size," the man is saying.

The voices creep into Lester's brain.

His stepfather's death rises up through his suit, through the pant-legs and jacket arms.

"Simon Terri went in after him—couldn't get him."

"Simon is gutless," Havlot says.

"Tried to pull Simon down with him—didn't he?"

"Simon's just gutless."

The voices fade. The star they were looking at shines through even now, on the houses like curious departments of hell, on McDonald's with its smell of ovens.

Bobby is kissing his father's blue lips and touching his hands.

Bobby is kissing his father's blue lips. Clarence stands to the left, his beads folded.

"Kiss him goodbye, Clarence," Bobby says.

"No."

"Kiss him goodbye, Clarence."

"No."

"I'm tellin Mummy you won't kiss him goodbye," Bobby says. "I'm tellin her you won't kiss him goodbye."

Clarence kisses the blue lips, acurious odour of mint on them. Bobby rubs two beads together, his face serious, his bow-tie slightly crooked. Bobby looks about, a remote look of self-confidence at his father's expense comes over his features. There are candles lighted at the head of the corpse that wrinkle against the nose shaped like an egg and seem to make the eye-lashes wink.

"I'm going to grow up to be like Daddy," Bobby says, because when he said it earlier his mother cried and the men nodded. Bobby burps and takes a fit of giggles.

The night is like wet lice on the window—and the infernal stink of the van humming. In town the German and Greek sailors in for the evening, the Greeks walking the streets with their hands behind their backs, the Germans sitting in the taverns. The *Dapo Antiklia* and the *Fnjlenes*—

"I'll help ya Lester—go right ta court for ya—" Ramsey saying. Ramsey shuddered suddenly—

"No," Lester said.

"Innocent are guilty Lester, eh—(heh heh) innocent are guilty?" Ramsey smiled.

The parlour was tiny, the lace table-cloths yellowed with age. There was brown wainscotting along the wall and a silver tea-tray on one of the tables. A large flowered couch dominated the room, roses perhaps, though he didn't remember. He remembered Bobby hitting Lazarus with a shovel and his mother going out to fight for him.

Clarence stared at the couch with the flowers.

Th house smelled of tea, of dark flowered couches, of pictures of the dead Christ with a red background, as the sun came out in the evening Masses. His mother would gnash her teeth at the boys. Bobby would run home. Bobby would sit on the chair.

"They're chasing me again," Bobby would say. "George Terri's chasing me."

His mother told them about the Indian men—about Tom Proud who murdered his sister Emma Jane Ward in 1889, and he heard that from others too. She never told him who was involved in it or what was involved, just the brains of Indians infected by alcohol, the dark stretch of water, the butcheries of the Reserve. She didn't tell them not to talk to Indian men or Indian women—these things were well understood. She looked out at them as they passed on their way to Alewood's, as she'd looked out when she was a child upon the Orangemen marching. Or sometimes she'd say: "Looka that one now—all dressed up."

His mother was at the windows watching whoever walked upon the road: "Looka that one now, look at the hat on that one, looks some spiffy."

The obscene gratification of gossip between his mother and other women rose toward him now, rose above the chair as he noticed the hair-tonic, and this obscene gratification of gossip rose in him, and he knew that it wasn't only his mother who gossiped or laughed about the Indians when they tried to get into the dances. The Indians weren't allowed into the dances then. But it was himself sitting in the parlour while his mother and the company told him about the squaw who tried to get into one of the dances by sneaking through the back window.

"First the squaw's head pokes through, Lester," his mother said. "And my God, then a leg—a head and a leg—and there she is stuck—all perfumed, you could smell her stink a mile—"

"Did you see what her stockings were tied up with?" the woman said.

"By God—I didn't look that far," his mother said. Bobby giggled. He took a fit of giggles.

"Well she was on plain view to everyone—"

"I could smell what was between her legs—I didn't have to look," the man said.

"Oh my God, did you hear that?" the woman laughed. His mother looked at Bobby, straightened the cuffs of her blouse and shook her head.

"I could smell what was tween her legs—I didn't have to look," the man says again, looking about, his cheeks puffed, winking both eyes at Lester. Clarence looks horrified. He is looking horrified.

There was a slight silence. Bobby pretended to fart. Then they all burst out laughing.

"Ya that's about what she smelled of," the man, winking both eyes, said.

"I should get him home now before he embarrasses me to kingdom come," the woman said.

"It was some sight with the bucks haulin from behind and the men haulin at her from inside—she was pretty well tore in two," his mother said.

And growing up he learned that it was cowardice—all this talk. And that he partook in the cowardice and listened, and appreciated it. And that squaw meant nothing more than cunt, and buck nothing other than cock.

Nobel readjusted the chair. And something became incorporated into his brain, a thousand little tragic fissures as Nobel cleaned away his head. Freddie Silver and the whole crusade team up from somewhere in West Virginia.

"I have some pain here," he said, flinching suddenly. He hadn't even realized he'd said it.

"What's wrong—did I hurt you?" Nobel said.

"No no now," he said. "No." His false teeth, with the false orange gums, clicked against each other.

"Funky town—take me down to funky town,"—came the song.

His mother folded her hands neatly. She watched the window and sat on the flowered couch gone dowdy—herself with too much rouge on her cheeks, her lips grey the two wrinkles coming down to her chin—her hair curled below the ears, flat on top. She watched. Clarence stood in the hallway as still as he could, and the apoplectic, horrified look had come again.

Suddenly Havlot came in.

His mother stood, brushed her dress down.

"Are ya comin are not? Haven't got all night," Havlot said. His mother smiled. She glanced at Clarence.

Then Havlot came in the morning or evening. Havlot would walk in and out. Havlot would grab his mother as she walked by. "Here," he would say, and he'd kiss her mouth.

"They're in love," Bobby said. "They're in love—aren't they?"

"Havlot," his mother would say. "Not in front of the children." Then her mouth would go soft as he kissed it. He'd hold her chin with his hand

and kiss her mouth. Then he'd lift his mouth and whisk his hand quickly away. Her lips would tremble and she'd smile.

"Get to bed children," she'd say.

"I'm staying up," Clarence saying.

"You're not staying up—go to bed," his mother saying. She'd smile. The smell of perfume and imported cosmetics, her chin powdered whitely.

"There's something Protestant about Clarence," Bobby saying. "Just something Protestant about Clarence—I'm going to bed—but there's something Protestant about Clarence—isn't there Mummy?"

"Get to bed."

"I said 305 *mea culpas* for Clarence," Bobby said.

That evening his mother was happy. Havlot told her to dance in the middle of the parlour.

"I can't," his mother said.

"Sure you can," Havlot said. Havlot was eating a piece of lemon-meringue pie. It was his favourite pie. His mother was laughing.

"I can't dance—not alone."

"Sure you can," Havlot said.

"No," his mother said.

"Never mind then."

"Havlot I can't."

"Never mind then," Havlot said.

"Well eat your pie—finish your pie."

"Never mind."

"But—I can't dance alone."

Havlot put his pie down. He yawned.

"Well how do you want me to dance?" she said.

Havlot shrugged. His mother began moving. She began raising her arms and moving her hips. Havlot watched her, taking the pie up with his hand and putting it into his mouth. Then he wiped his mouth with the back of his hand.

(Tonight Donnie wore an orange-peel moustache. So there was nothing to be done about it. And even if he lived another twenty years he'd still see Donnie with that moustache. When people came into the house, just at the wrong moment, the most wobbly moment of the conversation, down the stairs would come Donnie, with his pant-cuffs dragging, wearing an orange-peel moustache.

The old man's hands were trembling, and he closed his left hand, became aware of the smell of his own aged sweat relinquishing itself through his pants and jacket arms. His false teeth, with the false orange gums, clicked against each other. Yet in some way he was beginning to look like some shining splendid little old fellow. There was a cluck-cluck in his throat, like a clot of blood. And yes, a hair-ball or two floated.

Suddenly he heard Clarence bumping and throwing things above him.

"Clarence,' Ida was saying.

"Please please please—leave me alone." It was Clarence's voice. Lester cleared his throat, sniffed.

"How's yer dad?" Lester said.

"Pardon?"

"Dad—how's yer dad?"

"Good—they're gone out tonight."

"Gone out are they?"

"Gone to a movie," Nobel said.

"I see," he sniffed, cleared his throat.

Alewood's money sent the first lumber down to the mill and out across the ocean, and helped finance the last square-riggers to be built on the river. He now saw the last of it coming. Life of course would go on, and go on merrily, the lumber might still go out, the vacant-looking ships. The paper boats glided over the surface of the oily water, fathoms down salmon would struggle through flecks of fibre and swill. New faces would rise up with the expedients to make it rich.

Boys and girls passed by in the street. Lazarus, carrying a tin box, followed the fat man with tiny feet. Clusters of hair crabbed their way across the floor in the evening breeze, grey-white or colourless. The fluorescent light-bulb hummed.

"This song," the radio said. "This song's for you—'shake your booties —shake, shake shake your booties."

The night Oliver Brown thinking Russell Peterson was making too much of his wife, Sandra, and challenged him to go outside. To see his face, to see that he'd lost a cuff-link, his small white hand covered with mud—and why wouldn't he stay down? Why wouldn't he, beaten as he was, stay where he was? But no, he was obliged to rise again out of the mud. And going back inside, looking completely baffled and saying, "I deserved it—I mean, that fight, that was my fault, that one," and Russell looking sad, saying, "You've a good left on ya, that's all I can say there Brown," when everyone knew Oliver never landed a punch. And Sandra reprimanding them both sharply: "There you acted like two fools," and everyone laughing.

And then Sandra danced with Russell Peterson, her cheek close against his neck, and Oliver Brown drank in the corner, and gloomily seeing nobody seated near him went home early; and the next day Russell Peterson took friends of his to show them the blood.

The van itself is past misery.

And Packet, where was Packet?

Nobel dusted him off.

He gave Nobel a $10 bill and when Nobel began to give him back the change he said, "There there."

Nobel put the money in the cash-register, and silently took the broom from the closet. Lester was looking into the mirror, mumbling. How thin his skull was, with tiny blue veins running along the inside of his head. His new suit hung limply, the arms wrinkled.

"Anything wrong Lester?" Nobel said.

"I just didn't know how ugly I was," he chuckled.

"You look pretty dapper there."

"Me head looks like a pin-cushion—don't it?"

"Oh—I don't think so—"

"No?"

"No more than most—"

"It'll sorta stand out in court—won't it?"

"Of course not," Nobel said.

"Have ya ever been ta court Nobel?"

"No."

"Oh—I just thought that maybe ya might have been ta court there."

Lester stared into the mirror blankly, and then moving his head, first to look at one ear, and then the other. For years his ears had been covered, and now—there they were.

"Lester—did you know that Simon Terri was found this afternoon?"

"How's that?"

"They found him—when they were digging out there."

"Well what then—what I mean found him—dead?"

Nobel cleared his throat. "Yes."

"Dead eh—?"

"Well—yes."

"I knew it—I knew it, he finally found some place he couldn't shovel out of, eh—I knew he would—" He shook his head. "Shovel outta—eh?" He looked quite old, and with his haircut, shiny.

"Ya know by this time of year—I'm usually invited to Bryan's cottage fer lobsters—eh?"

Nobel fidgeted with the broom.

"No lobsters this year though eh Nobe? Eh Nobe?"

"Oh I don't know," Nobel said.

"No backyard lobsters this year," Lester said. "Eh Nobe my boy—ya know Nobe—the fishermen trap only mini-lobsters now anyway, mini-lobsters eh?"

Nobel smiled.

"And all those minilobs—eh Nobe my boy—minilobs—have various complaints; their eyes like black bugs protruding—eh Nobe; saying, 'Well well well' just before we boil them and for thirteen years I've listened to Mrs. Bryan saying, 'I think it's a bit cruel,' eh—into the oldpot, bubble bubble toil and trouble—eh Nobe—every year—I think it's a bit cruel, one year to the next—that's it, one lobster to the next—matter of fact I've never met a woman who smelled more like a lobster than she does—eh Nobe?"

Nobel smiled.

"As a matter of fact Nobe—we're all sort of lobsters to her—she's boiled me for thirteen years, and now it's Ceril Brown's turn—use margarine for him though—eh boy?"

"Yes," Nobel smiled.

"Margarine for that lobster—right?"

"Right," Nobel said.

"He finally found some place he couldn't shovel out of eh—well I knew he would—knew it—knew it," Lester said, suddenly speaking to himself. Nobel fidgeted with his broom. The old man looked at him. He held his birch stick, and kept tapping it slightly (tap tap).

We only want to get up and dance, came the song.

There was discomfort down his left side.

Now you might feel some discomfort.

"Lester its been ages," Karen said to him this morning. How far away that seemed now, when they met, she asking him if he'd seen her husband. The skin gone blue where the slash mark was. Her small wrist, the veins having been explored by a kitchen knife, the morbidity of too much valium in her blood. Then she having the remarkable spunk to tell him how much fun she'd be having in Bar Harbor—

There was discomfort down his left side—

"The thing about it is Nobe my boy—you know you don't have much of a chance when you take a walk and see—even though my eyes are pretty well gone—your lawyer and the men who've just managed to put an end to your business out chugalugging Kool-Ade with one another, on the tennis-court you happened to build for them—eh Nobe; and both

228

of them wearing those sweatshirts from American universities—right or wrong Nobel—right or wrong?"

"I can't see them doing too much to you—there Mr. Murphy," Nobel saying.

"Oh—I had to do it Nobel—had to! And I'll tell them that tomorrow."

"The best thing—Nobe, was how I got from the building—I was almost hit by a police-car there and then, he couldn't have been two feet from me—(heh heh)."

Nobel looked into the mirror, saw the back of Lester's head. When Lester spoke the back of his head moved up and down—

"I don't think too many people know too much about it," Nobel said. He whispered suddenly, as if he wanted to caution him.

Lester too whispered. "Of course they do boy—of course they do. I was dressed like a pumpkin," Lester said. Grinning slightly.

"Pardon—"

"Pumpkin—the whole bit—pumpkin eyes, pumpkin body—how in hell could they tell it was *me* if it wasn't for that goddamn telephone?"

"I don't think anyone knows anything much about it," Nobel cautioned again.

"Had littler pumpkins jiggling from the pumpkin body," Lester said to no-one in particular. "Took me a week ta get it ready."

Nobel said nothing.

"You know," Lester said, "what's the worst they could do to me?"

Nobel turned to put the broom away.

"Nobe my boy—eh, the worst." Lester spoke solemnly—again almost as if he were speaking to no-one in particular—how one side of his head moved up, the other down as he spoke. Nobel stared at the broom for a second. He could feel Lester's eyes at the back of his head—from McDonald's the smell of modern ovens. Lester's hand now rested upon the shelf. A draught of sweet-smelling air came through the opened door. Lazarus, head bowed as if expecting the crush of some weight, followed the fat man with tiny feet back along the cooling sidewalk.

"Hooga hooga hooga," came the insulting horn. Dale laughed.

"Ah ha ah—haaa," Dale laughed. Lazarus carried the tin box, its small silver key attached to it by a piece of string.

"Hooga hooga—"

"Ol pumpkin-suit Murphy," Dale yelled. Nobel looked at him. Lester smiled and shrugged suddenly, his teeth biting against each other awkwardly, his false orange gums. Nobel could see the old man's head trembling— The way he stood with his legs bowed out wrinkled his pants, and made the back of his pant-cuffs drag. He tapped Nobel upon the shoulder with the tip of the cane (tap tap)—

"Nobel eh—you understand there—I always looked upon Clarence's children as my own—eh (tap tap)."

Nobel nodded, looking away.

"Do you want a drive home Lester?" Nobel said.

Lester looked about. His hands fidgeted.

"No no."

"I can drive you back, no problem," Nobel said.

"No no," Lester said. "No is all—no is all." Sweat broke out and dotted his forehead, the thousand inevitable pinpricks of hair. Nobel put his head down.

Lester said, "$350,000 insurance." His eyes dimmed. He tapped Nobel with the tip of the cane, smiled suddenly.

Brown-eyed girl—la la la la la, brown-eyed girl—came the song.

In the gloomy night, the steel girders of the bridge they were building ran along its cement podiums to the middle of the river. There the white boulders lay, and children lay upon them in the summer. All of Cold Stream was being cut. Brice Pool having been poisoned by mistake, a thousand parr with translucent fins and bellies like death, foaming on the surface. The mercury-vapour light-bulbs gleamed wetly, one in front of each widow's house—a policy he'd implemented as member of the village council. The lights in the barbershop flicked off, and the darkness and the terrible sound of his own clumsiness washed over him. He looked back toward the barbershop, waited. A car passed him suddenly out of the grey night. Water splashed his London Fog coat, and his Johnny Carson suit-pants. He turned his birch-stick toward the car and cursed. It was Bobby Simms driving his new black Cadillac.

"Don't you know who I am?" Lester roared, a cluck-cluck in his throat. The car continued at 35 miles an hour in the direction of the discothèque.

"Pretty," the boys said. "In Vietnamese—how do you say pretty?"

He spat. White sewer-pipes lay along the side of the road. This summer they'd build a new sewer system. Years ago when men were putting in those road-signs that spoke of bends and turns and deer-crossings Lazarus Masey wasn't able to find work with them. And he'd gone to ask Lester for help. And Lester gave him $20 and said he would see what he could do. And Lazarus looked as if he'd expected this, and he calmly took the handout and patiently asked for work. And his mother sat in the shack where they lived, and little wisps of white snow came curling through the bottom of the door in winter—and they actually went and got a Christmas

230

tree. And the day after he was at the dance, in that tweed coat, he hit his mother, ho ho, and she had to complain about her twisted spine, and cry and go on about it. No, then they all tried to calm him down and his mother was crying about her twisted spine, and they all said:

"Oh lazey—oh lazey."

So he hit his mother again.

"I'll teach you—I'll teach you," he said to her. And his mother kept clutching her saucer, the one with the picture on it of Saint Veronica of Milan, and her halo was like lightning, like the shooting stars.

"Oh lazey—oh lazey."

So he hit his mother. The saucer had tea-stains on it. And he got so mad because she was clutching the saucer, just to make everyone feel sorry for her—and then they ran to get Father Murtree. And the old lady was all crooked with her crooked spine.

"Don't you know—don't you know?" Lazarus said. The bald patches of his scalp looking like the naked back of a downy chick. He sneezed and hardened mucus came from his nose.

"I don't joke—I don't joke—I'm too honest—and I'm going to—I'm going to work for the police cause I'm honest," and he was crying. And his mother was shaking and holding the saucer. And at Christmas they just had to go and get a Christmas tree, a little one which his mother called a *Crimpsmas* tree. Understand. He roared, "Understand," and his mother was crying!

"I'll pay yas for findin him."

A small owl screeched suddenly. There was an old barn, supported by pit-props. In the flat darkness the grass grew yellow, the grass tips red. Again came the screech of an owl, then silence.

"Pretty," the boys said. "In Vietnamese—how do you say pretty?"

Behind him the yellow M winked out in McDonald's parking-lot. Behind him the school with its children reaching toward the crêpe ceiling the band members, on uppers, playing Doug and the Slugs, "Too baa. Too bad."

Before him stretched the uncertain road. Now and then a dog barked, snarled out of the darkness at him, houses with their black windows seeming like shocked computers, holding the commodities, the utensils, the refrigerators.

"Too bad. Too bad."

Anne Murray seemed to wag her finger at him from the chimneys.

Dark clouds raced above him, but could not hide the peculiar aura of the moon, the stars themselves. He stabbed his birch stick into a puddle in

231

front of him. His throat went, *cluck cluck* and he fell, a tasteless bit of liquid came from his mouth. His right hand searched numbly for his birch stick. In the puddles of rain-water and mud, elongated worms gone white as death stretched their pores.

He searched for his birch stick; clumsily his hand moved. A vacant cigarette pack, its tin-foil gleaming in a puddle. Far away, a flame seemed to come up from the river itself, shoot up out of the water. The white flat rock Hudson Kopochus lay upon, on his journey to kill a man in 1825.

There was perfect laughter and shouting. And on television he remembered an old war movie, as if out of some past age—the American infantry were moving through Europe, and he left the porch-light on in the evening. For a second, two seconds he tried to stand.

It didn't matter. 105 degrees the day Daniel Ward died. His hands on a bottle of lemon-scented after-shave lotion. There was no need for Simon Terri to feel guilty about it but he always did. Comparing it to his own death, it wasn't much different.

He heard cursing, laughter somewhere. Oh yes, they sent someone here to help him. His hand stretched out for the stick, searched arthritically in the dirt and he thought he might pay someone to take him home. Pay them $10.

The van honked its horn somewhere: "Ahooga-hooga."

Were they screaming? He was aware of the fleck of bugs above his head, the terrible light glowing from up out of the water; and didn't he hear:

"Sexy eyes—sexy eyes." The song.

A girl screamed, who might or might not have been fifteen.

Victoria

So Packet followed his mother about the Maritimes, from Saint John to Halifax, to Dartmouth, to Charlottetown. For no reason he'd end up working in a city where she lived. She left Bennie in North Sydney. All this he knew, but she never met him, never saw him in any of those cities. Even in Halifax he had a manager and boxed with the tough black boys, who if all be told had much more finesse and quickness than he. He wore his hair short then, his eyes furious. Songs of the Beatles and Rolling

232

Stones came on the radio. He was carry-out boy for Sobey's, wearing a black tie and a white short-sleeve shirt. He sported a small quick moustache. He shovelled out the garbage-bin and spread Dustbane over the bin in the basement of the store. When $50 was missing he was let go, even though they couldn't prove it was him. He woke up in a rooming-house with a blood slick on the bed from bed-bugs—

Then he began to go up North, first for three months, then for four or five. Always he'd come back to his part of the river. He was hospitalized by a beating in Calgary, but he'd gotten them back with a baseball bat. Up north he'd hung a man over an open stope and made him recite nursery rhymes, because the man had stolen his oilers and his lunch. Whenever he came back from up north there were presents for Lois and Little Simon. He'd rub Little Simon's head playfully and drink with him into the night. Perhaps Little Simon led *him*, for there were things he did, and his conscience, soaked with alcohol, preyed upon him. He'd wake in the night and grab his head. Little Simon would watch him from the corner of the room. To wake in the night in the midst of a shuddering hangover when the dismal past threatens you, when faces form in slow motion before you, so every particle of their flesh breathes misery, and their voices say.

"What a hard time we're having here—what a hard time—isn't it all a bit like *Jude the Obscure*, ha ha?"

There were books in his back pocket and books in his suitcase, and books on the trailer floor. And there were wine bottles and rum bottles and winter came onto the earth. Kenneth Ward's widow visited him in the night.

"I like you, Packet Terri—do you like me? I like you very much, you tink I don know—dose cocksuckers take my money all da time—I have my period an dey still don care, not dem, for me—you like me—I put my head on your shoulder right here."

Little Simon sold hallucinogenics.

"My brother—my brother isn't frightened of a goddamn thing," Little Simon would say. And he'd pat Packet's shoulder. Packet would tip his tequila glass and suck a lemon.

And the faces came. They came and wouldn't leave him. Elizabeth Ripley Terri on the street with a man-friend with the Salvation Army soldier standing below a dead window, the parking-meters naked.

He told Little Simon how he'd bitten a man's ear off. That it was at dusk in Calgary, and four men surrounded him. He went first for the most dangerous and bit into his ear while the rest heard the shriek of terror.

And instead of coming at him they backed away. He with the man's ear in his mouth. Little Simon shook his head.

"A regular godzilla movie, Pack," he said. And the nights came, the white nightmarish winter with the cottagers' hideaways, and Old Simon going for walks along the river, and on the Reserve fires from faulty wiring or dripping key-macks.

Lois said, "Get ta bed you little bastards and the next time—the next time I bring a boyfriend here the firs' one who asks is he gonna be yer father—why, you'll run the switchin of yer life—why, I'll take a belt to ya—ruinin my fun."

He visited Old Simon and read to him. Then he'd be gone again, down to some woman or other—some married woman. Sandra Brown (née Simms) and him seen. Then coming home, the winter like withering ash.

"Oh God help us—fuck ya fuck ya," I said. I said I do what I goddamn well please, I said—Sandra Simms' body, and they lay in Oliver Brown's new house while Oliver was on business in Portland, Maine, looking at a black band that might play at his disco—

If you wanta sing the blues
Then you gotta pay your dues
Cause ya know it don't come easy—

So Packet lived in the night. And he lived constantly, like all men of the river, with memories. Memories of up north and what he saw of the men working, spending their money on frivolity, their marriages wrecked, or the broad-shouldered Newfoundland twins he was friendly with who left home four years before, with the intent of making enough money to buy land along the Humber River—and who'd made and spent over twenty times the amount needed and had a cocaine deal going. And the Indian girls who came to their boarding trailers, one who was murdered —the fight starting over a pair of panties that said Love on the crotch, in pink, with the O widened. And the Vietnamese veteran, a marine who drove a truck and spoke to no-one no matter what they said to him, but who always came back to the trailer with enough beer for four people, himself, Packet and the Newfoundland twins. And when there was a fight in the bar or tavern, they locked the doors so no-one could get out, and people went at each other with fists, boots and glasses. When the fight was over, the people paid for the damage and went on drinking.

"Ha ha—what—ha."

And he reading "The Death of Ivan Ilisch" a dozen times but not looking at one other story in the collection—

"What a thing to think of—you'll hurt yer brain," Little Simon said.

Sandra Brown saying, "Tch—you're so naive Packet—you're so naive, whatever shall I do with you—take care of poor Oliver, he's frail, he's not as strong as you are dear—"

What—ha ha—what?

"Fuck ya fuck ya."

"Tch, you're so parochial Packet—so—so much like the river. Whatever am I going to do?" Sandra Brown would say.

On the divan in the corner lay her underwear, her brassière with the cups turned inside-out, the half-smoked marijuana cigarette with its colourful pink paper emitting a stench from the ashtray, the new mall being built, the sound of cement and jackhammers. Through the window came the sunlight catching and recording the dust flecks like whimsical planets. Upon the organ top was a miniature statue of two lovers embracing, polished and shiny, and behind the rocking-chair Oliver Brown's slippers with their fur-ball tops. The fur off some dead domesticated rabbit, or some hard-pressed squirrel, some harassed mammal or other. In the evening Russell Peterson let his pigs out, and showed how they were well trained and obedient pigs, could fetch sticks and turn on the outside water faucet.

Back to his house, with George and his girlfriend, and Little Simon coming over, and Lois with her children—all fighting at the kitchen table and talking politics, with George ending the evening before Packet put him to bed, singing the song:

Pearl Pearl Pearl,
Oh don't you marry Earl—
He will lay you on your back
and he will open up your ——
Oh Pearl Pearl you are a horny girl—
Ha ha—what ha?

He'd caught his father running, in a nightmare, for cover from some enemy. And he remembered how he'd locked his food away once and threatened them all with eviction, like some grubby little man in a Chekov story. Behind Irving Layton the rum bottle sat—sweetly positioned in the centre of his thought.

If you wanta sing the blues,
Then you gotta pay your dues
Cause ya know it don't come easy—

In the night, when the young girl—George's—had come back from
the pole that branched the stream, and was sitting in the kitchen playing
Snap with Jeffrey, and the hairy-bellied bee ran up and down the screen
like a humming magnet. And the girl in the kitchen could recite, for she'd
remembered it since she was nine years old, "The Song My Paddle Sings"
by Pauline Johnson.

How they all fought with one another, cursed, in coarseness. He looked
about his room. What with it all, his rollicking records, his stereo, his
brick record-shelf and bookcase, his bear rug from a slaughtered sow, his
pouch with its marijuana—a few obvious pictures on the wall. And outside, near the stream that flowed down from Cold Stream, from the
mountainous area—the wooden water barrel lay with its silted water. A
barrel with a corroded iron top.

The clothes he wore, his pleated pants, his shirts open with the chest-
hair sweating, a golden medallion glittered under the 60-watt light-bulbs
at six o'clock—

And he? He drank from the rum. When he had a bad night there were
dreams in black and white—a long roadway somewhere, a dog blocking
his way. Sometimes there were dogs of various breeds, poodles, Dober-
mans and Shepherds. And every dog a bitch—a bad omen or something,
or the old barrels with the letter S, as there was the night he ran away—
and thought of the monkey with the sad mouth.

He went away and came back again, always to his part of the river. And
always there were fights, an affair with a woman—a deal made to earn a
profit, a week where he did nothing but stare at the ministerial programs,
a month where he caroused and became drunken, brawling and infected
with gonorrhea or pubic lice; arguments, unlawful netted salmon—Little
Simon playing a trick on someone—George.

Programs for better education—a course on homemaking, the social
workers wanted Lois to take a course on homemaking for unwed mothers
sponsored by the Catholic Women's League. For himself he kept away
from anyone who had the look of a punctual idea behind his eyes. She
went to the course in homemaking for unwed mothers, listened to each
one telling her story, and the nun directing them, and standing up said:

"Huh hell, I don't know what's wrong with me—guess I jus like ta
screw—" she stammered. "But not as much as I use to."

236

A thousand half-solid plans rose day after day, month after month, and then crept away again or, distilled by alcohol, lay preserved in some recess, forgotten. Ceril Brown's laughter in the warehouse with Elizabeth Ripley Terri, the night she swung her hips for him, teaching him, she said, how to twist.

Daniel Ward fell down, yes, but he was an Indian and he was drunk. And Little Simon kicked him to wake him up, but as soon as he woke, Little Simon stepped back and gave him the biggest boot he could across the head, and when they heard Ramsey's truck they ran. And then Little Simon fell down laughing, because he'd stolen a cucumber out of Daniel Ward's pocket—

"Who," he said, lying flat on his back kicking his legs and laughing, "just who among ya wants a cucumber samwrich?"

And Ceril did twist that night. That was part of it. Ceril twisting, Elizabeth who moved her hips. He twisted to the right and he twisted to the left, without music. His left foot forward, his right foot back, his right foot forward, his left foot back, with the feed-sacks smelling of the humus of mice. His mother saying, "Ceril, you'll never be a fantastic dancer—you're just too much of a man."

A steel rod of pain, as exacting as a surgeon's instrument at the centre of his life, while all around him sat the beauty of the earth, the stars forever, and the sun gracing the window after rain, or Donnie Murphy walking along collecting bottles silently.

He drank from his rum. Sitting very still in the night, he could feel his sweat drying, his loaded .22 pistol with the enamel-coloured handle, sitting on top of the book inscribed "Sow not in anger." Many times he had a foreboding of someone putting that pistol to their temple and squeezing. A rush of torment. It was always himself.

So, he was bred from the river, born in 1949. He'd grown up, more or less, and enjoyed it, took pleasure in the fights. When his father hit him, he hit him across the face and sent him sprawling under the kitchen table, and when he stood up his father hit him again hard on the other side of the face, and again sent him sprawling. Wasn't there compassion in that —in compulsive violence? And couldn't he still smell his father's hand? And didn't his mother say:

"The goddamn baboon arse—I tol him when he beats ya not ta beat ya on the head—now look at the bruise there—shit. We'll be late for church with all this racket—now get yer hand out of yer nose or ya'll sit alone—"

And after church they had ice cream. And weren't they all invited to

Lester Murphy's with Old Simon, and George got so drunk, and he and Lois were fighting, and Elizabeth kept saying:

"They embarrass me, Lester, really and truly," and he noticed, with George lying on the grass, with his new shoes with the air-holes, white shoes, sticking straight up in the air, and a blade of grass sticking out of each, didn't he notice the smile on Lester's face as he squeezed Elizabeth's shoulder, and laughed when George stood up, wiped his mouth, told a joke about the Indians and invited them all to dinner.

And what did it matter, what roadway where—and didn't he know that he couldn't have his picture taken with the monkey even when the Spaniard with the slick black pants was adjusting his camera and Ceril Brown was saying he'd pay $10 if the monkey would pull at its pecker. And didn't Elizabeth Ripley Terri say "Oh oh" and hide her head between her hands?

And didn't he grow up and fight in the school and fight on the way home from school and drown the cottagers' kittens if they paid him a quarter, by putting them in a feed-sack and standnig on them?

And didn't he corner Billie Masey one afternoon with his sister Susie? And while they crouched down in the corner of Alewood's store holding hands and huddling against each other, crying, did he or did he not threaten them with a burning cattail, the smell of black oil. Susie's white dirty underwear.

And didn't Susan Masey have her first period in school without knowing what had happened? Which outraged the teacher. And didn't he make people he didn't like sit in her chair after that, and smell the Kleenex at the bottom of her desk?

He drank from his rum, sitting very still in the night. A cat in heat might cry in the field, or a rainbow make a fading prism against his dirty window.

And didn't he talk of love to women he didn't love? And those women, knowing this, and not loving him, talk of love also—like Dale on downers collecting unemployment stamps? Or the man (who was that?) selling hats he'd stolen out of a bargain store, in twelve-below-zero weather, with the Catholic bell chiming a funeral. And weren't they all happy? And didn't they sit about in rooms, with yellow-papered marijuana cigarettes, listening to Cat Stevens? And didn't that woman Rhonda (did he remember her?) say something under her breath, after it was explained to her that Lois had three children and didn't believe in contraception. And wasn't her boyfriend, didn't her boyfriend laugh, vacantly, and then didn't her boyfriend introduce her to Ceril Brown? Where was this?

Didn't they listen to Cat Stevens? Didn't they all go down to the tavern later? (Where was this, had he forgotten already which tavern for Christ's sake? Was it Lester's?) And didn't they talk? Didn't a singles bar in Calgary sell thigh openers?

He drank from his rum, sitting very still in the night. The odd shudder, remembering the light-heavyweight—Danny Miller—he fought in a tournament, and was cut for seven stitches. In a clinch he tasted the salt of Miller's sweat—

Was there then the 50 condoms flushed into the blue toilet-water of women he didn't know or care about, in houses that smelled of aerosol, the used prophylactics and diaphragms, loins that carried the memory of knifed babies. Was it in Halifax, or here on the river, or both, where the little girl and boy came into the tavern to try and get their mother to her feet—didn't she say:

"Leave me alone now—it's Christmas—go over to the store and look at the turtles—I wanta have my Christmas drink." And didn't she look through her purse when the men started laughing?

And wasn't the river, gutted, finished, looking like white fingers, tree-stumps like corrupted sores—river blocks like ash-heaps in the twilight. However, wasn't this beautiful—somehow?

He drank from his rum, sitting very still in the night. On the radio, while Georgie's girl was buttering Jeffrey's toast, came the reports—all around him gathering in black electrical currents through those silhouetted wires. At twilight the rats came from under the rags and paper, their tails like greasy wire.

He' drink from his rum.

Somewhere a brooding cat might whine in heat, the salty bloody moisture between the clothesline and crooked fencing.

So Little Simon, self-appointed friend of youngsters, sold his marijuana, his mushrooms, hallucinogenic wonders. And in the late sixties he ran with the town boys, carried in the car he'd bought a baseball bat. And he went to work for an undertaker, draining the blood out of cadavers. It, he said, didn't bother him. It, he said, made him "humble." He kept his hair long, wearing black army boots.

"Little Simon," the boys would yell. "Little Simon."

"Get a grip," he'd say. "I'm busy as a cake at a wake, can'tcha see," and he'd turn off on a side lane or get into a building. Every few months or so there'd be a trip to St. Stephen/Calais, when he carried the .22 pistol in a holster in his army boot. The RCMP watched him, and more than once took him in and stripped him down and searched his car. Always they'd be left scratching their heads—for no matter when he was brought in—once on the way home from Bathurst—when they were sure he was carrying close to a pound of marijuana, they found nothing but the birth-mark on his left leg. He'd look at them, disappointed, and shake his head: "Ke-rist boys—jus cause I come from a poor family—" he'd say. "How many times ya wanta look at me little nob anyways?"

"It's only a matter of time Little Simon," the constable would say. "You don't want to go to Dorchester, do you—God, you're a brighter boy than that—" The constable would look at him with sharp, compassionate eyes. Little Simon would look back, a smile at the very corner of his lips. The sergeant would wave his hand irritably. Sunlight would filter along the counter-top, the clack-clacking of the large manual typewriter. Little Simon would rub his eyes, shake his head. On the way out he'd pull a cap from his pocket and put it on, down to his ears.

"Hey Little Sim—what's goin on—what's goin on?"

"I can't talk ta yas now boys at all—might just haveta get a lawyer to stop this harassment."

"What?"

"Sure—boys, once a month now they have kinda a slow day, so they say ta one anothers—'Less haul in Little Simon and look at his scrawny little pecker—same as we did las month—that always brightens us up—don't it?"

He wore a navy-blue woollen cap down to his ears, and the peak down to his brown, lovely eyes.

"Why do you carry the baseball bat?" the RCMP would ask.

"I don know where it come from—it wasn't there las weekend. Oh Jesus yes, yes I give Hank Aaron a lift—".

"Don't be smart—"

"Never was before—"

And the constable would take him into a room with a white radiator and two ancient leather-back chairs. The constable would offer him a cigarette. Little Simon would stare at the dust-ball floating between the constable's leather boots, and it would remind him of limp moss upon ancient cedars, the thin spider-webs against translucent light-bulbs. Or earlier still, the sound of something bubbling in fat, the squalid smell, his mother's blouse soaked with sweat, enhanced with perfume, the scent of instant coffee in styrofoam cups.

The constable would clear his throat.

"Well Little Simon, how old are you?"

"I don't know—seventeen I suppose—"

"Yes—seventeen. That's a good age. Your whole life before you at seventeen—"

"Except seventeen years," Little Simon would say. He'd fumble with his hat, and sniff. "And if a lad has eighteen to go—that means he's done most of her by this time—"

"All right then—"

"Well don't it? I mean it's easy to say, a person seventeen or however has a bunch a years ta go—but if he don't feel good in the morning like I never do then he might figure that she's about done—ya think?"

"Okay that's enough!"

"Well—how old are you?"

The constable would look annoyed, but then shrugging he'd say, "32."

"And ya look a reasonably healthy 32 also," Little Simon would say. He'd stop speaking abruptly, and drag on his cigarette. The smoke a soft green in the weak air.

The constable looking, waiting for him to continue speaking, but Little Simon would flick his ashes, yawn, sit up straight and smile.

"How much education do you have Simon?"

"Grade 8—completed."

,"Don't you think you're far too intelligent a boy to have left school in Grade 8—what if I could get you into technical school would you go— I mean," the constable would say, "you're as intelligent as most people I've met. There's no reason to waste a brain is there?"

The constable looking with measured intensity and sadness. Little Simon a smile at the very corner of his lips.

"Of course," he'd say, "you're right—"

"You mean you would go?"

"Sure—"

"What would you like to take?"

"It'd be a choice between electricity or mechanics."

"Well then."

"Sure."

The constable would stretch. Like all RCMP officers on duty, he looked peculiar with his hat off. Little Simon noticed flecks of dandruff in the parted hair. The heat from the radiator had the taste of grey metal. The constable's face was freshly shaven. He'd bright cheerful eyes and a prominent Adam's apple. There was a pin of some sort on his black tie, and the moons of his fingernails were white. Simon saw all this. The typewriter clacked like metal, having the same smell as the heat. Little Simon knew this. He knew that this officer liked to help young men, tried to be kind to them. He coached a curling and a volleyball team. He'd asked Little Simon twice to be on the volleyball team. Each time he asked, Little Simon would say "Sure," just as he said "Sure" about technical school. The easiest thing to do was to say "Sure," and just forget all about it. Little Simon knew this. He'd smile at the constable, and leave. Going by the desk he'd turn, smile again at everyone and snatch a ballpoint pen as a joke, wink at the sergeant.

Oh yes—the sergeant! The sergeant was a small quick-looking man—the man who'd come to talk to Elizabeth Ripley Terri about her son Packet one Christmas afternoon; and Elizabeth kept saying:

"Come in officers—the place is a mess but we've just had a Christmas—Packet, you don't have to tell me a thing—a thing gentlemen—I knew he'd get his arse in trouble."

And the officers told how Packet had come upon Kenneth Ward in his car with the children, with the hose leading from the exhaust, and how he'd managed to get them out, and tried to resuscitate them. How Kenneth Ward that Christmas Eve belly-cut the Ginnish man with a putty-knife, in a shed that smelled of netting and dried fish-scales. How the Ward man had gathered his children into the car and drove around until they were asleep; Sharon Ward with her favourite blanket and Teddy and Emma Jane and the two boys and the baby. And once they were asleep he put a hose into the exhaust and through the back seat, and sat quietly. Quietly. And the Sergeant asked Packet questions—asked him what position the oldest girl was in, the two boys and the baby—and Kenny Ward himself. As if it mattered. Then the sergeant asked him how he managed to get Emma Jane out, and was she the only one he tried to get breathing? Packet stared at him. He asked Packet if he'd seen a putty knife or a quart of Hermit. Yes, Packet said, he'd seen the wine.

"What did you do after midnight Mass?"

"I followed Jerard McGraw home—"

"Why did you do that?"

Packet shrugged.

"Why did you do that?"

Packet shrugged.

"Come on now—"

"He's payin me a dollar a week to look out for him—some lads we know are after him—anyway, he takes fits—I made sure he got home—"

The sergeant stared at Packet. Packet stared at the sergeant.

"And you cut through by the Catholic church on your way home?"

"Yes."

242

"And you saw the car?"

"Yes."

The sergeant looked at him. He stared at them.

"Did you take the hose off the exhaust?"

"Yes."

"What did you do with the wine?" the younger police-officer said.

"Drank it."

"What?"

"I drank it."

"Why?"

Packet didn't answer.

"Why would you want to drink that old wine?" the young officer asked.

"It was Christmas," Packet said.

"I knew the little bugger was up to no good last night—I knew that out all hours—those men will take you to jail now, serves you right," Elizabeth said. "Eh Lois—doesn't it serve Packet right?"

"We're not taking him anywhere," the young constable said. Elizabeth shrugged and smiled, and then for some reason winked—

"And then what did you do?"

"After I hauled the hose away I broke the window—an got them out and tried to get them breathing—the young one, Emma Jane I think, started coughing—"

"Why didn't you wait for us?"

Again Packet shrugged.

"Why not?"

"Why should I? You would have just taken the wine—"

"Fine Christmas this has turned out to be—fine Christmas," Elizabeth said, her lips puckered, staring at one officer and then the other. "Fine Christmas—gettin mixed up with squaw trash, you little bugger—"

"You hauled them from the car—and saved one—we know that Patrick," the young officer said. Again Elizabeth seemed confused. She smiled, nodded to no-one in particular, and for some reason winked.

Packet stared at all of them, his eyes believing/disbelieving, his gaze steady and quiet. Three years before, the man in that same car, Kenneth Ward, had given him a drink of beer and had talked to him. Sharon Ward hugged her teddy-bear, and Emma Jane had her thumb in her mouth. When he came through the Catholic church he saw the hose sticking into the exhaust and hauled it away, saw the green fumes crawl across the snow. Snow was coming down over the windows and he had to rub them to look in. The girl's head rested on her teddy-bear and there was a sweet smell in the air, a long-time smell, and the quiet oaks were catching snow in the topmost branches. Just down the way he saw lights along the quiet river. Everything was quiet then.

Then the next day and the day after they heard that Kenneth Ward had taken the children while their mother was out. He said he was going to take them to see Santa Claus. He drove around until they were asleep. Sharon wouldn't go to sleep. She was too excited. So he went back to the Reserve and got her teddy-bear for her, and she and Emma Jane cuddled up next to him in the car.

So they brought Little Simon in for questioning, and they'd telephone Lois. They'd tell her that her brother was heading straight to jail—that they never caught him with a stash, nor did they know where he hid it—but sooner or later they would—sooner or later. Lois would worry. She'd sit with a blanket about her, smoking cigarettes. She'd try to get in touch with Packet if he were at home. Sometimes she became sick to her stomach. "You leave my brother alone"—she'd yell on the telephone.

One warm night in April they saw him leaving a house in the centre of town. It was just after six, and the streetlights shone on patches of blue pavement. They put him in the cruiser and took him to the station, with the same search, the same result. They knew he'd been capping mescaline, but again he'd eluded them.

But the sergeant wanted him for something else.

Little Simon standing in his underwear, in the white room, with his two pairs of socks, the birth-mark along his left leg from his thigh to his knee-cap.

"Listen," the constable said, 'we have a written statement—signed by John Delano and his girlfriend—that you were involved in an accident—and failed to stop at the scene."

"What?"

"There was an accident you were involved in?"

"What accident—'"

"You're telling us that your car didn't go through the red light by the Bank of Montreal—didn't run into a car driven by Bobby Simms, from the nor'west and that you didn't drive off, straight to the high school, failing to stop at the scene of the accident, and that you didn't proceed to sell marijuana to high-school youngsters?"

"What accident?"

"It's all down on paper—with a signed statement by John Delano and his girlfriend—both seen with you at the time—their word against yours."

Little Simon lifted his toes and looked blankly from right to left. The sergeant looked at him. Little Simon tried to think. No-one had seen him, not even Bobby Simms. And it wasn't a red light he went through either. And he did hit Bobby Simms, but it was from the rear (and since it was Bobby's car—one of those cars he managed to get Lester Murphy to buy for him—he felt inclined to hit it—justa little bump—or as he said at the time, "a bumperoony"). Yes they were in the car with him—he was driving them home. Certainly John Delano wouldn't report it, no—but what about the girl?

It was just a little bump—just enough so Bobby Simms in his brand-new car was jolted forward and hit his head on the steering-wheel, and ran slightly into the back of a truck. But by the time the trucker got out of his cab, Bobby Simms was still clutching the steering-wheel staring straight ahead and Little Simon in his beat-up 1962 Chevrolet was gone through the liquor-store parking-lot. And no-one had seen him. And yes, he did sell marijuana to smug-faced Malcolm Bryan who said he really wanted to try it once and for all, but that was in the evening, long after he'd driven John and Cathy home. How had they found out about this? Why would John Delano, who'd been in jail himself, sign a statement like that?

He tried to think. Confess everything or what? As always there was that compulsion inside him to confess everything while they stared at him. The radiator perked softly, hissing.

"You know you have an important friend," the sergeant said.

"Sure I do," Little Simon said. Desperately he tried to think. He stared at the papers in the sergeant's hand, and looked at his own plaid shirt with the fabric around the buttons torn—his pair of jeans with a picture of Goofy on one pocket, and a picture of Mickey Mouse on the other. The first pair of socks he had on came up over the tops of the second. His three sweaters lying at different angles on the chair. He felt very lonely. As lonely as the scent of the fish he'd held at midnight during a netting.

Little Simon thought. The sergeant talked, passing the papers, signed statements, to the constable.

"You have an important friend—who telephones us now and then," the sergeant was saying.

"Ya—who's that now?" Little Simon was shaking, being almost naked.

"Mr. Les Murphy—he's interested in your welfare."

"Who—ole Murph—Jesus, now what d'ya think he'd want with me?"

"I don't know—but with him backing you—you don't have to get into this row—"

"Is that right? Listen, tell me the name of John's girlfriend," Little

Simon said. He stared at the constable's hands.

"Murphy has kept you out of a lot of trouble—let me tell you," the sergeant said. "But he can't keep you out of it forever—he'd probably feel much better if you just admitted this—hell, you probably won't get any more than a fine," the sergeant said.

"Old Murph—he's one of the rich old coots on the river—owns I don't know what all—you sure you got his name right, when he called?"

"Oh yes," the sergeant smiled.

"And yer sure—certain you got John Delano's name—and his girl-friend's?"

"Oh yes."

"Then I'm caught ain't I?"

"Oh yes."

"That you've got their fuckin names on those pieces of paper—"

"That's enough now," the sergeant said. Little Simon yawned, looked about.

"Fuck a duck," Little Simon said.

"Simon that's enough," the constable said. You could see blue veins in the sergeant's face.

"I mean I may's well confess too then," Little Simon said. "What do you think?"

"It'd be best," the constable said.

He was silent for a moment. Stared at them comically. The sergeant's hands moved, the radiator hissing, a bug or two with roving eyes on the window-ledge. He looked at the sergeant. The constable fumbled with the paper. Of course, Little Simon thought—why weren't the town police handling this? Simply because it was a trick. The sergeant wanted him so badly he was trying to trick him. Little Simon wiggled one foot and then the other.

"You want me to admit leaving the scene of an accident—last week you wanted me to admit to selling acid—two weeks ago you couldn't think of anything you wanted me to admit to, but ya brought me in here anyways. All this because the sergeant has a burr up his arse to put me away—"

"All right now."

"All because of Murphy—"

"It's up to us," the constable said, "to decide when or when not to bring you in, and right now we have two written statements—"

"From John Delano and his girlfriend?"

"Yes."

246

"I don't think you do!"

"Well we do—"

"Lester Murphy telephoned, after that Simms telephoned him, thinking it might've been me—which it wasn't atal—and each time Lester Murphy telephones you gather me up—"

"We do have those written statements."

"Okay—sure," Little Simon said. He grabbed his pants and began to put the things on. "What's John Delano's girlfriend's name?"

The constable fumbled with the paper. The sergeant's veins blue, stood out on his marble-coloured forehead.

"What's John's girlfriend's name?"

They didn't answer.

Little Simon was putting on his shirt, buttoning it rapidly.

"Girlfriend—you kept saying girlfriend—you think they were in the car with me, and you think my car hit this other car—and you think with two pieces of paper in your hand you're going to get me to admit to something you don't have an ounce of proof of. Well, grapple onta yerselves." He was putting his second sweater on.

"What's John Delano's girlfriend's name—with a signed written statement you should know—" he said. He sat in the chair and grabbed his boots, which were a size and a half too big for his feet. "I mean, even a girl from downriver can write her name—"

The sergeant looked at the constable, grabbed a piece of paper quickly, and looking at it, twisted his head sharply and abruptly threw the paper down.

"Bah—yer not even close." Little Simon was pulling his cap out of his pocket now and shoving it down to his ears. The constable, for some reason, smiled as he watched him. He was shaking excitedly, thinking rapidly, and his mouth and lips were going without him speaking.

"Lester Murphy," he muttered, "phones you guys, and you guys pick me up, on any goddamn excuse—I should get a lawyer—Lester Murphy has it in for me, does he then—we'll see about that."

"Yes, get a lawyer," the sergeant said. "Get a lawyer—go on."

"Lester Murphy is concerned about you—just like your grandfather."

"Lester Murphy is a pile a dose," Little Simon said. "The money-grubbin son of a whore."

"Settle down now," the constable said.

"Yes get yourself a lawyer—go on—get one," the sergeant said, touching the piece of paper one more time. Little Simon picked it up and began to make a paper airplane. The sergeant tore it away from him, his hands

247

shaking.

"I love to see you guys get lawyers," he said.

But Little Simon wasn't looking at him, he was staring at the constable, who was looking at him. The sergeant's forehead slicked with sweat stood out like marble. A roving bug or two on the inside window. From the dampened soil the smell of copper and ammonia.

"And you," Little Simon said, staring at the constable. "I thought I was gonna have a great time now—going to Tech. school—of course ya neglected ta tell me, which I went an' inquired about, is I haveta finish Grade 10—did you inquire—well I inquired—ya. So I was gonna go and get Grade 10—and then—why you woulda had yerself the star volley-ball player on the river—I'm as small as a Chinaman—eh? Well ya missed out on that buddy—playin a dumb trick like this—"

The constable stared at him, said nothing. His rather prominent Adam's apple.

"Who missed out?" the sergeant said, laughing.

"Oh ya—I forgot about you—you missed out too all yer life—sorry."

The sergeant laughed cruelly.

"Yes my little man—get yourself a lawyer—"

"Lester Murphy," Little Simon muttered, walking to the large white door, with the white handle. "Tech. school—I went an inquired about that there—"

The constable stared after him helplessly.

Little Simon had to walk back to his apartment. The streetlights at intervals of 50 yards shone on the blue pavement, the white rocks, the lawns. A hatred for everyone filled him and he saw clearly his own postur-ing, his staggering brutal adolescence. The sergeant he didn't care about. If the sergeant were to lock him up, or even slap him, as the town police had, he'd take it in stride. The sergeant would be efficient all his life—the type of man you'd hate to see in an embarrassing position, but the consta-ble? And Lester Murphy—he remembered Lester Murphy, all he could about him. How he stood amidst a group of men, saying something in a low voice, and how all the men laughed and shook their heads. How Lester Murphy would have corn-boils and lobster-boils, and invite some Americans, a few cottagers, into the back rooms of his tavern, but never the people on the roadway—

"Let them have their Jesus corn," he thought. So what in the name of Christ would Lester Murphy have to do with him? That Lester Murphy drank gin with the Americans, or bourbon—but now and then, invited over to Old Simon's, he'd have a glass of rum. Why all this infuriated him he didn't know. All those glasses of bourbon infuriated him. Their laughter infuriated him. Murphy infuriated him. He walked on, his hands shoved into his pockets, his eyes watching the shadows from under his peaked cap.

The lights from the houses shone on the cement walkways, the half-frozen soil in the stone flowerbeds, the wisps of futile paper across naked parking-lots, the theatre's marquee, its broadsheets behind cold wire showing naked pelvises, the guttural sound of a tractor-trailer loaded with pulp for the mill across the river, its tires floating in the haze of watery fumes. The sound of teenage laughter. The smell of sulphur like fouled human gas, the lace curtains over upstairs windows, the United Baptist Church, its plots allotted to the sober dead, and the black iron fence-grates—teenagers with ponchos and belt-wallets wandering to the park, where they'd sit on the benches in semi-hallucinogenic wonder. They said, all his life, that Lester Murphy had been mixed up in shady back-room deals. A queasy feeling of weak hatred and pity overcame him. For himself, for the constable with the enlarged Adam's apple. For Packet, for himself, for Murphy—for the hundreds, the thousands of men gone from the Maritimes to work and to build the rest of the country, and then to come home—a land bought and played with by foreigners, in a country that didn't know them.

He lived that summer in a one-bedroom apartment. From the living-room window he could see the bridge, the span opening when the ships manœuvrd, the wharf oil-tanks as the orange twilight flushed against them, or they sweated; the sailors coming and going from the wharf between the black ore tarps, their powdered footprints. There was a murder/suicide in the paper that he took interest in. He wasn't bothered by the RCMP any longer and this worried him. His apartment had a couch that he slept on, he'd tacked up a print or two. He had a beer-cooler instead of a fridge, and a hot-plate instead of a stove. He had two pairs of jeans and three shirts, cowboy boots and a pair of sandals, a pair of cut-offs for swimming, and a small Honda that he drove to and from the enclosure. He was drunk much of the time that summer. Everyone seemed to be drunk much of the time. He didn't see his brother/sister, or his grandparents. He lived alone—he was never that interested in chasing teenage girls, and for extra money he worked at the undertaker's. He was also involved in (but this couldn't be proven) a break-in at the liquor store. But this was because he was drunk and thought it'd be funny to break into the liquor store, and once they were inside he got everyone laughing so much they left without taking any more than 48 beers.

Sometimes he was ill, and once he broke out in a rash that made his skin feel, as he said, "like a ham rind," but all this cleared up.

He went to the undertaker's for extra money. The man he worked with sometimes, was a thin little man of 35. They told each other stories while they did the job. The man wasn't a good man for the job. After every job he got sick to his stomach, and Little Simon liked to tease him about it. Little Simon liked to say:

"Some day now you'll be like this here and I'll be here doin you up," and he'd wink and shake his head. The man would turn pale at this inconceivable insult. He'd try to laugh it off. Little Simon would take the scalpel. "Like this here—yer body still twitchin—eh?"

"Shut up now—shut up—that's not very Christian, that's not very Christian—"

"Oh God no—I know—not Christian at all."

"No it isn't, with Christian people here—"

'Oh God yes," Little Simon would smile.

"There's something wrong with you Little Simon, oh Lord—there's something wrong."

"I like how their faces giggle sometimes—don't you?"

"Them's Christian people yer talkin about—"

Little Simon would walk back to his apartment, where they'd disconnected his telephone for not paying his bill. He'd sit in the darkness drinking his beer half-warm, the vexing colour of urine in a spotty glass. Alone he'd begin to think. Some day he'd do something spectacular. Yes—perhaps he'd leave in a month or so—perhaps he'd drive a tractor-trailer from one end of the country to the other, down to California, Arizona—perhaps he and Packet would start a business—the peculiar scent of ointment on his hands. He'd roll some bits of hash with tobacco, soft warm breezes came through the window, and the lights shone sleepily against the oil-tanks and against the open spaces between. The sound of an anchor clanking, its iron chainlinks covered with river mulch, smelling like sewage; the stars so quiet, the flickering of lights from pont-shaped river-buoys, answering. Far off, in open bends, between outer islands and river turns, the four-inch mesh gill-nets where men with deft and subtle strength did not sleep—did not sleep.

Smoke furled from the mills, ebbed away softly and died in the heavens; the town smelled of cement fissures, aristocratic wooden structures. On the radio came talk of unemployment, and in the paper an article by a social worker, on the disturbing plight of youth. He walked the streets. The sound of young girls in doorways laughing, the boys in the drug-aid

250

centre playing Bob Dylan at 3.30 in the morning while a fourteen-year-old on acid was talking—he walked the streets. On Sunday evening, being called back to the undertaker's, he walked in jauntily, pinched the man to scare him. He turned about smiling, jumped up and clicked his heels and saw, while in mid-air, Blinky strapped to the sickening adjustable board.

When he landed he fell sideways into the enamel basin.

"This is a suicide," the man said. He smelled of alcohol. Little Simon straightened himself, took a deep breath, "A hanging—"

Little Simon didn't answer. There was a blue discolouration of the throat, the cartilage, esophagus crushed. The nearsighted eyes, with their thin albino-coloured eyelashes half-opened. Little Simon took a deep breath and breathed through his nose. The man moved forward, weightlessly. "He was found earlier near the cemetery—hung himself; rumour that he got some youngsters to help him out—hands tied, glasses broken —and then put back in his glasses' case—ya know they're not even gonna have an inquest—or nothing—fix him up, pump him full and bury him," the man was saying. "He don't have a goddamn parent in the world."

Little Simon didn't answer.

"Seventeen or something—he was mixed up, can you imagine, with a *man*—tried to take out a girl but—he was mixed up with a *man*—you know. The girl was there this evening, now, it wasn't her fault—a man who let him drive his car—for favours, you know—somethin rotten evil about that, a *man*—"

Little Simon whispered something. The naked body had an unearthly quality to it. Its sandy hair out of place.

"Worked for this man now—'magine—"

He was saying—

"The old man upstairs is pretty pissed off about the funeral arrangements they want—caterin to them he says—on welfare or some damn thing—the ole man's on the pills tonight anyway, and has a funeral tomorrow—that's why we're here—some goddamn thing—"

He was saying—

"It's not Christian atal—is it? Eh?"

(Yes, Little Simon thought—Blinky would complain constantly that he couldn't hear the TV because he had "poor ears." He'd have to sit as close as possible to it, and have the sound turned up, but then the clock in the hallway that hummed would bother him all night—and once, waking Little Simon, he said he could hear a noise downstairs. Little Simon said he could hear nothing, but Blinky insisted. This noise was driving him crazy. "Stuff a wad a something inta yer ears," Little Simon said. But

Blinky kept complaining.

And he got up and pulled on his pants, and then he asked Little Simon to follow him, because he was also terrified of the big house in the dark. So Little Simon obliged and down the stairs they went following the noise Little Simon couldn't hear. Along the long cold hallway, past the mahogany table with its smoky vase (there was also a smoky vase in the living-room) and into the kitchen that always smelled of potato peelings.

"You hear it—you hear it—it's driving me crazy," the young fellow said, blinking and bending over to scratch his knee-cap.

"Oh yes," Little Simon said, who could now hear the cricket clearly. It came either from under the stove or behind the fridge. "Well boy," Little Simon said, who was just a boy himself and who said, "Well boy" or "Well me son" to almost everyone, even women, "Now ya know what it is let's go back to bed and get some sleep."

"What is it?"

"A cricket—you can tell the exact minute of the day just by the way they crick—if they crick so many cricks it's one time and so many cricks it's 'nother."

"A cricket—well I'll have to put it outside before I can get some sleep."

"We'd have to move the stove and the fridge ta find the goddamn thing," Little Simon said.

"It'll keep me awake all night with its racket," the boy said. "I won't be able to sleep—I'll be listening ta it all goddamn night." He looked at Little Simon, his voice was shaky, as if he might start to cry. Little Simon shook his head, grimaced. The stove would be an easy matter to move— they could do that, but the fridge was on blocks to keep it level—as soon as it was tipped in any way the motor would start—and what an awful sound that was—more than that, if they tipped it the wrong way in trying to catwalk it the door would open and things fall out. Although there was never very much in the thing, that unbearable self-righteous frugality demanding that the metal racks support nothing but metal racks, a bottle of dill pickles with three pickles and a lot of juice, the crisper with two tomatoes and the freezer with the next day's meat (it being on this occasion three pounds of bony stewing meat already taken out of the freezer and left on the rack to thaw). It was cold in the house, the cricket cricked, the moon shone down on the dark tile roof, on the roofs of other houses, the dumb scrub shrubbery growing up at the side of the houses, with their solid foundations and their tangible white siding, their windows black, cars in the dooryard, an odd rusted barrel with a hole here and there, two-by-fours and sheeting browned and rotted from a torn-down shed. It

252

shone down upon all of this. The boy looked at Little Simon.

"Well c'mon," Little Simon said. "Get a holda that end," he said grabbing the stove by one side. As soon as they moved the stove outward the cricket stopped. They turned on the light and looked under the stove. No cricket. They were silent and the cricket started again.

"Oh for goddamn sure," Little Simon said. "It'd be under the fuckin fridge—that always happens—it's always that way," he said painfully, trying to take a kick at the stove. "Ya want a fuckin cricket ta be one place and it's another," he said. "Always been that way—an' always will be—from time began ta time begone," he said. He was standing in his underwear.

"C'mon," he said going toward the fridge. The boy followed him obediently. The cricket stopped and started. "Let's move her," Little Simon said, giving a thrust forward. The fridge came off its blocks, and the door swung open as the motor started and the dill pickles fell out and crashed on the floor.

"Oh yes now—here we are up ta our neck in pickle juice," Little Simon said. And just as he said that the woman came out in her housecoat with her grey hair in curlers and went at both of them with a broom—accusing Little Simon of leading Blinky on, and trying to steal pickles. And they were grounded for two weeks over that. But the strange thing was the next time they were allowed to watch the *Ed Sullivan Show* on television, Blinky sat as close as possible to the TV and, on the point of tears, complained he couldn't hear it, because of his bad ears.

Little Simon thought of this, and thought of the time he'd banged the boy's head against the wall—the last time he'd seen him Blinky turned in another direction. Little Simon had heard about the *man* and he'd heard about Blinky with this man. He watched the man's movements and said nothing. Then he heard himself saying:

"Get away from him—I don't want you hackin it up no more than already is there—" and steadily, precisely, without taking a breath he did the work.

That night the undertaker's daughter, a girl with buck teeth and fuzzy red hair, told him excitedly that man had landed on the moon. That night he got drunk and the RCMP picked him up and found on his person, stitched into the lining of his jacket, 22 mescaline caps and ten joints of hash. The town police, advised by the RCMP constable, locked Little Simon up. The constable stared through the bars at the boy. Little Simon stared back, smiled and gave him the finger.

Packet sat very still in the night, drinking from his rum—thinking, what did this road, these V-roofed buildings, these corner stores, this Reserve, this maddened river—these thousand and one families (all coming from Alewood it seemed, every one of them did—seemed that from his aristocratic long-legged wife brought back after the Civil War from Boston, which she always called Boston, Massachus—hass, her name being Amanda and Hitchman calling her Manna; Manna, he'd say—so that he and she started a roadway, a village themselves—he hiring Swedish boys, saying they were the only ones to understand the lumber business), this McDonald's fast food, this shopping-centre, all this (or the ambulance which came to the Reserve to take the boy away, who happened to be in the wrong position when a Francis man and a Proud man, both wearing shirts and sweaters, haircuts and boots identical—went at each other with imported black-market switch-blades, the handle of one saying, "I buy my beer in Milwaukee," and the boy tried to intercede, was knifed in the eye, the ambulance streaking along toward town the whipping of slush from its tires, its men ashen-faced in the dark, the corpulent cement plant ashen-sided), all this Packet thought—*means?* And the protracted shopping-centre floors, the smell of sterile Dustbane like burnt popcorn, the rustle of women's nylons under their skirts as they moved through the hospital corridor—how one of them—a Pamela Dulse—her face showing sensitivity and compassion toward other people's pain—how others giggled when they saw him—all this Packet thought, sitting still, feeling his blood—*means?*

The humped-up backs of cars, the querulous tires, the smell of the blood of jacked animals emanating from the trunks, along perhaps with rusted jacks, dated papers, all this as the breeze blew the scent of saddened grasses, the lovely brown withered branches that struggled upward like crooked fingers, holy holy holy Lord God of hosts, and when he came from Communion that morning, in one city or another, all faces anonymous, all buildings ashen-sided, all cement crookedly cut out, wisping from the funnels of alleys an odour of swamps—like the bog Ceril Brown was lost in; seeing the shaven men on their way hunting, leaving their wives for the great adventure—*means?*

Means that we too, Packet thought, have joined, and bragged about having and wanting, the great unwholesome anonymity of North America —houses, like ideas, straggly corpses from one end to the other, and it is what we wanted, what we bragged about having until we succeeded in having—*means?*

Loneliness, like a spectre in alcoholic nightmares, his own alcoholic nightmares, loneliness when the face of his brother/sister winked out of the lonely bear-rug eyes, and he envisagd the woman with sweating buttocks as she wrote editorials and human-interest stories for the local paper proclaiming her hatred of men—the anonymity and death that Hitchman Alewood (God bless) had started and that perhaps someone like Lester Murphy would finish—Hitchman who hired Swedes because he paid them next to nothing, and Murphy who smiled at certain men who frequented his tavern: *means?*

The steam whistle, spouting in Hamilton, like the wind withering across the fields, over the humps of pale snow toward the trailer-park Lois lived in, the lime-green trailer windows, the yellow window-sashes like closing eyelids, the dogs with their excreta amid the porch-boards, the ice glistening—and somebody, one afternoon waving and shouting, and mentioning? Doris Lessing?

That day he was drunk, being driven back from Saint John by a certain woman, whose name he happened long ago to have forgotten, and on the road the tar-blots, and the great crushing-machine not far off with its awful belt, and the piled, quick blue and brown crushed rock—the woman content to say that he must see the West Coast—

Of course, the man in Hamilton said, the man who sat drinking in a bar with coasters a long long time after lunch-hour, and who might have been charging their drinks on a credit card—of course the man said *you Maritimers,* he said, *think a hell of a lot differently than we do. Now I don't mean that you yourself are backward, but the region itself has backward sorts of ideas, and I certainly was wondering, what do you think of cities like Hamilton?*

The very best.

The man smiled, called to the waitress for another two scotches. Outside, across from the bar, in a cement parking-lot-playground children with book-bags played and wandered. The bar, with its reddish neon sign blinking its wire-shaped name in the afternoon light.

The man showed Packet his credit cards, smiled and winked, as if this in itself was some tremendous accomplishment, showed Packet a picture of his house, with its yellowed sashes like dead eyelids. Outside the cement fissures on the street like fouled waste, the naked worn sign on and off—

"There was a woman up here a while ago—a Maritimer—by Jesus I had a good time with her—let me tell you." He smiled and grabbed Packet's elbow.

"I suppose sometimes in the winter there's nothin else to do there but—you know." He smiled merrily. "What's your name again?"

"Patrick Terri."

"Oh a mic—a mic—" the man laughed. "How old are you Mickey?"

"Sixteen."

"There was a woman up here a while ago from the Maritimes—do you like women? You know my grandfather was from that area—somewhere —sixteen," he whispers now. "A little young to be in a bar by yourself. Do you like women like I do—you know?"

"I can take care of myself—"

"Oh don't go on like that."

"No."

"How did you get way up here?"

"Hiked—"

"Well would you—like to—have a place to stay—I mean with your *own bed*—"

"No."

"Of course, with your *own bed*—"

"No."

"Well Mic-a-mic, we'll have another drink anyway—hey aren't you Catholics all mixed up with the French anyways—eh? Ha ha."

(Ha ha what—ha—)

The rain, that day, was a showery mist against the spectre-like buildings, the ruined litter, cigar butts and ashes from used cigarettes. Packet drank in the bar with the man.

"Have you—do you get the Beverley Hillbillies on TV—do you know what the Beverley Hillbillies are—on TV? We get it here—"

"Oh yes."

"Do you like Jethro? Jethro is my favourite."

"Oh yes—"

"What?"

The man laughing and lurching forward (and how much, Packet would think, can you tell about a man by the way he lurches forward— how much, the scent of his shirt like the steam-press of a laundry, the window-sashes of his house like floating eyelids, the rain against the sign *Bartime*), grabbed Packet's upper thigh. Then serious again, calmly positioned in the centre of his thought, he said:

"Jethro—is—all *man*. Natural—that's why I like you—you're a natural—I bet. Let me ask you a question—and you tell me—I bet—when you sleep, you know—if you slept at my house you'd have your own bed —that you sleep—*naked*."

The man's hair, a spot of oil, his lips flushing sensually—in his manner-

256

isms that sad Americanism that most Canadians affect, down to his suit-pants, his brown leather shoes. In the bar then, that day the woman was talking to him: "You come here my dear—come over here love—come here—you're from the East—a Newfie are you, come here dear, come here my love—my husband was from the East—"

"Two more scotches," the man said.

"Come over here love—come here."

"You want another scotch?" the man asked Packet. Packet nodded. The woman's thick dark skin and heavy makeup—showing perhaps, who knows, some Spanish blood, the monkey with its face turned down while the world laughed at it.

"Come here dear, come here love, don't sit with him—"

The scotch came, Packet took his drink and left the man. The man: "Hey," he said. "You come over here—get back over here now."

Packet stared at him, smiled and sat with the woman. The faint scent of dead flowers permeated her—or maybe herself a dead flower. He sat with her, in a bar reeking of unattractive decorations, coasters, swizzle-sticks with the name of the bar stamped on them. The sign flickering numbly, while the man glared at Packet and Packet let the woman pat his hand as he drank.

The man fumbled with a napkin as he wiped his mouth. On the juke-box came the Animals' attempt at "The House of the Rising Sun"—and at that moment there was a shuddering and a lack of sunlight in the bar, the drizzle came down on the streets, filled with the clank of engine-gears, and buses' diesel exhaust, running their obvious and lonely courses. Hamilton, the man said—how, he said, do you like our cities?

A poster upon the far wall saying: "The proper interpretation of your dreams—the key to success." The man drank his scotch, wanting to show that he was totally put out and offended without raising the ire of either Packet, who mocked him, or the woman, who'd begun to curl her lips when looking at him. The woman patted Packet's hand, Packet looked at the man and shrugged off his stare. The smell of the man's oily hair and after-shave lotion ebbed away in the pleasant tang of scotches and ice. "*The interpretation of your dreams—the key to success, the key to mental, physical health—*" The woman too was now touching his thigh, lightly, telling him something, on her breath the scent of alcoholic ginger—her large circular ear-rings on stretched ear-lobes, hair held by a comb, brown and hidden in folds, her teeth shimmered with cigarette plaque, and she held the cigarette in continual desperate affectation. The man, who'd tried to impress and seduce Packet by his talk of credit cards, of city life or of his house and television—now was yelling at the bartender—

"Hey look—that boy there isn't of age—I sent him away from my table—he's only sixteen, a little young—this is a place I like to come to drink and—"

The man looked back toward Packet angrily, and then helplessly batted his swizzle-stick against the table.

("Do you like—women, you know like I do?")

Now too there was something colicky about the woman's talk. Like the man she tried to influence him, seduce him. Packet smiled at her. She smiled at him and looked through her purse.

"So," said the woman. "This is your first time away from home—are you homesick? I suppose you're homesick—?"

"No."

"Oh you don't have to say that—" She touched his arm. Her pores, with hair, flecks of dead skin, her two-day fingernail-polish stranded like shredded red paper, "Admit to me—"

They had to leave the bar. They walked out on a street in a dirty rain, Packet's curly black head above most of those they met, his powerful sloping arms in a ludicrous navy-blue suit-jacket. Workers waiting for the hulking tin buses. In third-storey windows green shades were drawn. In a small area between two streets, amid the rising and ebbing of sound, a naked tree rose shapelessly toward the sky, whiteish. It was late afternoon, and there was the woman walking slightly ahead of him. There was the curious laughter of children, streams of steam amid the vaulted buildings and brownish hedges where hidden litter looked sad and faraway. And Packet sitting very still in the night drinking rum, or in some alcoholic purge would remember, the stars winking in the sky, softly, obsessively waiting—

"Wait dear—" the woman said. They were up four flights of steps. The number of her apartment "4 – –," the last two numbers having fallen off once too often. She had a thin remade key and was struggling with the lock. In the long corridor red fire-extinguishers, with snug rubber hoses, sat in cylindrical basins, beside certain pots of flowers. You could see the bus-stop from the window.

The woman laughed.

"Do you know," she said, "my husband was from down east—are you a Newfie dear?"

Packet nodded. It didn't matter. He was in a country where a person's gloating ignorance of his fellow countrymen was considered the height of achievement. He sat watching her. She was 45 or 50, he didn't know.

She looked at him, her mouth wrinkled.

"Do we frighten you up here?" she said.

"Not atal," he said.

"Oh—yes dear, don't be impatient with me, eh?" (Ha-ha.) "I suppose a man needs his beer, eh?" (Ha-ha.) *Don't be impatient with me.*

"You know why we don't frighten you?"

Packet shrugged.

"You're already a man dear—you know, already a *man*—"
(Ha ha what ha.)

"My husband died—on an oil-rig—did you know that?"

"No."

"A beer—I must get you a beer—a man needs his beer."

Packet sitting very still in the night would remember. His corrupted stinking youthfulness when he felt obligated to feel better than she— *means?*

Means he wandered from one end of the country to the other three/four times with all the buildings, the gigantic smoking factories, the American advertisements watching him, the sky the colour of pale lamp-posts, the rain-streaked windows of offices that took in money and signalled successes, the jaunty talk of dim men/women he now no longer remembered. He played hockey in an industrial league in the Gaspé, and learned how to speak French passably—but quit when he found out that the coach wanted him to do nothing less than ruin the knees of fast-skating opponents—and then a fight in a bar where the father of a boy threatened to knife him and he spreading his arms broadly—

The face of his mother and Lester Murphy walking to the door—

He found himself, voluntarily, in the psychiatric wing of the out-patient ward asking a young woman psychiatrist he didn't know, had never seen before, to help him to stop drinking—and she asking him what was the cause of his drinking—and he saying, "Violence—"

"Violence?" she saying. "Explain violence—"

She sat behind a thin metal desk. Her hair soft brown, her eyes intent and grey. He sat upon a metal chair, his huge arms on the thin arm-rests. A flower, a coffee percolator and a note-pad, the finely sharpened pencils, a poor painting of a brook in May with too many Black-eyed Susans, the scent of pressed board, the fair-skinned plainly pretty woman—outside the sky was too blue and widely globed the bright girders, the walkways, where wind over the sharp cultivated lawns tasted of hunger.

"My own violence," he said.

"Yes—" she said, "but how—in what way are you violent, why are you violent?"

Her pretty hair without brooch or pin, the aura of sunlight from the window falling on it, creating a sensitive but nullifying corona—

"When do you feel yourself getting upset—or violent—and toward whom?"

"Everyone—"

"Why everyone?"

"Every—everyone."

She might have been scarcely older than he. Her plaid skirt when she stood and offered him coffee reminded him of a young Cape Breton girl doing the dance of the swords in beautiful sacrilege, but there was that numb taste of aluminum siding, and somewhere in the heavens beyond the little room, with now a modest scent of ground coffee, a plane was droning. (The styrofoam cups almost religious—) The whiteness had come, the nightmarish—

The wind that blew between buildings later that day, the sky so blue it crippled the walk of the countless hundreds—made him feel.

That at least in a bar, near the back corner, a cascade of drinks without too much said, and very little laughter brought at least for an hour the bright unspoiled serenity of the drinker, the spiritualism of the incomplete, the dead country gone.

After George set up at Old Simon's Packet was alone in a house he'd built. And he began finishing the wiring and fixing the upstairs. He'd go out to visit his grandfather and on his way home he'd talk to Little Simon. Little Simon had a tattoo on his arm now. His once-beautiful eyes (though still occasionally beautiful) flirted in a kind of darkness; he was doing speed now—though he thought no-one knew this. But he told Packet the pathetic story of seeing Lester Murphy trying to offer entertainment to customers—and standing at the tavern door in a suit and shaking hands, hiring a local country-and-western band.

"Did you know—that he's our great-uncle?"

"Oh yes—"

And the local country-and-western band, with the country-and-western shoelace ties, the spangled shirts—

"Did you know—he'd be Old Simon's half-brother—"

"Oh yes."

Or of a night walking along the road to the fishing camps.

Atlantic Salmon Centre of the World, to men who now came up from Vermont and scarcely knew him; and turning he would go in the other direction, follow the roadway, turn down a gravelled lane, with the perpetual sad smell of pine-boughs, across the little walkway to Bryan's cottage—

"Oh Lester Murphy—it's been ages."

And back he would walk.

"Donnie—"

"Donnie—"

"What's wrong Lesser dear, boys oh boys what's wrong?"

"You awake?"

"It seems—it seems Lesser I am—yes, now it seems I am."

"I'm sorry to wake you—"

"No—no—it seems I was awake Lester—what time is it?"

"Three o'clock."

"Oh God boy—God boy—I was awake—awake—what's wrong?"

"I thought you might—want to come into the room and have a glass of porter with me—but it's three in the morning, if you don't want to—"

"Oh ya know Lester—tonight you were out—seems I watched—on the television—seems I watched, Daffy Duck—"

"Oh yes—"

"Daffy Duck—Lester—on the television—"

"Oh yes—." Lester would watch Donnie sit up.

"Now don't upset your pipe tabacco!"

"No no—sorry Lester—no—the can's under the bed, safe under the bed—member you told me to put it there—member?"

Or he would sit in his tavern, chairs and transparent ashtrays like ghosts that have spoken, the draft taps solemn, with a resigned wisdom. The lone waiter who closes the curtains too easily in the evening; or if not, from out the tavern windows in the twilight he might see the jaunty boys and girls walking to the disco—

Alone.

Where was all the bright, unspoiled laughter, that day at the picnic (ha ha), when Mr. Bryan said—

Alone.

Old Simon looked upon it—as if from a great distance, when even Mr. Bryan—was smoking a marijuana cigarette to try it out, and the young woman who was attached to the Department of Social Services—saying—

Alone.

Mr. Bryan smoothing his hair in the wind, to hold his tie to his chest, and calling Old Simon the salt of the earth, saying that even if he, Mr. Bryan, were to become something as significant as Minister of Fisheries he would always recognize (I know what I'm saying is difficult to say and

I might be laughed at—but I will always recognize and understand), and grabbing Simon by the elbow. Then realizing Simon's elbow was far out of place, Mr. Bryan let go his grip, smoothed down his hair quickly and—to Lester watching him walk back to the barbecue—how much cleanliness and propriety did one man need in his life?

Alone.

Who seemed to know much about Ottawa and the men in Ottawa, Canadian reports on the penal system tabled—where not only did Little Simon see the bars of the jail, and the clean limited space of a Canadian cell—

"Did they getcha mad Lionel?"

But a thousand others saw the bars of cells and jails, and once inside were dragged, beaten by men, corrupted—the steam of anger and frustration. When even in the courtrooms you could see the scars of prisoners—

"Did they getcha mad Lionel?"

"Lionel—I know Lionel—and all you do is don't get Lionel mad."

"That's the first sacred rule right there—don'tcha get me mad—"

Mr. Bryan to table his report on the penal system—how much cleanliness and propriety did one man need in his life? The dull parliamentary bell sounding.

The old man stood at the tavern door, smiling at the customers, his false teeth with their false orange gums, the country-and-western bands wearing the frilled neckwear, lace ties.

(Hank Williams' dream is Canada's dream.)

The empty protracted floor. Finding out when Ceril Brown was having bands at his disco.

In Packet's mind, the day he saw his father trying on the raccoon coat. Yet when his father made a joke of it (of how he looked like nothing more than a big raccoon), Packet became furious—he began screaming and yelling at them. How he screamed at them, when his father joked about that coat—

No, Little Simon said. It's very simple. He sits in the damn dark for the longest time—or he'll wake up Donnie at four in the morning. No-one now even bothers to torment him; perhaps they are tired of painting his doorknob—no-one does it anymore. Nor did he close the tavern when he should have. It would have been quite sensible to have shut down two years ago. But he kept it open. There was something infantile about that —something terrible about he and the lone waiter sitting there and waiting—for the few customers to make their daily appearance. He didn't even know how much money he was losing. Day by day his private savings were dwindled and scraped away (that money you might have seen him carry off into the darkness).

He wanders about the house with dirt on his shirt-cuffs, his large hands. Or sits in the dark staring down at the cold lifeless flowerbeds, cement circular jugs for flowers, withered grasses the colour of blond hair.

Everyone in the village—or on the river itself—knows what he's been up to—it's October now and he's planning something for Hallowe'en.

"I don't think anyone knows too much about it—"

Everyone knows about it. And perhaps too, again in some way, he wants them to know.

Little Simon said: You see it's all damn foolish; Dale had it all over the river a week after he hired him—paid him $1000 to torch the place. They met near the rear of the cement plant that rose corpulent and dirty above them. The money paid over. Then the old man waited for something to happen—

When it didn't Lester had to drive out to meet Dale again—again in the cement plant. It was night and only one light shone in a back window. The old man had to climb across those cement bricks to meet with him. The old man inched his way along, and met Dale in a little opening surrounded by cement blocks.

"You can count on me Mr. Murphy."

"This is just between you and I Dale," Murphy saying, "Eh, heh heh?"

Dale nods his head, coughs quickly.

"I ripped my pants," Lester saying.

"There's a new type of patch out Mr. Murphy—just have to iron it on—" Dale says. Lester looks away. Dale fidgets, coughs quickly. All those handguns, all those greased engine parts, in crates brought in in the evenings, in the helter-skelter adolescent fittering and noise of rose-cheeked boys wearing their cut-off denim motorcycle colours, of small-time drugs and amusements; Dale who Murphy didn't realize notified Ceril Brown on any action taken, went quickly to Ceril's office, stood before the desk, and scratching between his buttocks quickly told Ceril what Lester had proposed. Dale who'd grown up thinking of Ceril Brown as some sort of economical saint, because he would hand Dale a quarter or 50¢ for the movie on those lonely winter Saturday afternoons—Ceril tells Dale not to mention it, but Dale has it all over town in a week.

So the police put a tap on Lester's phone.

Dale enjoying his instant success; buying the carpet, the gadgets for his van—whistling as he lays down the bloodrose carpet and cuts away the excess about the edges.

"Spending the night together—oh oh oh oh," comes the song.

Lester waits in the evenings for his building to go up, taps his birch cane. The money of course is for Donnie, not for him. Even the memory of his tavern is faded in the minds of villagers, and the new and corpulent disco lights revolve in the dirty air. Lester goes back to Dale.

Dale at first doesn't know how to act. He is almost about to run away and keeps scratching his face nervously; as Lester waves his cane at him— but there are witnesses this time, boys wearing those cut-off denim motorcycle colours. Dale keeps looking away. The old man with dirty shirtcuffs, his white T-shirt showing at the neck.

"What's he blamin on you now Dale eh? Eh?" one of the boys says. Dale lowers his head. The old man looks at Dale, remembers the times Dale's mother walked to Ceril Brown's bottle exchange, and the times the boy's father was tormented, even the times the old grandmother put snuff under her lip, and sat in the room with her crooked spine; all those incidents in a life that was without clean linen, was without money for Pepsi at lunchhour in school, was constantly audited by the woman from the social services, who told his mother where she could get the best buy for her money—was with the nurse who told Dale he needed glasses, and they bought him a heavy-rimmed welfare-recipient pair, glasses that could be worn to school like a badge—was with his sister Susie.

"Ahooga-hooga," went the insulting horn—

Was with the nurse who reprimanded him because he took his glasses off and smashed them; and then the long nights when he struck out on his own—was helped along by Little Simon.

"Why does everyone blame everything on you Dale—eh?" the boy said angrily. Dale's lower lip began to tremble—his face looked peculiarly white. Lester shook his head sadly, and turned to go home.

"Hey," the boy said, jabbing Lester with his finger so Lester had to back up. "You're not invited here Mister—Dale's in our company and our—*protection*." He said protection emphatically, yet seemed at once surprised at the word.

"Hey hey," Lester managed, but the boy kept pushing him back, the jeans he wore loosely about his hips, his healthy face flushed and a bit of blond down on his upper lip.

"Protection," he kept saying now. "Eh—protection from old pricks like you—eh?"

Another boy giggled. When the first boy heard the giggle a slight smile came across his face, the corners of his mouth twitch thinly and then, all the more angry, his mouth sneered, his nose seemed to take on a prominence it never had before.

'Maybe we should get the police—eh Dale?"

Dale nods quickly and tries to smile, and then laughs and scratches himself nervously between the buttocks. "Don't get grumpy," the boy said.

Dale laughed nervously, took a mouse out of his pocket and patted its head with a finger.

"You you," Lester kept saying. "You you."

"You too. You too," the boy answered. The other giggled.

"I named my mouse Lester," Dale said, grinning.

Lester kept trying to slap the boy's hand away—the boy kept plucking at strands of Lester's long hair—

"You you," Lester managed, his head trembling. "You you—"

On the wall a calendar with chorus-girls wearing studded, glittering diapers. The boy smiles and blows smoke into Lester's face.

"You you," Lester says furiously. The hair on the boy's upper lip trembles.

Dale now begins dancing with the mouse on top of his head, in a little corner of the room, his head pecking like a static robot—the grey evening against his skull, the mouse wandering around on top of it.

Little Simon shook his head. His face, hands coarsened by various addictions; his breath smelling of unpleasant amphetamine. He still wore his three sweaters, his coat, too large, with his pockets bulging with things. His boots the same size as his brothers's. Sometimes he'd bare his left arm to show the tattoo—a grinning devil with a pitchfork.

He worked at the disco for Ceril Brown four nights a week. He sold drinks, and with three other men kept order in the house. He had his own float—so all his cash-flow was his own, and he was also on unemployment—having had worked at Calvin Simms' Irving garage before that. So, at times, he'd be earning more than $400 a week—but the money was nowhere. He lived nowhere. He drank and found himself waking in strange rooms at five in the morning with the adroit plenum smell of the furnace escaping, the eerie unfamiliar shades; with no means to get back home. The river went on around him—but he was the river.

"A woman come ta see Old Simon, at the house," Little Simon said.

"Why's that?"

"She's writing a history of the roadway—come yesterday."

Packet said nothing.

"She's a damn American who moved here six months ago—and already she's decided to do a history of the roadway—"

Packet said nothing.

"A course they got all our hockey players, and they got all our iron ore and our fish—so they got her pretty good; they deserve it—they got it they deserve it; a lot more'n the boys in Fredericton or Ottawa—"

"You tell her that?"

"Tol her she had a mouth on her like a sucked lemon—told her her eyes were the same as shots of piss, things like that—not cruel things; teased her a bit till she left—I didn't want her in the house—cause well, my incident the other night with the door-knobs—I mean some of them are still lying about the floor—"

They were silent. The car rolled on with its hood-pins shaking and the valves ticking. The sky bright blue, a day with the withering branches still and golden, frost in the ground about the small white church buildings, a penitent coolness about their windows.

"Ya well, I'll get out right here Pack—I've a person ta see about business."

"I'm not bootleggin anything now," Packet said.

"Oh no—not bootlegging—"

"Well why don't you come back to the house with me—have a steak and a drink of wine?"

"I'd like to, Pack—but I gotta go—gotta go eh?" Little Simon said.

Little Simon said: "You know that's a sad bastard of a way to turn out, abandoned by friends, tormented by youngsters and alone in a house with a retarded boy."

Little Simon said: "There is something terrible—I mean you see how he is, after all these years—after those thousands of dollars spent on modelling his house after Alewood's, the money spent on entertaining people from Vermont—after all these goddamn years, you see him putting on his suit and tie, and going over and standing at the tavern door, waving at people as they pass on their way somewhere else—" Little Simon shakes his head.

"I makin any sense—ya know I always liked tormentin the old bastard—"

And he was gone through the dry field in an October afternoon, with his hands in his pockets, his cap over his ears—and Packet would love him entirely, and be sad.

He wished to be alone that fall. He read in the mornings, put the door-knobs back on after Little Simon left. He went from the house in the afternoon and walked along the hill bright with dying foliage, the bled

266

trees. At the midpoint of the hill (though he didn't know this) he was at the place where Old Simon and Daniel Ward had seen the eastern panther years before. He stopped to drink there. In the distance the porters balked, and the saws with rhythmic loveliness cut trees to be sold, pulped, transported to the United States, made into toilet-paper and sold back to us. The sound was lovely. A jay gabbled and a chipmunk rustled. He thought of the northern mine where he'd crawled into a shoot and shut off his light, while below him a man, with a light gleaming weakly from his black hat bragged about stealing his oilers. He remembered what he'd done and then forgot it—but it would always be there. Everything would always be there—the American man's laughter when he fed him the chocolate-covered Ex-Lax, the sad monkey—with Ceril Brown boldly showing off his money. He drank the water and it came down along his mouth. His back ached with physical strength—and suddenly the trees, the bleeding leaves, the metrical saws, the wind, the stumps soggy with rot and the lingering smell of humus—the twisted fossilized toadstools like stiffened bird-wings; and he reached forward into the hunger of the day, and went back to his room—

Light gleamed weakly on the frozen soil, the fading scent of manure. So we have wanted and finally achieved our discos, our McDonald's fast food, our shopping malls and bookstores with biographies of American politicians and Hollywood movie-stars, he thought. Quite a legacy left by Alewood, by Randolf himself whom Old Simon took hunting. He, Randolf, must have realized it was absurd to find himself in Burma just at the wrong time, in a pair of shorts you see in British films, running away, while men laughed and taunted him in a strange language with bayoneted rifles, and he fell down and put his arms over his head and screamed when they began stabbing him—all this seen and witnessed, the degradation and disgust, his blood spotting the hands of the Japanese conquerors— how too, with a brash wave of his fist, did he face his adversaries—looking about in terror for a sign that it was all a joke and they really did know that he was Randolf Alewood, who went to university in Boston where he sang songs like "Barney Google, with the goo-goo-googly eyes" and whose grandfather was a Canadian millionaire. And all the money that was channelled out of here by Rosemary Alewood and her husband in the late fifties and early sixties to banks in Boston where they set up and still controlled a thriving plastics' factory—yet who could blame them for not being as sentimental as Old Hitchman himself, who until the end of his days was writing briefs and tracts about the strength of an unattached

Maritime country.

Or how with action garbled by Scotch that Alewood might have given him—perhaps they talked in a shed somewhere (in one of those curing-sheds Alewood had for his salmon)—did Thomas Proud walk into Alewood's house, while his half-sister sat at the dining-room table. He wearing the white shirt, the dirty bow-tie below his thin muscular face—

The carriage with the thin golden-coloured wheels, the indoor toilet, the little Emma Jane Ward (already going fat on childbirth and chocolates, and not really discriminating between one and the other). "Same's now eh—I mean," they said, "you know how good, how horny a young squaw, I mean can look—eh?"

"You come with me," Tom Proud said.

"Why?"

"Oh you'd be surprised what I got for you."

In some strange imitation of Alewood himself, his eyes pouched and swollen, like a boxer's mouse at 22 years of age.

"I want to show you dis present—"

She noticed in his peculiar eyes a deep fear of her, and her lips turned slightly upward. She ran back into the house to collect her purse and bonnet and along the roadway she sang "la la la," her face powdered with imported cosmetics under the dead moon, the stars in the sky; Tom Proud watching, the important arrogance of her subtle gait, constantly adjusting the purse on her arm as if fed up with everything.

"Where are we going?" she saying in Micmac.

"In here," he saying.

"Where are you taking me then?"

"No."

"All you have to do Tom, is pray to me the same as yesterday," she saying, "and you'll get money—pray on your knees to me that same way, and you'll get money—"

"No."

"Well see if I care—you won't get any money then, la la la."

"No."

"Pray on your knees now, like yesterday—I command."

"No."

"Well—you think then you'll get my money—I command, like yesterday."

"No."

"La la la—ha ha ha Tom, ha ha Tom—Mr. Hishman will run you away, same as Saturday—la la, ha ha Tom—ho ho ho."

"You pray on your knees."

"Tch."

"You pray on your knees to me."

"For you—for you—ha ha ha—ho ho ho Tom—Mr. Hishman says—ho ho ho."

"Pray on your knees to me."

"To you on my knees."

"Better start to pray—"

His lips quivered and opened and he couldn't look at her. The forest engulfed them with crazy refracted shadows of the dead moon. She hit him on th shoulder with her purse.

"La la la Tom—I make everyone pray to me—Tom I command—okay?"

"No."

"Remember when we splashed you with the waggon—Mr. Hishman said, 'Who's that' and I said, 'Tom Proud.' Hishman said, 'He don't look much proud to me girl—ho ho ho—what does he want?' 'Money.' 'Then he better pray for it because he won't get it any other way'—Mr. Hishman said to me—said to me." She hit him on the back with the purse and stamped her feet.

"Where we goin Tom—I demand."

"No."

"Mr. Hishman knows all about you Tom—we laugh at you—la la la Tom, everyone—I get the pants for you Tom, an everyone laughs. I get the shirt for you Tom and everyone laughs, ho ho ho—so there Tom—ho ho ho."

"No."

"Remember when you prayed to me and I wouldn't give you the money and then you prayed again and I gave you the money?"

"Hishman's lumber is stole in town—I stole his lumber in town—"

"You stole his lumber—you stole his lumber?"

"On my back—carried it on my back."

"Oh—strong Tom—steals undershorts from Mr. Hishman and lumber on his back—strong Tom."

"Be quiet."

"You think I'll be quiet—I won't be quiet—where are we now Tom, where are we now Tom—I'm going home, you help me."

"No."

"Help me go home Tom—no more pants, no more money."

"No."

"Help me Tom—help me and I'll pay you—I'll pay you, like Mr. Hishman, I'll pay you—"

They were at Cold Stream then, and the guttural sound of water over precious stones, and she stamped her foot and when he turned to her under the light of the dead moon she saw that he was deeply afraid of her. She smiled sullenly.

"I just knew you'd help me Tom—for money I knew you would—la la la, I knew you would—"

Music, sweetness of Micmac.

The day Packet left for out west was the day Old Simon left the hospital. He now wore, not the pleated pants, the loafers, the medallion—

A week before he gave the medallion to George. George's face now, red to the top of his bald head, looked permanently sunburned. He put the medallion on immediately and wore it with steadfast determination. He didn't see Little Simon, but told George to watch over him.

"Watch over him—God yes, what do you mean watch over him, I always do; he gets away with nothin when I'm around—nothin—" George said.

"Say hello to Tully—if you're out that way," George said. "And tell him," George said, with his eyes closed, his face sweating, "that I'm earnin a hundred bucks a day, eh?"

"Tell him," George continued, "that I've a woman here now who went to technical school—hey—is that where you went?" he said to the girl.

"What?"

"Where in fuck did ya go—technical school or what?"

"Yes I went to tech. school," Beth yelled. "Ya know that—Jesus Christ!"

"Ya," George said to Packet. "Tell him I'm married to this one that went to tech. school and that she keeps my books." He smiled, looked about.

An early snow fell when he waited for the train, across from the ancient bank vault where the pigeons roosted, down from the churchyard, the white statue of the crucifixion of Jesus Christ. Now and then, between the flumes of white smoke, the rails glimmered, the smell of diesel. New white metallic freight-cars rested, or shunted, or a small tractor hauling a trailer filled with baggage rolled by.

The train would be filled. They would go west together—in the barcar patrons telling inconceivable stories, their eyes blinking, the stains of smoke against the blank windows, where now and then a house, a station

—Drummondville where the houses shuddered, onward. He'd work north in a camp of 60 men, where the cook, perpetually drunk, would be fired, where 45 of the men were Maritimers like himself, where the second cook came as drunk as the first one left and was known to spit into the food when he was angry.

He entered the train, noticed a woman putting on lipstick, another laughed loudly and grabbed him saying, "Hi ya darlin—where the hell is this?"

And he passed on; from behind him now came the sound of a guitar, a man trying to sing Hank Williams in a broken pitch. The train started, jolted and swayed.

Off on a sidestreet beneath a burned-out streetlamp a woman in an absurd dress and hat danced crazily with a broom.

Not that his life was on a course irrevocable and damned, Packet thought sitting on his bunk one night—the night he received a letter from Lois informing him of her win on Atlantic Loto—but that there was something in him that would want it that way, or something in the laws of coincidence that would make it that way. George also wrote him a letter about Lois' win. Lois had a dream about the number and the series and went to every drugstore and candy-store in town until she found the number, so said George. But perhaps it was true. Why did he think of her spending it gullibly on nothing, buying the children useless toys and George a new car? And yet this is what would happen. Why couldn't he be happy ior her no matter what she'd spend it on, no matter what she'd end up carting home to her trailer?

Only the fear, as he had whenever he took a motel room with the furniture all synchronized, the vases, sea-bird pictures and sprayed plants in some glowering city—

He read Marlowe's plays, introduction by Edward Thomas, Everyman's Library No. 383.

Only the fear of Susie Masey with her hands covering her eyes, and he standing over her and Billie with a burning cattail in the back of Alewood's store. Susie's spindly chicken-bone legs; it was not the legs so much as the blue stockings sewn to her one piece of underwear—and that she tried to protect her brother.

He flinched. The men about him who'd come north, most of them Maritimers like himself, lay down for the night.

"Patrick," they would say. "Patrick—tell us about the light-heavyweight there—Danny Miller—that musta been one fight—Packet, you asleep

Packet?"

No there was always whispering noises—like perhaps his grandfather heard in the gauze-coloured hospital corridors.

In the morning there was snow. There was snow. In the quiet light, reflected through the trailer window, the pictures of unblemished women with wet clitoris posted on the walls. The sound of music before breakfast droning on, Doug and the Slugs.

And didn't he hear, "Too bad—too bad"?

Packet worked, and his bunk became his hideaway. At night the lanterns set in motion the shadows, against those pictures of women, the shouts of card-players. He'd let his beard grow, and sitting on his bunk watched nothing again, and evening, and then again. He'd heard now the rumblings from the east, the talk of Lester Murphy, from the lame shadows the mummified smiles of women disrobing; the pumpkin with the hideous carved grin climbing the back stairway with the canister of gasoline creaking, below him the tennis-court where leaves scudded; the memories of the Bryan children thwacking the ball: "Too bad—too bad."

(Now you might feel some discomfort.)

Packet worked and ate with the men and sat with them at supper. Then returning one afternoon he saw a new duffelbag in the bunk next his.

"Hello Packet Terri," the man said.

It was the man who'd stolen his oilers five years before, the man he'd held over the open stope—

Packet said nothing. The man smiled as Packet took a bit of frozen biscuit from his pocket. He wouldn't bother with the man, and setting his piece of biscuit down seemed to imply that.

Packet wouldn't bother with him. The music came—

He looked about for his small shoe-box of letters from his family. The man smiled.

"Oh I just looked through these," he said. "Just wanted to see if it was you."

He handed the box over. Packet stared at him. Breathed quietly. There was something about the man—what was it? The girls' eyes flashed upon the wall, their smiles knowledgeable. The man, still holding one of the letters in his hand, began to read it aloud.

"Oh Pack," the man said, imitating someone. "Oh Pack," the man said again, "Little Simon is on some type of drugs all the time—all the time—he's sick, every day is he sick—and just laughs at being all pilled up and sick—" Perhaps this was all funny. The man laughed and kept reading,

272

now and then his eyes would twinkle at Packet—merrily they'd twinkle out, the bunks like cold heavy objects. Perhaps it was all funny. Packet remained still, his arms hanging over his knees, his shoulders sloping. Everyone listened. The man imitated someone quite well—perhaps, Packet thought, Truman Capote.

"Pack—Little Simon fell down at the disco—jus like he was taking a fit—and Dale Masey tried to pick him up—Little Simon couldn't get up —almost choked his head off—"

The men moved about in their bunks. The man still read for a second. He kept trying to imitate someone. The white biscuit on the bed was cold and formless, hardened and durable. Packet remained very still. The man folded the letter, gave a sudden grunt and handed it politely toward him. The letter fell at his feet.

Packet lay very still in the night. The next day the man told him that his brother was the foreman. His eyes shone as he told Packet this. Within a week he had the promotion Packet was promised a month before. And that night walking about non-committally from bunk to bunk, as the men laughed at his stories, he told of the two Newfoundland twins who were caught selling cocaine, and the American, the ex-marine who had to be sent away after Packet and the two Newfoundland twins left, and of how violent he suddenly became one day. His amused eyes, as he scratched his groin through his white Stanfield underwear, with the spot of urine and his two big toes black, made all the men laugh.

Packet said nothing. It wasn't there. The raspy breathing of a mummified pumpkin suit was. A thousand insults were. But the man, with the spot of urine on his Stanfield underwear, laughing about the accent of the Newfoundland twins or how the ex-marine became erratic and started to break things, wasn't—

Nothing was important. (Important?)

The food wasn't hot, the cups had a greasy film when you drank tea, and no-one felt like eating when they saw the cook drunk. So the men became angry with one another, and then pacified themselves with great amounts of hashish or marijuana, and then gobbled up the cook's food. The women shone upon the spotted walls. The wind howled or was still.

I'm going to sleep now though, Packet thought. I've the damn uncomfortable feeling—

The stars were blue. He could see them. There was a rumbling noise somewhere. In the end though, he thought—enough money will buy ploughs. Who has written that we must go back to the garden? Oh yes, Voltaire—

273

In his dream François Villon stealing wine—
Then Packet knew someone with a knife was coming at him—

He's gone to sleep now. She stands by the door. There will be no wandering about the house tonight. Though he sleeps in the hallway, alone on his
side, he sleeps with his right arm extended, his hand curved like the
renaissance painting of Adam in the Sistine Chapel.

She knows now there will be no long night—whore of night, Packet
calls night. He is afraid of it. And sometimes when he first lived with him
in Victoria—more out of obligation because she couldn't leave him alone,
she would wake on the foam mattress at three in the morning and see him
crouched in the corner near the balcony window, in that artificial night-
light watching her—studying her sleep, as if he wished to be a student of
a subject he never understood.

He sleeps. As if in one of those childhood pictures she likes, of the
archangel spreading his wings over him—keeping away devils, the chat-
tering beaks that always collect in the grey darkness—of guilt dancing on
his shoulder, small pitch-forks extended—

She first met him there—in Victoria; he saw her from across the hotel
floor. And up on the street it was raining, the buses were moving in the
grey traffic. The hotel had the iridescent smell of beer upon the felt table-
tops, the golden-coloured exit curtains. Men with unclipped beards drank
the hours away. Other men, homosexuals, along the far side of the room
beyond the partition, laughed and taunted each other. It was the dead hour
of ten o'clock on a Saturday morning. The homosexuals and the hookers
sitting near them taunted each other. A man held a pink cigarette holder
and blew smoke here and there through his pressed colourless lips, while
his friend, a boy of twenty, dressed in the slacks of a bullfighter, danced
to the disco music from the juke-box, and a girl coaxed him to do pirouettes. Packet sat near the bar, drinking Guinness, his fingers with their violent brass rings circling the glass. The man with the cigarette holder, a
spot of undried beer upon his belly, curled his colourless lips. The boy
tried frantically to do pirouettes at ten in the morning. The back exit was
opened. The curtains billowed and the scent of Victoria's streets, somehow
a little too fresh, seeped into the room. Packet drank, watching them. The
man held the boy on his knees for a second; each laughed in turn.

Canadians moved through the rain with umbrellas. The cold brick of
insurance and employment offices, shut. The electric light now shone
upon the boy, strutting.

He sleeps now. Sun bathes their lane in the mornings, and when it's raining it makes the lane as ruby as grease. They have come back from the field. The last of it is planted. Not even his usual drink of red wine tonight, which would make him settle, talk about his days as a potato picker:

"Ahundred-barrel-a-day man is a good man," he'd say. "Only one of your Indians could keep up with me," and he'd wink.

He'd come out of the northern camps. And he'd ended in Victoria. The lights of the legislature and the Empress Hotel—above the streets and colourful plazas where street-musicians played for coins, and boys married to women wrote film-scripts after ten years of reading Kurt Vonnegut.

They met out there, sitting across the floor from one another, with the dancing and the young prostitute on downers crying at her girlfriend. On the streets the Canadians walked, dressed for the rain, rain over the city, against the gutters of suburban houses, and the ice-breaker tied up at port.

"Hello," he said. "Do I know you?"

He watched her. There was no use to smile at him. For years she'd tried to thank him—and she'd seen him coming and going, where he'd stayed in the small pump-house in the back of Alewood's General Store one summer, when his clothes stank of the various bait-sheds he slunk to at night.

Right out of the northern camps, where he'd left for back east and being Packet turned west.

"I know you Packet," she said.

He flinched. She could see his shoulders. His eyes drew inward trying to remember—the rash of freckles on her face, her black eyes. He stared, but not like old Havlot would stare as she crossed the lane from time to time singing la la la. What incorruptible part of them was left anyway, listening to the talk of homosexuals at ten in the morning while the sad boy did pirouettes for his lover—tried to attract his attention.

The hooker on downers crying at her girlfriend, the girlfriend cursing. She thought suddenly—they took Susie's clothes off that day—in Malcolm's car when they were all fifteen—it wasn't even shocking to hear what Malcolm said—as he put them out, threw their clothes, scattering them. "Silly Susie," one yelled. "How dirty is yer hole?"

And the snow came down, and under the tire-treads there was a rivulet of dirty, icy water.

"Not into a squaw's paunch of a dirty hole," the same boy yelled in a terrible voice, a pimple on his right cheek and a pimple on his left—and both the pimples dry, as Susie, her thin body looking grey in the evening air, kept chasing after her belongings— There was one instant when

Malcolm seemed to realize something, how grey Susie was wandering simple-mindedly about the snowflakes, the rivulet of dirty ice-water; she happened to catch Malcolm's eyes, and then becoming suddenly angry he drove away—

Packet sat with her. She remembering being asleep in his arms a long time ago. But of course this was Victoria in March, buildings as snug as dead white crabs rested in the rain, the legislature closed, its brick steaming; and men and women, and in St. James Park the ducks snuggled together under the small wooden bridges, where people walked primly, and beyond that the giant drift-logs resting in the sand, or along the highway, rain, and in many streets the dormant lights of apartments, where she saw the hearse pull out, a small procession.

He looked at her freckles, her lips curled, the curvature of her breasts heaving there, in the dark place, in the little slice of torment beneath the streets where she came every Saturday, because she found it less tormenting than the streets themselves. She remembered being in his arms a long time ago.

"Emma Jane Ward," she said.

He lifted his eyes from the glass, nodded and drank.

The rocks in the river are hushed in different hues tonight, rose and violet and darkened. Rose and violet and darkened.

In Victoria then, in the pleasant house of his uncle and aunt—Tully had retired early and moved to Victoria, and Packet had taken her to visit them —in the house, with its artefacts, its antique desk dating from, they said, one Hitchman Alewood.

On the table there were two-pronged forks, large black olives and whole mushrooms in glass bowls—

"I know someone who'll have a hangover," Devoda said.

"Pack—I think your aunt will have the wrong impression," Emma Jane said.

"Of who—wrong impression of who—me or you?" Packet said. Devoda smiled at him, winked. His shoulders flinched, his hands when he picked up the glass. His fingers with their vicious brass rings.

And Tully wanted to tell her something—show Emma Jane his Indian artefacts, tell Emma Jane that his wife Devoda worked with Indian children, taught them how to enunciate their vowels properly (which Indians never seem able to do). Devoda smiled at Packet.

Packet stared at them—and the horrifying crushed look (perhaps of peop.e showing Indian artefacts) had come over him—perhaps of a thousand children, Indian and white, in the white schoolrooms of docile farm communities being taught how to enunciate their vowels properly —Kanada, ferry bad, that boy who loved some idea of storm-troopers, the Leningrad blockade, shouted, and then George had the misfortune to shoot him through the pelvic girdle.

Tully sat beside her, kept telling her the price of one of the hand-carved Eskimo boys that sat, assuming perhaps it was an Eskimo boy, on the piano—the ivory keys monotonous and stiff. And she knew that Packet more than anything wanted to be like them, to say—oh yes how right— truly how you seem to have understood it—and she knew Packet hated himself.

And Packet drank his alcohol, the ice in the glass. And Tully, what was he saying—wanted to show Packet his miniature computer, which was programmed to turn on the oven. The thumbnail of Packet's hand black where he'd squashed it on a piece of machinery, and later that night the young man with urine spotting his Stanfield underwear came at him with a knife while he slept. The black thumbnail with its ridge of raw flesh.

"Why aren't you drinking?" Packet said to Emma Jane. "For all their enunciation, don't they give Indians anything to drink here?"

"I don't want to drink," Emma said.

(Pretty, in Micmac.)

"Have a fuckin drink," Packet said.

"She certainly can have a drink if she wants," Devoda said. "But if she doesn't want to drink then no-one should try to force her—"

(Is that how you say pretty?)

"Squaws," Packet said. "You know they don't usually rip off their clothes, or get thrown out of little boys' cars until they have five or six drinks—eh Devoda, certainly you must have learned that by now—eh Devoda?"

"She is not a squaw—she is an Indian woman," Devoda said. Devoda said, "She is not a squaw—she is an Indian woman—"

(Now you might feel some discomfort.)

He shivered again.

"Oh I've a message for you Tulland," he said.

"What's that Patrick?"

"My old man is earning a hundred bucks a day now—has his own private secretary—"

"Is that right?"

"Of course."

"Well I'm glad to hear he's doing so well—what's he doing now?"

Devoda asked.

"That depends—when we were youngsters he used to put our heads into toilet-bowls—my squaw can vouch for that, he was famous for it—he did it in front of Ceril Brown to impress him. Whenever the children were naughty, and Ceril Brown was there, well sooner or later Little Simon and I would find our heads in the old toilet-bowl for a flush."

(Ha ha—what ha.)

Tully took a sip of wine, stood and went over to play a record.

"What would you like to hear Emma?" Tully said.

"Anything," Emma said.

"Tom-toms—" Packet said. Merrily he swished his feet back and forth. "Eh Tully—tom toms."

He had the bottle beside him—pouring another glass.

"You're talking like a damn fool—trying to shock someone," Emma Jane said.

"Listen to the squaw," he said. "The only thing Indian about her is her cheekbones—Alewood's great-grandchild—did you know that? I mean she deserves her inheritance—part of their chemical factory in Boston."

"Ah Patrick—it's not chemicals they own—it's plastics—" Devoda suggested.

"Chemicals," Packet said.

"I'm sorry," Devoda ventured, "but it's plastics."

(She managed to wink—)

"Plastics then—she should have her plastics, but will she—will she ever have a piece of plastic? Or that desk maybe?" (Ha ha—ha.)

"Christ Packet—shut up—I think we should go now."

"Go—home was never like this—never was."

"Let's go," Emma Jane managed.

Packet said:

'They complain they're not fed right eh—but do ya see?" Here he tapped her with a finger. "There's T-bones there, and there—looka the pork chops there."

(And Little Simon fell down, how terrible it was that Little Simon fell down—)

And Tully stared at him; and Devoda in her powder-blue dress was Devoda at his grandmother's funeral—not knowing quite what to do—more than that it was Devoda's hundred letters to his sister couched in the same way, about boys and hygiene and habits that she must not only have told Tully and her children about, Packet thought, but told her bridge-club composed of managerial wives in northern BC—who would above

278

all talk about nasty little ploys and how to prepare trout cheeks. And how they must have discussed it all, during those outings when they bought, he imagined, hand-carved Eskimo bathroom fixtures.

And Emma Jane saw how he would love to be like them—how in fact he'd love to say: "Oh yes truly—I think it's an absolutely honest assessment."

"You can stay," Emma Jane said. "I'm going home."

He called the houses dead shells of white crabs. She didn't listen. There was a certain cindery scent from the monkey trees, branches curled like monkey tails. She didn't listen. And the monkey trees, he said, all seemed to be—sad, like Devoda managing to wink, and the diamond pin she wore —and when they left Tulland was filling the dishwasher—and then it hummed like an incessant vacuum, and the plastic bottle of Joy soap liquid squirted just as sadly when Tully asked them if they'd enough money for a taxi. A bubble formed and exploded.

And the monkey trees, he said, all seemed to be—the Empress Hotel rose up, the lights from the ice-breaker twinkled. They could hear the generator.

His face was twitching horribly and he couldn't stop a convulsive shiver—

His face twitched horribly under his beard. He couldn't stop a convulsive shiver as he walked. And their orange dishwasher, he was saying— was in fact like their orange stove, and there were oven-mitts, he said, hanging in their oven-mitt place, with ludicrously happy thumbs on them, and salt-and-pepper shakers carved, he said, like Mexicans doing the Mexican hat-dance (holla).

She didn't listen. The smell of the roasting-pan, of lukewarm blood went away, and with it Devoda's smile.

The chained garbage-cans in line, on Fort Street a bus, solemn. A dense smell of diesel suddenly—

He tried to grab onto her—

She walked away from him—

"Emma Jane," he yelled.

He began to choke. He leaned against the side of the building. In the plaza a musician sat huddled with his guitar. Packet was choking. He tried to get his breath. The muscles in his throat convulsed, and under the plaza's pale light she could see his temples blue and beating.

"No," he managed.

"What's wrong man," the musician said. "Hey lady, what's wrong?"

"No," Packet managed. The boy shrugged, hung closer to his army

279

jacket, pressed against the coloured tile.

The tile, the young man slouched against it—and farther up the street the lights of the Chinese/Cantonese restaurant winking—a place where Packet had already found out you could buy wine at three in the morning; and behind, in another building, a partition of glass beads, in a certain room (only on the outside was there the Western alley, the grey cement).

He couldn't catch his breath. It was strange, he had no sensation at all in his fingers. What if Emma Jane had kept walking? No she held him up and he could feel her body—certain tiny purple pebbles on the street near the garbage-can—

"Packet," she was saying. "You'll kill yourself—that's what you want —try to breathe."

"Hey man—what's wrong?"

(Bullet pierced the aorta—death was almost instantaneous.)

"No."

"Hey man—what's wrong?' He smelled the army jacket, the man, slighter than he, tried to hold him up by lifting him under the armpit. All movement created—death—

(Ha ha what ha.)

At least Little Simon could make them laugh.

The pebbles were so damn important, every sensation brought the pebbles moving to the right and left, the warmth of a generator stank in his mouth. The Indian woman, Emma Jane, her river the same, the same history—

"Too much Lester—I got a little too much today—hey, hear about the Indian bought the hot-dogs at our restaurant—one for himself and one for his—squaw?"

"Well there was this buck with his squaw, eh?"

"Oh Georgie," Elizabeth said.

"And they come up and ask me fer two hot-dogs and I give them two and put on the mustard and the buck says to the squaw after openin up the bun and lookin at it—hey squaw—what part of the dog did you get —eh?"

"Oh Georgie."

"Shut yer Jesus mouth, it's just a joke—hey kids stop yer fightin and mind yer Jesus manners in front of Mr. Murphy—"

He felt himself falling, falling slowly, and then suddenly too fast, like a reel of an old movie, the ancient blue sidewalk, the smell of dust and the spittle of dead men. Why did he fall? Why was he frightened?

"Ya know Mr. Murphy—don't I have a good-lookin wife—a Jeesless good-lookin wife—there are a lot of men—a lot who'd love to well—she sticks to me—sticks ta me—" (Ha ha.)

"Oh Georgie don't be a fool—shut up."

"Ya know Mr. Murphy, Packet is a scaredy cat—scaredy cat—wouldn't get his picture taken with a monkey—and wet the bed when he dreamed of her—eh?"

"Georgie shut up—"

"Scaredy cat—scaredy cat— tell him about the murder of Emma Jane Ward Mr. Murphy—a squaw was murdered in Cold Stream Packet—her ghost is still hauntin us—just like the monkey Packet—just like the monkey—"

"Oh Georgie shut up."

"Boys—I jus love teasin Packet Lester, in fun ya know—it's all in fun, Elizabeth thinks I'm mean—it's just in fun—all in fun, eh?"

"Oh George shut up."

"Packet's a scaredy cat that's all I know about her."

"Please Packet—" Emma Jane was saying. "Get up—you can't lie here Packet—"

"I have to go," the musician was saying. "Hey listen, you need a taxi—hey listen I gotta go—"

"Please Packet." The sidewalk was so warm. He was far into the sidewalk.

"C'mon Packet for Jesus Christ's sake."

'Hey," the musician said. "Tell yer old man they got a lot of Billie boys here that love taking people in back alleys and beating them, real Starsky and Hutch—"

"Oh for Jesus Christ's sake Packet—please Packet."

The musician's footsteps retreating, with the clickers on the Texas-style boot-heels along the sidewalk scattered with refuse. The lights of the Empress Hotel make it look larger and across the broad harbour beyond the relaxed, grinning totem-poles the Parliament Buildings signal to the boyish footsteps of the Canadian musician. The monkey trees, under the street in the Churchill Arms now, with its gold cords hanging by the entrance, the hooker flushed high on coke shows under her willowy shorts the tight black-laced panties that rushed blood to his penis until her smile reminded him of Susan Aitkins—

"Please Packet—I'm all alone—all alone—you can stand—Packet I'm going to cry—you're making me cry."

"Packet is a show-off Mr. Murphy, that's what Packet is—jus ask Elizabeth—"

"Oh Georgie shut up."

"Then why did he run up the side of Cold Stream 'Lizabeth—just a show-off and why does he think he's the big know-it-all around the restaurant—'bout pourin ketchup—wouldn't even let me pour some ketchup—just a show-off, that's what I think—likes makin big scenes—what I think—"

"Oh George really, you're embarrassing everyone."

"Well I like the truth."

"Yes," Lester saying.

"Jus the truth about my kids."

"Yes."

"Boys it must be awful because of Donnie—Lester you have my sympathy about Donnie."

"Thank you—"

"No now ya do—I don't like to see a boy like that, eh Simon? I mean what chance do they have?"

"It's just terrible," Elizabeth saying. "Lester has my sympathy—"

"Well he has everyone's sympathy as I was predictin—"

"Yes."

"Lois stop pullin at yerself, what's Lester gonna think." (Ha ha.)

"They embarrass me—all of them Mr. Murphy," Elizabeth saying.

It's not all that disastrous to lie on the sidewalk, the generator that stank of currents of electricity in his mouth, vibrating like a humming magnet, and there is a little wind in his ears. The smell of dust like crêpe-paper at some sad graduation—or clowns with painted faces maybe, the spittle of this generation and the last. Emma Jane—what was she doing? (Didn't she know it was dangerous?) She was slowly lying down beside him now. He must be shivering, and his lips must be blue again. Because she was holding him. He could feel her warm hips and breasts, holding him, her arms under his head. The little wind caught at her hair, and he thought, ridiculous, and then Maxim Gorky. Her hair wisped sadly in the wind, a cigarette-package made a racket. He opened his eyes. Above the Empress Hotel a meteor burst suddenly—like a buzz-bomb he'd heard it, and then it burst—seeing a piece break off in flames and crackle. The whole sky lit up. There were shrieks of laughter from people leaving the Chinese/ Cantonese restaurant. All faces looked toward the sky. The light it made was broad and pale. How many worlds had it travelled? Small, wonderful —the wooden sign above the shop in the cobbled alleyway where tourists strolled at noon, past the glass case where there was a letter written by a notary circa 1889, his pen and marble-topped pen-holder—all to be sold

282

for $440, and the Jewish man from East Germany showing the jacket with embroidered sleeves of a man killed in the Boer War (a man who'd met Merlin Terri on the *HMS Sardinia* in 1898—when it sailed that October), the Boer War then—the bullet-hole blackened with powder—saying: the stiff fashions of yesteryear like starched phantoms—

There was a slight rumble. The meteor piffed—

OIGOA/Sepoitit—

THE NEW CANADIAN LIBRARY LIST

Asterisks (*) denote titles of New Canadian Library Classics

McCLELLAND AND STEWART LIMITED
publishers of The New Canadian Library
would like to keep you informed about
new additions to this unique series.

For a complete listing of titles and
current prices – or if you wish to be added
to our mailing list to receive future catalogues
and other new book information – write:

BOOKNEWS
McClelland and Stewart Limited
25 Hollinger Road
Toronto, Canada M4B 3G2

McClelland and Stewart books are
available at all good bookstores.

Booksellers should be happy to order from our catalogues
any titles which they do not regularly stock.